R. A. Adkins

The Hum

Copyright © 2010 by Rachael Adkins

All rights reserved, including the right to reproduce this book in any form whatsoever.

This book is a work of fiction. All characters and events, names and places are either the work of the author's imagination or are used fictitiously.

For Lindsey and Faith, who cheered me on with the kind of enthusiasm I've always envied, and for my mother, who knew I was a writer long before I did.

Chapter 1 ❖

I didn't need to look at the clock to know it was five in the morning. The hum always came at the same time, starting from somewhere within myself; a resonance that made every cell in my body sing me awake. It was a feeling like none I'd ever had, euphoric in nature, and at this point in my life extremely welcoming and very nearly life-saving.

For a moment I lie there, relishing the happiness that engulfed me. I'd been having these…episodes… for eight nights now, and every night the feeling would cease to exist the moment I discovered its source. As much as I wanted to capture it, I was afraid that it would vanish as soon as I attempted to do just that, and so I allowed myself a few minutes of this blissful sensation before the desire to find it became too overwhelming.

Finally giving in to the temptation of locating it, I lifted my blanket back and stepped onto the floor. Immediately I sensed that the happy feeling that was flowing through my veins came from somewhere outside the house, and if I could find it I could have it all, and then every amount of pain I've ever felt would be erased forever.

Slowly I made my way to the door of my room and let my hand rest on the knob. The feeling was still with me, and I sighed with relief. This had been the point where it had faded into nonexistence on the first night, and I was pleased to know that at least this wasn't a cycle. I wouldn't get closer and closer until I was finally thrown back to the beginning. Tonight I would find it.

I crept down the stairs, careful not to wake my parents, although I knew they would stay asleep no matter what kind of noise I made. The joyous sound inside me was getting stronger, and I wondered how I was the only one who could hear it.

I reached for the dead bolt on the front door, knowing this was where it ended last night, and a little afraid that maybe this was the farthest I was allowed to get near it. Somehow I found the strength to turn the knob, though, and when I pulled open the door the wave of pleasure that engulfed me was so strong that I dropped to my knees.

Finally, I composed myself and stood, knowing that once I reached it, I would become it, and there could be nothing better than not only feeling euphoric, but being euphoria itself.

Crossing the threshold, I stood on the weathered front porch and looked to the left, knowing that it would be waiting for me beside the maple tree. At once I bounded to the tree, the crisp smell of autumn leaves under my bare feet sweeter than it had ever been. After only a few steps, I stopped, awestruck at the most beautiful sight I had ever beheld. Floating face high to me was a perfect glowing sphere. It was as if the sun and the moon had combined and intensified, making it impossible to distinguish the difference between the two. It was a glittering yellow, yet somehow a glowing silver at the same time, and it was pulsating without actually moving. I wanted to reach for it, but intuitively knew I couldn't. For reasons I couldn't understand, I knew my touch would cripple this extraordinary magnum opus.

Somehow I became aware that it was pulling its energy back from me, and my euphoria slowly faded into the hum it was before I was lured outside. I was a little disappointed that the exhilaration had to go, but glad it let me keep the hum, which made me feel as if I were a tuning fork.

Knowing what I was supposed to do next, I cleared my throat. "Why are you here?"

It answered me then, not with a voice, but inside of me, as if it had rewired all of my nerves to understand its own Morse code. "It is time to awaken."

My eyes flew open just before my dad tapped his knuckles against my bedroom door.

"You up yet Gabs?"

My pulse was racing from the dream I'd just had, and I inhaled deeply through my nose before I could answer. "Yeah, Dad."

I heard the familiar creak in front of my door as he walked down the hallway toward the stairs that led to the kitchen. I knew it would be him. No matter how many times my mother swore she was going to get herself together in the morning I knew she wouldn't.   Not that she didn't want to.

Up until eight days ago I knew what it was like to wake up in the morning and have him be the first thought. I knew she was agonizing over losing him, and so I was patient, forgiving, and understanding when she fell through with her promises of getting better.

Devon, my twin brother, will have been gone for a year tomorrow. His disappearance was nothing short of devastating to my family. There were no leads, no evidence of foul play, nothing anyone, including his closest friends, could think of as to why he would have gone away. It was almost as if he never existed in the first place, which was partly why I'd been in his room a little over a week ago.

I needed a good look around, not only at the posters on his walls, or the pile of CD's that were stacked neatly on his dresser. I needed something more than that, something he created, maybe, just to prove to myself that he really did exist once. I opened his closet first, just to see if maybe the clothes that were hanging there still had his smell. After sifting through most of his things, I found his leather jacket. He had outgrown it about a year before he came up missing, and I put it on. The sleeves landed just beyond my fingertips, putting into perspective just how big he was. I wasn't sure if my mother would be upset if she saw me in it or not, so I wadded it up and snuck it across the hall to my room before she could see it. After quietly shutting the door, I slipped the jacket on while standing in front of the mirror.

I shoved my hands in the pockets, my fingertips brushing against a folded piece of paper that lay curled up in the corner. I held it in my hand a moment, hoping that it wasn't a girl's phone number or a class schedule. I needed it to be something he had written himself, anything - as long as it proved my brother lived and breathed and made a mark on this world. I pulled it from the deep pocket and unfolded it carefully so I wouldn't tear it. On the middle of the page was a hand drawn symbol - an infinity sign surrounded by a ring of fire.

I examined the yellowed paper carefully, wondering what connection this design had with my brother. Obviously it was drawn by him, but was it his own creation, or was it something he'd seen and tried to reproduce while suffering through some boring lecture at school?

For some reason, I couldn't let the matter of the eerie symbol rest. Questions were gnawing at me, and I finally gave into my curiosity and booted up my computer. I typed in its description in the search bar and selected the image icon. It took a while, but I finally found a very similar rendition. Shock seized me as I read the caption under the picture.

'Lucifer's noose: known as the symbol of one of the oldest satanic cults in history. Predates the birth of Christ.' It was the symbol of an ancient satanic cult.

What was Devon doing with it? Perhaps it was a mistake. He could have picked it up anywhere. There were always a few people at our high school who claimed to be involved in such things, but no one ever took them seriously. It was possible that one of these hooligans could have dropped the drawing in the hallway at school, and Devon just happened to be the one to pick it up. He was always very talented at drawing; it most definitely would have piqued his interest.

Slowly I started to breathe again. I knew Devon could never be involved in something as twisted as a cult, but then again, rumor had it that sometimes these groups didn't take no for an answer. The worst case scenario would be that whoever drew this symbol could be involved in his kidnapping. With this thought, anxiety overtook me.

The smart thing to do would be to tell my parents and let them handle it, but with my mother being so devastated and my father trying to forget that he ever had a son to begin with, an accusation like this could only bring back the pain. I decided to do a little more investigating before I alerted them to something so serious without enough evidence.

That evening, after I finished the dishes and my parents sat down in front of the television to pretend they were watching it, I pulled on my jacket and headed for the garage. It was a long shot since the entire house, garage, and both vehicles had already been searched in the initial investigation, but the police missed the symbol in his pocket, so I had to try.

The last year Devon was here, he spent hours in the garage. We assumed he was fixing up his old Chevy Silverado, but looking back I realized that I had never actually seen him work on it at all. I had to admit this worried me a little bit.

Once in the garage I looked over the obvious places. The truck was, of course, the first place I investigated. I also checked in every single tool box, storage box and closet, and found nothing interesting. I had searched for nearly an hour and couldn't find a single trace of anything that would suggest he was into any type of cult, gang or group that he shouldn't have been. I was just about to exhale with relief when I spotted it. Engraved on the rubber handle of his hammer, as if it were a logo, was the symbol.

My heart was hammering so hard in my chest I had to sit just to calm myself down. I breathed through my nose, willing myself to get a grip. This didn't have to mean anything. I decided to carry the hammer back into my room to investigate it further. I didn't want to upset my parents, and being in the garage for a long time would have done that.

Carrying the hammer across the living room in front of them did not worry me. For the past year my parents had been only semi-aware of my existence, and I knew I could all but do a tap dance in front of them and the most I would get from them in return would be a glazed-over half-hearted smile. I knew it was a petty thought to consider, but if I'm being honest I'll have to say that I have wondered if they would have acted the same way if I would have been the one to vanish.

I walked up the stairs to my room quickly, shutting the door behind me, and threw the hammer onto my bed. It bounced a couple of times before sinking into the brown and aqua patterned comforter, the symbol glaring back at me in defiance. My hands trembled slightly as I sat down beside it, and at once my head was throbbing behind my left temple.

Instinctively I covered my eye with the palm of my hand and clasped at the pain with my fingers. "Damn," I muttered to myself. I started getting headaches the day Devon went missing, but they started easing up within the last four months. Now my headache was back with a vengeance, and made worse by catching me caught off-guard. I breathed through my nose, preparing to battle it. When I finally had a grasp on my determination to go on despite it, I picked up the hammer to examine it closer.

I had always known Devon was artistic, but I had to stare at the intricateness of his carving in awe. Had I not seen the symbol on that piece of paper beforehand, I would never have looked twice at it on the hammer. It was carved on the rubber covering of the handle with such precision that it looked as if it was done in the manufacturing process, sent through a machine and stamped there before it was packaged and shipped to the hardware store.

I traced the infinity sign with my index finger. It was like an elongated number eight that toppled over on its side, graceful and elegant. The halo of fire that surrounded it, however, could not be mistaken for anything less than sinister. Although it too was meticulous in the extreme, there was nothing soothing about it. It almost seemed like it was mocking the infinity sign, ensnaring it inside a confine of wrath. I shuddered at the thought and tossed the hammer aside. *What did I think I would find?*

The hammer missed my pillow and landed hard against the wrought iron designs of my head board. "Crap," I muttered, sure that this would pull my parents from their reverie. I heard them mumble something to each other downstairs, but a few moments passed and I knew they were not going to make any attempt to leave the comfort of their couch.

I reached behind my bed, feeling my way down the wall to get the hammer. I felt something soft and oval shaped and pulled it out to look at it. It was the end of the hammer, the menacing emblem against my palm. I flattened myself against the floor then, sticking my head under the bed, to see where it had gone. Reaching my hand across the thick carpeting, I felt something cool against my fingers. Afraid of touching it before I actually saw what it was, I bounded downstairs to grab a flashlight.

To my surprise, both of my parents were looking at me, interest blazing in their eyes.

"What are you up to Gabrielle?" My mother was trying her best to act casual, but I knew that she was really asking, *'What was all that noise about?'*

"Oh nothing. I just need to grab the flashlight."

"What do you need a flashlight for?" My dad asked. He wasn't one to care about being nonchalant. I should have considered this before being so truthful, I guessed, but it would have been too obvious a lie if I told them something different then went upstairs carrying a flashlight.

"Oh. Well I dropped something behind my bed."

He looked at me, expecting more.

"A coffee mug. I just wanted to make sure it wasn't busted into a thousand pieces or something before I reached for it and sliced my hand open." *What kind of lie was this? A coffee mug?* I decided that in the future I should come up with a lie before being put on the spot.

"A coffee mug?" My mother reiterated my thought. "Since when do you drink coffee?"

I shrugged, not knowing what to say, then turned on the spot and ran to the junk drawer in the kitchen to grab the flashlight. Once again I could hear my parents mumbling to one another in hushed voices, and when I tried to avoid them on my way to the stairs, my dad stopped me.

"Gabby, just a minute."

I could feel my face heat up and hoped that after a year of steadily ignoring me they would have forgotten how that meant I was anxious. I turned. "Yeah, Dad?"

"How did a coffee mug just fall behind your bed?"

Crap, crap, crap, I thought. I was no good at lying. Besides my obvious lack of creativity, which everyone knew was the first prerequisite of a good lie, my body was always determined to rat me out. My hands and knees started shaking, my brow furrowed, and little beads of perspiration threatened my hair line.

"It didn't just *fall*, Dad. I was setting my alarm clock and I knocked it off the stand. It hit the headboard pretty hard - didn't you hear it?" I hoped this last statement would convince him it was plausible. Instead, my first statement was what caught his attention.

"Why would you be setting your alarm clock? You get up at

the same time every morning don't you?"

Well, hell, here I go again, I thought, before I perjured myself once more. "I have to get up a half-hour earlier tomorrow. April can't pick me up for school so I thought I'd catch the bus instead." I was making things worse with every word. Now I was going to have to call April to tell her not to pick me up, then I was going to have to get up at five-thirty in the morning just to catch the stupid bus where I would be the only senior in a world of immature underclassmen.

This seemed to satisfy my dad. He scrunched his nose and said, "You can take my car if you want. Bob won't mind to pick me up for work; he's always trying to get me to go to breakfast with him and the other guys. I can catch a ride home with him too."

I sighed with relief. Lie accepted, bus travel thwarted. "Thanks, Dad." I meant it sincerely, although I did feel guilty about the lie.

"Yeah, well, maybe I'll see what I can do about getting you a car," he said, his eyes finally traveling toward the television again. "Can't believe the thought never crossed my mind before now." He mumbled his last statement to himself, and I knew I was off the hook.

Back in my room, I shined the flashlight under my bed, illuminating the chilly object that spilled from the secret cavity of the hammer. A glint of gold caught my eye, and I could just make out the shape of a key. I reached for it, the texture not at all what I would have thought.

I held the key in front of my face, absentmindedly shining the flashlight on it for a moment. I turned off the light and stared at it, awe pulsating throughout me.

The key looked as if it were made of a metal I had never seen. It was golden in color, but only slightly. It was the same width and length of any normal key, but much heavier. I closed my hand around it and shut my eyes, trying to get a feel of how heavy it was. I estimated that it weighed about the same as a roll of pennies.

I flipped the key over in my hand, eyes still shut, and felt along the length of it with my thumb. There were tiny bumps all along it, smooth like glass. On the face of the key I could feel a smooth oval. I looked down at it, the gems shiny now from my inadvertent polishing. The shaft of the key was encrusted with what looked like onyx, intricately lining the indentations that led to the bottom. The red oval gem on the face was something I didn't recognize, the color a mixture of ruby and amber. In the center of the unknown gem was the symbol again, convolutedly etched beneath the surface.

My hands started trembling uncontrollably then, and the headache that was brewing behind my left eye seemed to explode, sending shrapnel throughout the rest of my head. I clutched my head in agony, the pain so terrible it trapped my voice in my throat, rendering me mute. I'm not sure when I blacked out, but the next thing I remembered was feeling the hum.

I reached over to turn off my alarm clock before it sounded. I wasn't quite sure why my dad had suddenly started waking me up every morning, but I was sure it had something to do with my mom. The screeching sound of my alarm was probably starting to get to her, and I knew my dad would have preferred to let her sleep.

Ugh, I thought, seeing the time. *Why must he insist on getting me up before six?*

I rolled out of bed against my most heartfelt wishes, and slogged toward the bathroom, considering the outcome of my dream as I showered.

Now that I reached the source of the hum, would the dreams continue? What else could happen if they did? Would the beautiful orb absorb me or something? I had to laugh at myself for that last thought. I've always had crazy dreams, but somehow this one seemed quite logical to me. Absorption didn't quite fit.

The shower perked me up, and since I had some extra time, I decided to put a little makeup on. I lined my blue eyes with black liner, careful not to overdo it. There was a fine line between looking sophisticated and looking easy, and since I didn't consider myself either, I applied somewhere between a lot and just enough. I brushed on just a small amount of blush, having never mastered the technique. My lips always seemed too dark, so instead of lipstick I used a cream-colored gloss that tasted like French Vanilla.

I looked at myself in the floor-length mirror that was attached to the inside of my bedroom door. I could definitely use a haircut. My thin dark hair was getting a little too long for me, resting just beyond my shoulders. Normally I kept it short and fun, but after Devon went away I wasted most of my energy grieving, and my looks didn't seem the least bit important anymore. My skin could definitely use some sun. I've never had a very dark complexion, but I'd never actually considered myself to be pale skinned, either. My pants were sagging, and my shirt was baggy enough that I looked like I had not developed past the age of thirteen. I definitely needed to put on a couple of pounds; I was beginning to look unhealthy. Suddenly I wished I hadn't put on any makeup. It was wasted effort. I sighed, forcing myself away from the mirror.

My dad yelled at me from the kitchen, pulling me from my thoughts. "Gabby, there's coffee if you want a cup!"

This was our new morning ritual. We had a cup of coffee together, and then he offered me his car, which I accepted only when I knew for sure he would be having breakfast with Bob. Then I would grab my book bag and give him a peck on the cheek, and remind him to pass it along to Mom. But this morning was different. This morning he decided we should have an actual conversation. No wonder he woke me up so early.

"Hey, Gabs, I was just wondering if you needed a new dress or something," he said, leaving me completely confused.

"What? Why would I need a new dress?" I guess the shock

on my face was a little embarrassing to him, because he went slightly pink around the ears at my reaction.

"Well, I mean, isn't the homecoming dance coming up? Bob said something yesterday about having to buy Gina a dress, and I just meant that, well, you can ask for a dress you know. I don't expect you to go in an old skirt or anything." He was looking into his coffee cup, his brows furrowed.

"Oh. Homecoming." When was the homecoming dance? How did I miss that? "I really haven't given any thought to homecoming. I don't think I'm going."

"What do you mean you don't *think* you're going?"

I rolled my eyes. "Dad, you don't just *go* to the homecoming dance. You have to have a date." How embarrassing. Did I really need to be having the 'boys don't notice me' conversation with my own father?

"Oh. Well if anything changes just let me know. Like I said, it wouldn't be a big deal to get you a dress. I know they can be expensive, but that's not the issue. Gina's really looking forward to it. Bob says it's all she's been talking about for the last two weeks- "

I cut him off. "When did Gina find enough time to crawl out from under a guy to tell her dad all about a dance?" It was rude, and I knew it, but if I had to stand around listening to what a perfect daughter Gina Kupfner was it was bound to come out.

"Gabby! What has gotten into you?" As soon as he said it, I could tell he wished he hadn't. And just like any other time something went wrong, he pretended it never happened. "Here." He handed me the keys to his car. "Bob's going to be here in about five minutes, and you're going to be late if you don't get a move on."

When I pulled into my parking space at school twenty minutes later, April raced to meet me at my door. I had to laugh at her expression. Her eyes were open wide with a mixture of excitement and anger, and I could tell that part of her was dying to tell me something, and the other part was really frustrated at having to hold it in so long. I was ten minutes late.

She was so jumpy I had to roll my window down to let her spill it while I grabbed by bag from the passenger seat. I knew if I made her wait another second she would probably just attempt to bust her head through the glass to get to me. "Seriously, Gabby, can't you get to school on time without me? I mean, I've been dying to tell you something since I got here and now we've only got another five minutes until the bell rings!"

I shook my head. "So why are you wasting those oh-so-precious five minutes yelling at me? Tell me what it is that's so important."

Honestly, I don't know how April and I manage to be best friends at all. We are polar opposites and undoubtedly always will be. April is beautiful. She has waist-length blonde hair - the good kind; it holds curl during hurricane force winds when she wants it to, and can stay pin straight no matter what the humidity. She's five-six, slender, and has the figure of a swimsuit model. She's also the chattiest person I know, and everyone at school loves her - faculty and staff included.

I finally made it out of my dad's car, nearly taking April's right thumb off when I shut the door. "Well, I was just talking to Travis, and he said Curtis told him he was thinking about asking you out!" She jumped toward me with jazz hands, her mouth open in a huge smile as if she had just jumped out of the shadows screaming, 'Happy Birthday!'

"What?!" I started walking for the school, April hopping to catch up, looking crestfallen with my unenthusiastic attitude.

"Yeah! He really wanted to ask you to Homecoming, but he figured since the two of you really don't know each other that well it would probably be awkward, so he's going to see if you'll go out with him after school first." I looked at her with confusion. "You know, so by the time the dance comes around, you'll have a few things to talk about."

"So he wants to try me out first?" I didn't hide anger well. I could already feel the heat crawling up my neck.

"For crying out loud, Gabby. Don't you think you'd rather get to know him a little before getting all dressed up just to be staring at your feet at the dance? Because that's exactly what you'll do. You'll be all shy and refuse to dance with him and the two of you won't even talk at all. Don't you think it would be better to get that out of the way beforehand?" April was talking a mile a minute, but even though it was hard to keep up I kind of got what she was saying.

"Yeah, I suppose so." A smile started creeping across my face, which made me furious with myself. "He is kind of cute I guess, now that I've actually pictured him in my head."

"So you're going out with him then!" She started jumping up and down, clapping her hands.

I suddenly wished I carried a straight jacket in my back pocket. I would have put April in it just then.

The bell rang before I was prepared for it, scattering students in all directions, and before rushing off to Government, I made a mental note to tell April about the conversation I had with my dad this morning the next time I saw her.

Making my way through the crowd of students, I suddenly became aware that the hum was with me. The closer I got to Mr. Enoch's classroom, the stronger it became, although it was nowhere near as powerful as it was in my dream. It grew steadily inside of me, starting in my chest, then making its way down my arms, my fingertips finally quivering with the strange sensation.

It was odd, really, how I was pleased with it. Usually I considered myself to be quite the hypochondriac, any change in my body sending my nerves into a frenzy of panic. But this was different; it was welcome. I could only describe the feeling of the hum as fluid relief coursing through my veins. It was as if I had been instantaneously vaccinated against worry and pain, and I was glad for it.

When I reached the classroom, a smile on my face, I realized that there was only one other student there - a new guy. He was sitting at the desk beside mine, cocked back in his chair with his feet resting on the wire book rack under the seat in front of him. His thin dark hair was somewhat long, pieces of it curling around his eyes and resting on his cheekbones. His complexion was a buttery tan, his small nose and perfect lips set in an all-fact, no-nonsense expression.

"Hi," I said, hoping he didn't mistake my feel-good smile for something different.

"Hey," he answered, his expression unmoving.

"Where is everyone?" I wondered aloud as I took a seat next to him.

"The bell just rang. It's another five minutes before anyone has to be here." He was talking like I was the new student.

"But I'm always late for Government," I said with surprise. "I was all the way down by the office, and it takes forever to get clear up here." I got up from my seat and looked out the door. The hallway was still crowded. I was extremely perplexed, and looked at the new guy as if he could explain it to me. He pointed to the clock, proving to me that I had somehow made it here in around five seconds.

I scrunched my nose. How was it possible to get here so fast? I supposed I could have been mistaken about where I'd been when the bell rang. Maybe I wasn't by the office. I sometimes get to thinking so deeply that I end up in the places I intend to go without any memory of having gotten there. That could be the only explanation.

New Guy interrupted my thoughts. "I'm Julius Carter. I just moved here from Ohio." He extended his hand.

"Gabby Spencer," I said, grabbing his hand to shake it. All at once, I was a tuning fork again, the hum so loud in my ears I was sure the entire first floor of the school could hear it. I jerked my hand away in shock, as if Julius had just electrocuted me.

"Oh, sorry," he said. "I didn't realize my hands were so cold."

"It's fine," I managed to breathe out. The sensation was leaving so quickly I was starting to wonder if I had only imagined it.

A few students started to pile in then, and I turned to face the front of the classroom, ignoring them. Curtis was in this class, and I didn't want to make eye contact. I wasn't sure if April had told him she talked to me, but just in case she had, I didn't want him to think I was sitting on pins and needles waiting for him to ask me out.

I was able to sit back and relax when Mr. Enoch started class. He was filling us in on Robert C. Byrd, the Senator of West Virginia, and I knew that all I would have to do to get caught up on everything he was teaching us would be to search the internet when I got home. Besides, this was Kentland, Indiana. Why did we have to learn about a Senator from West Virginia?

I was just about to let my mind wander off when I heard someone sniggering in my direction. I looked to my right to see Gina Kupfner rolling her eyes at me. She was sitting beside Curtis, whispering in his ear while keeping her eyes on me, an evil smile twisted on her face. I knew she was talking about me. She must have overheard what April was telling me this morning and decided to use all of her sluttish charm to intervene.

Curtis shook his head at Gina, and I watched her face flood with angry shock before she turned toward me with an evil glare. I flashed a big smile and a fingertip wave in her direction. She reeled around in her seat, her honey colored waves bouncing against her too-tight sweater, to face the front of the class.

I knew I was being immature, but I couldn't help myself. I was giddy throughout the remainder of the class, knowing that Curtis would ask me out as soon as it was over.

Honestly, I didn't know why I was so happy about it. It wasn't as if I'd been harboring a big crush on him or anything. Hell, before April mentioned Curtis's potential interest in me I'm sure I wouldn't have given him a second thought. But for some reason, (even though it killed me to admit it) I was just excited to be noticed. It could have been anyone, and I still would have had the same butterflies-in-the-stomach feeling.

But what topped it all off was the fact that Gina Kupfner had been scoffed at. And the guy who did it was about to ask me out as soon as the bell rang.

I was lighthearted throughout the rest of the class, daydreaming various scenarios of Gina being rejected by assorted football players and wrestling team captains.

I had to admit to myself that this was turning out to be a pretty good day.

When the bell finally rang, I gathered my notepad, book, and pen as slowly as I could, acting as if I was having trouble fitting them into my book bag. I was trying to let the class empty out as much as possible to give Curtis a chance to approach me.

I quickly looked around to see that most of the students had already left. As I was throwing my book bag over my shoulder, I looked up to see Gina walking swiftly toward the door. Before she made it, she ran into me, shoving her right shoulder into my left one, knocking me to the floor. I was so angry I barely heard her gleeful cackles as she left the classroom. My neck was heating up, goose bumps rising on my arms.

Curtis was behind me, picking up a few things that spilled from my bag when I hit the floor, and suddenly my anger switched to humiliation.

"She's not exactly what you would call kind, is she?" I looked up to see Julius extending his hand to me.

"Definitely not," I answered, before letting him help me off the floor. I grabbed his hand and nearly fell again. The shocking sensation was traveling up my arm, the hum so loud in my head I wanted to cover my ears. The wind was knocked out of me, my knees becoming weak. I was sure that another second of this would render me unconscious, and I jerked my hand from Julius's.

All of my senses came back in a fraction of a second, the feeling of electrical shock completely negated. I stared into Julius's eyes, searching them for an answer. He stared back into mine, as if in silent respond, admitting the odd sensation came from him. The eye contact lasted only a second, but I was sure about what I saw in them. He nodded at me, and then turned toward the door, my eyes following him, willing him to wait for me. He slowed down and stopped just outside the door, leaning against the frame.

Curtis handed me a couple of my pens and a few cough drops that he'd picked up from my spill, then gave me a faint smile. He ran his hands through his blonde spikes, the muscle in his forearm flexed slightly. I wondered momentarily if this was for my benefit, and I could feel the warmth crawling up my neck. "Gabby, I've been meaning to ask you if you'd like to see a movie with me this weekend?" His statement turned into a question, and he looked at me with hopeful eyes.

I stared into them for a moment, thinking that for a fraction of a second his gaze was more eager than hopeful. An odd feeling shot through me then. It wasn't the hum this time; nothing like it. It was something more like fear, and I took a step back. "I appreciate the offer C-Curtis," I stammered, "but I've already made a date for this weekend. Maybe some other time."

I thought I noticed a flicker of fury in his eyes before I chanced a glimpse in Julius's direction, but when I whipped my eyes back to Curtis's there was nothing in them but calmness.

I shook my head, trying to rid myself of the insanity that seemed to be slowly seeping into me. First I was sure there was some kind of electrical current running through Julius, and now I was imagining I saw something evil in Curtis's eyes.

"Yeah, some other time. I'll give you a call," Curtis said, his voice peaceful. Then he walked past me and glared at Julius.

This time, there was no denying it. There was fury in his eyes, and I knew I did the right thing in turning him down. (Well, lying to him anyway.) The anger in his eyes was a flashing yellow light screaming caution.

Just then the tardy bell rang, wrenching me from my contemplation, and I groaned. I was supposed to be in Chemistry

II with Mrs. Barnes. She always shut her door after the tardy bell and vehemently refused entry to any latecomers without a written excuse from the office.

I sighed. So much for this turning out to be a pretty good day. There was only one thing left to do. I was going to ditch the rest of the day. It wouldn't be too hard to convince my dad to write me an excuse; I would just tell him I was having cramps or something and had to leave school to go home and lay down. Of course, my mom was there, and she would know I didn't actually come home. Oh well, I would have to figure out the details later. All I knew right now was that I was definitely leaving.

I made it all the way to my dad's Buick in the parking lot before I realized Julius was walking with me. I jumped at this realization, and Julius laughed.

"Ditching? You don't really seem the type," he said.

"How would you know?" I retorted. I was pretty annoyed by now. It was only ten minutes until nine, and my day had already taken a drastic turn for the worse.

"Just an observation really." He leaned against the Buick. At first glance he looked cocky and arrogant, but looking into his face all I saw was thoughtfulness. "That Curtis guy thinks you turned him down because I convinced you to go out with me before he had a chance to ask you. I've officially just made my first enemy thanks to you; the least you could do to make up for it is try to be pleasant." He smiled at me, flashing a dimple.

"How are his assumptions my fault?" I tried saying it sharply, but his grin softened the bite, and I inevitably found myself smiling back at him.

Julius changed the subject quickly. "So where are you headed?"

I really hadn't thought that far ahead. I knew I didn't want to go home, but I really didn't want to be hanging out at the grocery store either, which happened to be the most exciting place in Kentland. "Watseka," I said suddenly. Where it came from, I'm not sure, but it did make the most sense.

"Ah, crossing state lines - a fugitive. Mind if I come along? I haven't been to Illinois yet."

I looked at him a moment then said, "Well, my mother always told me not to pick up strangers, but seeing as how I'm officially a criminal now I don't see how breaking one more rule would hurt." I unlocked the doors and we both got in. As I started the car I said, "This makes us even; sneaking you away from school counts as being pleasant."

Julius laughed, and I felt the hum trickling through my veins once more.

Chapter 2 ❖

It was Saturday morning, and the crisp autumn sunshine that filtered through my window woke me up before nine. I realized this was the first night I hadn't dreamed of the hum, and I was racking my brain to remember what it was I had been dreaming. I gave up after a few minutes, unable to grasp at the fleeting images for more than a fraction of a second.

I climbed out of bed and stretched, then pulled my hair into a ponytail and headed to the bathroom to brush my teeth.

Midway through my morning ritual, I heard my mother's soft sobs coming from my parents' bedroom, followed by my father's reassuring voice. "Nina, please. You have to stop doing this, it's been a year."

My heart dropped. Devon had been gone for a year today. How could I have forgotten? I rinsed my toothbrush and placed it back in the purple plastic cup by the sink.

I closed the toilet lid and sat down on it, the chill from the ceramic creeping through my thin pajamas and sending goose bumps up my back.

My mother's sobs became harder, and I heard her stutter through them, "Just go, Vick. If you want to go on pretending you never had a son then that's your business, but *I'll* never forget. Just go. Leave me alone."

I heard my father sigh and then the creaking of the bed as he left it. Their bedroom door opened up, and I could tell he was paused in the doorway. "I miss him too, Nina, but we have a daughter to think about. I can't allow my grief to take over, not when it could mean losing both of our children." He shut the door quietly behind him, the sound of the latch catching sending an eerie silence throughout the house.

I waited until the sound of his feet against the soft carpet in the hallway faded before I drew a breath. Tears were stinging my eyes, the lump in my throat finally winning. I grabbed a tissue and dabbed my lashes, trying as best as I could to keep myself from crying. It would be too hard on Dad to have to deal with Mom *and* me. When I felt I had it under control, I looked at myself in the mirror. He probably wouldn't notice, but I turned on the cold water and splashed my face just to be sure, then made my way down to the kitchen to make a pot of coffee.

Dad was sitting at the table, his laptop open, trying his best to convince me he'd been typing a column for the paper all morning. "Morning Gabs," he said a little too enthusiastically.

"Morning, Dad. You and Mom want a couple of eggs or something?"

"Mom's pretty upset this morning. I don't think she'll want anything." I could hear the hurt in his voice, and the attempt to cover it.

"Don't worry, Dad," I tried to reassure him. "She'll come out of it sooner or later."

He sighed. "I know." He shut his laptop quickly, and then turned to me with determination. "You know Gabby, I'm really proud of you. At first I thought you'd never get better. The way you locked yourself in your room and refused to eat, crying until your eyes were swelled shut, I thought I'd lost you. But you slowly crept out of it. I know the pain will never go away, at least, not until he comes home, but you've done a great job of making an effort to live."

I didn't know what to say to that at first, but then I realized he was really thanking me for not being like Mom, and I understood what he wanted to hear from me. "It's just going to take her longer is all. She'll get there; she just needs something to reach for. Maybe we should start asking her to do things for us. If we let her know we need her, it might help."

He thought about that for a moment. "You know, I think you're right. We've been taking care of everything around here; it's probably making her feel like she has nothing to contribute." He smiled then, which made me feel so much better.

"Let's start tomorrow. Today her grief seems kind of appropriate," I said, trying to hide the somberness in my voice.

Dad's face fell slightly. "Yeah. I know." He released another sigh.

I poured us each a cup of coffee, and sat at the table with him, trying to think of anything but Devon. My thoughts turned to yesterday, when Julius and I went to Watseka instead of finishing the day at school, and suddenly I knew I had to tell my dad now instead of waiting until Monday to bring it up.

"Hey Dad," I started, approaching the subject reluctantly. "I have to tell you something. Yesterday after Government class I left school and went to Watseka for the rest of the day."

"Why?" He sounded a little angry, which made me glad for some odd reason.

"Gina Kupfner shoved me down after class, which made me late for Chemistry, and Mrs. Barnes won't let you in without an excuse from the office. I was really upset, so I just…left. I know I shouldn't have let her get to me like that, but, I don't know, I just needed to get away. Sorry." I paused before adding, "I'd appreciate it if you would write me an excuse." I dropped my head and put my hands in my lap, waiting for the reprimand.

There was a long pause while my father thought. Then, finally, he said, "I'll write you an excuse. I definitely don't want you to ever do that again though. If you do, I promise you I won't be so lenient." He said it harshly, and I knew he meant it. Then, in a softer tone he asked, "Why did Gina push you down?"

I sighed. "She thought a guy in our Government class liked me, and she wanted to humiliate me in front of him."

"Why would she want to do that?"

"Because she's a -"

Dad raised his hand to stop me before I could get the word out. "Never mind. I should have known better than to ask."

We sat in silence for a few more minutes, and then he said, "I think I found a pretty decent car for you. Do you want to go look at it?"

My eyes perked up in surprise. "Really?"

"Sure."

"What kind is it?"

"A Ford Focus. Used, but in pretty good shape."

I wasn't sure what a Ford Focus was, but I figured if he was willing to buy it for me I wouldn't worry about it.

"Let me get a shower before we go," I said, enthusiastically jumping from my chair.

"Take your time, these car lots don't open before eleven on Saturdays anyway."

I hopped up the stairs, a little excitement in my step. In just a few short hours I would have my very own car, and that helped to take my mind off of Devon.

"I want you back before dark," my dad called before I pulled out of the driveway. "You aren't used to driving at night yet."

"No problem!" I was trying to keep the smile out of my voice, but I wasn't sure I was doing such a good job of it.

"I love you, Hon. Wear your seatbelt and say hi to April for me." My mom was waving from the porch, which was part of the reason it was hard for me to repress my grin. It was close to three and she was still in her robe, her short dark hair sticking out in various places, but she was trying to force a smile, and that told me that she *wanted* to get better. I learned in my Psych class last year that that was the first step.

"I'll never take it off, I promise. Love you!"

I backed out of the driveway, my legs a little shaky from excitement.

I hadn't called April to tell her I was coming; I wanted to surprise her. She and I hadn't talked since yesterday morning, and I expected her to be a little sore with me for turning Curtis down. She was always telling me I needed to get out more - to have a little fun, and when I seemed somewhat happy with her news of Curtis's interest in me she felt like I was taking a small step forward. She was happy for me, and I kind of felt bad knowing I let her down.

I knew she would forgive me as soon as I told her about my day with Julius. I actually had a pretty good time with him. He was casual enough that I didn't feel self-conscious around him and funny enough to keep me laughing, which was a good thing, considering I kept worrying about the trouble I was going to get into once my dad found out what I'd done. Julius didn't seem to worry about getting in trouble at all, which I found odd, considering he only attended one class on his first day at a new school. He laughed at me when I pointed that out to him and told me he wasn't in school because he had to be.

We ate at Dairy Queen around noon. Julius bought us both hot dogs and a shake, and when he handed me mine our fingers touched and I was certain this time that I felt the hum. I tried to search his eyes the way I had after he helped me off of the floor in Government, but this time he wouldn't look at me. He acted as if he hadn't noticed anything, so I let it go.

Maybe I really did have an overactive imagination. Maybe I was slowly going insane.

After slurping up the last of his milkshake he asked, "So what's the deal with this Gina girl? Why does she have it in for you?"

I groaned silently to myself. The afternoon was just starting to get pleasant and he had to go and bring her up. I shrugged. "It's not just me, really. She has an aversion to any girl who's just about to be asked out by a decent-looking guy."

"Oh. One of those girls, huh?"

"Yeah." I rolled my eyes. "Her dad and my dad are pretty good friends. They work together at the *Rensselaer Republican*. Bob picks my dad up every once in a while and they have breakfast on their way to work. Dad sort of gave me hell about Gina this morning - 'Gina's *excited* about Homecoming. Bob just bought her a new dress' - ugh. I've never really talked to her or anything. I guess it's wrong to judge her, but…"

"After what she did to you this morning I would say your judgments couldn't be more correct." He tossed his empty cup into the dumpster. He seemed to be pondering something for a minute, then said, "Are you sure that's the only reason she did that? I mean, I saw the looks she was giving you in class, and she and Curtis were whispering back and forth all morning."

"What? I saw her whispering something to him after she caught my attention, but I figured she was just counting on Curtis to flirt back with her and she wanted me to see it. When he shook his head at her she glared at me like she wanted to leap across the classroom and decapitate me." I had to laugh a little.

"Actually, they were in a pretty deep conversation before that." Julius looked worried, like he was trying to solve a murder mystery.

"I didn't notice. Anyway, it isn't a big deal. I don't plan on going out with him, even if he does call, which he probably won't." I knew it was stupid, but I sort of wished he would call. I was being honest; I wouldn't go out with him, but for some reason it felt nice to be noticed.

"He'll call," Julius said, his brows still set together as if in deep thought. His expression never changed when he asked, "Why did you tell him no?"

"I didn't tell him no. I told him I already had a date."

Julius rolled his eyes and let his face settle into a smirk before saying, "Okay, let me rephrase my question. Why did you lie to him?"

My face twisted into a mixture of embarrassment and shock. Was I so repulsive to the opposite sex that it was considered common knowledge that I couldn't get a date?

Julius read my expression well, and immediately became apologetic. "I'm sorry, that came out wrong. What I meant was, well, I could read it in your face. You're not a great liar."

I took a deep breath. "I guess that's considered a bad thing."

Julius cocked his head to the side, contemplating. "No - actually, I happen to think it's a quality to be admired. It's just that for most people your age it seems to be a requirement for living."

I cocked a suspicious eyebrow toward him. "What do you mean 'your age'?"

"Did I say that? Slip of the tongue. I meant *our* age."

I wasn't totally convinced. My eyes squinted instinctively as I asked, "How old are you?"

"Eighteen," he said quickly, without hesitation.

I tried to catch him off guard. "When's your birthday?"

"September first," then catching my mouth opening with another question he added, "1991."

We sat in silence for a few minutes, then he asked, "So when's *your* birthday?"

"August twenty-ninth – 1991."

Julius flashed me a smile that warmed my insides. "So you're just a few days older than me."

Another moment of silence and he said, "You never answered my question."

I looked at him with confusion.

"Why did you lie to Curtis?"

I shrugged. "I don't know, really. April told me he was going to ask me out and I was all prepared to say yes, but when he asked me..." I trailed off. What was I supposed to say? That Curtis scared me? I could just imagine Julius laughing at me for that one.

"What?"

"I'm not telling you; you'll laugh at me."

"No I won't. Seriously, Gabby, do I look like the kind of guy who would laugh at you?" He had that cat-that-ate-the-canary grin spread all over his face and I had to smile.

"Alright." I paused, rolling my eyes at myself. I couldn't believe he talked me into embarrassing myself. "He had a weird look - like he was way too eager for me to say yes." I could feel the heat climbing my neck. "I guess it just scared me a little."

I turned my head away from him, not wanting to see his reaction. I was sure it would be one of suppressed laughter.

"I figured that was it," Julius said, surprising me.

I whipped my head back toward him. "What do you mean?"

"I saw it too. It only lasted for a second. There was something sinister in his eyes, but he caught himself and recovered quickly. He just wasn't fast enough." The tone and facial expression Julius had was serious. His elbow was resting on his knee, his chin in his hands, reminding me of Auguste Rodin's sculpture, *The Thinker*. His eyes were squinted as if he were grasping at an idea that kept extending, never quite able to reach the end of it.

I don't know how long I was staring at him, but when he looked up and saw the wondering on my face Julius checked his watch. "We better get going, school lets out in fifteen minutes and I'll need to get my car."

We made it back to school with perfect timing. All the other students were piling into their cars, making it easy for us to be inconspicuous. When Julius got out of the Buick, he waved with a smile.

I honked the horn of my little blue Focus when I pulled into April's driveway. I saw her peek through the curtains of her room and I waved as I opened the door to step out. Before I even made it to the door, April wrenched it open, nearly yanking it from the hinges.

"You finally got a car!" April had a way of stating the obvious without sounding extremely annoying.

"Dad took me to get it today. I know it's not the coolest thing in the world, but at least it's mine." I patted the car's glittery blue hood like it was my pet.

"It's really cute Gabby!" I could tell she meant it, and that pleased me for some reason.

"Plus, at least you didn't have to get a job to get it," she said sourly. "My parents laughed at me when I asked them to buy me a car."

April still held the job thing against her parents, even though she liked working at Murphy's Grocery. She would never admit it though.

"So do you want to go for a drive?" I was dying to be behind the wheel.

"Where do you want to go?" April had a big smile on her face, unable to hide her happiness for me. Maybe that was why I liked her so much; she was one of those people who could be genuinely pleased for others.

"I don't know. Anywhere's fine with me."

April rolled her eyes. "Jeez, Gabby, do I always have to be the creative one? Let's just go to Watseka and grab a pizza or something. Mom's been starving me. She just found out about this diet where you put pureed vegetables in everything. Honestly, she's never been much of a cook before this; I don't know why she thinks we're actually going to eat the crap she's attempting to make now."

We jumped in the car, (fastening our seatbelts as promised) and headed down the road toward Illinois.

Once April finally stopped gabbing enough to take a breath, I leapt at the chance to talk. I told her all the details of my adventurous Friday, starting at the part where Gina sniggered at me, and ending with the part about dropping Julius off in the school parking lot. April interjected a gasp or a giggle every now and then in reference to my play-by-play commentary. When I was finally finished, she practically exploded with her opinions of Gina, calling her all the things I hadn't thought to.

"So you're not peeved at me for the whole not going out with Curtis thing?" I was a little surprised that she hadn't gasped at that part.

"Gabby, please. You really need to stop worrying about other people's feelings so much. If you don't want to go out with him that's your business. I was just excited to see you smile about something."

I heaved a sigh of relief. I knew she was right. Getting over other people's feelings was something I definitely needed to work on.

"So what does Julius look like? Is he good looking?" I caught the inflection in her voice when she said his name, and I knew she thought I was interested in him.

"Yeah, I guess he's good looking." I pulled into *The Pizza Shoppe* then and killed the engine.

We were walking across the parking lot, April chattering happily in my direction, when I noticed a ragged old woman staring my way. Her face was bony and her skin so translucent I could make out every vein that crisscrossed her features. Her long white hair was thin, wispy, and yellowed from lack of washing. Her eyes were set deep in their sockets and rimmed in deep purple. Meeting my gaze, her face contorted into an ugly snarl.

She backed up toward the white painted blocks of the restaurant, as if my presence was terrifying. When I looked at her, puzzled, she lifted a bony finger at me and said in a coarse dialect, "The owner of the secret walks among us, and all must be prepared for the upheaval she will place upon us! It is she who seeks to open the gates of Hell!"

It sounded like an accusation, and I turned to look behind

me, sure I couldn't be the one she was referring to, but everyone in the parking lot was staring at me.

The old woman seemed as frightened by me as I was bewildered by her. Her frail eyes darted left and right, stricken with terror. Her bony fingers clutched at the wall behind her now, as if she were backed into a corner by street thugs. Suddenly, something that sounded like a sob came from her throat, and she turned on the spot, running down the alley behind the restaurant.

I stood there, frozen. The entire parking lot was quiet now, and I could feel everyone's eyes scanning me. Goose bumps covered my skin, the hair on my neck and arms raised with a violent prickle. Slowly, whispers erupted all around me, and all at once I was thawed out by the feeling of the hum.

It started in my chest, radiating throughout my torso until it reached the tips of my toes. I suddenly became aware of a hand on my back, and I turned to see Julius staring at me with understanding in his eyes. "This might be a good time for an explanation," he whispered in my ear. "Take April home and meet me behind Murphy's." I nodded silently, and just like yesterday, as soon as he removed his hand from me the entire calming sensation was ripped away, leaving me weak-kneed.

"Forget the pizza, April. I need to go home." My voice was quivering and April grabbed my elbow.

"I'll drive," she said, making it sound more like a demand than an offer.

I nodded and handed her my keys. On the way back to her house, she made me feel better by making fun of the old hag, and commenting on Julius's good looks and obvious charm. She thought it odd, though, that he seemed to come out of nowhere. When she offered to have me stay the night, I refused politely.

"No, thanks. I need to get something to eat anyway. Sorry we didn't get to have any pizza."

"Don't worry about it, it wasn't your fault. I have to work tomorrow, so I'll grab something decent there."

I jumped into the driver seat and said, "Oh, I almost forgot. Mom said to tell you hi."

April's face turned into a wide smile. She knew how hard my mom was taking Devon's disappearance and she looked as relieved as I was to hear she was making *some* progress. "Tell her I said hey!"

I backed out of the driveway and honked as I headed down the street. Murphy's Grocery was only about a mile away, and I wasn't sure that was going to give me enough time to get my thoughts in order.

First, there was the matter of the hum, which I was completely and beyond a reasonable doubt convinced had something to do with Julius. Secondly, there was the scary old woman who accused me of seeking the gate to hell, whatever that was, and third, I wanted to know what all of this had to do with me.

As I pulled into Murphy's I noticed Julius at once. The door to his car was open, and he was standing with his left foot on the ground, his right foot still on the floor board. His left hand was tightly gripping the door, his right one beckoning me impatiently.

Instinctively, my jaw dropped. Was this the same car I dropped him off to at school yesterday? I couldn't remember if I noticed his car or not, which told me that it most definitely could not be the same one; there was no way I could have *not* noticed *this* vehicle.

I jumped out of my Focus and ran to his car, dropping into the black leather passenger seat. Before I got my seatbelt on, he hammered the gas pedal, gravity slamming me against the durable interior. My heart was beating against my ribcage furiously, and at once I was weak with fright. Sensing this, Julius rested his hand on my shoulder, the hum taking over my senses and calming me in record speed.

We were turning corner after corner, maneuvering the tiny town streets much more easily than should have been possible at our current rate of speed. I watched serenely, (thanks to the hum), as familiar streets became distorted, indecipherable blurs.

I must have been much calmer at that point than I should have been, because the first question I asked him was, "What kind of car *is* this?" I was running my fingers along the sharp contours of the interior, the sleek black leather slightly giving under the pressure of my fingers.

Julius laughed, and he started to pull his hand away. I quickly jerked it back.

"It's a 2009 Dodge Challenger - 6.1 liter Hemi V-8, 425 horsepower."

He could have been speaking Greek for all I knew. "Oh. How fast are we going?"

He cocked an eyebrow, and slowly released his hand, waiting for me to object. When I didn't, he continued. "Relax. We're only going 55. Once we get on the highway I'm planning to open it up, though, so you'll want to hold on."

"What do you mean 'open it up'? You're going to floor it?"

Julius laughed again. "Yes."

"How fast does it go?" My anxiety was reaching an all-time high now that Julius's hand had abandoned my shoulder.

"I really don't know," he said unworriedly, "It's registered for 180 though. Hold on."

I gasped. We hit the open highway with enough speed that I was sure my seat was about to swallow me whole. The roaring sound of the engine was deafening, and the faster we went the more it felt like floating than driving. I clutched the console, my fingernails tearing into the heavy leather.

Somehow, amidst all of the horror, I found my voice. "What is going on?"

Julius stared straight ahead, his eyes concentrating on the highway, his foot focused on the pedal. "Curtis is up to something. He knows."

"Curtis knows what?!"

"As soon as I'm sure he's not anywhere near us, I'll fill you in. Right now it's best if I concentrate."

I couldn't argue with that logic. I kept my mouth shut, not only because he asked me to, but also because I found it difficult not to. We were registering 180 now, but I was sure we were going faster, as the needle on the speedometer was threatening to do a three-sixty. Nothing outside of my window seemed to exist, all of nature was a blur of browns and reds; it was as if we had been sucked into an enormous vacuum.

Finally, after what seemed like a lifetime, the car started to slow down. I could feel my seat releasing me, and the blood returning from the back of my head to the front. I eased my grip on the console and breathed.

Julius pulled the car over into a small clearing, my head bobbing idiotically as he crossed a ditch, then smacking hard against the passenger window as we slid sideways into a stop. He turned the Challenger off and stared out the window for a moment, his eyes investigating the field. I watched as his expression changed, as if he had stopped searching with his eyes and started listening instead, hearing something I couldn't. He looked at me with surprise, and suddenly I heard it.

A low rumble was coming from the earth, like a subway train traveling quickly below us. The rumbling steadily grew louder, and all at once the vibrations turned into tremors. It felt as if a storm were brewing below the surface of the Earth, thunder roaring beneath us, and I gasped in horror when the realization hit me. We were in the middle of an earthquake.

With the speed and agility of a panther, Julius leapt up, putting one foot on his seat and the other foot between my knees on mine. He forced his hands against the ceiling of the car, his face strained and his muscles hard and tensed. It took a moment for me to realize what was going on, but when I looked out the window from my crouched position beneath Julius, I understood.

All around us the earth was changing. I watched in awe as the ground sprouted thick rock; ragged peaks of soil and stone heaving upward. I watched as trees toppled over, their thick trunks lifted from the ground. I watched as the land cracked, forming small canyons throughout the clearing. I watched as everything around me was consumed by destruction. And all the while, I was still, the earthquake never moving me, Julius putting all of his unnatural strength into keeping me safe.

Then, all at once, everything became calm. Julius slumped himself on top of me, whether from exhaustion or relief I couldn't tell.

The earthquake lasted only a few seconds, but it had been enough to throw me into shock. My chest was heaving, my breath heavy. A chill came over me, and it was if a frost had silently crawled up my spine, maneuvering itself in such a way that it settled in my stomach. Sweat had saturated my thin cotton shirt, Julius's warm breath against my chest sending goose bumps up my neck.

Finally, Julius lifted his head from my body, staring into my horror stricken eyes. He reached toward me, and instinctively I shoved his hand aside.

"No, I don't want you doing that!" My voice was cracked, and I was trying my best to keep my composure.

Julius looked at me, confused. His olive colored eyes were filled with concern, and I could tell it took everything he had not to reach out to me.

Without thinking, I grabbed him by his jacket and pulled his face an inch from mine. My breath was heavy in his face, but I didn't care. "I need to know what you are!" My voice was quivering now, a lump quickly swelling in my throat. Julius paused, contemplating. I shook him. "Explain!"

"Alright!" He pulled away from me, opened my door, and effortlessly maneuvered himself around me. As he stepped onto the ground he offered me his hand, which I refused with an accusing glare. I stepped out of the car, and he sighed as my knees buckled beneath me and I fell.

Julius extended his hand once more, this time offering a promise. "I won't do it if you'd rather I didn't." I hesitated, and then accepted his offer. He lifted me with ease, grabbing me around the waist and hoisting me onto the hood of his Dodge. He stared into my eyes, and with a look on his face akin to quickly ripping off a Band-Aid he said, "I'm a sentinel."

Chapter 3❖

    I swallowed. "You mean like a guardian angel or something?" My voice was a mixture of fear and awe.
    "No." Julius bowed his head, thinking. A moment later he said, "It would be impossible for you to understand unless I started from the very beginning." He sat down on the hood next to me and tossed his head back, thinking. Finally, after contemplating how to begin, he stood, his eyes calm, facing me.
    "Everything in the world has an opposite. Day has night, black has white, and good has evil. Heaven has Hell. Then, there is Earth. Can you think of its opposite?" He was studying me. His brows were furrowed and his head was tilted, waiting for a response.
    Shakily I answered, "The sky?" I knew it was ridiculous the moment it came out of my mouth, and I rolled my eyes at myself.
    Julius shook his head, much like a college professor would to a pupil. "The sky is a part of Earth. It can't be its opposite."

I thought for a minute. I contemplated the moon, but then figured the sun was the opposite of it, then thought perhaps it was outer space in general, but that didn't seem to make sense to me. The sun and the moon existed in outer space just as much as Earth did, so that definitely wasn't it. "I can't think of anything."

"That is because Earth has no opposite."

I didn't understand. "But you just said everything in the world has an opposite."

"Perhaps I should have said everything that *has to do* with the world has an opposite."

I raised an eyebrow. I should have known it was a trick question. Julius was starting to get on my nerves. "Just get on with it," I said sharply.

Julius chuckled, but before I could reprimand him he continued. "You obviously believe in angels, since you thought I might be one, so I'm sure you know the opposite of an angel is a demon. Just to clarify, angels come from Heaven; demons come from Hell, and the two places clash - severely.

"From the beginning, Hell and its creatures have tried to gain control over Heaven, and so Earth was created, surrounding Hell on all sides, acting like iron bars on a prison cell, only much, much more effective."

"Earth was eventually covered with life. God created man, beast, and vegetation, each in male and female form - opposites of one another. Everything was given free will, as every creation had before the earth was made."

"So Earth was created as a barrier between the opposite worlds, and the only way for Hell to take over Heaven would be to conquer Earth first. However, since Hell was located in the center of the earth, it was impossible to know what it was like. This left the demons very vulnerable, but eventually they found a way to penetrate the bars of their prison without ever having to leave."

I interjected, unconvinced. "A loophole?"

Julius nodded earnestly. "Exactly. Just as the demons had

exercised their free will not to be part of Heaven, others did the same. There were new arrivals - human souls. They informed the demons of what the outer wall of their prison had become. The demons were furious. They felt as if they were being made a mockery by God and the angels. But the demons soon realized something that made them glad that Earth was filled with life. These human souls could easily glide through the walls of their prison and end up on the outside. They did not need access to the gate to get out."

"Soon, the demons devised a plan. They would use one of the human souls to enter an unborn child. These hybrids were called malefactors. The child would live as a human, and have no memories of its life among the underworld until the demons felt the time was right for it to 'wake up.'"

"The purpose of the malefactor was to recruit as many people as it could and form an army. The army of the malefactor would then turn on the good people of Earth, destroying those they could not control with fear, and use the others to find and unlock the gate for them. The location of the gate to Hell is unknown to everyone in the underworld. They believe now that only a truly good person can find it, so by taking hostages and forcing them to look for it, they assume they can make their escape, and conquer Earth. What they weren't counting on, or perhaps the thought just never occurred to them, was that everything has an opposite."

My eyes widened. He didn't have to tell me. I already understood what he was about to say. "Sentinels are the opposite of malefactors."

"Yes," Julius said. He seemed pleased that I was smart enough to figure that much out on my own. "But I think it is important to tell you how my kind came to be." He cleared his throat as if he were about to make a very important speech. "The way this works is a very miraculous process." He blushed, a little embarrassed about admitting his feelings of reverence before continuing. "When a malefactor is made - when a soul enters a fetus - something else happens. Another child is created in the same womb. It is an exact contradiction to the malefactor. If the malefactor is a girl, a boy is created. If it is a boy, a girl is created. This extra child, miraculously conceived, is a sentinel. Twins."

"I don't understand what all of this has to do with me," I interrupted.

I wasn't being completely honest. I *had* found a connection. The symbol I found on my brother's things was one of a satanic cult. Now all of a sudden I had a sentinel following me around, telling me about demons that make malefactors. The malefactors recruited armies. Was my brother a part of this army? Did one of these malefactors talk him in to joining, or did they just scare him with threats against my family to get him to agree to do their bidding?

Or was it something more? Was Julius trying to tell me that my brother was a malefactor, and as his twin I was a sentinel? I shook the thought off. If that were the case, wouldn't I know it? The twin thing had to be a coincidence.

Then there was this whole business of the old lady who accused me of seeking the gates of Hell. Did she say I wanted to *open* them? I couldn't remember, but it was becoming evident that I did fit into this bizarre story in some way. I just wasn't sure how yet.

Julius sighed and scratched the back of his head, his shoulder length hair sticking up in the back. "This is the rough part." He bent his head back, trying to think of the easiest way to tell me the rest. Finally, after a few seconds he said, "The old lady in the parking lot."

I cringed at the thought of her. "What was she talking about?"

"First of all, I should tell you what she is," he said.

"A malefactor?"

"No. She is what we call a remorseful one."

"A...remorseful one?" That definitely didn't sound good.

"What is that?"

"There is only one way to escape from Hell. You have to feel remorse -"

I interrupted him. "Wait. You just said that human souls could come and go. They wouldn't need to escape would they?"

"It's a little more difficult than that," Julius said, his face strained with frustration. It was hard for him to find the words he needed in order to explain everything correctly. "Souls need to be where they are most comfortable. Imagine everything you feel, everything you believe in - in its concentrated form. There is a reason we have bodies while we walk the Earth." He sighed in aggravation. "The only way I can think to explain it is this: A car has a check engine signal that comes on whenever something is not working right under the hood. When that signal light starts flashing, we take it to a mechanic to get it fixed. If that signal didn't come on when there was something wrong, we would probably just keep driving the vehicle until it broke down."

"Souls are very similar. Our earthly bodies act as a check engine signal. If we get scared, we shake. When we're happy our hearts beat faster. Without these signals, our souls would be out of control. That's what I meant when I said they have to be where they are most comfortable. If they were evil, and you put them in a place where they had to deal with good things, it would be really bad. Same thing goes for a good soul. Souls in the wrong places are very unstable. Without a body to inhabit, they wouldn't want to be on Earth for very long."

I took a deep breath. Things were really starting to get confusing, and I wasn't sure if I would be able to keep track of it all. I released my air and said, "Okay. So the old woman was a remorseful one?"

"Yes. As I was saying, the only way to escape from Hell is to feel remorse. No one who feels something so unselfish could live there. That is the total opposite of what it was made for."

"When a soul feels remorse for the things it has done, it is expelled back to earth, and immediately enters a fetus. It then has to go through a life very similar to the one it had most recently lived through. The process is not pleasant, but it is necessary. It makes the soul, for lack of a better word - healthier."

I raised an eyebrow. "How? If someone is going through pain, wouldn't that make their soul that much more bitter?"

Julius nodded. "It can. Some souls end right back where they came from, but for some it is very successful, and after their time on earth is over, they are glad they had the opportunity to do it again."

I still didn't understand how it could in any way be considered healing. It seemed almost cruel to me.

Julius read the expression on my face and continued. "The healing comes from getting past and obstacle. When a remorseful one is going through its second life, it is actually going through a rehabilitation process. There are parts that can hurt, but once you realize you can make it past the rough spots, you start to feel better about yourself."

That was hard to swallow. Not that I didn't agree with the reasoning behind it, but because I was imaging the worst parts of my life, and having to relive them. I couldn't fathom having to live another life where my brother disappeared.

No matter what anyone says, there is no getting better. You don't slowly get back to normal, you just get used to the pain. The happiness my brother gave me is gone. In its place I've acquired a dull ache, and I've adjusted to fit it into my life. I've gotten used to its presence, so it's a lot easier to deal with now, but it never goes away.

I looked up to see Julius giving me one of those you-poor-thing smiles. I got the impression he knew what I was thinking, and that scared me.

"I haven't gotten to the worst part yet," he reminded me. "The old woman knew something about you."

I gulped. I remembered what she said vividly, and after everything Julius had just told me, I really wasn't sure I wanted to know how I fit into opening the gates of hell. "I came to you to tell you. I have to prepare you." Julius took a deep breath and said, almost reverently, "You are a sentinel too."

That did it. I leaped from the hood of his car in shock. My ears started to ring, my knees started to shake, and a cold sweat came over me. My body was shivering violently, and I was getting very dizzy.

Julius jumped to my side, putting his hands on my shoulders to steady me. "If you want me to calm you down I will, but I won't do it without your permission anymore."

I wanted to say no, to tell him to go away and never come back, but instead I said, "Just don't let me faint."

At once the dizzy feeling vanished, my knees stopped shaking, and the ringing in my ears and the cold sweats dissipated. My body was left with a pleasant tingling sensation, but I still felt the same anger and confusion I had before I nearly fainted. "Thanks," I said weakly.

"No problem."

"I wouldn't say that," I said sharply as I yanked his arms from my shoulders. Anger was ripping through me with the force of a hundred wild horses. "I happen to think there is a huge problem. What makes you think I'm a sentinel? Was it that old lady? Because she could have just been crazy you know." I was practically shouting at Julius now. I felt a little bad about it, because his eyes were screaming apologies at me, but I couldn't help it. I was angry.

"No. I knew before she said anything," Julius said regretfully. He led me back over to his car.

I refused to sit on it. I leaned up against it instead.

"I still have a lot to tell you," he said hesitantly. "You might want to sit."

I shook my head stubbornly, refusing to look him in the eyes.

Julius sighed, his cheeks puffing out, causing the hair around his face to flutter. Shaking his head he said, "Alright. Have it your way." He leaned against the car beside me and continued. "You understood what I told you about the opposites, right?"

A lump started to build in my throat and tears were prickling my eyes. "Yeah. If I'm a sentinel, my brother is a malefactor."

The tears started flowing down my cheeks the moment I said it out loud, and I turned my head away from Julius. I didn't want him to know how bad I was feeling. For one thing, it was a little embarrassing, and for another, I didn't want him to feel any worse than his expression told me he already was.

He put one hand on my shoulder. There was no hum, just the warmth of his palm through my sweater. I turned to look at him, wiping the tears from my face with the edge of my sleeve. His olive eyes were pained, and at once I realized why. He had been in this same position at some point during his life. He was remembering how it felt.

I threw my face into his chest then, knowing he needed comfort as much as I did, and sobbed, his arms wrapped tightly around my torso. He rested his chin on the top of my head, consoling me. I could have stayed there in his arms forever, and I knew he would have let me. There was something about the two of us sharing the same pain that made me feel like the dull ache that's been living inside of me could possibly disappear. Like two negative ends of a magnet, the pain was being repelled from both of us.

Finally, after what felt like forever, I had no more tears left, and when I lifted my face from Julius's chest I realized the sky had turned lavender. I had about ten minutes to make it home before dark.

I jumped away from Julius. "My parents want me home before dark." I looked around, letting the damage from the earthquake sink in. "Oh my God! I didn't even think to check on them!"

Julius was helping me into the car. "Don't worry. We're the only ones who got hit with it."

My eyes were wide. "How do you know?"

Julius hesitated. "Curtis did it. He's sort of working for the underworld now. He's part of their army." The engine of the Challenger roared to life, deafening me when Julius revved it. He maneuvered around the small ditches and trees almost too easily, and slammed the gas pedal into the floorboard the moment we were on pavement.

This time, my breathing remained steady, although I still clutched the console hard enough to make my knuckles turn white. I wanted to ask Julius more about Curtis, but I was worried I might distract him. We were going fast enough now that if we were to wreck, I was sure we would disintegrate on impact.

As I was looking out the window I tried to discern the surroundings that were flashing by. I had only just now realized that I had no clue where we had been. It was somewhere off of the highway, and it had only taken us about five minutes to get there, but that was with Julius going almost 200 miles an hour. I estimated that it would have taken about twenty minutes to get there doing the normal speed limit.

The car slowed steadily, and I knew we were nearing Kentland. The outside world was becoming discernable now; I could even make out street signs. "Do you always drive so fast?" I asked, suddenly aware that if the earthquake hadn't killed us Julius's driving very well could have.

"No, only when it's necessary. Too many bad things can happen when you speed."

I was glad I hadn't asked him that when we were headed toward the clearing; his answer certainly wasn't very comforting.

We pulled into Murphy's and Julius let the motor idle while he searched his glove compartment. He pulled out a pen and grabbed my hand, scribbling a phone number across my palm. "This is the number to my cell. Call me as soon as you get in."

I nodded, then got out of his car and walked over to mine. I looked back at Julius as I was unlocking my door. He was scanning the parking lot. *Probably looking for Curtis,* I thought.

I jumped into my car, my hands shaking enough to make putting the keys into the ignition difficult. I finally got it started, the little four cylinder engine sounding weak compared to the deafening rumble of the Challenger's V-8. I chuckled to myself at the sound of it, and then pulled out of the parking lot.

The sky was getting darker, and I was hoping that by the time I pulled into my driveway, (which would be in about three minutes) my dad wouldn't consider it night yet. I would have to try to convince him to let me drive after dark. Not that I had a whole lot of places to go after the sun set, but it seemed a little ridiculous to be eighteen and forbidden to drive after dark.

I rounded the corner onto my street and looked over at the clock, now glowing brightly in the dimly lit car. 8:01. When I pulled in the driveway and turned the car off, I noticed my dad's head peeking through the curtain. *Damn*, I thought. He'd probably been checking out the window for me since seven-thirty.

I checked my face in the rearview mirror, hoping my recent crying spell wouldn't be obvious. I knew I would have to act casual so as not to alert my parents, so I swallowed, willing the shocking revelations about Devon and I to find a spot somewhere in the already present pain that was located somewhere below my sternum.

I sighed as I got out of the car and shut the door. Dad had just stepped out onto the porch. He would probably demand the keys and forbid me to drive anywhere but school until I graduated.

Apprehensively, I walked up the steps and was surprised to see a grin on my dad's face. "Right on time!" He tapped the face of his watch proudly. "How did it do?"

"As well as the Buick," I said, not knowing the kind of car lingo he expected from me.

"Good, good." He still had that giant smile, like there was an exciting secret he had that was killing him to keep from me. He continued with the small talk, which made me that much more suspicious. "So did you and April have fun?"

I didn't know what to say to that. Had that been what the smile was about? Did he find out that she made it home much earlier than I did, and now was trying to catch me in a lie? I decided I'd take the chance. There was no way to explain to him what had happened during the last few hours. I drew a deep breath, preparing for the inevitable beads of sweat to start forming on my forehead. "Yeah."

"Good, good," Dad said, rocking back and forth on his feet, his smile as wide as ever. "Where did you go?"

I got the idea he was stalling, or maybe he was just trying to see how far I would take it before I finally cracked and told him everything. "Watseka. April wanted some pizza. Her mom just found out about this pureed-vegetable diet thing. April's been dying for some real food."

"Good, good."

Now I was convinced my dad wasn't even listening. He was making small talk on the front porch with me to keep me from going in the house. What was going on in there? I peeked around his shoulder, trying to get a glimpse through the window. He moved with me, blocking the view. I laughed. "What is going on?"

"I don't know what you mean," my dad said teasingly.

Now I was smiling. "Come on, Dad. I know you're trying to stall me. Nobody says 'good, good' to anything unless they don't really care what you're saying. Tell me what's going on."

Just then the lamp flickered on and off in the living room. I looked at my dad quizzically, and he laughed.

"I guess you'll just have to find out yourself," he said, opening the door for me.

I stepped inside and was surprised to see my mother dressed in a pair of new jeans and a pale pink sweater. She had fixed her hair; the short spikes I had gotten used to were now tamed into curls. There were quite a few grays mingled in with the shiny brunette locks, and it wasn't her usual style, but it was definitely nice.

Her face, though somewhat older than I remembered it being, was highlighted with blush and lipstick. Her pretty blue eyes were skillfully outlined, making them stand out as if they were demanding more attention than the rest of her features.

Mom smiled at me and I smiled back timidly. I wanted to run into her arms and tell her how much I loved her. I wanted her to know how happy it made me to see her smiling like she truly meant it. I wanted to tell her I missed her, but I knew how fragile she was. I knew that, like staring at a deer in the woods, one step toward her could send her sprinting in the other direction, so I was forced to admire her happiness from afar.

She cleared her throat, trying to find the voice she used to use back when she was happy. "I made lasagna."

I tried to smile as if it were the most normal thing in the world. "Sounds good." I sniffed. "Smells good too."

My dad interjected. "Hope you didn't get too full on the pizza." He patted his stomach as he said it, and I was glad he found it so easy to act as if everything was as normal as it always had been. I loved that he was able to act as if this hadn't taken Mom ten times the effort it would have a year ago.

He sat down at the table and began helping himself to the lasagna, salad, and garlic bread. I caught Mom's eye then and we both started laughing. It was such a good feeling that tears pricked my eyes, and I hoped that I could pass them off as tears of laughter.

As Mom and I sat down at the table, Dad looked back and forth between the two of us in bewilderment, as if he couldn't understand what was so funny. His expression was comical enough to send us into another round of laughter, and this time I was unable to stop. I bent over, clutching my stomach, tears spilling down my face. My mother was in a very similar position, and finally Dad tried to calm us down. Through a mouthful of food he said, "Awight. S'not that funny." The look on his face was serious, and it was too much. I was laughing so hard I couldn't breathe, and my sides hurt. Mom was smacking her leg, gasping for breath between peals of laughter.

The relief I felt was overwhelming. For a year my mother and I had barely spoken. She would ask me questions occasionally, verifying that she knew I existed, but she never gave any indication that she wanted to spend time with me. I stayed out of her way, sometimes hoping that we didn't cross paths in the hallway or kitchen. It was just too hard for her to look at me and know the other half was missing.

I'm not sure why, but there were times when her grief irritated me. It sounds horrible, I know, but sometimes I couldn't stand to look at her when she was overcome with sadness. I guess it was because I always felt like Devon was out there somewhere, and she was acting like he was gone for good. It was like she just gave up and surrendered herself to the thought of never seeing him again.

Now here we were, being a real family again. The best part was that it was so effortless. We weren't trying hard to make it work. It was all so natural.

The worst part was that the pain Devon left in my chest was still there, and my own laughter felt like salt to the wound. I was sure my mother felt the same way. Right now I was angry at Devon for leaving us, and I was trying my best to get back at him by having a great time with the rest of my family.

By the time Mom and I calmed down, the lasagna was fairly cold, but we ate it anyway. It was just as good as I remembered it being. I ate two pieces and a very large plate of salad. Dad ate most of the garlic bread, but I managed to grab the last slice before he did. It felt great to be full. I hadn't eaten like this for a long time, and it was making me very sleepy.

All through dinner Mom and I did impressions of Dad's serious expression, laughing at each other most of the evening. Dad found it pretty amusing too, once he saw what it looked like, but we never had an actual conversation until dinner was over. I had just set my fork down and emptied my glass of milk when

Mom spoke up.

"I hear the homecoming dance is in a couple of weeks. Who are you going with?" she asked indifferently.

Dad risked a glance in my direction. His expression was apologetic, and I knew he had filled her in on the conversation we had yesterday morning.

I slumped back into my chair. The homecoming dance made me think of Curtis, which made me think of Julius, which made me nervous. I just realized he told me to call him as soon as I got in, and I wondered what he was thinking now. It had been about forty-five minutes since I'd seen him. I needed to find a way to call him without my parents finding out. I didn't want them to think I wasn't enjoying our time together, especially since it had been so long since we'd really been a family, and I didn't want my dad to suspect that I lied to him about where I had been earlier.

I suddenly had an idea. Answering my mother I said, as casually as I could manage, "Actually, I'll be going with Julius Carter."

Dad tried hard to hide the surprise on his face. "I thought you said you weren't going!"

"Well, Julius asked me in Government class, and I said yes." I shrugged just to prove it was no big deal.

"Oh. So that's why Gina knocked you down."

My face turned red. I had forgotten I told Dad about that. "Actually, no. Another guy - Curtis - asked me to go to a movie this weekend, but I had already told Julius I would go to the dance with him. Gina had no idea about Julius. She was mad about the other guy."

"Curtis Desmond?" My mom asked curiously.

I was surprised when she mentioned his name. "Yeah. How do you know him?"

Mom pursed her lips and shifted her eyes to the table. Trying to sound cavalier she said. "He was a friend of Devon's. The two of them hadn't been hanging out for too long before..."

A wave of shock hit me. For some reason after Julius had mentioned it, I had been under the impression that Devon had simply woken up in a trance one day and walked out, but from what my mother had just said, I gathered that there had been some sort of planning with Curtis before he left.

"He was only here a couple of times. The two of them worked on the Chevy. I don't think he ever even came in the house." Dad assumed I was thinking I hadn't remembered Curtis and Devon being friends, and mistook my shock for guilt.

"I just forgot. Like Mom said, they hadn't been friends for long." I was trying to hide the tremor in my voice as I answered him.

How did I miss this? This should have registered to me, especially when Julius told me Curtis was part of the underworld's army.

"Well," Mom said, trying to turn the conversation to a more cheerful topic, "Have you thought about a dress? I could take you down to Lafayette to find one tomorrow if you'd like." I could tell Mom was getting excited at the thought of the two of us out shopping together. "With your dark hair you would look so pretty in something pink."

My insides were groaning. Why did I keep getting myself into these messes? For some reason, every time I told a lie I ended up inside a car. "Sure," I said with as much enthusiasm as I could muster. I started this lie as an excuse to call Julius, and now I was going to have to make a fool of myself by asking him to take me to the dance just to get by with it. What would I do if he refused? My neck started to heat up just thinking about it. I would definitely have to stop this lying business.

I started to clear the table to put some space between me and my parents. I hoped they hadn't already noticed the telltale signs of my apprehension; the beads of sweat that had been forming on my forehead were beginning to trickle down the sides of my face. "I'm just going to finish these dishes up and then go call him," I said, not looking at either of them.

As I was loading the dishwasher, the doorbell rang, interrupting my mother's suggestions about how I should wear my hair to the dance. The three of us shared looks of confusion before it rang for a second time and Dad went to answer it.

The hair on my arms rose when I heard a familiar voice. It was Julius. This was going to be the most humiliating moment of my life. My parents were sure to bombard him with questions about the dance, and he would have absolutely no clue what they were talking about. If there was one moment during my life when I wanted to curl up in the fetal position and hide under a rock this was definitely it. Julius was sure to think I was crazy.

"Gabby, Julius is here to see you!" Dad sang from the living room.

"Coming!" My voice cracked with fear and embarrassment. I quickly started the dishwasher and headed to the living room, my knees shaking ferociously. "Hi," I said weakly when I saw him.

"Hello," Julius answered politely. He was looking into my eyes as if he were trying to convey a silent secret. "I hope I'm not interrupting anything," he said to my parents. "I was hoping to talk to Gabby about the homecoming dance. I don't know if she told you, but I asked her if she would go with me."

My jaw dropped. Did he know that I had just told them this very thing, or, like me, was it the only thing he could think of to use as an excuse to talk?

Mom spoke up pleasantly, "Actually, she was just telling us about you, Julius." She extended her hand. "I'm Nina. It's nice to meet you."

My heart began beating wildly the moment I saw Julius reach for her hand. What would my mom do when she felt the hum? I sighed with relief when I saw her hand drop back to her side when the handshake was over. She was showing no sign of having felt anything abnormal.

Julius extended his hand to my dad who said, "Vick." He didn't seem to think there was anything unusual about his touch either.

Relief flooded me before I remembered that Julius had put his hand in mine earlier today without leaving me with the hum. He promised not to use it on me without my permission, and it dawned on me that he must have some control over it.

"I understand that it's getting late, but I wondered if it would be okay if Gabby could come along with me to a friend's house." Then he added, "If she would like to of course."

What was going on? There was little chance my parents would let me leave with a guy they just met. Or would they? I just realized I had never been in this position before. I had no idea what they would say.

Inquisitively, I looked at my parents. They were staring into each others faces, puzzled as to what they should say. There were a couple of shrugs and nods as they shared a conversation composed completely of body language, and then they seemed to reach an understanding. They turned to the two of us; Dad's arms were crossed and Mom was wearing a pleasant smile. I knew they decided I could go.

"Since it is a Saturday night, and your curfew isn't until midnight, I don't see any reason why you can't go. However, we would like to know where it is you are going exactly." Dad ran his fingers over his graying mustache when he finished, and I knew he was trying to intimidate Julius.

"We'll be at Evan Currant's. He invited the entire senior class over to his house to work on the homecoming float. It's the week after next and so far no one's come up with a very good theme to go on. Evan's a little worried." Julius was so convincing that I wondered if maybe he was actually telling the truth.

My parents obviously accepted it, because they both perked up excitedly. They were the kind of parents who hoped my high school experience would emulate those cheesy teenage movies from the eighties, minus the sex, drugs, and drinking. I imagined they hoped I would start a ridiculous new dance craze that everyone miraculously fell in step to at the homecoming dance. I cringed at the thought.

"Well, alright then," Dad said cheerfully. "Just be home by midnight."

"It was nice to meet you Julius," Mom trilled as we started for the door. Then she caught me in a hug and kissed my cheek. "I love you Gabby," she whispered in my ear.

I had to pull away before I started to get choked up again. It had been a long time since Mom and I had any type of sentimental exchange, but I'd done enough crying for one day. "Love you too, Mom. Dinner was excellent."

Dad waved to us as we stepped out the door, and once outside in the fresh air I exhaled deeply.

I hadn't realized I was sweating until the cool night air hit my face and sent chills all over me. I started to shiver, but I wasn't so sure it had anything to do with the weather. I was nervous. Once I got inside the car and buckled my seatbelt, I folded my hands together and tucked them between my knees to control my shaking. I didn't want Julius to notice, but evidently he did, because as soon as we pulled out of the driveway he offered me his hand.

I groaned. "Am I really that obvious?"

"Very."

I took his hand and smiled as the hum trickled through my veins, warming every part of me from my scalp to my toes. It was odd how the hum did exactly what I needed it to. This time it left me a little more comfortable than I normally would have been. I wondered if it customized itself according to my needs, or if Julius had total control over it and was making it do what he thought I needed it to.

Once I was entirely relaxed, I released Julius's hand and asked, "So where are we really going?"

Julius laughed. "You actually thought I would lie to your parents?"

Calmly I said, "We really are going to Evan Currant's? Huh."

"What?" Julius asked.

"Huh?"

"What did you say 'huh' for?"

I shrugged. "I just didn't think you would actually go to someone's house you haven't even met."

"Who says I've never met him?" Julius wasn't the least bit irritated. In fact, he was a little smug. I knew he was just dying to tell me how they'd met.

"Come on, Julius. You've only been to school for one day and only spent a total of forty-five minutes there. You ditched with me, and Evan isn't even in our Government class." I thought for a minute before asking, "Did you meet him outside of school? Is he your neighbor or something?"

Julius exploded with laughter, which really irritated me. When he finally calmed down he said, "Evan is in our Chemistry II class, our English class, and our Sculpture class. We've met. And no, we are not neighbors."

I was completely confused. The only other possibility that I could think of as to how the two of them could have met would be for me to have totally neglected to notice that Julius had been in school before yesterday. "When was your first day?"

"Yesterday," he said matter-of-factly.

I could feel my neck heating up, and I knew that the hum's effect was wearing off.

"Okay, obviously there is some sort of secret you are keeping from me, and I haven't figured it out on my own. Tell me what it is please."

Julius shrugged, and then pulled into the parking lot of the dollar store. He shut off the engine and turned to me, this time with a serious expression. "There are a few things you and I need to discuss. Actually, there are a few more things I need to explain to you, and you need to listen."

I was staring at him, my expression mute. I would listen to what he had to say.

Julius accepted my cooperation with relief, and then went

on. "As sentinels, you and I have a few attributes that normal humans don't. You saw what I did in the car during the earthquake. We have a lot of strengths. I just figured that the quicker you learned how to use them, the better."

I raised my eyebrows in anticipation.

"The first thing I need to teach you is how to bi-locate." He paused, monitoring my reaction. When he was satisfied that I wasn't going to gasp, he continued. "We can be in two places at once, and I think that it would be very wise for you to learn how to do this tonight, because while I told your parents we would be at Evan's house, there is another place we need to be as well."

"Where?" I asked.

"I need you to meet a very old friend of mine. He is my mentor, to be honest. His name is Cordele, and he is a sentinel too."

Chapter 4❖

After everything Julius had told me, this is what made me gasp. "There are others?"

"Absolutely. According to Cordele, there are now five of us including you."

He started to say something else but I interrupted. "Really? Where are they? How does he know? Is Cordele the leader or something?" I had more questions, but Julius raised his hand to stop me.

"This is why we need to see Cordele. He can answer your questions much easier than I can. And no, I wouldn't call him the leader." He chuckled to himself before adding, "He's much too modest to even entertain that idea."

He fell back into the seat and closed his eyes, thinking.

I couldn't help it. I had to stare at him. It was hard not to notice Julius. Everything about him was so...*good*. I particularly liked the way his dark hair looked against his toasted-colored skin. His face was a little scruffy, something you didn't see much on boys his age, and up until now I didn't realize how attractive I found it.

A tingling sensation was starting between my abdomen and my sternum, and I quickly turned my head to look out my window. I was breathing rapidly, and I hoped that Julius was in such deep thought that he couldn't hear me. I tried to calm myself down, wiping my clammy hands across the legs of my jeans.

What was I thinking? *The first time I'm alone with someone I am physically attracted to and my animal magnetism takes over.* I winced at the thought.

Suddenly Julius tapped me on the shoulder.

I jumped and let out a little yelp of fear.

My outburst must have scared Julius, because he jumped too. "Are you okay?" He asked after seeing me with my hand clutched against my chest.

I was breathing heavily again, this time due to fear, and the armrest of the door was jammed into my back. I nodded. "You just startled me."

Julius was nodding now. "I could tell." He reached for my arm and cajoled me into the seat properly. His expression turned apologetic before he said, "Actually, I meant are you okay with everything that's going on? I saw you staring out the window. Tell me what you were thinking."

My face instantly heated, and I was glad the only light in the car was the soft glow of the dusk-to-dawn light in the parking lot; I had to be red. There was no way I could answer him truthfully - at least not without dying of embarrassment. "Oh. I was just wondering about how the whole bi-locating thing works," I lied.

Julius's face perked up and his lips formed an amazing grin that threatened to liquefy my insides. "I know it sounds impossible, but it's actually very simple." He opened his car door and stepped out.

I watched closely as he shut the door and bent down, looking at me through his window. "When you can't see my head anymore, look out *your* window," he said.

I watched as his head descended below his window, then turned to look out mine. For the second time that night, I jumped and screamed. There was Julius, winking back at me. In a flash he had vanished, and I turned in my seat to find him sitting next to me once more.

I clutched my chest which was heaving uncontrollably. I immediately grasped Julius's hand and pressed it hard right below my throat.

He smiled at me, and I thought I caught a hint of awkwardness in his eyes. I released his hand abruptly, not wanting to make him uncomfortable, but his expression changed in an instant, and he returned his hand of his own accord.

My heart slowed as the hum infiltrated me, and at once I was relaxed.

Julius left his hand on my chest as he talked. "Sorry I scared you, but it was inevitable. I had to prove that it was possible, otherwise you would never be able to do it yourself." He was searching my eyes, trying to find out if I understood. When I nodded to him he smiled, then said, "All you have to do is think of the two places you need to be."

There had to be more to it than that. Nothing was that easy. I rolled my eyes. "*Visualize*," I said sarcastically.

"Exactly," Julius said, ignoring my cynicism.

"But you said we were going to see Cordele. I have no idea where that is," I pointed out.

"Actually, you don't need to. You just have to think that's where you need to be."

I looked at him, unable to understand how that was possible. How could I think of a place I needed to be when I had no idea where it was? It made no sense to me.

Julius sighed in frustration. "Tell me about a person I've never met, but don't tell me where they live."

I thought a minute. "My Grandma Fran."

Julius closed his eyes in thought. When he opened them a few seconds later he said, "Right now I'm at your Grandma Fran's. I'll be back in a moment to tell you certain things that I've seen while I was there, just to prove that it's possible. The thing is, you don't have to *imagine* the person or place, you just have to *think* the name of the person or place." He paused then, and I noticed his hair moving, as if a soft wind were blowing around him. He looked at me seriously and said, "Okay, I've made it back. Your Grandma Fran is asleep, thank God, because I ended up right beside her bed. There are four pictures on her dresser. One is of your family, one is of another couple and three children, one is of two boys on bicycles, and the other is an older man in a work uniform standing beside a train."

I nodded to confirm what he just told me. I remembered those pictures well. My uncle Roy was a couple years older than my dad, and they were the ones on the bicycles. He and his wife Sylvia have three kids - two boys and a girl, and my great-great-grandpa Jim was the one standing next to the train. He worked as an operator for the B & O Railroad, and Grandma talked about him often. He was her grandfather, and was raised by him and his second wife after her parents died in a barn fire.

"So see, it's very easy. Just think 'I need to be with Cordele,' and you'll be there." He talked as if it was something people did everyday.

I closed my eyes, thinking of Cordele, but nothing happened. I sighed in frustration. Had I really expected anything different? I opened my eyes. "Nothing."

"Sorry," Julius said. You have to think, 'I need to be with Cordele, *and* I need to be here with Julius.'"

I rolled my eyes and shook my head. This had to be the most ridiculous thing I have ever attempted. This was all probably just some enormously absurd joke he was playing on me. I had to be the most gullible person alive. He'd probably start laughing any minute and then tell the entire school about it on Monday. I glared at him.

As if he knew what I was thinking, Julius placed his hand on mine, filling me with the hum. He was proving to me that everything he told me was real, and it was hard to dispute anything when I was filled with euphoria. I closed my eyes.

"I'll meet you there," Julius whispered encouragingly.

Julius's words filled me with a feeling I had never experienced and I smiled, instantly thinking of the two places I needed to be. I wanted to meet Julius there, and so I knew I would.

This time, something happened. I could have been a wisp of smoke. I felt as if I were weightless; that I existed where nothing else did. It lasted for only a fraction of a second, and when I opened my eyes I was standing next to Julius in a very unfamiliar place. I was also aware of sitting beside him in the Challenger, beaming at him. It was extremely odd.

Julius patted my hand as we sat side by side in the car. "You get used to the feeling. Pretty soon it will feel as normal as swinging your arms while you walk."

I smiled and put my hand on top of his. "I believe you."

In the unfamiliar place, I let my eyes roam. Evidently I hadn't given much thought to how Cordele lived, because although this was easily the strangest place I had ever been, I wasn't surprised in the least.

The entire first floor was an open area, the kitchen stove and refrigerator on one end, a small bench with mismatched cushions and a tiny, rabbit-eared television on the other. Beside the couch was a door, which I took to be a closet, and beside the door was a set of stairs.

The size of the dwelling and its outdated furnishings wasn't what I found peculiar. The oddest thing about the place was that every object I set my eyes on had a duplicate in a smaller version.

Against the wall beside the refrigerator was a small dining table. Beside the small dining table was an even smaller dining table. Beside the television was a very normal sized desk, much like the one in my own room, and next to it was a small one. Bookcases lined every available wall; a short one following every tall one.

I heard footsteps on the stairs then, and Julius winked at me. Cordele was slowly making his way down the stairs; the sound of his hand sliding against the wall for support was very prominent. When he came into view, I was taken aback.

He was barely taller than me, his back hunched over slightly just below the neck, and his thinning white hair stuck out in shabby tufts on either side of his head. The skin around his mouth was wrinkled and long, giving him the look of a bulldog, and his nose was large, reminding me of the drawings of Neanderthals that were in my science book my freshman year.

"Julius!" He stretched his arms in welcome as he stepped off of the last stair. His appearance may have been that of an aging man, but his demeanor was very youthful. He embraced Julius in a tight hug, patting his back with gusto, apparently thrilled to see him. "I have to admit I wasn't expecting you so soon." Then, turning to me he said, "I am very delighted to see you here. Very delighted. Under the circumstances I assumed that it wouldn't be easy to convince you, but evidently I have underestimated Julius. I will have to find a way to make it up to him."

I was bewildered. What did he mean 'under the circumstances'? Was he referring to everything Julius told me, or was there something more? I got my answer soon enough.

Julius coughed, an invitation for Cordele's attention. With his eyes he was warning him not to proceed with the present conversation.

Cordele's expression changed suddenly; embarrassment and anger toward Julius taking over. His eyes were scolding Julius, who returned a diffident gaze. "Apparently I have been elected to fill in the blank spots," Cordele said to me. "Were you aware that there were any?" He glared at Julius while speaking to me.

"Not until this moment," I answered weakly.

I, too, was angry with Julius for not telling me whatever it was that was so pressing, but for whatever reason, I was furious with Cordele for reprimanding him. I wanted to stand in front of him with my arms stretched wide, preventing Cordele from demeaning him with his potent stare.

Cordele acknowledged my defiant appearance and smiled. Turning to Julius he said, "I apologize for my quick temper. There was no excuse."

I relaxed my stance, slightly embarrassed for the obvious profusion of emotion I felt toward Julius.

Clearly intent on changing the subject, Julius asked, "Where is Nayana?"

Cordele's eyes perked and a smile found his face. "She is asleep at the moment." He chuckled. "She so wanted to go to Los Angeles, but I am currently doing research in Rome, and she certainly can't be running about in a large city without a chaperone. She is a little sore with me."

"You mean you're in Rome *now*?" This bi-location thing was nothing short of miraculous to me.

"At this very moment," he affirmed.

Just then I heard soft footsteps on the stairs.

"Whether it is her inquisitive nature or her intuition I do not know, but whatever the reason Nayana has decided to join us." Cordele's eyes twinkled when he said her name, and he seemed pleased that she didn't appear to be holding a grudge.

The three of us turned our attention to the stairs, and once I saw her I gasped.

I had expected Nayana to be the same age as Cordele, and had assumed that she was his wife. In fact, by the way he had talked of a chaperone, I presumed she was in poor health. I couldn't have been more wrong.

Standing at the foot of the stairs was a beautiful dark-skinned child in pink flannel pajamas. Her dark, almond shaped eyes were mesmerizing, as if they were the source of all knowledge. Shiny waves of deep brown hair flowed to the middle of her back, and her small hands were folded in front of her. She couldn't have been more than six years old.

"Julius," she nodded in greeting. Then turning to Cordele she said smugly, "I couldn't resist meeting another female. I suppose that would make me inquisitive." She walked over to me and held out her hand. "It is nice to finally meet you, Gabrielle. I've been very curious about you."

I shook her hand gently, trying to resist the urge to bend down to her level and tell her how lovely she was. Something told me she wouldn't like being treated the same way other children were. "My friends call me Gabby."

She smiled at me, making it very hard to refrain from pinching her cheeks. "Please sit down," she offered politely. "From what I gather, there are many things to discuss." Then, addressing all of us she said, "I would like to ask that we be as quiet as we can, I'm sleeping upstairs and I really don't want to be disturbed."

"Of course," Cordele said, and he pulled a kitchen chair next to the bench.

We all exchanged looks while we were seating ourselves, and finally Cordele spoke up. "So, Gabby, Julius told you that you were a sentinel, and that you could bi-locate. What else did he tell you?"

I fidgeted, unsure where to begin. "Well," I started, "he told me that I was a sentinel, and that there are malefactors." I swallowed, the thought of my next statement leaving my throat dry. "My twin brother, Devon, is one of them." It was harder to say out loud than I had anticipated, and I had to pause while trying to subdue the lump that was forming in my throat before going on. "A boy I go to school with, Curtis Desmond, is part of his army, and he caused an earthquake earlier today to try and get to me."

After these words, Cordele's patient expression turned to one of shock. Of course Julius hadn't told him about this. Cordele had made it clear that he hadn't seen Julius today.

Julius interrupted. "It's true. The moment we made eye contact I knew who he was. He was trying to get Gabby alone, and when she declined his offer of a date he was furious. I knew he would try to get to her, so I monitored him closely all day. When I found out what he was going to do, I took her out to a remote spot while he performed the earthquake. He targeted her, and I knew if she were in a populated area the destruction levels would be high."

Cordele sighed. "Very quick thinking, Julius. You did the right thing." He looked up at Julius then and added, "But you should have told her."

My brows furrowed. "Told me what?"

Cordele and Julius stared into each other's eyes, and Nayana placed her hand on mine.

It's something horrible. Julius and Cordele are arguing with each other over who will tell me, and Nayana is trying to prepare me. I couldn't stand the silence. I needed to know what it was they weren't telling me. "What?!"

Finally, Julius spoke. "Gabby, I need to tell you what the purpose of a sentinel is."

I gaped at him. "B-but isn't the purpose of a sentinel to protect people from malefactors?" I had to be wrong. If I wasn't, his expression wouldn't be so crestfallen.

"That is...part of it, but that isn't our main objective," he refused to break eye contact with me. He exhaled sorrowfully and said, "Gabby, our purpose is to -"

Don't say it, I thought.

"We've all been where you are right now -" he tried to console me.

I closed my eyes, feeling the lump in my throat swell. *Please don't say it.*

"I know how difficult this is going to be for you to hear -"

Please, please, please don't say what I think you're going to.

"Gabby, our main objective is to eliminate our malefactors."

I slumped into myself, the ringing in my ears fierce. The

cold sweats were beyond my control, and the shaking that started in my knees quickly spread throughout me, my body jerking frenziedly. It felt as if my temperature had bottomed out, my insides were shivering with cold.

This can't be right. I have to have heard him wrong. But I knew I heard right. Trying to convince myself of anything other than the truth right now wasn't going to help. Right now I had to find a way to cope with this disturbing realization, and later I could find a way around it, because one thing was certain, I would *never* eliminate my own brother.

Tears were spilling down my face now. Why was this happening to me? Devon and I had been best friends up until the day he went missing. It was next to impossible to imagine him being anything less than perfect. He had always been polite, empathetic, kind, and mannerly. How did all of that change? How was I supposed to accept that he was evil, when I'd never known him to be any such thing?

Grief was swallowing me, leaving me somewhere deep within its entrails. I could have fought it, but there was something about the horrible pain that felt wonderful, and I suddenly realized why my mother found it so difficult to climb from its belly. I was ingested by it, and I knew that if I let it, it would break me down into a million pieces, using me as its source of survival. I fell deeper within the pain, willing it to take me, hoping it was strong enough to destroy me.

Guilt was ripping through me now. I deserved to be eaten alive by it, because I dared to entertain the thought that what these people were telling me about my brother was true. How could I have done that to my brother? I shouldn't have listened to them. I should have defended Devon the moment Julius insinuated he was anything but faultless.

I couldn't stop crying; couldn't stop the pain. I didn't want to. I earned this anguish, and I owed Devon my agony.

As I was delving deeper and deeper into my heartache, I slowly became aware of voices penetrating the wall of pain.

They were familiar, and I liked them, but I refused to reach for them. I didn't deserve the pleasure they gave me. The farther I strayed from them, the stronger they became. The voices were so forceful that I could no longer focus on my pain. They were strong and I was weak. I tried to fight them, but the more I persisted, the more adamant they became, until they had evolved from voices into feelings, and suddenly I was filled with the strongest feeling of happiness I had ever experienced. I had to have died and went to Heaven. There was no earthly feeling that this could have been compared to.

I felt as if I was gradually drifting upward, the feeling of exhilaration guiding me from the agony that had briefly encapsulated me. I was grateful for the escape.

I don't know how long I was drifting, I only knew that the relief it gave me was wonderful. I never wanted to be anywhere but there in that existence of infinite happiness.

Eventually, however, the happiness resumed its original form of voices, and they seemed to be getting louder and louder until finally they were right in my ear. My eyes fluttered open due to the increased volume and I saw Julius's face staring at me, his eyes wide with concern.

There was a damp cloth on my forehead, and I reached for it instinctively. My hairline was soaked, but I wasn't sure if it was from the cloth or if I had been sweating that profusely. I tried to sit up but Julius gently pressed his hand against my shoulder, silently letting me know it was better for me to lie down. Nayana noticed me stirring and was quickly at my side, retrieving the spent cloth from my forehead and preparing a clean one. *It must have been sweat.*

"How long have I been out?" I asked Julius feebly.

"About fifteen minutes. I'm not sure if that's normal or not, but Nayana and Cordele were sure you'd be fine."

He fell silent after that, letting me process my thoughts.

I tried hard not to think of the whole elimination process, but the thought was branded in my brain. I tossed the idea around my head, coming up with no other solution to escape it other than ignoring it completely. I had made my decision; I would walk away from Cordele, Nayana and Julius and never look back. If it was up to me to destroy my brother it would never happen. I wouldn't do it.

Timidly, Julius disrupted my thoughts. "It's hard. I know it is, but you have no other option. You were created for this."

A tear trickled down my cheek at his words.

Cordele bent down to me, offering what he thought were encouraging words. Quietly he said, "Who Devon once was and what he is now are two totally different things. The moment you see him you will understand, and your instinct will take over."

My heart pounded at the insinuation that Devon and I would see each other again. "When will I get to see him?" The excitement in my voice was obvious. I sat up, this time ignoring Julius's gentle shove.

Cordele, Nayana and Julius all exchanged glances, and this time it was Nayana who silently volunteered. She placed her small hands on mine and said, "We all dealt with this situation in a very similar way as you have. First we refused to accept it, then we tried to find a way of escaping it, and finally, when we realized we would be able to see our loved ones again we were hopeful." She bowed her head and released my hands. "Perhaps it will be easier for you if you are prepared in a way none of us were." She exhaled, and then looked into my eyes. "You have never experienced grief like you will the moment you see Devon again. The sight of him will inflict torturous, unadulterated pain. He isn't who you remember him to be, nor has he ever really been who you thought he was. Everything good in him was a ruse; trickery built into him before he was ever delivered from your mother's womb. It was a necessary tactic. It is harder to defeat someone you love and care about, and so every malefactor in history has been equipped with all of the necessary traits to acquire love. He was unaware that it was only a defensive weapon while he was younger, but as soon as he discovered who he was, he acknowledged the fact that all of the goodness in him was false."

I didn't know what to think or how to feel. I became numb. Julius reached for me, but I held my hands up to stop him. I needed to think. I stood up and walked around the small area a couple of times, trying to process what Nayana had just told me. After a couple of laps I had finally grasped what she was trying to get me to understand. "Are you trying to tell me that Devon is equivalent to a robot?"

She nodded sweetly.

I looked at Julius, my eyes stinging from the crying I'd done. "I have to eliminate him?"

"Yes."

"And if I fail?"

He looked at me with the most serious expression I had ever witnessed. "Eternal damnation. All life will be reduced to pitiful existence. Happiness and love will be reduced to nothing more than a hopeless concept. Pain and misery will take on new meaning. Hell will be right here on earth, and everything and everyone will exist in it."

I was void of speech. There was nothing more to be said. At this moment I had a choice. I could attempt to eliminate my brother, which would cause me pain, or I could give up and let him and his army convert the earth into their own personal torture chamber. Why did the greater good always have to suck? I sat down and put my head in my hands.

"So tell me what I have to do," I said stoically.

Cordele sat down next to me looking solemn. "There is much preparation to be done. It would be unwise to look for Devon without the proper groundwork. The first thing you must know is that yours is a very unusual case."

I looked up at him, stunned. In what way was this anything but unusual?

"Your case differs significantly from ours. For one thing, Devon rejoined his ranks a year before you rejoined yours, and you had assistance." Cordele's expression was quizzical, as if he'd thought this through many times and never came up with a decent conclusion.

"What - the three of you just woke up one day and thought, 'Oh, that's right, I'm a sentinel'?" I really hadn't planned on sounding so sarcastic, but it certainly ended up that way.

"Something like that," Cordele replied. His voice held no hint of cynicism at my tartness.

"So why didn't *I*?"

"I'm not sure." Cordele looked somewhat worried.

"If Julius hadn't told me...?" I let the question trail off. It was evident that Cordele had looked at this from all angles, and that this was a question he had already asked himself.

"I can't answer that either." He sighed. "Of course, we deliberated for a year on the issue of telling you. We weren't sure what the outcome would be either way, but in the end we all agreed that telling you would be best. Thankfully our theory about the possibility of insanity was incorrect."

I rolled my eyes. If my earlier demonstration wasn't considered lunacy I wasn't sure what was. If they had known how stolid my personality was before they found me, I was convinced they would have concluded that I was, in fact, insane. I'd experienced more emotional shifts in the past eight hours than I had in the last six months. "How else is my situation different than the rest of yours?"

Cordele studied me. He was obviously considering whether or not I was stable enough to tell me what was on his mind. Either he felt it couldn't do much more damage, or that I was mentally stable, but for whatever reason he continued. "Devon is no longer trying to gather troops. I believe he may have already rejoined the underworld."

My breathing sped up. "Are you telling me he's...?"

Julius grabbed my elbow. "We don't know that for sure. His signs were everywhere, but now they're nowhere to be found. He may have just found an extremely good hiding place."

"Signs?" I was sitting now, trying to regain my composure.

"You've heard of auras?" Nayana asked. This must be her area of expertise.

"The light that surrounds people?"

Nayana giggled at my crude definition. "Yes. Everything has an aura, even malefactors. The difference is that the aura surrounding a malefactor is much heavier than the normal aura. It actually leaves a trail. We don't think they are aware that they do this. It makes it very easy to pursue them."

"And Devon's aura trail is gone?"

"Right," Cordele said. "And there are two possibilities, both of which you just heard. I personally hope that he has just found a good hiding spot. If he is in Hell already, this is going to prove much more difficult than we have ever experienced."

"How so?"

Julius spoke up. "Well for one thing, once a malefactor is created, a sentinel has to eliminate it - or die trying. A sentinel can not go to Hell, obviously, so it would be a catch-22. If the malefactor found a way to do its work from home, it would have it made."

There was silence. My mind drifted back to the night almost two weeks ago when I had discovered the satanic symbols on Devon's belongings. "What's the key for?"

All eyes quickly turned to me, confusion registered on all of their faces.

"What key?" Evidently my statement piqued Cordele's curiosity, because he was staring at me in awe. I got the impression that he was usually the one to introduce new concepts and discoveries, and he had an insatiable thirst for new developments.

"I was in Devon's room a little over a week ago and found a piece of paper in the pocket of his jacket. It was a hand drawn symbol of an infinity sign surrounded by a ring of fire."

Cordele interrupted me. "Lucifer's noose."

"That's what the website I found called it," I said, nodding in agreement. "They said it was the symbol of one of the oldest satanic cults in history."

Cordele was pacing the floor now. "They're wrong. It isn't the symbol of a cult. It is the symbol of Satan himself."

At this point, nothing surprised me, and I continued on with nonchalance. "After I visited the website, I went looking for more evidence. At the time I was hoping the symbol was a misunderstanding, but when I found Devon's hammer I realized he was actually a part of whatever this...*thing* was. He carved the symbol into the rubber handle covering on the hammer. The center is hollowed out, and inside it I found a key. It's made of some kind of metal I've never seen, and it's encrusted with what looks like onyx and some other kind of stone. The symbol is etched into a big gem on the face of the key."

Nayana and Julius were looking at Cordele for an explanation, but he was too captivated to respond. "Fascinating," he whispered.

When no one said anything more, I continued. "That's the same night I started having the dreams."

"What dreams?" Julius asked.

"You know, the dreams about the hum."

"What hum?"

I blushed. How embarrassing. Of course he wouldn't know what I was talking about, it was a term I invented in my head to describe the feeling. "Well, you know - that thing you do when you touch me - that feeling that calms me down." I turned my head, expecting Julius to be choking back laughter.

"That's a very interesting way of putting it," he said calmly, surprising me. "Cordele calls it 'electromagnetic remedial waves'. I like 'the hum' much better."

I smiled.

"So you dreamed of the electro - the hum?" Cordele asked.

"Yes."

"Tell us about the dream," he said.

"Well, really it wasn't always the same. I would dream that I was feeling the hum while I was sleeping, and get out of bed to find it. The first night I woke up as soon as my feet hit the floor. I would get closer to it every night, but I never actually reached it until Thursday night, or rather, Friday morning." I was smiling. It was hard not too smile when I thought about the dream.

"What happened when you found it?" Nayana was enthralled with the dream. She was hanging onto my every word.

"Well, when I finally reached it, it was a beautiful orb. I wanted to touch it but I didn't, and it said, 'It's time to awaken,' so I woke up."

Everyone was quiet again, overwhelmed with their own thoughts and theories.

Finally breaking the silence after a few minutes Julius said, "What are you thinking, Cordele?"

"Well…" He was still in mid-thought, and I could tell Julius didn't want to interrupt him, despite his impatience. After tapping his chin with his cupped fingers a few more times Cordele said, "One thought I was having was that Gabby was seeking us out on a subconscious level. It was almost as if some unseen force was holding her back, and after she found the tangible evidence - the symbol and key - her subconscious mind decided to search for us without the help of her conscious mind."

"But what would have held me back?"

"I'm not sure, but it does seem odd that there were clues left where only you could find them. I'm sure the police led an investigation?"

"Yes," I said. "But I did think it was weird that they didn't find the drawing in his pocket. It was in his favorite leather jacket. He wore it all the time," I paused, thinking. "I don't know, maybe they did find it and thought it was nothing." I shrugged before continuing. "The hammer I can understand - the carving looks more like a logo that was stamped on there with a machine. I never would have noticed it if I hadn't found the drawing first."

Cordele and Julius exchanged glances and then Julius said, "She would have noticed the trail, if not while she was awake at least while she was dreaming of the hum."

"Unless they found out about it and discovered a way to disguise it." Cordele was pacing again.

"Are you suggesting that Devon came back after the investigation and placed the drawing there?" I couldn't think of any reason as to why he would do that. What would be the purpose? Cordele and Julius seemed oblivious to the fact that I was there. They kept asking each other questions, ignoring mine. I would have been offended if their questions weren't so intriguing.

"What would be the reasoning behind it?" Julius was obviously much more comfortable sitting still while trying to solve a problem. His head was leaned against the wall, the back of the uncomfortable bench much too short for support.

"I don't know."

Since neither of them was getting anywhere, I was beginning to get frustrated, and finally spoke up. "Okay, let's just say that everything about me is normal by sentinel standards. How would I go about destroying Devon?" My throat burned with these words; I had to swallow hard to keep the bile that was creeping into my esophagus to a minimum.

Nayana bounced over to me, her dark waves springing jauntily against her back. Her mature nature was one of the things I found so adorable about her, but I did my best to refrain from saying *'what is it?'* in a childish manner when she approached me. It wasn't easy treating her like an adult. "I'm afraid you're mistaken, Gabby. Sentinels cannot destroy. We are the opposite of malefactors, whose goal is destruction. We can only create."

I was overcome with surprise, and a little aggravated. I ran both hands through my thin hair, wishing I had something to pull it up with. This was becoming a long night, and I wished that I could get a little more comfortable. I exhaled, asking the inevitable question. "How is it that their souls can enter an unsuspecting fetus, and this is not considered creation?"

"They are merely using the resources of others. In other words, they are thieves." Nayana's almond shaped eyes were staring at me with sincerity.

"Okay, then if we can create, why haven't we come up with some type of malefactor vacuum or something - just sweep them up and be done with them?" I was sure that one of them had an answer ready, which was something I had suddenly found quite annoying.

"We can only create what they destroy."

I had just officially reached the end of the proverbial rope. I jumped up in exasperation, my fists clenched. "Well, now that makes a whole hell of a lot of sense doesn't it. We're nothing more than some type of supernatural maintenance crew?" My face was getting hot and my hands were clammy which only succeeded in irritating me further. Why did my body have to tell on me every time it experienced some type of emotional change? I tried calming myself down by breathing through my nose, and slowly exhaling through my mouth. It helped somewhat, and I sat back down on the uncomfortable bench. "Sorry, I guess I'm just a little tired."

"I know it can be frustrating, but just remember that we're here to help you. We won't let you do this alone." Nayana smiled at me, her tiny nose scrunched up with little wrinkles.

What she was telling me made me wonder. "You three are planning on helping me?"

Julius laughed. "Of course. It would be a waste to just stand around and watch you. Besides, Devon will have his army. It won't exactly be a fair fight any way you look at it."

I leaned back in the bench and cocked my head back, overcome with curiosity. "What about your malefactors? Did any of you have help?"

Cordele cleared his throat. "I didn't, but Nayana, Daniel and Julius did."

"Daniel is the other one?"

"Yes. His time came after Nayana's." Cordele settled back into the kitchen chair that he had pulled up earlier. His excitement over the new developments in my case was gone. Now he was calm and I could tell he was going to tell me a story he had repeated three times before. "We all 'wake up' at different times; there is no specific age. As far as I can tell, I was the first of our kind, and I woke up in 1257."

I gasped. This was something I hadn't counted on. I started tallying on my fingers. "That would make you over seven hundred years old." My mouth was agape as I studied Cordele closer, examining his every wrinkle - his every age spot. I was overcome with wonderment.

"Actually, I'm closer to 830. I was born in England at the turn of the twelfth century. My birth was never recorded, or celebrated, so I had no way of knowing exactly how old I was, but I estimate that I was nearly eighty before I woke up." He paused to let me breathe, watching my mouth close finally. "My twin sister Barbara and I were a bit of an anomaly - if you were lucky enough to survive past the age of sixteen in the middle-ages, your life expectancy wasn't much past the age of sixty. To live into your seventies and eighties was not exactly uncommon, but many people found it strange that a set of twins were stretching the boundaries together."

"I can only speculate as to why it took so long for us to reach realization. Perhaps they hoped that Barbara would have gathered enough wisdom in her long lifetime to work in their favor." I noticed how he winced when he said her name; the pain still present after all those centuries. I deduced that it must have been harder on him than the rest of us - he had spent an over average lifespan with his sister - they must have been very close.

"Barbara and I both outlived our spouses by many years. By the time we were in our mid fifties, I had outlived my wife by four years, and Barbara had outlived her husband by ten. We had no intentions of ever looking for love again, and we decided to combine our resources and live in the same household. We were aging, and with age comes loneliness, and as we both became more nostalgic after our spouses had passed it seemed like the logical thing to do. We lived together for many years before she left."

"One evening, when we were close to eighty, she left our small stone hut in Wales to pick greens. I fell asleep before dusk, trying to pass the time before our evening meal. When I woke up, the sun was breaking over the horizon, and I knew she was gone."

"I was filled with a strange sensation - a wonderful feeling I had never experienced. But my first instinct was to find Barbara. I knew immediately what she was, and I was deeply pained by how strong the impulse to eliminate her was. I tried to fight it. I told myself that if only I could find her - if only I could see her - our reunion would be enough to eradicate that burning desire to rid the earth of her presence."

"She wasn't difficult to find. I followed her trail out of Wales, and found her amongst a group of men who were known for their open defiance of King Edward III. They had escaped execution only by cowardice; they spent most of the end of their lives running during the nights and hiding in crop fields to sleep during daylight. They were trying to recruit enough people to revolt, and these were exactly the kind of people Barbara needed for her own army."

"I waited until I knew they were well away from dense population, and I visited them. Barbara was furious when she saw me. She attacked. Her physical strength was more than I bargained for. Her touch seared my flesh, and the bones of her fingers slashed through my skin as if I were made of parchment. Somehow, amidst my shock, the instinct to defend came over me, and I stood tall and straight, exercising all of my energy into the pit of my gut. I was strong as steel, and Barbara's fists broke against my chest."

"Her small group of minions was terrified. Some of them

fled, and some of them stayed for fear of what Barbara would do to them if they didn't. There were a few, however, who stayed for the sheer enjoyment of the fight. I knew I had found my weapon in them, and so I pretended to surrender."

"Barbara planned on using me to open the gate, and for a week she dragged me across the country, looking for unusual landmarks that might be hiding the entrance. While on this journey, I managed to convince the ruthless few of her minions that she was using them; planning to steal their glory after overthrowing the king. I knew I couldn't destroy her myself, so I used them to do it - they decapitated her while she slept." Cordele bowed his head, the torture prominent in his posture.

I tried to hide the tears that were stinging my eyes yet again. His story terrified me. I could relate to the anguish he lived with before he eliminated his sister, but the torment he felt afterwards was what frightened me. Centuries had passed, and still the love he felt for Barbara had not waned. Obviously time did not heal all wounds. Why?

If it was our purpose - our undeniable instinct - to rid the earth of our malefactors, shouldn't the love we feel for our siblings dissipate? If we were created to exterminate them, shouldn't we be able to do it ourselves? The concept was disturbing, and I found it very difficult to comprehend.

Julius's voice intruded my thoughts. "Gabby?"

"Hmm?"

"It's eleven-thirty. We should probably get going."

My head jerked up, Julius's announcement dissolving my contemplation entirely. "Oh," I crooned with apprehension. I hadn't been paying any attention to the time, and hadn't given any thought as to how smoothly the return connection to my other half would be.

"Once you get used to bi-locating it won't be necessary to be so cautious, but since this is the first time you've ever done it, I think it would be best not to take any chances."

Chances? He was insinuating that things could go wrong,

and I suddenly felt the heat rising up my neck. Momentarily I imagined a scenario in which one half of me was stuck in limbo - stranded in some abysmal dimension. I quickly shoved the thought from my mind, breathing deliberately through my nose as if this would keep it at bay.

Turning to Cordele and Nayana, Julius said, "We'll check in with you in a few days. With Curtis on the loose I think it best to keep watch for Gabby."

Cordele nodded to him then transferred his attention to me. "I can't promise you this gets easier Gabby, but I will remind you that your duties will not be in vain." He gestured to Julius and Nayana as he said, "Love lost is oftentimes compensated in tremendous amounts."

I smiled at him consolingly, and hoped he didn't find it condescending. I understood now why Julius was so fond of him, and I found myself hoping that Cordele was satisfied with me.

Nayana bounced over to me eagerly, and to my surprise, lifted her arms up, signaling me to hold her. I hoisted her up to my eye level and she hugged me. "I'm glad you're a female. I was beginning to get tired of being the only one," she whispered in my ear. I laughed quietly at her. She retreated from my arms and joined Cordele next to his chair to watch us depart.

Our good-byes finished, Julius said to me, "This time you need to become aware of your other half."

I closed my eyes, blocking out the scenery around me, and concentrated on trying to focus in on the scenery of the other place I was at. It turned out to be very simple. I found that I was very conscious of everything that had happened at Evan's house, which was extremely surprising to me.

I was waving to April, promising to call her, and listening to the comments of the envious guys who were practically lusting over the Challenger. I blushed a little as Julius opened the door for me, even though he seemed to be doing it absentmindedly - he was answering questions about exhaust systems and carburetors. I distinctly heard the word 'Edelbrock' come from what must have been five different voices simultaneously, and I wondered what it meant.

Once inside the car, Julius smiled at me playfully. "Watch them," he said as he started the engine. He revved it up a couple of times and I watched as several of the guys were clutching at their chest in mock reverence to the car. I laughed, and Julius waved as he backed out of the driveway.

After a few minutes of silence, we pulled back into the parking lot of the dollar store. "Okay," Julius said, not bothering to kill the engine this time. "Are you aware of being in both places?" I felt his hand squeeze mine back at Cordele's. I knew he was doing it so I wouldn't have to open my eyes, and I was a little embarrassed about how his attempt at proving his tangibility sent chills up my spine.

"Mm-hm," I said, nodding.

"Alright, so now all you need to do is make both of your minds aware of the one place you want to be now."

I did what he instructed, and at once I was the wisp of smoke again, but only for the smallest of moments. I opened my eyes to find myself - my whole self - sitting next to Julius.

His hair did that moving thing again, and he opened his eyes and looked at me, smiling. "Now that wasn't so hard, was it?"

I had to admit that it wasn't.

Chapter 5❖

I spent much of the next few days pondering the events that unfolded the previous Saturday. While my mind frequently replayed certain scenes over and over, my abrupt inattentiveness was making me an easy target for most of my teachers.

My Chemistry teacher, Mrs. Barnes, seemed delighted with the change, as she felt that her top priority as a teacher was discipline. On Friday afternoon she shamelessly humiliated me in front of the entire class by interrupting my thoughts to suggest that maybe I would find it easier to concentrate if I wore my homecoming gown to school everyday. Perhaps if I had it on I wouldn't have to spend so much time imaging myself in it. My neck reached a temperature I was sure wouldn't have registered on any traditional thermometer, and I found myself wishing I was able to inflict intense pain on her. At least Gina wasn't in this class - it would be outright impossible to live down if she heard it.

My creative writing class was the worst. Not because Mrs. Jameson declared it her personal mission to insult me - in fact, she was as pleasant as ever - but because I couldn't concentrate on the topic. We were supposed to be writing a review about our favorite book, and I completely butchered mine, not bothering to be creative in the least. Was it considered irony that I had written about the first book that came to mind - *The Catcher in the Rye?* I imagined being face to face with the main character, Holden Caulfield, cringing while he pointed at me and called me a phony.

Lunchtime couldn't have come soon enough. I sighed with relief as the bell rang dismissing class. Julius laughed at my cantankerous disposition when he caught up to me at my locker.

"Having a bad day?" He asked teasingly.

I glared at him incredulously. "You had to ask?"

"Hey, some people might consider Mrs. Barnes's cruelty as something more like playful banter," he said lightheartedly.

"*I* am not one of those people." I shut my locker a little harder than intended, and was reprimanded with a scolding glance from Mr. Enoch as he passed us on his way to lunch.
I rolled my eyes, exasperated, and trudged alongside Julius to the cafeteria.

April was waving us to her table, surrounded as ever by a plethora of friends and her boyfriend, Travis Minnard.

Julius had acquired instant popularity, thanks in part to his car. In a school this small it wasn't too hard to find a few shallow individuals.

I was easily accepted into the crowd based on the fact that I was April's best friend. I'm sure I still would have been accepted even if it weren't for this fact, not because I fit in that well with these people, but because I most definitely wouldn't have fit in anywhere else.

There were really only three cliques here at Kentland High. There was the group I belonged to, which was composed of two-thirds of the senior class; we were considered your normal, every day, stereotypical teenagers.

Then there was Gina's group. Her group was made up of eight people, and she was their ring leader. I'm convinced that most of the other seven wouldn't have been there at all if she had been able to consider herself a group without them. Hers was the narcissistic group. She considered herself ultra-popular, so much so that she had to alienate herself from the majority of the school to prove it, sharing herself with only an elite few.

The other group of friends was nearly as large as ours. This group was the mature group. Anybody was welcome to join, but only on the condition that their attitude and personality was kept to a minimum. If the stolidity of the circle wasn't taken into account, it would actually have been considered a very diverse crowd. I could easily have fit into it the first few months after Devon left, once the numbness set in anyway. I could actually picture myself finding a niche somewhere between the girl who always had her nose stuck in a book and the guy who was constantly cleaning his glasses. But it wouldn't have worked. While I might be like them in many ways, there was one significant difference. I liked to live vicariously through other people. I wasn't one to jump on the bandwagon, but I heartily enjoyed watching others leap onto it headfirst. I'm sure that made me morbid on some level, but what could I do about it? The mature crowdies were much too boring for me, and I would have become frustrated with them quickly. They would have eventually exiled me.

Normally, there was a seat reserved for me across from April, but today there were two. Either people were starting to get used to seeing Julius and I together, or April asked that everyone make room for the both of us before we sauntered into the cafeteria side by side.

After we got our lunches - pizza was always on the menu for Fridays - we settled into our seats. April immediately went into a tirade about Mrs. Barnes's 'playful banter'. "She had no right to say that to you! As if you spend your time daydreaming about homecoming! It's hard enough to get you to admit you're even going!" My face detoured red and went straight to maroon. Julius had never really asked me, although we both told my parents he had, (I still hadn't worked up the courage to ask him if he knew I had told them that before he got there) and anyone who asked while we were at Evan's working on the float. I wasn't sure if we would actually be going, or if it was just an excuse for us to keep everyone off our backs.

Before April could say anything more to deepen the hue of my face, I interrupted. "Do you care if I borrow your notes? If I fail that test on Monday she'll probably draw some horrid caricature of me and give anyone who laughs at it extra credit." Ashley Forte, a blonde-haired girl with thick makeup heard me and laughed. I hadn't meant to be funny, but I let it slide.

"Don't let Mrs. Barnes get to you. That's what people on power trips want, and if you ignore them, they'll eventually move on to an easier target," April said, shrugging.

"In that case, maybe I shouldn't ignore her. I'd feel like crap knowing I could have prevented someone else from public humiliation."

"I agree with April," Julius said. "It's not so easy being a martyr."

I caught on to the inside joke and chided under my breath, "Martyrs have a choice."

Julius opened his mouth to say something more, but was quickly interrupted by Evan. "Did you hear about Curtis?"

Julius tried to maintain an indifferent expression, but I had already noticed the blazing interest in his eyes before he had a chance to recover. "What's going on with him?" He asked as if he could really care less.

"He got jumped by a couple of guys over in Watseka last Saturday. He was in Iroquois Memorial for a few days. He's home now, but he's not sure when he'll be able to come back. You should see him. His face is messed up pretty bad, and both of his arms are broken. The guy looks like hell."

I chanced a look at Julius, hoping no one would notice.

"That's too bad," he responded, trying his best to sound sincere.

"Yeah, tell me about it. He's our center. I hope Ryan Phillips knows what he's doing. He's supposed to play Curtis's position. It's gonna suck if we don't win the homecoming game." He muttered the part about Ryan under his breath, but everyone heard it anyway.

"Hey Gabby, weren't you and Curtis supposed to go out or something?" It was Ashley again, and she was looking at Julius even though she addressed me.

"No," I said flatly.

Ashley kept her eyes on Julius's face for a moment longer, no doubt hoping to catch a glimpse of anger. She wasn't doing a very good job today of hiding her grudge toward me. She obviously had a crush on Julius.

When lunch was over, Julius and I walked in silence to our next class. I knew we were thinking about the same thing. What really happened to Curtis? I pondered this all the way to English, and all through class. The dismissal bell rang in what seemed to be no time at all. I was so deep in thought that I jerked fiercely in my seat when it sounded, my heart racing wildly.

My next class was Probability and Statistics, and I groaned to myself. There was no way I would be able to concentrate now, not with the recent developments involving Curtis, and there was no way Mr. Howell would let me get away with daydreaming.

Julius could sense my mood and pulled me aside, letting the crowd pass. I was just about to object - we were going to be late to class - then realized I didn't care. I'd already had a bad day, I might as well go for the gold.

Julius had me by the arm, pulling me close to him to whisper in my ear. I tried to ignore the warmth that was spreading throughout my system while he had me so near. I wondered if he could feel my temperature rise or the blood rushing quickly through my veins. I hoped not. "It is easier to concentrate when the part of you that's uninterested isn't there," he whispered quietly in my ear. I could feel his smile even though I couldn't see his face, and the hair on the back of my neck rose.

I pulled away from him quickly, trying to play my abrupt movement off as surprise at what he'd suggested. "Bi-locate?"

He shrugged, "Why not?"

"Does that really help?"

"Absolutely."

I glanced at my watch. "It's a quarter after one - we only have an hour and a half to get back to our cars."

Julius rolled his eyes. "Honestly, Gabby. I thought you understood the concept of bi-location. The parts of us that are here will be able to drive home."

This time I rolled my eyes at myself. "Oh, right."

"Meet me at my apartment as soon as the tardy bell rings."

I was taken aback. He had an apartment? "I don't know where that is," I said, trying to hide my surprise.

Julius sighed in frustration. Tapping his head he said, "Think it."

Why couldn't I grasp that concept? Attempting to conceal my embarrassment, I quickly jumped past him and headed for our next class. The bell rang just as my foot landed inside the door, and everyone turned to look as Julius's sneakers squeaked against the tile as he stopped himself abruptly mid-run.

Mr. Howell's eyes narrowed on us, and then shifted angrily toward the students who were stifling laughter. Sharply he said, "Take your seats."

I shuffled to my desk and sat low in my seat, waiting for Mr. Howell's eyes to stop boring into me. I knew he wouldn't have been so severe if Julius wouldn't have slid into the doorway the way he did, making it look as if the two of us were so involved in each other we barely remembered to go to class. I made a mental note to start walking to class without him. Maybe people would stop assuming we were together if we weren't side by side so often.

When Mr. Howell was satisfied with the duration of his dramatic pause, he turned to the blackboard, focusing his efforts on drawing a graph. I stole a glance at Julius then, who jerked his head toward the door, signaling for me to go. Had he already left? I nodded in his direction, and then stared at the girl's hair in front of me, making an effort to block out everything around me. *I need to be at Julius's apartment and here at school*, I thought.

In a split second I became aware of being in two separate places. It was as if I were watching a news program in split screen, both of them jabbering about something different. It was extremely annoying, and if it really were a television show I would have changed the channel. I finally heard Julius calling my name, and at once Mr. Howell and his graphs were extinguished from my mind.

Now that I was focused, I had a good look around. The apartment was studio style, a very large open space with thick, round beams running from the ceiling to the floor. One end of the elongated area was sparsely furnished. There was a large comfortable looking couch against the left wall, (directly across the stove and refrigerator) taking up a small fraction of the enormous space. It was a creamy beige color, and folded neatly on one of the cushions was a brown fleece blanket topped with a pillow that looked like it was bought sometime in the last decade. The couch was obviously bought for its comfort; he slept on it.

There was no kitchen table, only a simple wooden coffee table in front of the couch, topped with a stack of cheap coasters. There were a couple of tall bookcases next to the couch, although I wasn't close enough to see the kind of books he kept. An oval, braided rug covered the rustic wooden floor under the coffee table, giving the small corner a cozy ambiance.

As I took in the rest of his apartment, I was heartily astonished as to how little I really knew him. Where were the pizza boxes filled with leftover crusts? Where were the empty coffee cups that should have been strewn all over the place? Why weren't any of his dirty towels thrown over the back of the couch? And where were his filthy socks that should have been scattered all over the floor? The entire place was spotless, and I felt a little intimidated. My bedroom at home wasn't quite this orderly, which was saying something; I always considered myself to be quite organized.

"It's pretty plain, but I don't need much," he explained.

"It's very...clean," I opted, unable to think of another compliment at present. My disbelief at his lack of griminess made it impossible for me to say anything different.

Julius shrugged. "I'm not here often enough to make a mess." His ears were a little pink, and I could tell he was slightly embarrassed, especially when my eyes wandered back to the neatly folded blanket. Trying to preoccupy my wandering eyes he said, "Do you want a soda or something?"

"Sure," I said, following him down the empty space, listening to the echoes of our footsteps.

I sat down on his couch, careful not to mess up his blanket. It was very comfortable, and I yawned. I hadn't been sleeping well since I'd stopped dreaming of the hum. My dreams had become fleeting images of color - swirls of bright yellows and rich reds. The oddest thing about them was that there were also sounds - not conversation or soft whispers, but horrible, unsettling noises. It was as if every radio station in the area had used me as an antenna, and I heard all their signals at the same time, blaring and undecipherable. My eyes became heavy, and all at once I couldn't stay awake.

There was a knock at the door. I turned to look at Julius, who was standing next to the refrigerator, dropping ice into two glasses. I was surprised that he seemed to be ignoring the now incessant pounding. Grumbling, I stood and stretched. I would have to leave the comfort of the couch and answer it.

Slowly I made my way across the empty expanse of the

apartment, the knocking becoming more persistent the closer I got to the door. "I'm coming!" I shouted, frustrated. I rolled my eyes when I reached the knob, the continued knocking extremely irritating. I swung the door open, my sour expression fading the instant I saw him.

It was Devon.

A whirlwind of emotion took over me, each feeling counteracting the other, neutralizing my nervous system. I was frozen, unable to compute the thoughts that were swirling in my brain. Finally, one thought stood out. I remembered Nayana telling me what would happen the moment I next saw him. I recalled the feelings she explained to me vividly, and I narrowed my brow. She was wrong. Devon was exactly as I remembered him, and the sight of him invoked no instinct to eliminate.

He stretched his arms toward me, offering a hug, and tears spilled down my face as I accepted his invitation. My chin was resting on his shoulder, my feet floating above the floor as he held me in a tight squeeze, and I breathed in the scent of his leather jacket.

Suddenly, my eyes flew open in fear. He didn't have his leather jacket when he left. I had it now, folded painstakingly on the shelf in my closet. Carefully I released him. Sliding down his chest until my feet touched the floor, I slowly lifted my face to meet his, and frightened by what I knew I'd see. When my eyes finally met his, my blood turned to ice, and from the depths of my stomach came a terrorizing scream.

My eyes flew open, and I clutched my chest. My heart was racing wildly, and sweat had saturated my shirt, the thin cotton sticking to my torso. The light was all wrong. It could have been dusk or dawn, the sunlight a faint trickle through the unfamiliar windows. For a moment I was disoriented, unable to recognize my strange surroundings, until Julius opened the bathroom door, struggling to get a clean t-shirt over his head.

Thrill punctuated my fear as I caught a glimpse of his torso, pale in comparison to his face and arms. He had obviously been in the shower, his dark, shoulder-length hair now coal black and wavy with dampness. My face flushed, but I knew he would think it was from fear of the dream I'd just had.

"Are you okay?" he asked, concern flooding his face.

I nodded. "I was just...dreaming," I said, trying to infiltrate calmness into my voice.

Julius sat beside me on the couch. "Sounded more like a nightmare than a dream by the way you were screaming."

"I can't remember now," I lied; I was starting to feel childish. "What time is it?" I asked to change the subject.

"Well, it's close to seven here, so that would make it close to six in Kentland."

Did I really sleep that long?

Crossing times zones in Kentland was no big deal. Benton County, directly south of Newton County, (which is where Kentland is located) runs on Eastern Standard Time, so it was no big deal when he mentioned the difference.

"Where are we?"

"Cleveland," he said noncommittally.

I knew I should have been surprised, but after last weekend, nothing about Julius surprised me much anymore. It did make me think though. I didn't know much about him really, except that he was a sentinel and exceptionally good-looking, at least in my opinion. I decided that if we were friends, I had a right to ask him a few questions.

I turned to him with a serious expression and asked, "How is it that you came to have an apartment in Cleveland? You only just turned eighteen, and you never mentioned anything about a job." This question suddenly inspired others. "You have an exceptionally nice car, which is in Kentland at the moment, and if you come back here every night, where do you keep it?"

Julius laughed. "I wondered when you were going to start the interrogation." He paused for a moment, contemplating, and then said, "You know, you are really very patient."

"It's a virtue," I said with mock insouciance.

"So I've heard." The corner of his mouth was turned up in a half smile.

"What?" I asked innocently, as if I hadn't meant to be funny at all.

Julius snorted through his nose and shook his head. "Nothing." He straightened his face then and said, "So, I live in Cleveland because it's familiar to me. I grew up here." He winced before he admitted the next part. "And I didn't exactly just turn eighteen. I'm actually seventy-eight."

I repeated him aloud and very slowly. "Seventy-eight."

"Yes. Although, as you probably already understand, I will never develop past the age of eighteen, well, twenty to be precise; I always did look younger than I actually was." He was looking at his hands as he talked, and I could tell he was nervous.

"Why?" I breathed.

"I don't know. Cordele seems to think that not only is it our duty to eliminate our own malefactors, but to help the new sentinels too. We wouldn't be able to do that if we grew old."

"But Cordele didn't wake up until he was around eighty," I interjected. "His age hasn't made a difference."

"Yes, but that was the age he was when he eliminated Barbara. If he had grown any older, he wouldn't have been able to help Nayana."

I nodded understanding. "How old is Nayana?"

Julius smiled. It was hard not to when thinking of her. Just imagining her pleasant little face was enough to make any heart melt. "Physically she's six, but she's been with Cordele since the fifteenth century. She had it pretty rough. She and her brother, Samar, lived in India. When she woke up, her brother had already recruited their parents. He convinced them he was some kind of messiah, and that Nayana was evil. She sought out Cordele by his hum, and together they followed the trail of her brother. When they caught up to them, her parents attacked. She and Cordele managed to overtake them, and they bound them up in an attempt to keep them safe until they were able to run Samar off. They hadn't come up with a plan on how to eliminate him, so their first objective was to save her parents. They knew they could trail Samar easily, so they tried to scare him away to give them time to take her mother and father home. Unfortunately, her brother didn't give up that easily. He started to attack them, and while he was fighting Cordele and Nayana, he accidentally killed their parents. Samar became a remorseful one, and Nayana went to live with Cordele. He thinks of her as a granddaughter."

I sighed. Her story was even worse than Cordele's. I hoped this wasn't a pattern. I didn't even want to think about how it would turn out for me.

Julius must have been able to tell what I was thinking because he said, "Daniel and I had it much like Cordele. It was nothing more than simple cases of making their minions turn on them. It turns out they are very predictable creatures."

If he was trying to make me feel better, it wasn't helping. He did a fairly good job of hiding his anguish, but I knew it was there; I had seen it in his eyes the day he told me about Devon, and I caught it now in the subtle cadences of his tone.

Trying to preoccupy my own thoughts, I asked, "Do we *ever* die?" I was holding my breath as I waited for his answer.

"I believe we can, although I've seen no evidence of dying in the traditional sense." His expression was thoughtful as he considered his carefully chosen words.

"Meaning what?"

"Meaning I don't think our bodies expire with age. We are extremely healthy.
However, I do believe we can be killed as easily as any other human."

My perplexed appearance must have registered to Julius, because he delved into another story about Cordele. "In the late fifties, Cordele and Nayana decided to vacation in India; Nayana loves to visit her homeland every now and then. While they were there, Cordele fell from the balcony of their hotel. I'm not sure how he managed it, but it happened nonetheless. It was a twenty foot drop, and he broke his neck, his hip, his collar bone, and both ankles, not to mention the damage that was done to his internal organs. He was in the hospital for months, the first two spent in a daze between unconsciousness and reality. Nayana, Daniel, and I were convinced he was going to die. We performed the hum on him the entire time he was lying there, feeble and meek. I don't know if it did any good, but once he recovered, Cordele told us he was sure he would have died from the pain alone if we hadn't intervened."

I exhaled, a mixture of relief and apprehension flooding through me. "But why?"

Julius shrugged. "I would assume it has something to do with the balance of nature. If we weren't expendable on some level, malefactors wouldn't be either."

I thought about what he said for a moment, and decided it probably made sense.

Attempting to smooth the abrading texture of our conversation, I returned to my initial questions. "So, you grew up here in Cleveland, and you're actually seventy-eight." I tried not to flinch when I candidly mentioned his age. "Tell me more about yourself."

He flashed a flawless grin in my direction. "You can be unequivocally persistent when you want to be."

"Another virtue?"

"I wouldn't count on it," he said, tossing me a scintillating grin that caused my heart to stutter.

I sighed. Evidently the fact that he was old enough to be my great-grandfather hadn't registered to my heart; or whatever part of me it was that decided to quiver shamelessly whenever he bared his charm.

"I do have a job, actually," he continued, apparently unaware of my minor heart failure. "I'm a mechanic at a repair shop just around the corner. And as for my car -" the pitch in his tone rose when he said *car*, "I've been keeping it in your garage."

"How is that possible? It's very loud, I would hear it." I lifted my eyebrows and added, "We have extremely...*curious* neighbors. It doesn't seem likely that they would miss something like that."

"Where is your creativity?" He rolled his eyes at me and I caught a hint of aggravation in his tone. "I do have relatively privileged resources at my disposal; being a sentinel - and a rather gifted mechanic - comes with advantages you know."

I had no retort for his heaping sarcasm; I had been much too skeptical even though logic was clearly irrelevant. "Okay," I sighed. "I surrender. From now on I will be utterly gullible."

"I'm not sure gullible would be the right word here; it implies that you're easily tricked. I come off bad that way." He contemplated for a moment, then said, "Assumed belief would be a better way of putting it."

I found myself quickly getting aggravated with him. "So from now on, I'll just take for granted that anything I previously considered impossible is absolutely normal considering sentinels have supernatural abilities, which - I might add - have never been revealed to me. Is that better?" I ranted angrily, hoping he understood the meaning behind my jumbled words.

Julius got the point. Raising his hands in defense, he said, "Okay, I understand, I shouldn't assume you understand anything about what we can do when I've neglected to inform you in the first place."

"Thank you," I said harshly, my irritation still fresh.

Julius frowned and turned away from me, his posture sour.

I was immediately stricken with guilt. "I'm sorry," I blurted.

Hesitantly, he spoke. "I'm sorry I hurt your feelings." He sounded surprised at himself, as if he found his own words hard to believe.

I blushed. "Actually, I'm not normally so easily upset. I've been a little cranky the last few days because I haven't been sleeping well."

"Still -"

I interrupted him. "So, how about those privileged resources?"

He smiled, rising from the couch with renewed enthusiasm. "Okay, you know how to bi-locate, so that's one down, but there are many other things. Sentinels are naturally very stealthy, but it wouldn't hurt to practice, although I don't know how we'd go about it here. We also possess a very potent defensive strength," he said with an impish grin, and I could tell it was his favorite.

"Sounds like something that requires practice."

"Well, it *is* better to get a good understanding of just how powerful you really are. It tends to take you off-guard the first time you use it." His smile was radiant - his eyes alight with excitement.

"Are you going to do a demonstration?" No sooner had the words come out of my mouth than Julius's closed fist rushed toward my nose. I caught it a couple of centimeters away from my face, its momentum backfiring on Julius, causing him to clutch his shoulder with his free hand. Stunned, I released his fist and stepped back, my hands covering my gaping mouth.

"See what I mean about catching you off-guard? If I would have been Curtis or Devon, you would have just given me a tremendous advantage."

I was still too astounded to respond.

"I'm fine, really," Julius said, and then took another swing at me to prove it.

This time I pivoted quickly, simultaneously grabbing him by the fist and the inside of his elbow, then heaved him easily over my head and onto the floor. He lay there motionless for a minute and I rushed down to him, aghast at what I'd done.

A groan escaped him, and I panicked. Bending directly over him, each of my hands on either side of his head, I pleaded with him. "Julius! Are you okay?" My eyes were wide with fear.

In an instant, I was under him, my head hitting the wooden floor loudly, but feeling no pain. He had flipped me over, my vulnerability a weapon in his hands. My breath was heavy as he leaned over me, adrenaline rushing through my veins. I wasn't sure if it was due to the strenuous activity or the longing that burnt deeply within me. Perhaps it was a mixture of both.

This time, I thought I saw a flash of something meaningful in Julius's eyes, but he quickly turned his face away and stood, reaching for my hand. I let him pull me to my feet and said, "I think I've had enough defensive strength training."

Julius didn't say anything, but nodded in agreement.

Not wanting to meet his gaze, I bent down on the pretense of tying my shoe. "Maybe next time we should work on the hum," I rattled off, trying to dispel the obviously awkward feeling that was hovering between us. "I mean, I've only ever done it while I was sleeping." A thought suddenly occurred to me as I stood up, finished with my shoe tying feign. "Maybe I could use it on my mother. She sort of fell apart after Devon left. Last Saturday was the first time I've seen a real smile on her face in a year."

Julius displayed a velvety smile. "That's a very good reason to use it." Studying me he added, "You are very kind, Gabby."

My neck heated up from his compliment. "Most people would do the same. She is my mother after all." I couldn't understand why he thought it was a big deal.

"And modest," he muttered under his breath, unaware that I heard it. Then, speaking directly to me this time, he said, "We should probably get back."

I checked my watch. It was almost nine. "Do you have to work tomorrow?"

"Yeah, but I'll be able to get away. No school on Saturday," he reminded me.

Something occurred to me then. "The first day you were at school you didn't go to work, and you didn't go to work today either. Are you off on Fridays?"

"Thursdays and Fridays are my days off. Why?" he asked suspiciously.

"I just wondered. Most people have the weekend off."

"Well, since it's quite easy for me to get away, I volunteered for weekend work. That way, there are only three days when I'm completely tied up."

I smiled. "This bi-location thing is pretty convenient, isn't it?"

Julius beamed.

Chapter 6 ❖

Mom woke me up at seven the next morning so we could spend the day in Lafayette dress shopping. It was only about an hour drive and I had to remind her that it was in the Eastern Time zone now; if we left here at eight it would still be eight when we got there and most of the shops didn't open until nine.

The damage was already done though; the extra hour of sleep I was hoping for wasn't going to happen. I tossed and turned, trying to force my eyes shut, but it was no use. I finally gave up and headed for the shower.

Mom had the whole day planned out for us, so I felt too bad to try and convince her that going all the way to Lafayette was unnecessary. Julius hadn't mentioned the dance again, and I wasn't sure what to tell my parents. *Maybe I should start thinking of a lie now*, I thought. I was sure to come up with something decent in a week's time. But right now I couldn't begrudge my mother this opportunity. I would have to suffer the day out, pretending to be excited; the way a normal daughter would behave.

I dressed carefully, knowing that the better I looked, the more pleased my mother would be. She would think I was taking this homecoming thing seriously. If I pulled on my velour sweats and Perdue University sweatshirt she would undoubtedly think my heart wasn't in it.

I was wearing my yellow v-neck sweater with a white tank top underneath to conceal my minimal cleavage, and the dark, boot cut jeans I picked out for myself last Christmas. I was trying to decide if I should wear my brown shoes or my black ones, finally choosing the black ones since they were easier to get off and on; Mom would probably have me trying on every dress in my size. I was wearing my hair in a ponytail, which felt a little unusual; I wasn't used to my hair being long enough to wear up.

Since she had mentioned pink, I planned on getting the least expensive pink dress I could find. That would save us some time, and I figured I wouldn't feel so horrible about the entire lie if it didn't cost my parents so much money.

I gave myself one last look in the mirror, hoping Mom would approve of my attire, and then headed down to the kitchen for a cup of coffee.

Mom was sitting at the table when I walked into the kitchen, an empty look on her face. She was staring out across the living room, focused on nothing. I ached to be able to fill her with the hum, to prove to her that the feeling of happiness that used to fill her wasn't imaginary.

I took a deep breath and exhaled through my nose, then fixed what I hoped was a convincing smile on my face. "Do you want some coffee?"

Mom whipped her head around, yanked from her disparaging thoughts. An instant smile appeared on her face when she noticed me. "No, thanks, sweetie. I already had a cup." Looking me over, her smile widened. "You look very nice."

"Thanks," I said, pleased that she was satisfied with what I was wearing.

I poured my coffee into a paper cup and added enough milk to turn it a warm, light brown color. I stirred it around a little with a spoon, and then took a sip to test the temperature. It didn't burn my tongue; the milk had cooled it down a little. I tapped the spoon on the side of my cup before tossing it in the sink, and then said, "Are you ready?"

Mom stood up and straightened her green button-up shirt. She inhaled deeply with her eyes closed, and I knew she was trying to rid herself of the depressing thoughts that had been swimming through her mind all morning. She was preparing herself to spend the day with me, making room for all of the good moments we would be spending together by exorcising her brain of the bad memories that continually crept up on her.

I realized at that moment that I was actually looking forward to our day together. The whole morning I tried to convince myself that I needed to do this for her, but I quickly recognized that I needed this day too, and all at once a genuine smile captured my face.

I did the driving at Mom's suggestion; she had never ridden with me before and decided she needed a first hand observation of my driving skills. I was a little apprehensive at first, thinking that the ride to Lafayette might be filled with nagging; but Mom promptly made me feel at ease.

Noticing my hands tense against the wheel as I backed out of the driveway, she patted my shoulder and said, "Relax, Gabby. I really don't expect you to drive us into a tree or anything." That made me feel better, and my grip loosened instantaneously.

Halfway to Lafayette, I found myself having a really good time. Mom and I shared another laugh about Dad's expression during dinner last week, and I confessed my dislike for Mrs. Barnes, filling her in on the humiliating remark she made about me in class on Friday. Mom seemed sincerely miffed about this, telling me she wouldn't get angry if I told the old hag off, and I promised her I would the next time.

We stopped for breakfast just before nine, (again) neither of us wanting to stand in front of the shops before they were actually open. After looking over the menu of the small diner, I opted for the apricot-cheese crepe, while my mother chose the waffles. It took us forever to finish our meal; we talked far more than we ate, and our waitress raised her eyebrows in our direction frequently, our laughter evidently bothering her.

We didn't make it to the first boutique until nine forty-five, and I found myself sifting through the racks longingly. I actually did want to go to the dance with Julius, although I never would have admitted it aloud.

The dresses were arranged according to color, and I went straight for the pink. There was every hue imaginable, ranging from silvery pastels to violent fuchsias. I picked through each and every one, grabbing all of the dresses in my size, and once in the dressing room, I only tried on the ones that were less than what I considered to be reasonably priced.

Mom insisted on seeing every dress on me, making faces at the ones she thought were unattractive. I was down to the last one when she handed me a knee length, pale yellow dress with an empire waist and scalloped bodice. I had to admit, it was very pretty, but when I looked at the price tag I cringed. It was more than I would have expected her to spend, even if I *was* sure I had an actual date.

As soon as I stepped out in the dress, Mom clasped her hands to her face and said, "Oh, Gabby, that really looks beautiful on you! Your dark hair really sets it off."

I smiled insipidly, knowing how upset she would be for me if Julius didn't pick me up on Saturday night. I would have to come up with something really good to tell her. If she thought he stood me up she would never forgive him. Maybe I would tell her his uncle was in the hospital. She might be too busy feeling pity for Julius to treat him derisively if she pictured him suffering at his bedside.

She paid for my dress with the credit card, which I knew was reserved for emergencies, driving the guilt in even further.

Back in the car, she reminded me about shoes. "Something with straps will really go nicely with your dress," she said excitedly.

I couldn't bring myself to do anything but nod.

"So," she began in a sprite-like tone, and I knew what she was about to say had nothing to do with shoes. "You and Julius have been spending a lot of time together lately."

I could feel the temperature rise in my face, embarrassment seizing my body. "I guess."

"Well, you spent most of last weekend with him, and he's been over to the house twice since then, and then last night the two of you went with April and Travis to get pizza. I know it's been awhile since I was a teenager, but I don't think the rules have changed much since the mid eighties - the two of you are dating, Gabby." She looked very smug, as if she had discovered who the murderer was in a mystery novel long before one was expected to.

"Really, Mom, we're just friends," I said, rolling my eyes. My heart fell a little when I admitted it out loud, but I tried to ignore it.

"Please, Gabby. If he isn't technically your boyfriend yet it's only because you're too shy to admit your feelings to him. He's obviously very smitten with you."

The hairs on my neck stood up in delight at my mother's last statement. "I don't think so. He's never insinuated any such thing." But my mind flashed on that brief moment last evening when I saw something in his eyes. Could I have just been hopeful?

"But you are smitten with him?"

I rolled my eyes. "What - do I act like a slobbering little puppy or something when I'm around him?"

Mom laughed. "No. You just act *way* too casual. I'm your mother, remember - I can tell when you put on an act."

"Ugh!"

"What?" She asked, genuinely surprised.

"Now I'm putting on an act?"

"Honestly, Gabby, I've lived with you for the past eighteen years; it's easy for *me* to notice the subtle differences but it isn't obvious enough for Julius. Trust me, he doesn't suspect a thing."

"How can you be so sure?" I asked, still appalled at my apparent difference in behavior.

"Because he likes you. If he were certain you felt the same way about him he would have told you by now." This didn't make me feel better in the least.

"Oh, great!"

"Now what?"

I sighed. "What if he does notice my 'act'? If he has, and he hasn't mentioned it, that would mean he doesn't feel the same way! I've probably been embarrassing him, and he's just too polite to say anything!"

This time it was my mother who rolled her eyes. "Good grief! The boy asked you to the homecoming dance Gabby! He likes you!"

The conversation ended abruptly then. My heart was in the pit of my stomach. He hadn't asked me to the homecoming dance - not really. He only mentioned it the night he met my parents, and I was sure he only did it then as an excuse to get me out of the house. We would undoubtedly be spending a lot of time together as sentinels, but he couldn't very well profess this to my parents, so I was convinced that he only used the dance as a ruse.

When we pulled into the shoe store, I let the car idle. I didn't want to make this any worse than it was. Shopping for shoes to go with a dress I would never really wear was bordering on insane, and I couldn't make myself go in.

"What's wrong?" Mom asked.

"Nothing," I lied. "I was just thinking - those shoes you wore to Amanda's wedding would look really good with my dress. I think I'd like to wear them if you don't mind."

Amanda was my second cousin. She was thirty-six when she got married two years ago, and my mom was one of the bridesmaids.

"You know, they would be perfect, actually," she said after thinking about it for a moment.

"Well, I suppose there's nothing left to do then. Should we head home?"

We pulled in the driveway around noon, and I took my dress upstairs immediately and hung it in my closet. I put it on the end, right against the wall so I wouldn't have to see it every time I opened the door, then I went downstairs to the kitchen to make myself a sandwich.

My dad was sitting at the table, reading the paper. He looked up at me when I came in and asked, "So how did the shopping go?" I knew he was really asking me how Mom was. This had been her first real outing since Devon's disappearance, and I knew he had been worried about her all morning.

"Great," I said truthfully. "Mom and I had a lot of fun."

His wary expression instantaneously turned to one of relief. "Good." Satisfied, he turned his attention back to the paper. "Hmm. You'd think they would have written about it in here," he said, thinking aloud to himself.

"What?" I asked curiously.

"Last night the eleven o' clock news mentioned something about an earthquake that happened a little ways north of here off of highway 41." Flipping a few more pages he added, "But there's nothing about it in the paper."

My hands started shaking, and I shut the refrigerator, leaning against a kitchen chair for support. Trying to subdue the quiver in my voice I said, "An earthquake?"

"That's what they're saying. The news said a team of geologists is all over that place." He chuckled. "I bet they're going insane. After all of this time, thinking that the crater was made by a meteorite." Perking his brow he faced me. "You know they thought at first that an earthquake could have caused that thing, but after a while they ruled that out." He snapped his paper, his eyes delving into the print once more. "I bet they're kicking themselves now."

Dad was referring to the crater in Kentland which was discovered in the late 1800's by a couple of farmers. After a considerable amount of research in the 1960's, a group of geologists decided it was an impact crater created ninety-seven million years ago by a meteorite.

I had to agree with Dad - the fact that there had recently been an earthquake so very close to the sight of the crater would definitely have geologists scratching their heads. Of course, I knew that was no normal earthquake, so my first concern was not the crater.

I suddenly realized that Julius and I hadn't discussed Curtis at all yesterday, which I now found very strange. After Evan had explained Curtis's absence to us in lunch yesterday, I figured his mysterious beating would be the topic of discussion between the two of us. Now that I pondered over it, I became suspicious. Forgetting about the sandwich entirely, I bounded back up the stairs with the intention of calling Julius, my curiosity getting the best of me.

As soon as I shut the door behind me, I turned to see Julius sitting on the end of my bed. I jumped in fright at the initial sight of him, clutching my chest, my heart racing.

Once again I found myself wondering if he could read my mind, and I was extremely horrified. He would know everything my mother and I had discussed today, and I couldn't think of anything more appalling. I rounded on him with anger. "What, are you a mind reader or something?" I hissed in a sharp whisper.

"Hardly," he said, stung by my accusation. "A person's thoughts are their most private sanctuary. That would be equivalent to breaking and entering wouldn't it?"

"Then how-"

"Your hum. I can always tell when you're thinking of me."

Now I was past mortification. I felt my ears turning fifty shades of red and I cringed, revulsion showing in my eyes. "Always?" The moment it was out of my mouth I instantly regretted it. My tone implied that I thought of him often and in such a way that I didn't want him to know about.

I could tell he wished he wouldn't have said it. He realized now that he could have spared me a lot of embarrassment. "Well-," he stammered, "really only when you need to see me. It's like our own private telephone line."

I tried to recover, hoping he hadn't read too far into my implicative mannerism. Coolly I sat down beside him. "If we have the hum, then why did you give me your phone number?"

"Because at the time I gave it to you, your hum was very weak. I barely felt it that whole day."

I remembered the consoling embrace we shared when he told me about Devon, and was surprised that he had felt a hum from me at all. "If I have a hum, why can't I feel it?"

Julius shrugged. "I never feel mine unless I'm transferring it to someone else. It is very distracting when you feel it. It takes a lot of practice before you get to the point where you have enough control to let go. The first few times I did it, I was so swept up in the feeling that I didn't want to stop."

I sat down next to him on my bed. "That's understandable." My mind flashed to the last dream I had of the hum. I remembered falling to my knees with the pulsating happiness, hoping at the same time to feel even more.

"So, what's on your mind?" He patted my leg when he said it, having no idea how distracting his meaningless gesture was to me.

I tried to act as if it hadn't affected me at all, and suddenly I realized what my mother meant about my act of casualness. Now that I was aware of it, I was worried that it was obvious, so attempting a reverse tactic, I smiled at him, acknowledging his light touch, and patted him playfully in return when I said,

"Curtis."

Julius's expression turned cold. "What about him?" he asked icily.

"How did he end up in the hospital?"

He grunted. "Why does it matter?"

I gasped. "Was it you?"

Julius stood, his posture stiff. "What if it was?"

I couldn't understand his contempt. If it *was* him, it certainly wasn't an unwarranted action. Was this not part of the job description? "I'm just surprised that you kept it from me. I don't understand why you would."

Julius sighed, sitting next to me once again. "I just didn't see the point in worrying you is all." He turned to look out the window as he thought, wondering if he should tell me the whole story or just a brief synopsis. After reaching his decision, he kept his eyes on the window, never looking at me once as he spoke. "His powers are extreme. I've discussed it with the others, and none of us have ever seen such strength in a minion. We worried that they would evolve, and it seems we were right. Causing such a catastrophe as an earthquake is usually something you would only see in a malefactor. Their capabilities have surpassed adaptation. We have no idea what to expect from the malefactor. We can only hope that your strengths have evolved as well."

My throat was dry as I tried to speak. "So you fought him, to test your own strengths before I had to use mine."

He nodded. Facing me again, I saw something that resembled sympathy in his eyes. "He was very weak. Too weak for a minion. I think that maybe he found a way to concentrate all of his energy on you - that he borrowed all of his reserve power that he would have had to use on those you recruited - to destroy you. If this is the case, then all we have to do is make sure there is always someone else to defend you, which should be easy."

He was trying to make me feel better, but I knew there was something more, something he was very hesitant to tell me.

"But?"

"But you are the only one who can eliminate Devon. We can help, but ultimately the final act will be up to you."

"And you are afraid that he has evolved so well that he will be ready for anything? It won't be as easy for me to turn his minions against him as it was for you?"

"We think he'll be ready for anything." He stopped, shaking his head as if he were disgusted with himself. When he looked back at me I could see an unfathomable amount of sympathy in his eyes. He took my hands in his, ready to administer the hum. His mouth opened in an attempt to speak, but he was unable to find the words. His face was twisted in pain, and I knew what he was about to tell me; I had prepared myself for it ever since Cordele had brought up the possibility the night I met him.

"He's already there, isn't he?" Tears stung my eyes, eventually spilling over onto my cheeks.

"Gabby, I'm so sorry." He wrapped his arms around me in another consoling embrace.

"I think I always knew," I whispered into his chest. "Why else would he have left the key? He wanted me to have to come to him."

Nothing was said for a long time after that. I kept my face hidden in Julius's chest, sobbing quietly for an immeasurable amount of time. His arms never left me, willing me to grieve as long as I needed to.

Finally, I lifted my head and wiped my eyes, now red and puffy from all of the crying. I realized that my parents couldn't see me this way, but it was impossible to turn myself into stone. My brother was dead, and no one besides me could know. I grabbed a bag and packed a few changes of clothes.

Julius understood immediately. "I'll meet you there. I need to check in with Cordele and Nayana."

When I bi-located to Julius's apartment it was empty, and I wondered for a moment where the other part of him was. I dropped my bag on the floor as I fell into the couch and curled myself up into ball against the fluffy armrest.

I was shaking uncontrollably, my insides freezing, so I carefully unfolded Julius's comfortable brown blanket and wrapped it around myself. It did little to warm me, but it's softness against my face was comforting. When my tears finally exhausted me, I fell asleep, the couch and the blanket creating a safe-haven for me.

Thankfully, my dreams were nothing more than the indiscernible flashes of colors that I had recently gotten used to, and the sounds that accompanied them were much quieter, to the point where they were almost forlorn. I was aware that I was dreaming, the fact that my brother was dead still very real. There was no escaping my grief.

My dreams began to change with this realization, the colors forming themselves into Devon's face, smiling, the way I most liked to remember him. His hair was the color of my father's - light brown with a red tinge whenever the sun hit it. He had my dad's eyes, too - a very light hazel color that was easily confused by the color of clothes he had on. It was strange how vivid he was; like I could actually touch him. I knew better though; if I reached out to him he would fade away, and how could I be sure if he would be this vivid in my next dream?

Even my dreams started to become too exhausting, so I gave up on them and decided to open my eyes. This time, Julius was beside me, calm, reluctant to say anything or make any sudden movements. I smiled at him, though my eyes were swollen and refused to comply with my intended expression.

"You've been asleep for a very long time; I wasn't sure whether or not to wake you." His face was full of worry.

"I'm fine."

"No," he said softly, reaching out timidly to touch my face. "You're not." I shuddered as the back of his hand grazed my cheek, and he withdrew it. I only had room for one emotion now, and grief was the least confusing of the two.

"I ordered a pizza," he said blankly, acknowledging my need

for his lack of compassion. "You should eat." He put a couple of slices on a plate for me, and brought me a soda. He shrugged. "I would have made your favorite meal, but since I don't know what that is, I decided to go for the one thing I was sure you liked."

My tone was stoic. "Close enough," I said flatly. I took a couple of bites, but my stomach turned, and I set it back on the plate.

Julius didn't object, and I was grateful to him for that.

When Devon first left, and the realization finally set in, I locked myself in my room. My dad pounded on the door with food at least six times a day, sure I was going to die of starvation. It was very aggravating. People seem to think you should eat twice as much as normal when you are upset.

After the failed attempt at eating, I rested my head on the back of the couch, covering my eyes with my forearm. The tears started coming again, and I wished Julius wasn't sitting right beside me to witness me completely fall apart. My chin shivered as I tried to stifle the sobs that my lungs were threatening to expel.

"Gabby, would you like to be alone?" Julius asked hesitantly.

"It's your apartment, Julius, I can't ask you to leave," I managed through sobs.

"Yes you can. I don't mind," he reassured.

There was a long silence. I raised my arm from my face and discovered that he was gone. Suddenly, I was stricken with panic. I jumped up from the couch, adrenaline coursing through me. I felt like I should be running, like I should be doing something.

Devon was gone, but he couldn't really be dead. Somehow, I had to do something to prove it. I ran toward the door, the echo of my pounding feet reverberating ominously against the bare walls. By the time I was close enough to reach the door knob, however, my panic retreated, and once again I was overcome with misery. I crumpled to the floor, my agonizing sobs dense in the atmosphere of the apartment.

Amidst my anguish, I found that I regretted sending Julius away. I needed him - I needed someone to keep me calm. As soon as the realization set in, I felt a warm hand on my back, and I felt another one around my waist. He gently lifted me onto my feet, and my sobs quieted somewhat. "I'm sorry. It's just that I don't know what to do," I said, trying to keep my tears back.

"Do not apologize." He looked into my eyes, his gaze soft and understanding, and walked me to the couch, where I fell asleep once again.

The next day wasn't much different. The exception was that I was past the panic now. I didn't move from the couch until Julius sat on the coffee table holding a clean towel and a bar of soap. "You might feel a little more comfortable once you've showered," he said politely.

Somehow I had forgotten all about hygiene, and I was a little embarrassed that Julius had to remind me.

On Monday I made an effort to rejoin reality. I ate two donuts for breakfast, which was a relief to Julius; I could tell he had been on the verge of force feeding me. I didn't have to be reminded to shower either, although I did have to ask him to retrieve my toothbrush and deodorant for me, which I left at home in my haste to leave. He quickly reminded me that I would need them there too, and offered to buy me an extra set on his way home from work - the other half of him would be skipping school today to be with me here.

I was aware of everything my other half was doing now. The more time I spent separated into two parts, the easier it was to detect what was going on in both places at once. I was doing well at home and in school, although I was much more detached than normal. That part of me could still feel the grief, but it was much more tolerable than the part of me that was staying at Julius's apartment.

He returned to himself at five that evening, handing me a

few toiletries, which I thanked him for graciously. I noticed him leave immediately after that, and I wondered where he was going. He'd rarely been completely here for the past three days, and I speculated as to whether or not this was his normal routine. Was something going on he wasn't telling me about, or was this just his typical pastime?

I did the dishes for him after we ate, (I couldn't cook worth a damn so I figured this made up for it) then returned to the couch to once more wallow in my sorrows. Julius was engrossed in his magazine, *Motor Trend*, on the other end, giving me my space.

I was almost asleep when I heard a knock at the door, and I jumped, peeking out from over the top of the blanket to look at Julius, expecting him to be looking back at me with the same mystified expression I wore.

Instead, he calmly laid his magazine on the coffee table and made his way to the door noncommittally. I was even more perplexed by the casualness of his gait, as if he were answering the door to a friend who called to say they were stopping by.

I stretched my neck to see around him when I heard a couple of muffled voices, and was surprised to see two men in midnight blue overalls. They handed Julius a clipboard as they walked away, then came back momentarily carrying a large rectangular something wrapped in plastic.

"Where do you want it?" The tall skinny one with the thick beard asked.

"Just set it down against that wall there," he pointed. He signed the clipboard when they were finished, then handed it back and closed the door behind them as they left.

A surge of guilt ran through me when I realized what the men had delivered. It was a bed. "I am so sorry."

Julius's brow creased and his bottom lip stuck out before he asked, "Why?"

"For taking over your couch. I've been so selfish, I didn't even think about where you were sleeping."

"Gabby, you are quite easily one of the most selfless people

I've ever met. And you needn't worry about where I've been sleeping. I can promise you I haven't been uncomfortable." He started tearing the plastic from the mattress as he said, "I've been meaning to get one of these for a while, and it's just that I haven't had a lot of time recently."

I got up from his couch and helped him with the frame. There was no headboard, and he didn't have any sheets, but we set it up regardless. We stepped back to admire our work, then satisfied, sat down on it to test its comfort. It wasn't bad.

"Now you just need some sheets and you'll be all set," I said as I patted the bed.

"Do you want to go with me to buy a set?" He asked hopefully.

I hadn't realized how used I had gotten to being here until the subject of leaving was brought up. I really didn't want to leave, not even for a quick trip to a department store, but not wanting to ruin his high after getting his new bed, I agreed. "Just let me pull a brush through my hair," I said. "I've been sleeping on and off all day, it probably looks horrible and I wouldn't want to embarrass you."

Julius rolled his eyes and shook his head. "You could never embarrass me. Nothing you do makes you unattractive."

I smiled, my face red from his compliment before heading to the bathroom to brush my hair.

Bi-locating in Cleveland was not easily done. There was always someone around, and Julius finally admitted that he usually thought of the parking lot of the senior assisted living facility. Elderly people slept a lot, he mused, so it wasn't likely that they would see us. Also, he confessed, it wasn't unusual for people to ignore them when they complained about supernatural events.

Once outside the facility, it was only a short walk to the store.

We went straight for the linens, and I pointed out the full sized sheet sets. Julius contemplated a moment, and then decided he would rather have a comforter set, and I scoured the aisles for the ones that could be passed off as masculine. He seemed to like neutral colors, and I pointed out one with brown and blue stripes.

"You like this?" he asked, disbelieving.

"Sure. It matches the rest of your things."

"My things being my couch?" He tossed it back on the shelf and grabbed a soft, moss green set with brown decorative stitching. "What about this?"

"It's very pretty. A little feminine -"

"It looks like something you would pick out for yourself." He looked up at me, his face scrunched as if he were trying to recall something. "Aren't your bed covers brown and green?"

"Aqua, actually. But really, I think you should pick something out according to your own taste." My face was pink. How could he remember anything about my bed?

"I don't know what my own taste is. I've never had to buy this stuff."

"Well, just pick one that catches your eye."

We walked all along the aisle, scrutinizing every set. Finally, Julius grabbed one from the shelf. "I like this one. What do you think?" It was faux suede, soft, but masculine. The colors were soft tans and moss greens, sectioned into four squares to make a pattern.

"I like that one a lot, actually." Smiling at him I added, "See, you have taste."

Once we were back at Julius's apartment, I made his new bed for him. He had to lift the mattress for me so I could put the dust ruffle on, and he laughed when I grumbled about having excessive strength that could only be invoked in defense. He tried to help, but I told him to just stand back and watch, and once it was done we both stepped back to look at it.

Julius seemed pleased. "My very first bed."

I rolled my eyes in disbelief. "Are you saying that in no time during your seventy-eight years on earth you've had a bed?"

"I've had a bed; it's just that I never had my own. I've never slept in one alone before."

My eyebrows rose of their own accord, and before I could recover, Julius spotted my reaction.

"I had a big family growing up. There were three of us to a bed."

I sat down on the bed, interested. "Really? How big?"

Julius sat down beside me on cue. "There were twelve of us kids - nine boys and three girls."

"Wow. What are their names?"

Julius exhaled through his nose. "I knew you were going to ask that. Let's see - Ralph, Thomas, Jonathan, Arden, Mildred, Erma, Mathias, Me, Suzanne, Eugene, Arnold and William."

"That's a lot of kids. What are your parents named?"

"Ralph and Caroline."

I scooted up on the bed to rest my back against a couple of pillows and patted the spot beside me. "Are they still -"

"Alive? All of them actually, except, of course for my parents - and Suzanne." His eyes fell when he mentioned her, and I felt my own heartache swell again.

Timidly, I asked my next question. "Do you ever see them?"

"Yes. I visit them occasionally."

"So they know?"

"That I'm a sentinel? No. You see, after I eliminated Suzanne, I became a different person. I knew it had to be done, for the sake of humanity at least, but that didn't mean I didn't feel remorse. I loved her, and I had her killed, and I was haunted by what I had done. My family assumed I was merely distraught over the disappearance of my twin, of course, but my suffering caused theirs to grow. I loved my family too much to let them agonize over me, so one day I announced I would be moving to Oregon to get work as a lumberjack. I actually did do it, too. I wrote them letters often, but then on my thirtieth birthday something happened. One of the guys at work mentioned how young I looked. He said it very strangely, and I could tell he thought there was something very odd about me. Cordele had warned me about this, but I was too caught up in my new life to worry about it. A few days after that, my sister Erma sent me a letter saying her husband needed work and they were planning to come to Oregon. I didn't know what to do. What would she think if she saw me? I left, and didn't contact any of them again until just a few years ago. I wrote to my brother Arnold and told him I was Julius the third, and it is on that pretense - that I am their nephew - that I get to visit them."

"I bet they were relieved."

"Very. And they are flabbergasted by the uncanny resemblances between their brother and his grandson." The corner of his mouth turned up in that dazzling grin that stimulated my nervous system, sending every hair on my neck into a frenzy.

I noticed that he hadn't said much about his twin, Suzanne. I could understand that. Every time I thought about Devon, my stomach curled into a ball and my chest became heavy. Would I always feel like this? Probably. Even Cordele's eyes filled with despair when he talked of Barbara.

I blew a strand of hair away from my face. Evidently waiting for the pain to go away was useless. I made up my mind right then that after tonight I wouldn't be staying here any longer. It had been hours since I last cried, and I figured that I couldn't hope for anything more than that.

"What are you thinking?"

I jerked at the sound of Julius's voice. "Oh, I was just thinking I should probably go home tomorrow."

"Really?" His tone was indifferent; I couldn't read the feeling behind it.

I sighed morosely. "It's never going to go away."

"No, it's not." Cautiously he added, "But at least you can know that you weren't the one who took his life."

I found solace in his words. I knew he was right. I don't know how I would have dealt with the pain if I had to do what the others did.

"Well, anyway…" I said, signaling the end of the conversation. "I need to get some sleep." I slid off the bed and headed for the bathroom to brush my teeth and put my sweats on.

When I returned from the bathroom I noticed Julius curled up on the couch, covered up with his brown blanket. "What are you doing?"

"Going to sleep," he said as if I were the single most clueless person he'd ever met.

"Why aren't you in your bed?" I asked quizzically.

"Give me some credit, Gabby. I do possess a touch of chivalry. Besides, it isn't as if the bed is only going to be here for this one night. I'll get to sleep in it soon enough."

Repeating what he told me the first time I came here I said, "You are very kind Julius."

With a wonderful grin he replied, "Most people would do the same."

Chapter 7 ❖

By Tuesday I was back at school in my entire form. Apparently the part of me that was sensible had been at Julius's, because somehow April had me talked into being an active participant in spirit week. Today was eighties day, and I cringed when I saw myself in the mirror wearing shoulder pads, stirrup pants and faux snakeskin flats. April made it worse by showing up to crimp my hair before school.

Why was it getting so hard to just fade into the background?

Not only did I have to worry about making a fool of myself against my better judgment, I was also growing nervous about what I was going to tell my parents when they found out I wasn't going to the dance. I'd given up hope of Julius mentioning it by the time I returned home. We'd been together for three days straight and he hadn't even hinted at it.

But dealing with these nerve-wracking situations paled in comparison to the inner turmoil I was going through over finding out my brother was dead. I couldn't tell anybody, and when people asked me what was wrong I had to say I was tired. It wasn't a lie, but it wasn't exactly the complete truth either.

Of course, Julius laughed at me the moment he saw me walk through the doors of the school with April. My face burned with embarrassment, and he promised not to do it again. "I don't think I've ever met someone as self-sacrificing as you," he said.

"How does dressing up like a fool classify as me self-sacrificing?" I demanded.

"Please, Gabby. If it didn't please April you wouldn't be caught dead like this."

He had a point.

One good thing about Tuesday was the fact that Mrs. Barnes was absent. At least she wouldn't see me like this and torture me over it. Her substitute, Mr. Marks, was actually a pretty decent guy. He gave us our homework assignment as soon as the bell rang, then quizzed us on eighties trivia for the remainder of the class. After the dismissal bell rang he complemented me on my convincing attire, which I quickly accredited to April.

During lunch that day, I was swathed in eye rolls by Ashley, who evidently blamed me for Julius's lack of interest in her. She was going to homecoming with Evan, but it was apparent to everyone that she really wasn't interested in him. It was April who finally said something to her, which surprised everyone, as she was normally so neutral. The fact that April told her off on my behalf caused everyone else to alienate her. After all, if April's high tolerance toward annoying people was compromised, you had to be obnoxious.

I spent much less time with Julius after school that week. After having spent so much time at his apartment, I was sure I was going to start getting on his nerves anytime, so I tried to give him some space. When he asked if I wanted to go get some pizza in Watseka Tuesday afternoon, I told him I really just wanted to spend some time with my parents. It was very hard not to go with him. After spending all that time with him I found it harder and harder to ignore the feelings I was having for him.

By Thursday I was running out of excuses, (the fact that I could bi-locate made it impossible to dodge him for long) and I agreed to go to Evan's once again to help with the final touches of the homecoming float. The two of them had become pretty good friends over the past couple of weeks, and although Julius wasn't really into all of the homecoming traditions, he didn't hesitate when Evan asked him to help.

I drove home and changed out of my camouflage outfit, (another spirit week calamity for me) and donned my Perdue University sweatshirt and an old pair of jeans. I was relieved that tomorrow was simply school color day. I wouldn't have to do anything more stressful than wear a school tee-shirt.

I told Julius I'd meet him there, trying to keep him away from my parents for the time being. They would undoubtedly bring up the dance, and Mom would unquestionably go on and on about my dress. I wasn't so much of a masochist that I would intentionally invite torture upon myself, so I told him I needed to change my clothes and do my homework. Thankfully he didn't object, although he did look somewhat suspicious.

When I pulled into Evan's driveway, Julius was already there, sitting on the tailgate of Evan's truck. He had a crescent wrench in one hand, tapping it absentmindedly into the palm of his other. He was talking about spark plugs and manifolds, and trying to explain what these things had to do with Evan's truck backfiring and missing. I really tried to understand what he was saying, but he lost me on the missing part, so I walked over to where April was standing.

She was handing out tissue paper to everyone, demonstrating how to shove it into the holes of the chicken wire without crumpling it into a tattered mess. I grabbed a handful and began helping. I was concentrating on trying to do it the way April taught me, so when she tapped me lightly on the shoulder I jumped. She didn't say anything, but her eyebrows were raised and she nodded in Julius's direction.

I looked over to see Gina Kupfner leaning against the tailgate next to Julius, her cleavage in her throat. I walked around to the other side of the float so I wouldn't have to strain my neck and be completely obvious. April followed me, cussing Gina under her breath.

"What are you going to do?" She asked me.

I shrugged. "What can I do? Julius isn't my boyfriend."

"Maybe not officially, but he's as good as."

I stared in their direction for another few minutes. Julius seemed oblivious that Gina was there beside him, never skipping a beat in the conversation he was having with Evan. She looked like she was getting impatient, and finally, instead of waiting for him to notice her, she tapped him playfully on the thigh. He jerked at her touch, which sent her into a spasm of simulated giggles. Coyly she batted her eyes and said something to him that I couldn't hear. It must have been fairly suggestive though, because I saw Evan's eyebrows raise in a mixture of surprise and envy.

Julius slid from the tailgate and landed on his feet, his posture stiff. I couldn't tell what he was saying, but according to the scornful look Gina was now wearing it was something she hadn't counted on. In obvious contempt, she stomped off to her car and squealed the tires as she sped off.

Only when the sound of April's voice pulled me from my trance did I realize my knees were shaking.

"Did you see her face?" She asked gleefully. But her delighted expression changed in an instant to one of trepidation. "First Curtis, now Julius. You know she's going to make it her personal mission to make your life hell now."

Great. That's all I need; more hell.

I sighed. "Oh well. I'm sure she would have found someone to torture eventually - might as well be me I guess."

Julius caught my eye then and waved, the wrench still in his hand. There was grease on his cheek where he touched his face with his dirty hands, a long streak of it that started at the top of his cheekbone and ended somewhere amidst the scruff on his face. He winked at me, his way of silently conveying to me that Gina didn't stand a chance with him, and with that one simple gesture, I couldn't hold back any longer. By its own volition, my face turned upward in an illuminating grin, conveying all of the feelings that were churning inside of me. I looked down quickly, afraid of measuring his reaction to my telltale expression.

Beside me, April sighed in exasperation. "What is wrong with the two of you?" It was a rhetorical question, but I wouldn't have known how to answer it even if it wasn't.

I chanced another look at Julius as I went back to stuffing tissue paper through the holes in the fence. He and Evan were deep in conversation now, and I wondered what they were talking about.

"So what are you going to wear tomorrow night?" April was part of the homecoming court, and although the subject of homecoming was one I normally would have avoided at all costs, I brought it up hoping she would forget about Julius and me.

She rolled her eyes, proving she understood what I was thinking, but graciously accepted my need to change the subject. "A skirt suit. You would like it. The jacket is that black and white checkered material, and the skirt's black. There's a wide shiny belt that wraps around the jacket and I'm wearing a red shirt underneath it." It sounded hideous to me, but I was sure April would look beautiful in it. "I'm not sure what the other girls are wearing - I probably should've asked."

"It's not going to matter what the other girls are wearing. You're going to win," I said matter-of-factly without taking my eyes off of the tissue paper I was stuffing into the small wire holes.

It only took about an hour to finish the float, which depicted a football cleat getting ready to stomp on a small devil. Everyone seemed pleased by it, but I seemed to be the only one who found it symbolic.

After the float was finished, we all stood around and talked until it was dark. After the trip to Lafayette with Mom, she gave me her blessing to drive at night, having dubbed me an excellent driver, but I didn't want to push it. I waved to everyone as I headed to my car, which Julius walked me to.

Just when I had my fingers on the handle he asked, "So what time should I pick you up Saturday?"

"Huh?" My confusion was sincere. I couldn't remember having made any plans with him.

His face reddened at my response. "I guess that was a little presumptuous of me." Stammering, he continued, "I mean - I guess I never officially asked you -"

It dawned on me then that he was talking about the dance, and my heart immediately started its gymnastics routine. "When you mentioned it I thought -" but I couldn't finish. What was I supposed to say? *At the time I thought you somehow overheard me lying to my parents about you taking me and used it as an excuse to get me out of the house?* I couldn't tell him that.

"That I was just saying it to get your parents off your back after your dad kept going on about Gina and all." He said through an embarrass-laden cringe.

I was taken aback. That thought never really occurred to me, but the fact that he remembered what I told him during our lunch in Watseka made my heart swell that much more.

"That was part of it," he went on, "but when you didn't object I thought -" He stopped, his greasy hand wrapped around the back of his neck and his eyes staring down at his feet. I could tell he didn't know what to say, so I was just about to speak up when he suddenly looked me in the eyes. "I would like the two of us to go to the dance together. Not as a favor to your parents, but because I really enjoy spending time with you."

I was speechless, dumbstruck. I didn't understand what he was saying. Did he mean he liked spending time with me as a friend? I really didn't *think* that was what he meant, but what if it was? It took me a few seconds to regain control of my senses. "I really enjoy spending time with you too, Julius," I said softly, holding his gaze. I was hoping his reaction would give me a little further insight into what he was thinking, but the smile he returned was very abstruse. "Pick me up at seven." I flashed him a friendly smile, trying to express the same monotonous look he was giving me, and then hopped in my car.

Just as I started the engine, Julius knocked on my widow. I rolled it down and he leaned against the car, his hands gripping the door. "Do you have a dress?"

It seemed I was destined for embarrassment. I really didn't want him to know about the whole shopping trip to Lafayette. "There's one in the back of my closet somewhere." It wasn't a lie, but it insinuated that I'd had it for a while.

"What color is it?"

"Yellow."

Julius gave me one of his ethereal smiles. "Yellow looks lovely on you." He stood back from the car then and said, "See you tomorrow."

I waved to him as I backed out of Evan's driveway, keeping my eyes on his glorious smile as long as I could before he faded away in the distance behind me.

As soon as I got home I ran upstairs and retrieved my dress from its hiding spot in my closet. I carefully unwrapped the plastic and hung it on the hook that protruded from my bedroom door, painstakingly smoothing out the wrinkles with my hands, then stepping back to admire it. It really was a very beautiful dress - I just hoped it wasn't too much for a homecoming dance.

I checked the clock on my side table. It was five minutes after nine, and I wondered if April would be home yet. My adrenaline was pumping hard, and I needed to talk to someone who was a little more experienced speaking guy language than I was. April would definitely be able to tell me whether or not my excitement was warranted. I leaped onto my bed and grabbed the phone, my hands shaking so hard I had to redial her number twice.

When I finally got it right, April answered the phone midway through the first ring. "I was just getting ready to call you!"

"I wish I would've known that, it would have saved me a lot of trouble," I said impatiently.

"What?"

I immediately started filling her in on everything Julius had said, including the facial expressions he used and the intonation of his voice when he said certain words. Then I told her how I had perceived all of the above, and ended with telling her how I messed up her phone number because I was shaking so badly.

April half laughed, half sighed with frustration at my inability to read between the lines. "Do you seriously need him to spell it out for you? Because if that's what your expecting it probably won't happen; guys don't compute that way. They expect you to understand everything they feel without proper communication."

I sighed. Why wasn't I built to understand everything as clearly as everyone else could?

"Look, he made the first move, now he's waiting for you to reciprocate. Flirt with him. It's all gravy after that, trust me."

I lied awake in bed that night, thinking of how to go about flirting with Julius. I knew it should just come natural, but anymore natural didn't seem to apply to me. I tossed and turned all night, waking up every couple of hours with a new worry.

What if he laughed at me? What if he really did like me, and then I did something stupid that changed his mind about how he felt about me? What if April was wrong and he didn't like me to begin with? Julius wasn't your average teenage boy after all; maybe the rules didn't apply to him.

When morning finally came, I was exhausted, and had the bags under my eyes to prove it. I didn't have the energy required to make myself look decent, so I didn't even attempt to.

After getting out of the shower, I towel dried my hair and pulled it up into a messy knot on the back of my head. I didn't put on any makeup, and I opted for my black velour sweats instead of jeans. I didn't look at myself in the mirror; I just grabbed my jacket and bag and headed downstairs for a cup of coffee before I left for school.

Julius met me at my car as soon as I pulled into the school parking lot, the sight of his dazzling smile stimulating my every nerve. I suddenly wished I would've put a little more effort into my appearance; Julius looked better than I had ever seen him, and here I was dressed in a sloppy pair of sweats with my damp hair tied back in a messy lump.

"So, how is it that you always manage to pull up exactly two minutes before the bell rings?" He asked with a mischievous smirk.

"Hey, what can I say, I'm punctual." Remembering April's advice, I winked at him before adding, "Could be another one of those virtues I'm so full of."

He tossed his head back in a hearty laugh before gently cupping both of my cheeks in his warm hands. "Among other things," he teased.

My heart was beating so hard against my chest from his touch that I couldn't think of a decent retort, so I just nodded, which sent him into another peal of laughter. The bell rang then and he grabbed my hand as he turned to enter the school. I didn't realize how stunned I was with his actions until I felt a slight tug on my arm. I was frozen in place, and Julius all but dragged me through the parking lot before I regained my senses enough to walk on my own.

Walking through the crowd of other students with Julius's hand entwined in mine was exhilarating. We received a few smiles, but for the most part, no one seemed to notice. It seemed as if being side by side with Julius was the most natural thing in the world, even to everyone around us, and the genuine smile that stretched across my face was unwavering.

When we finally made it to government, Mr. Enoch coughed in our direction, signaling us to release one another's hand. I blushed slightly and took my seat beside Julius, who winked at me when he noticed the pink tinge my face had taken.

I copied down the notes Mr. Enoch had written on the board, trying to force my mind to focus on something other than Julius, but it was no use - by the time I was finished I realized I hadn't absorbed a word of what I'd written.

Was it normal to be so consumed by someone? Would I ever be able to concentrate on anything else again? I had spent a lot of time during the last few weeks thinking of Julius, but today was different. Today it was if my feelings had taken on a life of their own; an incorporeal being that fluctuated between Julius and me. Did he feel the same way?

I was ripped from my contemplation when I heard the hard taps of heels against the tile floor. Looking in the direction from which they came, I saw Gina Kupfner entering the classroom. She was dressed in a short, fluffy, beige skirt and a white spaghetti strap shirt, but it wasn't her scandalous attire that caught my attention. I was more aware of the muddy, olive green light she was encased in. It was her aura, and it was extremely loud to me. I shot a furtive glance to Julius, who raised his eyebrows back at me in confusion. He didn't understand the reason for the shock that was registered on my face.

I ripped a piece of paper from my notebook and wrote:
Did you see the green?

I hoped that if the note was intercepted, the words were vague enough to not be easily understood.

I handed it to Julius while Mr. Enoch was busying himself with the pass Gina had just handed him. Julius took it from my hand so stealthily that I didn't even notice it was gone. After reading it he nodded, then wrote something back and handed it to me. I opened it and read:

Did you notice anyone else's?

I looked around the room at all the other students, none of which I noticed any type of aura from. Looking back at Julius I shook my head.

He reached out for the paper then, and I gave it to him, hoping he was going to explain. When he handed it back, all it said was:

Cleveland

I kept my eyes on him until I saw the subtle movement of his hair as he divided, then closed my eyes, willing myself to meet him at his apartment.

Bi-locating was becoming second nature to me, and it wasn't at all as uncomfortable as it had been the first couple of times I did it. I was completely aware of being in two places at once now, able to focus easily on both thought processes that were simultaneously going on inside my mind. I opened my eyes to see Julius sitting patiently on his couch, and I immediately followed suit.

"You should stay away from Gina as best you can," Julius said gravely, his face twisted in earnest contemplation.

His words startled me; they insinuated that he had discovered some sinister plot Gina had planned for me. "Why?"

"I'm not sure - I would have to talk to Cordele and Nayana to get their opinions as well - but I think that maybe you have inadvertently discovered one of your evolved strengths."

He was *The Thinker* once more, but this time my blood turned cold as I looked at him. His elusiveness reminded me of the day he told me about Devon's death, and I found myself frightened by his new revelation.

"Wh - What do you mean?"

"Remember when Nayana told you about our abilities to see auras?"

I nodded.

"Well, we can see everyone's, and it's been like that since the moment we woke up. When you never mentioned seeing them, I just figured that you never would. Cordele, Nayana and I have discussed it, and we thought it had something to do with the fact that you never got a chance to see Devon's. The first ones any of us have ever seen were from our malefactors. We thought that maybe the sight of them triggered our ability to notice everyone else's." He looked into my eyes then and added, "Evidently we were wrong."

"But why can I only see Gina's?" My voice was shaky now, and I was ringing my hands in nervous anticipation.

Julius shook his head. "I have a theory, but I can't be sure how accurate it is. I think that maybe you only see auras that directly affect you in some way. Yesterday, Gina was furious with you when I told her how I felt about you."

I knew it was completely inappropriate of me to be focusing on anything but the topic of auras at this moment, but the fact that Julius just admitted he had feelings for me made that sensation between my sternum and my stomach extend throughout my entire anatomy. Trying hard to ignore it, I listened intently as Julius went on.

"I watched her aura change before my eyes to the exact color you saw her in today, so I know very well it has to do with you. The fact that you saw it today is what makes me think she might be planning something to harm you in some way." Then he added with a laugh, "Of course, she has no idea who she's dealing with. There is no way she could actually do you any physical harm, but I wouldn't doubt that she is going to attempt a shot at public humiliation."

"Great - that's just what I need - more humiliation." I slumped back into the couch, angry at the world. Why was it that every horrible thing that could possibly happen to me seemed to come to fruition? I was a marked woman - a universal scapegoat.

Julius wasn't one to allow me to wallow in self pity for too long. "There is no way anyone will let her get away with doing something to you. The more attempts she makes, the less people will like her, and in the end, the only person she will succeed in humiliating is herself." He gently lifted my chin with the tip of his index finger, raising my eyes to his. "You are a gift to all of the good people of the world, Gabby. They may not know to what extent, but they feel it, and people have a way of standing behind the ones they believe in."

I smiled at him, unable to escape his hypnotic gaze. "I believe you," I said much more softly than I meant to, and before I thought about what I was doing, I slowly closed my face in on his in a spontaneous reaction to the overwhelming feelings that were stirring fiercely inside of me. His hands cupped my face as he kissed me back, a cascade of thrills surging throughout me as I felt his rich lips against mine, and with one hand on the back of his neck and the other on his chest, I felt his heart beating rapidly against my palm.

Somehow amidst our abundance of fervor, we managed to pull away from each other. We were both wearing radiant smiles, and I, at least, was breathless from the excessive amount of adrenaline that was now pulsing through me.

"That was unexpected. Wonderful, but unexpected," Julius managed to breathe out.

"You captivated me. I'm sorry for the ambush, but you are partly to blame," I teased.

"I'll take all the blame if that's the kind of punishment you deal out." Julius's roguish expression was hard to disregard - I wanted to kiss him again the moment he flashed his green eyes at me in that way, but somehow I managed to tolerate it.

"Back to the aura thing," I demanded. "If I only saw the auras of people who wanted to harm me, why didn't I see Curtis's?"

Julius thought for a long moment. "I don't know unless…" his train of thought seemed to take a route of its own, and suddenly he looked up at me with surprise. "Unless he didn't actually want to hurt you. You have to remember, he's forced into doing Devon's bidding. Remember how Cordele told us that some of Barbara's minions stayed with her out of fear? Perhaps that's the case with Curtis. While he certainly would have went through with whatever Devon told him to do, he may not have had the underlying desire to do it."

"So there's hope for Curtis? Do you think we could convince

him that he's on the wrong side?" I was optimistic. If there was a chance to save someone's soul I wanted to do it.

"I'm not sure that's likely. For one thing, he made the conscious decision to join Devon, so there has to be something in him that desires evil. I don't think he could ever be entirely trusted, even if he *has* realized he made a mistake." Hesitantly he added, "Plus, I did hurt him pretty badly. I doubt he'd want anything to do with something that I was involved in."

I thought about what Julius had just said. It made a lot of sense, and although I understood that we shouldn't recruit Curtis, I still felt a twinge of sympathy for him. "Isn't there anything we can do for him? I mean, is he doomed to Hell alongside Devon just because he has poor judgment?"

Julius shrugged. "Where he ends up is his decision. I wouldn't know what direction he's headed." Frowning he offered, "I'm really not as concerned with him as you are. He tried to kill you Gabby."

Oh yeah, that. Some sentinel I was turning out to be. I sighed in frustration and slumped into the couch once again. Leaning my head against Julius's shoulder I said, "How am I going to do it, Julius? Devon's in Hell and I'm out here, if I open the gate to find him they win by default, and if I stay out here and do nothing, he'll continue to find a way to recruit people into his army until the human race is all but destroyed. I don't understand what I have to do to eliminate him."

Julius put his arm around my shoulder and kissed the top of my head. "We'll figure it out. If there's a problem, there's a solution."

I hoped he was right. There was something that was bothering me, something that I didn't want to bring up to Julius. If Devon and I truly were evolved, and I actually succeeded in eliminating him, what would the next sentinel have to deal with? I knew it was unnecessary speculation at this point, since it couldn't happen again for a few years, but it was still a worry. It did make me think though. Instead of waiting to find out all of the ways in which I had evolved, wouldn't it be more prudent to try and find out beforehand? With this sudden enlightenment I turned to Julius. "I need to know all of our strengths. I have to be able to test them so we can find out what I have evolved in and exactly how they work in comparison to yours. I think it would give me a good idea about what I have to deal with."

Julius rubbed the scruff on his chin, thinking. "It seems very logical, but there is only one problem. You can never really know how strong you are until you are faced with evil. When you and I did defensive strength training, you were strong, but that was only a fraction of the strength you really possess. I didn't really intend to harm you, and that was taken into account when you defended yourself against me." He lost himself in thought again before continuing. "I really don't know how we'd go about testing you."

He was lying. I knew he was thinking the same things I was. Curtis and Gina. "I need to find out, Julius, and I know you and I are thinking the same thing. Why are you trying to protect me when you know I can't get hurt?"

Julius looked at me almost apologetically. "Actually - I was thinking that you would hurt *them*. That's one reason I told you to stay away from Gina whenever possible."

Now I was confused. "But I thought sentinels couldn't destroy."

"Well, as far as Cordele, Nayana, Daniel and I are concerned, that's certainly been the case, but we can't be sure about you yet. Besides all that, we may not be able to kill, but we can certainly seriously injure and debilitate. I don't think you need that on your conscience." He rubbed my cheek with the back of his fingers as he added, "You are very sympathetic. What would you think the minute you realized you hurt someone?"

I knew what he was getting at. I would probably vow to never hurt anyone again, no matter what someone did to provoke me, and that probably included Devon. I rolled my eyes. "Please. You don't really consider me that frail do you?"

He raised his eyebrows as if to ask me whether or not I was joking.

I huffed. "This is humanity we're talking about - life and death, the greater good and all of that - I think I could manage to consider those things while I was inflicting pain on those who deserve it."

Julius laughed. "You have a way with words, Gabby. But you certainly know yourself better than anyone. If you say you could do it, then I don't doubt you." Then, checking his watch he said, "Let's get back, it's lunch time and I'd like to be there when I eat. I'm starving."

We made it back just as we were entering the cafeteria, and the smell of cheeseburgers and French fries made my mouth water. I just realized that I hadn't eaten anything the night before, and I hadn't had any breakfast this morning either. I got in line with Julius, inconspicuously combing the room for Gina. I didn't see any sign of her, or the people she ate with, which made my stomach turn. They were probably somewhere right now, talking over the finalities of their plan to humiliate me.

We sat at our normal spot across from April and Travis while we ate. The conversation was strictly homecoming, and I was glad my mouth was too full to talk. I would have felt too ridiculous joining in with the other girls while they gushed about their dresses and shoes and hairstyles, and I didn't know anything about football, which the guys were now discussing. I ate in silence nodding in agreement to everything that was being said. I was glad to hear the other girls describe their dresses, though. I worried about what everyone else would be wearing - I didn't want to stick out in any way - but the other girls seemed to be describing dress styles very similar to mine, so I was relieved.

When we were finished with our lunch, Julius and I threw our trays away and stood just outside of the cafeteria waiting for the bell to ring. His hand was holding mine, and he stroked the back of it with his thumb. A few other people were standing around the same way we were, whispering something back and forth, but I was too busy staring at Julius to notice them.

Eventually the whispers caught his attention, and when his gaze turned to them I followed it. It was Troy Davis, Grady McKitrick, and Kaitlyn Summers, a group of kids who normally sat with us at lunch, but were frequently absent from our table due to their love of pranks, which often led to them getting into trouble. They had lunch detention today, which was held in the guidance office. I couldn't understand what they would be doing here. Usually the kids with lunch detention were sent straight to class after they were finished eating.

"Hey guys. Didn't you have lunch detention today?" I wasn't usually so nosy, but their behavior seemed odd to me for some reason, so I had to ask.

"Yeah," Kaitlyn said quickly. She turned her back to me then and faced Troy and Grady.

It was odd that Kaitlyn didn't elaborate in some way. On any other occasion, she would have went on and on about how unfairly she'd been treated, and how she didn't do whatever it was that got her into detention in the first place. Her peculiar behavior left me suspicious.

Julius must have picked up on it too, because he scrunched his eyebrows in their direction and dropped my hand to join them. "So, what were you guys in detention for this time?" He asked subtly.

The three of them chanced a glance in my direction, and then started frantically whispering to Julius. His eyes widened, and he looked toward me instinctively. I thought for a moment that they were informing Julius of some horrible prank-gone-wrong that landed them in detention, but then I heard the vice principal, Mrs. Albright, yelling at the end of the long corridor.

"Ten days, Gina! No football game, no homecoming dance! I can't possibly suspend you for anything less than that after a stunt like this! Why, why, why, would you possibly want to hurt someone this way? You know, I could expel you for the rest of the year if I wanted to, we have policies against things of this nature!"

Gina's volume matched Mrs. Albright's, but her tone was mocking. "Like I care. I don't want to be here anyway. I'll finish the year at a private school."

"You obviously don't understand, Gina. Private schools have standards, and now that you have this on your record you will be hard pressed to find one that will accept you. They have a much lower tolerance for these sorts of things than public schools do. Our rules and regulations are dependant on the government, but they are free to make them up as they go along."

Gina had nothing to say to this, and I heard her heels tapping against the floor as Mrs. Albright escorted her toward the office.

My voice was shaking as I rounded on Julius and the others. "What did she do?"

No one knew what to say, they just stared at me with sympathetic eyes, while they thought of ways to approach me. Even Julius was timid in his method, walking slowly toward me as if I were a wild horse he was trying to break.

I opened my mouth to ask them again, but just then, the secretary, Mrs. Faulkner, went over the loud system. "All students are to stay exactly where they are until further notice. No one is to leave their classrooms. Thank you."

I was stunned. Was it really that bad? I had to find out. In a split second decision, I ran down the corridor, Julius quickly behind me. All I had to do was reach the end, where Gina was caught, and I was sure I would find out what she did.

It wasn't easy staying in front of Julius. I was ten feet from the end of the hallway when he caught me, but I didn't need to go any further.

I tripped over my own feet in shock, landing on my knees and catching myself before my head hit the tile. My throat swelled immediately, and all of the hairs on my neck and arms rose in synchronization. I tried to hold back the sobs that were in my chest fighting to break free, which resulted in desperate whimpers coming from my throat.

All along the walls of the hallway were posters of Devon. They were the same ones my parents and I pasted all over the county, the only difference being the caption above his picture. The words *Have You Seen Me* were now replaced with: *You would have left too if you had a sister like mine.*

Julius leaned down to where I was lying in the middle of the hallway and picked me up, setting me on my feet. His eyes were intense as he grabbed me by both of my shoulders and at once I could feel the wonderful sensation of his hum rushing through my veins, warm and soothing. My rapid gasps were slowing to steady breaths, and my shaking frame was calming down, leaving me still.

The principal, Mr. Wilcoxen, rounded a corner then, and his face fell when he saw me. "Gabrielle -" He was at a loss for words, and I could tell he wished he could've gotten all of the signs down before I saw them. There was a big stack under his left arm, and he nearly dropped them when he saw that my eyelashes were wet from holding back tears.

"Would you like me to call your parents and have them pick you up?" He asked consolingly.

"No." It came out much sharper than I had intended. "I would rather they didn't know about this. My mother..." I couldn't finish. If she found out about this there was no doubt in my mind that the recent progress she made would definitely take a downward spiral.

"Her mother hasn't been taking Devon's disappearance well. If she found out what Gina did it would devastate her," Julius finished for me.

Mr. Wilcoxen nodded. "If you can get your guardian's consent, Mr. Carter, I would be willing to let you escort her home. Under the current circumstances I don't think it would be wise to let her drive herself."

"Cordele won't mind." He looked down at me then before turning back to Mr. Wilcoxen. "Would you mind calling him for me? I shouldn't leave Gabby alone, and I don't think it would be a good idea for her and Gina to see each other at the moment."

Mr. Wilcoxen's eyes widened with understanding. "Of course." Then turning to me he said, "Gabrielle, this won't be counted as an absence for either of you. I'll talk to the rest of your teachers and have the two of you excused from any homework they might assign." Then, with nothing less than absolute concern in his eyes he said, "I'm deeply sorry you had to go through this today. You have my word that Gina and her friends will not bother you again."

"Thanks, Mr. Wilcoxen, but you have nothing to apologize for," I said in a lethargic tone.

He nodded for no other reason than to acknowledge he heard me. "I'll get all of this cleaned up before anyone sees it." He walked away then, toward a couple of teachers who exited their classrooms to find out what was going on. I watched as they shook their heads in disgust at the posters that were lining the walls. They started tearing them down as Mr. Wilcoxen headed toward the office to call Cordele.

Julius walked me down the hall, past the cafeteria and out the doors into the parking lot. Grady, Troy, and Kaitlyn were staring at us as we walked by, their sympathetic expressions more than I cared to look at. Julius stopped just after we passed them, and turned around. I heard him ask that they not tell anyone what had happened, and listened as they all promised they wouldn't.

My mom was very worried when I walked in the house, but I told her I was just having cramps. She questioned me about my car suspiciously, thinking it was odd that I wouldn't have driven myself home, but I told her I took a couple of Tylenol and they made me drowsy. She accepted the lie easily, knowing how I had a low tolerance for even the simplest pain medication. I promised that I would feel better after a nap, and that Julius would come back later to take me to the school so I could pick up my car. She felt better after my explanation, and left me alone so I could rest.

Once in my room I slumped into my bed. I really did need a nap after the restless night I had, so I curled up under my comforter and drifted off to sleep without any problems.

When I woke up, I realized that I had slept most of the day away, the evening sun a dull yellow against the white wall. I stretched and yawned, which felt wonderful, and rolled over on my side to check the clock. It was almost six. I couldn't believe Mom let me sleep so long.

When I sat up to get out of bed, I heard muffled voices downstairs. There was laughter, which puzzled me. Mom and Dad weren't ones to laugh with one another, at least not in the recent past. My curiosity got the best of me, and I rubbed my eyes and made my way downstairs.

I was surprised when I entered the kitchen and the first person I saw was Julius. I knew he would be coming over, so I shouldn't have been so shocked, but for some reason, seeing him interacting with my parents on such a natural level made me feel like I had just entered another dimension.

"Hey, Gabs," my dad said with the enthusiasm of a drunkard. He grabbed my shoulder, hugging me close to him. "Thought you'd never wake up." Then, turning to Julius he said, "Well, son, what do you think? She's covered in pillow creases and her hair's a little messed up, a little different than what you're used to seeing."

I had to roll my eyes at that; Julius had seen me look worse, contrary to Dad's beliefs, but at his sudden personality change I had to raise my eyebrows.

What was going on? Mom was giggling at Dad's every word, and Dad was talking in an obliviously obnoxious way. Maybe we had a gas leak. I looked Julius over, wondering if he was going to surprise me with some odd behavioral change as well, but my quizzical expression only sent my parents into another round of boisterous laughter.

"I'm just going to brush my hair and then you'll take me to get my car, right?" My words were slow and rhythmic, the way one might talk to a child. I was testing his sanity, worried he might be in the same condition as my parents.

"Hurry back," he said with a wink, in a completely conventional tone. I heaved a sigh of relief. At least there was some normalcy to the increasingly bizarre atmosphere I woke up into.

I bounded quickly up the stairs and pulled my hair down, brushing it hastily before I pulled it back up into the lump it refused to recoil itself from. After putting on my socks and shoes, I grabbed a jacket from my closet and met Julius once again in the kitchen.

My parents followed us to the door, and once we were inside the Challenger they waved as if we were visitors they wouldn't see for a long time.

"*What* is going on with them?" I insisted with a hint of accusation.

"I decided to take a page from your book - you know - good deeds for humanity and all of that."

"My book? You are the same thing I am Julius. It's in us to save humanity, remember?"

"There's a difference between saving humanity and making it feel better. I usually reserve my hum for more urgent cases, but I remembered what you said about your mom, so I decided to give it a try." He shrugged tactfully.

I raised my eyebrows. "Is it possible to overdose on the hum?"

Julius laughed jovially at my joke. "Your parents are fine, it's just been so long since they felt anything that good that they reacted to it a little differently than most people would."

I wondered if they noticed it came from Julius. I remembered being worried that they would feel it when they shook hands with him the first time they met, knowing what I thought the first time he gave it to me.

I didn't tell Julius what I was thinking, not because he might think I was being too worrisome, but because I realized that he knew what he was doing. I didn't want to insult his intellect.

When we pulled up next to my car, Julius let the Challenger idle. I could tell something was on his mind, but I wasn't sure I should pry. He would tell me what he was thinking if he wanted me to know, wouldn't he? Of course, there was another tactic I could try if I wanted to get something out of him. I placed my hand on his and looked into his eyes, trying to silently convey that he could tell me anything. He smiled at me with what looked to me to be sadness, then reached out and tapped my nose. Our silent communication was an easy language to understand. He was telling me he got the message, but it was something he didn't want to worry me with.

His inaudible statement left my insides limp. Julius was never so ambivalent, and I knew that whatever was worrying him had to be serious. If he wouldn't tell me what was bothering him, I had no other option than to assume it was something horrible. He left me with nothing to speculate over, no idea as to what could leave him with an expression akin to exhausted desperation.

Did his mood have something to do with me? Had there been some new developments with Devon that he wasn't telling me? Or did this have something to do with our newly established relationship? I decided not to think about it. When he had everything figured out he would tell me; it was obvious to me that he was analyzing something, and he hadn't come up with an answer yet.

I turned toward the door to let myself out, but Julius tugged on the back of my jacket and pulled me back into my seat. At once his warm hand was caressing my cheek, sending shivers all over my body. His breath was in my face, and the intoxicating fragrance of his skin was leaving me dizzy. He pressed his lips to mine, softly at first, then gradually becoming more passionate.

Instinctively I hugged his neck with my right hand and submitted, kissing him back vehemently. My heart was beating wildly beneath my chest, and I became aware of a new feeling -

something electrical in nature - recurring through my veins; intermittent charges that imitated the rhythm of my heart.

I pulled away then, finally comprehending the wonderful feeling that was flooding my body. It was my hum. "Julius, did you feel that?" My voice was shocked and breathy.

He smiled at me and leaned back in his seat, his face smothered with satisfaction. "Your hum?"

His words hit me with sudden realization. The worry I had seen on his face only moments ago was due to my previous inability to perform the hum. The fact that I had never before been consciously aware of it had him baffled, and his passionate kiss was an attempt to bring my hum to fruition.

I exhaled, pleased that I was now aware of my own hum, and relieved that Julius's uneasiness wasn't something more serious.

My only concern now was how to gain control of it. Julius could dispense his at will, and I wondered how much practice, if any, that he put into forcing it out of himself. I remembered what he said about it being difficult in the beginning to make himself stop when it was best, but I wasn't sure whether he found it complicated to administer.

"How do you do it? On purpose I mean."

Julius thought for a minute. "I just know that I can. I imagine the feeling I want to give, and when I touch someone, it's there."

I beckoned him closer, and then concentrated on remembering how my body felt as the hum was pulsing through me. I inhaled deeply, and when the sensation came over me I touched Julius's face, willing the phenomenon to extend beyond my fingertips and into him.

The result was incredible. The intensity of my hum had escalated, leaving me breathless with euphoria. I didn't want to release his face, knowing that the connection would be lost then, and that once again I would only be filled with that cheap, dull feeling I lived with on any everyday basis.

But somewhere within me, logic screamed. I knew I must let go, for in giving into the pleasure I would be losing everything else, and so it was with immense effort that I loosened my hand.

Julius shuddered as I recoiled, and at once I was sure that something had gone wrong.

"Are you okay?" I managed to gasp, my hands against my mouth anxiously.

He shook his head slightly and blinked his eyes. "Wow."

"What did I do wrong?" I positioned myself with my shins against the seat, sitting on the back of my heels. My back was plastered to the passenger door in fright, and the tips of my fingers were on my bottom lip, which was trembling slightly. I had never reacted that way to Julius's hum, and I was sure something went terribly wrong with my attempt.

"You didn't do anything wrong." His tone was one of pleasant surprise, his expression still filled with shock. He was taking rapid, shallow breaths, as if he had just run a mile, his right hand pressed against his chest and his left one holding onto the steering wheel for support.

"What do you mean I did nothing wrong? Look at yourself!"

"Gabby, I'm fine. It was just really intense. I think our hums connected somehow."

His breathing was becoming slower, more relaxed.

"Does that really make sense? I mean, I've never felt anything like that when you've given me the hum. Why wouldn't they have connected when you did it to me?"

Julius smiled dazzlingly, his green eyes sparkling with delight. "I think that maybe we uncovered another evolved strength."

Chapter 8❖

I was immensely relieved that I hadn't hurt Julius after all, but I couldn't understand what good it would do to be able to connect my hum with someone else's. How could that possibly be a strength? The intensity nearly incapacitated Julius, and if anything I saw this as a setback rather than a strength, although Julius vehemently disagreed with me, keeping a gleeful smile all the while we discussed it.

"This has the potential to make you twice as powerful," he explained. "I'll give you that it knocked the wind out of me, but you have to see that as a good thing. Malefactors aren't equipped to deal with happiness - it is the total opposite of their composition. If we could find a way to administer the hum to Devon while the five of us sentinels were joined..." He shrugged, knowing I had the gist of what he was thinking.

I thought his idea was nothing short of ludicrous. "And if it nearly kills you in the process, exactly how could that be considered a great tactic?"

His smile faded slightly. "I'm sure it would just take some practice. Maybe if we both put an effort into it, we could create a different kind of energy. Instead of you being the sender, and I being the receiver, we could both be senders."

I wondered if he had a point, but I also pondered the results. What if something went horribly wrong? Would we be harmed in any way?

Julius interrupted my thoughts. "Come on," he said, looking at his watch. "I need to get back to the game, I told April and Travis we'd be there in time to see her crowned."

I gasped. "Oh no! Did we miss it?" Guilt rushed over me when I realized I'd completely forgotten all about the homecoming game.

"No. The game just started a few minutes ago, but I was there earlier helping Evan with the float."

"But you saw April, right?"

"Yeah."

"Did she ask why we left school?"

"No. I think she was waiting to ask you." He thought for a moment, and then said, "You know, I like her. Ashley, Jamie, and Cassandra ambushed me with questions, not even caring that it wasn't any of their business, but April didn't even mention it. She is very thoughtful of other people's feelings."

"That's why she's my best friend."

We exited his car and walked across the parking lot and down the back field until we reached the football field. The stands were crowded with students, teachers, and alumni.

We made our way to the middle of the crowd and sat down beside Kaitlyn and Grady, who were sharing a container of nachos from the concession stand. They gave us a cautious glance, gauging my disposition. After what had happened today, they were leery of being even slightly buoyant around me. Apparently they came to the conclusion that I was fine, because their expressions became happy an instant later, and they waved their greetings.

The game was in the second quarter, and we were up by seven. I tried to get interested in the game, but ten minutes into it I found my mind wandering with boredom. Football was not my thing, but I managed to put on a good front. I cheered with the crowd whenever something good happened, but apart from the touchdowns and tackles I had no idea what we were applauding and whistling about. I was clueless when it came to the rules, regulations and terminology of just about any sport.

By the time halftime came around, my hands were stinging from all the clapping I had done, and my toes were curling from the cold that settled over the field when the sun went down. The floats were lining up on the track now, and the M. C. was giving the audience instructions on how to vote for their favorites. The voting was simple; you cheered loud and hard for your favorite, and whichever float received the highest praise won fifty dollars for its class fund. The senior class won, although in my personal opinion the juniors should have. Their float was very similar to ours, except they had a complete football player whose leg actually rose up and down toward a devil.

The homecoming court was announced then, starting with the freshman attendants, and ending with the juniors. Finally, after what seemed like hours, the senior nominees were introduced to the crowd. Ashley, Jamie and Cassandra all paled in comparison to April, who looked very chic in the skirt suit that sounded so hideous when she described it to me. To no one's amazement but everyone's joy, April was announced as the homecoming queen, sending cheers throughout the stands.

When the game started up once more, I slumped into the cold metal bleachers and rested my chin in my hands. The score was now twenty-one to seven, with Kentland in the lead, Evan having made two of the touchdowns. I wasn't sure what his position was called, but he seemed to really know what he was doing. He dodged a ridiculous amount of tackles, and I was surprised that someone so big could run so fast. Each time the clock stopped, he took off his helmet and shook his burly head, the sweat that flew from his messy red hair sparkling with help from the stadium lights. It reminded me of those sports drink commercials - the ones that glorified sweat.

The final score was thirty-four to twenty-one, and when the game ended, everyone in the stands cheered for our victory. I cheered just as enthusiastically as everyone else, but secretly I was only doing it because I was glad it was over. If it wasn't for April being part of the festivities I wouldn't have come, but I figured no one needed to know that but me.

After the game, I drove my car home with Julius following me. I parked it in the driveway, and when I didn't see any lights on in the house I didn't bother to check in. If my parents were asleep I didn't want to bother them. I hopped in Julius's car and we drove out to Evan's to celebrate.

His garage wasn't as crowded as I thought it would be. The past couple of times that I'd been there, half of the senior class was helping with the float, but tonight it seemed like more of a private party. The SUV that was normally parked there was gone, and Evan had a few lawn chairs set up so everyone would have a place to sit.

Kaitlyn and Grady were already there, and I noticed Ashley was standing next to Evan with her arm wrapped around his waist. I was waiting for the scowl to appear on her face when she saw me, but to my surprise she gave me an apologetic smile instead. I smiled back to let her know there were no hard feelings; I knew how easy it was to fall for Julius.

Troy brought Alexis Kimble, a girl with coffee colored skin and beautiful teeth, and April and Travis pulled up just as the rest of us had started congratulating Evan on his three touchdowns.

"Where are your parents, Evan?" Travis asked when he noticed the space in the garage.

"A bunch of their friends they went to high school with come in town every year to watch the homecoming game, and then they all drive down to Lafayette and stay out all night. It's sort of like a class reunion. They won't be home until tomorrow afternoon."

Now I understood why his get-together was only composed of the ten of us. Evan had gotten into trouble during his sophomore year over drinking. He and his friend, Matt Hensley, who was a year older than us, were out drinking one night. Matt was driving, and wrecked his dad's jeep. The vehicle went airborne after he made a turn in the road at a dangerous rate of speed, and landed on its top in someone's yard after rolling three times. The jeep missed the house only by a couple of feet, but Matt and Evan weren't so lucky. It took the paramedics four hours to get them out of the mangled wreckage. They both spent two months in the hospital, and after two surgeries to repair his broken knee, Evan had to do a year of physical therapy. He also sustained a head injury that left him deaf in his left ear. Matt broke his collar bone and his neck, but luckily everything healed perfectly and he didn't suffer any permanent damage. Evan refused to ever drink again after that, and I realized that he hadn't invited the entire class over for fear that things would get out of hand with his parents away for the night.

His parents were nice enough to set out trays of sandwiches and bowls of popcorn and potato chips before they left, and the ten of us sat around in a circle eating and discussing the recent victory of Kentland High.

Eventually the topic turned to music, which was a relief to me. Evan's stereo was tuned to a classic rock station - the same station I listened to in my car. April, Travis and Grady didn't care for the music, but they didn't object much. Instead, April thought it would be fun for Evan and me to compete against each other by guessing the names of the bands that were playing.

It was actually very fun, and the game continued throughout the evening with each new song that came on. I only missed two of them - one song by Peter Frampton, and another by Firehouse. I got Evan on Ozzy Osbourne, though, who has always been a favorite of mine.

My curfew was midnight, and when Julius pointed out that it was eleven forty-five, I groaned. I was really enjoying myself, and I didn't want to leave.

Before Julius took me home, we made plans with everyone to meet in Rensselaer for dinner the next day.

I fell asleep fairly easily that night, considering the long nap I took earlier in the afternoon, and I didn't wake up until nine the next morning. When the sun hit my face, I squinted my eyes, trying to remember what I had been dreaming about. Someone in my dream had changed into some type of growling, yellow eyed creature, but I couldn't remember if it was me or someone else. I gave up on it after a few minutes, and climbed out of bed, hoping Dad would already have a pot of coffee on.

When I opened my bedroom door and stepped out into the hallway, I heard my mother's familiar giggles coming from their room. Dad was laughing a little more loudly than she was, and I rolled my eyes. How long was the hum going to last on them? I was glad they were feeling better, but their chipper demeanor was starting to get somewhat annoying. It was reminding me of a movie I'd seen awhile back where a daughter was taken into protective custody because her parents were high on drugs. Both of the parents were laughing hysterically and the police eventually had to hogtie the mother. I shook my head, attempting to rid myself of the ridiculous comparison I'd just made, and then walked downstairs into the kitchen to put on a pot of coffee.

Our kitchen was actually quite small in comparison to the rest of the house. It was long and narrow, with a space for the table at the very end, which opened up into the living room. As I turned left at the bottom of the stairs to enter the kitchen, the smell of coffee wafted through the air. *So Dad has been up already,* I thought. I grabbed my favorite mug - the heavy one that came from the paper where Dad worked - and headed to the refrigerator to grab the milk.

As soon as I reached for the handle of the refrigerator, I

gasped, nearly dropping my mug on the kitchen floor. Julius was sitting at the table, reading the paper and drinking a cup of coffee. Completely ignoring my illustration of fright, he said, "You should really switch to decaf. Our kind doesn't exactly need a stimulant."

"How did you get in here?" My hand clutched at my chest as I tried to calm my breathing.

"Are you seriously wondering?" His face was turned upward in an astute smile.

Of course it was a stupid question. We could show up anywhere we wanted to just by thinking about it. I sighed in frustration. Was I ever going to get used to this?

"What I meant was, *why* are you here?"

Julius folded the paper diligently and placed it back on the table before answering me. "I thought it would be a good idea to check on your parents. They have to know the hum came from me, and I might have to modify their memories." His hands were folded neatly on top of one another, his voice steady and calm as if the topic of memory modification was as normal as discussing the weather.

"Modify their memories? Why? How? Can you really do that?" I was beginning to wish there was a manual that I could consult. There seemed to be a new surprise everyday.

"I keep forgetting about your little malfunction," Julius said.

"You mean the fact that I'm completely unaware of everything that has to do with being a sentinel, with the exception of what you've told me?"

"Yes, that would be the malfunction to which I am referring."

I pulled out the chair beside Julius and sat, curling myself up to rest my chin on my knees. "Any new speculations as to *why* I have a malfunction?"

He shook his head in response. I realized when he did that I wasn't expecting anything different. If he'd figured anything out he would have told me by now.

Figuring it wasn't doing any good to ponder my particular eccentricities, I returned to the subject of memory modification. "So how do you go about modifying memories?"

"Well, first of all, I need to know how your parents are feeling this morning."

I rolled my eyes and huffed. "Like they've inhaled too many paint fumes - the old kind that's full of lead. I heard them giggling together when I left my room this morning."

Julius laughed. "That's not so bad. Once it starts to wear off they should start feeling better."

"You make it sound like you gave them a dose of antibiotics."

He cocked one of his eyebrows. "Hmm. That's one way of looking at it. I like your analogies."

I shook my head in wonderment. How could he manage to be so cavalier?

"I'll also have to gauge their reaction to me. That's one reason I came here so early this morning."

"I wouldn't be surprised if they found it odd that you're here, Julius. It's a little after nine in the morning and they obviously didn't hear you come in. You might want to take that into account before you go messing with their brains." I got up to go to the refrigerator and retrieve the milk; I still wanted that cup of coffee. I continued questioning Julius while I was going about my business in the kitchen. "So how does it work anyway?"

"Well, it works the same way the hum does - application wise anyway. It requires touch. I think of a new memory and project it the way I would the hum, and the other body accepts it."

I sat down next to him again and took a sip of coffee. Thoughts and ideas were swirling around my head like frenzied dust particles that floated in a shaft of sunlight.

There were so many possibilities that came with memory modification. The entire world could change. If a terrorist who was about to bomb a building full of innocent people was suddenly implanted with a false memory - one where he was supposed to disable the bomb instead - lives could be saved. If people in third world countries were implanted with memories of being doctors and surgeons, perhaps suffering would decrease. The possibilities seemed endless to me, and I wondered why no one seemed to have thought of them before.

Before I told Julius what I was thinking, another thought occurred to me. If memory modification was so easy, why wouldn't he have used it on his family? Why wouldn't he have made them forget about Suzanne, and why wouldn't he have used it to make them forget he existed before he left?

Julius took my hand, pulling me out of the thoughts I was entrapped in. Stroking the back of my fingers with his thumb, he looked at me with thoughtful eyes. "Can I ask you what you're thinking?"

I wasn't sure if I should tell him or not. Julius was a very intelligent person, and nearly anytime I suggested an idea to him, he had already thought of it himself. It was unlikely that the thoughts that were running through my mind hadn't already run through his, so I didn't think it would really do any good to voice them.

On the other hand, I didn't want Julius to think I was trying to dodge his questions, so I gave up on the debate that was now consuming my mind and decided to answer his question. "I was just wondering why you didn't use memory modification on your family."

Julius smiled and nodded, pulling his hand away from mine. He leaned back in his chair and shrugged before folding his arms across his chest and tucking his hands underneath them. "I thought about it, but there were a couple of problems. For one thing, everyone I'd ever met in my entire life would have had to have been modified for the plan to work, and that would have taken some real time. First of all, I knew there were people in the world that I didn't remember having met, which would have screwed up the entire operation. Second of all, there were people whom I wouldn't have been able to find, and it would have been too risky to assume that those people would never again have contact with my family. Obviously, if any of those people had run into my family, there was the chance that they would have inquired about me and Suzanne."

He cleared his throat and looked out the window before adding, "But even if I had been able to find everyone I needed to, I wouldn't have done it." He looked back at me, his olive eyes teeming with earnest. "My family was all I had - the only thing that concurred my existence. They were the only solid evidence I had that proved that I was real; the only thing that confirmed that at one point during my eternity I was actually a normal human being. I know it was a selfish way of looking at it. It was horrible to see the pain in their faces before I left, and even now when I visit them the guilt is unbearable at times when they reminisce." He chuckled to himself sarcastically. "They always have a story to tell me about their long lost brother, and each one ends the same way - with them telling me how much they miss him, and how they wish they could have seen him before he passed away." He exhaled deeply when he was finished, and the sadness that clouded his face left me wishing I hadn't brought it up.

I grabbed his hand and squeezed it. "I'm sorry." It was barely more than a whisper, but he smiled back in response.

Rising from his chair, he stood behind me and gently wrapped his arms around my neck. "You have nothing to be sorry about. There is no way to describe the relief you've given me. For the last fifty-eight years I've had these feelings bottled up inside me, longing to have someone to talk to. Cordele, Nayana and Daniel are great, but the four of us have a sort of silent understanding. We've all been through the exact same thing, so there is really no reason to discuss how we feel. It's different with you. An explanation is required in order for you to understand, and somehow explaining things to you helps me too."

I rubbed his cheek as he rested his head against mine. Knowing that I helped him feel better in some way made me feel wonderful, and I hoped that it would always be this way between us.

We suddenly heard the sound of childish laughter coming from the hallway, and Julius released his embrace and settled once more in the chair he had occupied moments before.

I retrieved the pot of coffee and refilled his mug, then added a little more to my own to warm it up.

The moment my Dad rounded the corner into the kitchen his face lit up. "Coffee! You know, Gabby, maybe we should switch to decaf. I think the regular is starting to make me a little jittery." He wiggled both of his hands while he said it, which Mom found extremely hilarious. She laughed so hard that she eventually started rubbing her cheeks, trying to relieve the soreness that had developed in her face.

After Mom finally regained her composure, she spotted Julius. "Well, what do you know? I didn't even hear you pull up in the driveway. Have you been here long?"

"I got here about half an hour ago," he responded, checking his watch. "The two of you seem very happy this morning. Did you get a good night's rest?"

Mom and Dad looked at each other with matching quizzical expressions. "As a matter of fact, I can't remember when I had a better night's sleep," Dad said with confusion.

Mom nodded in agreement.

"So how was the game last night?" Dad seemed to be getting a grip on reality now that he was questioning his unusual night of peace.

"We won," I offered. "And April got Homecoming Queen."

"That's a given," Mom said with a smile on her face. I could tell it was her talking and not the hum.

"So what are your plans for tonight?" Dad unfolded the paper and began scanning it as he asked. I could tell he was trying to act as if it was no big deal, when really his curiosity was nearly killing him.

"A group of us are going to Rensselaer for dinner, and then we're going to the dance. It isn't over until midnight." I hoped they wouldn't tell Julius he had to have me home before the dance was over.

"Come straight home after the dance is over," Dad said sternly. It was nice to see he was slowly getting back to his old self.

Beside him, Mom just nodded in agreement.

"I'll have her back on time," Julius said with sincerity.

Mom smiled at him. "Thank you, Julius." She said it with such candor that I found it hard to believe there wasn't hidden meaning behind it.

I stole a glance at Julius, who was studying my mother's face intensely. By his studious expression, I gathered he caught the alternate connotation, and was now deciding whether or not he needed to modify her memory. After an awkward moment, he said, "Your welcome."

He stood to leave and shook my dad's hand. I knew what he was doing to him, and I wondered what part of his memory he was tampering with. Was it the part where he gave him the hum? Or was it the memory of him studying my mother's expression? Could it possibly have been both?

I watched as Dad's face changed from confusion to happiness while his hand was in Julius's. "We'll see you in a bit, Julius," he said with a wide grin.

Julius waved as I walked him to the door, and before I shut it behind me I heard my dad say, "Great kid, that Julius. It was nice of him to stop by just to fix the microwave, wasn't it?"

All I heard from my mother was, "Huh?"

I rolled my eyes at Julius when we were standing on the porch. "Fixing the microwave?"

"I couldn't think of anything good that quickly. I had to do something, he was getting suspicious."

"So did you fix the part where you gave him the hum, too?"

"No. He's much too skeptical to have thought it came from me."

"Evidently my mother isn't. Why didn't you fix hers?"

"I don't know. I know I should have, but there was something about the way she looked at me - like she was pleading with me not to take it away…"

"She's suspicious." I wondered… "What if she knew? What if somehow she found out?"

"There are people who know - the remorseful ones for example - but they've always just… known. I don't know how anyone would react if we told them ourselves."

I didn't need to ponder how my mother would react if I were to tell her. I knew that I never would, because explaining it to her would mean telling her about Devon, and I knew how devastated she would be. It was an impossibility, but I decided that I wouldn't dispute her suspicions. If ever she voiced them to me, I wouldn't lie.

"Well," Julius said, tugging me from my thoughts, "I'll be here around seven." He bent slightly to kiss me before he got in the Challenger and left.

By five that evening, Mom was yanking me from the couch to start on my hair. I hadn't given any thought to how I was going to style it, and I was a little nervous when I found out she expected to do it for me. The moment she mentioned it, images of pictures from her own prom materialized in my head. I didn't want to disappoint her, so I figured I would just stuff a comb and brush in my purse to fix what was sure to be a catastrophe the moment I entered Julius's car.

She dragged me upstairs to the bathroom impatiently, which resulted in me stubbing my toe on one of the stairs.

Once I was seated on the toilet, I started to hyperventilate. I spotted a giant can of hairspray - the kind that mimicked super glue. There was no way a comb and a brush could make it through that stuff without ripping your hair right out of the scalp.

Mom calmed me down by showing me a picture she'd cut from a magazine.

The model in the picture had a hair color very similar to mine, which was pulled up in the back and crowned with a rhinestone, wrap-around head band. It was very pretty, and I hoped she could pull it off.

I was afraid to look, when, forty-five minutes later she said she was finished. I squinted my eyes as I stood, apprehensive about seeing my own reflection, but opened them wide with pleasant surprise when I spotted myself.

Mom placed both of her hands on my shoulders while I stared into the mirror, a timid smile perched on her face. "What do you think?"

I was speechless. Mom's craftiness was a surprise, and I didn't know what to say, so I just nodded my head in amazement at her talent.

"If you hadn't washed your hair today I wouldn't have had to use so much hairspray. The natural oils in your hair really help to hold the curl, but I think it turned out nice anyway," she said, admiring her work. Finally she stopped looking at me and started cleaning up the bathroom. "You'll want to wait to do your makeup; you want it to be fresh for the pictures."

"You're not going to do it for me?" I wasn't the best makeup artist, and with the way my hair turned out, I had a newfound faith in Mom.

She smiled at me, thankful for the compliment that lay beneath my apprehension. "Sure."

By six forty-five, I was completely ready, my hair up, makeup done and dress on.

Mom handed me the shoes she wore when she was in my Cousin Amanda's wedding, and I suddenly wished I'd tried them on beforehand. The heels were higher than I thought, and I hoped I didn't make a fool of myself by falling on my face. I slipped them on just as I heard Julius's car pull into the driveway, and Mom rushed me upstairs to spray me with perfume.

I knew it was just an excuse so she could see Julius's face when I walked down the stairs, (the way it was done in those cheesy movies she used to watch) but I didn't object. After everything she'd went through today she deserved it.

I made my way back down the stairs after Mom did, and whatever reaction she was hoping for from Julius became irrelevant the moment I laid my eyes on him. The words handsome, dashing, and debonair all came to mind, but none were accurate enough to describe him. His dark suit fit him perfectly, and his yellow tie set off his carefully styled dark hair. He was clean shaven, leaving his face looking soft, and I longed to touch it. The sight of him left me breathless, and I didn't inhale until he spoke to me.

"You look…" He was tongue-tied as well, which made me blush.

"Beautiful, Gabs," my dad finished. His wide smile was unexpected. I knew he wanted me to be a normal teenager, but I thought that when it came right down to it, he would have grumbled somewhat when I started dating.

Mom pulled out the camera then, and started taking pictures. She must have taken about twenty before Julius and I finally managed to make our way outside, and was still snapping as Julius opened the car door for me. She and Dad stood on the front porch, waving and taking pictures until we were out of the driveway and on the road. I sighed with relief when they were no longer in sight, and Julius laughed at me.

It usually took about twenty-five minutes to get to Rensselaer, and we were cutting it close; we were supposed to meet the others by seven-thirty, so I was surprised when Julius pulled over on the side of the highway once we were outside the city limits.

"What's the matter? Is something wrong with the car?" I was confused, and instinctively my eyes flashed to the message board behind the steering wheel, searching for the check engine light.

"Nothing's wrong, I just realized my blabbering didn't do you any justice back there." His smile was radiant, and at once I wanted to reach out to him, but I knew he wasn't finished speaking, so impatiently I waited for him to continue.

"I really didn't think your parents would have been comfortable hearing the words that came to mind when I saw you come down the stairs this evening, so I decided it would be best to wait until I got you alone to tell you what I think."

With those words, my heart started racing at speeds that could have broken the sound barrier. His voice was hanging in the air like puffs of smoke, swirling in the atmosphere until its hypnotic dance left me intoxicated with adrenaline. My skin shivered with satisfaction as he cupped his hands around my jaw line, his fingertips resting calculatingly on the corners of my eyes as he rested his forehead on mine. I blushed when I realized how heavy and quick my breathing had become, but I made no effort to slow it down.

Julius's voice was barely above a whisper when he said, "Never in my life has the sight of a woman invoked such feelings within me as you did this evening." He kissed me gently on the forehead and then added in my ear, "You are the essence of beauty." He rubbed his nose along my cheek until our mouths connected, kissing me softly at first, and then becoming more fervent as I kissed him back. The hairs on the back of my neck raised as his hands lingered to my throat, and my heart, which was racing so wildly before, suddenly started to palpitate irregularly. I didn't want the moment to end, so when Julius finally pulled away I sulked.

He laughed when he saw the expression on my face, then ran the back of his hand tenderly along my jaw and said, "We're late."

I sighed. "I know."

Julius pulled back onto the road, driving ten miles faster than the speed limit. He looked over at me often, a grin stretched across his face every time. It made me nervous when he did; the roads were getting more narrow and the curves were getting sharper. I held my breath most of the way through the rural stretch, and exhaled deeply once the houses started getting closer together and the roads began straightening out.

We were still five minutes late, even with Julius's speeding, and the rest of the group was waiting outside of the restaurant when we pulled up.

"Where have you been?" April asked as soon as Julius opened my door. "We've been here for twenty minutes waiting on you! Kaitlyn and Grady couldn't wait any longer - they already put our names on the roster - they should be calling our table any minute now."

Julius grabbed my hand and pulled me from the car. April gasped when she saw me, and immediately forgot that she had been reprimanding me a moment ago. "Gabby! You look great!"

"Well, you don't have to be so surprised about it," I joked, but secretly I enjoyed her stunned approval. April was as beautiful as ever - she was wearing a teal slip dress with her hair halfway up, with long, golden curls cascading across her shoulders and down her back. Although she never acted even remotely conceited, she had to know she was beautiful, and it was nice to know that even if it was just this one time, she considered me in the same category as herself.

Her attention turned to Julius then, scanning him over. Her cheeks turned red at the sight of him, which was saying something - April rarely blushed. She quickly averted her attention back to me and I smiled with the left side of my mouth, my eyes looking in Julius's direction. She raised her eyebrows as she smiled back, tilting her head slightly toward him, silently telling me she agreed with what I thought - Julius was much more than handsome.

Kaitlyn waved us over then, letting us know our table was ready.

Julius hooked his arm around mine and together we walked toward the restaurant, April in front of us scurrying toward

Travis.

Right before we made it through the door, however, I glimpsed something out of the corner of my eye that made me stop dead in my tracks. I was frozen in place, adrenaline pumping through my veins so harshly I could hear the thud of my heart in my ear. I felt a slight tug on my arm as Julius kept walking after I stopped. Confused, he looked down at me, and, catching the direction of my gaze, his head turned to see what I was looking at. I felt him stiffen significantly as he saw the four strangers that were staring in our direction, their auras filthy green.

"What do we do?" I whispered frantically.

"You aren't going to do anything," Julius said after a moment. "They're obviously Devon's minions, and if they're anything like Curtis I should be able to take care of them fairly easy." His eyes were squinted in loathing and he was speaking to me through gritted teeth.

"But there are four of them!" My frame was shivering uncontrollably now, fear for Julius overpowering the shock that overtook my body the moment I saw the minions. "They came for *me* didn't they? I have to help!"

Julius's face instantly contorted into an expression of shock mixed with disgust. "Absolutely not! Didn't you hear anything I just said? If these four are anything like Curtis you could be in serious danger. They could kill you, Gabby!"

The minions slowly started advancing then, walking across the parking lot inconspicuously. My heart pounded in my chest with every step they took in our direction. The closer they got to us, the easier it was to make them out, and I was surprised that they were all females.

Two of them were blondes, although one was significantly shorter than the other. They were both wearing matching smirks. The third one was wearing a baseball cap, her long dark hair pulled through the hole in the back. The fourth one was behind the other three, but as they approached us she made her way to the front, her unmistakable honey toned locks bouncing in rhythm with her flamboyant walk.

Once I realized it was Gina, my fear turned to anger. Julius noticed this and pulled me behind him.

"Protecting your precious girlfriend are you?" Gina's face was alight with satisfaction at the apparent fright she instilled.

"On some level," Julius said calmly. "I would hate for her to be filled with regret after she severely wounded you."

Gina threw her head back and laughed with enough performance to land herself in a Broadway play. "Like I'm scared of her!" Her false humor had suddenly vanished, replaced by what could only be described as an expression of sheer loathing. Her eyes were squinted in rage and her voice was a low growl when she said, "At first I wondered what she had that I didn't; why all of a sudden did every guy seem to think she was so great? Then I realized that there was *nothing* she had that I didn't - everything about me is better than her. Finally it dawned on me that the only thing she had that I didn't was a sob story. Her twin brother up and left and now everyone feels sorry for her. What you guys don't understand is that she is using that to get you. 'Boo-hoo feel sorry for me because my brother ran away.' Give me a break. The two of them weren't even close. The fact of the matter is that she's glad he's gone. Now she doesn't have to see him *and* she gets whatever and whoever she wants just by mentioning his name."

The three girls behind her seemed shocked now, as if they were seeing Gina for the very first time. The murky aura around the short blonde one was beginning to fade somewhat, and I noticed she was shuffling her feet in an attempt to pretend she was too preoccupied to hear what Gina was saying.

"Everyone knows about you, Gabby. I told them all what kind of person you really are." Her own words seemed to give her a boost of confidence, and the loathing that was smeared across her face only moments ago was now replaced by a look of satisfaction. "You know, I heard you had to take some kind of nerve medicine when your brother left. I took the liberty of telling everyone how unstable you are. Why don't you go take some of that medicine now, maybe you'll feel better and then you won't torture me every time I happen to pass by."

I was too busy watching the auras around the other girls vanish to care too much about what Gina was saying now. She was trying to victimize herself, and in doing that she had totally contradicted what she had said before about how I used my brother's disappearance for my own benefit. Obviously she told these girls that I had been harassing her, but the fact that she sought me out to verbally attack me proved to them that she hadn't been honest.

The three girls still stood behind her, but their expressions had softened, and I could tell that they were somewhat frightened of Gina now. She had just given them an example of the kind of person she really was, and they didn't want to be crossed with her ruthless desire to punish anyone who stood in her way.

Julius let go of me. I knew it was because he could feel the calm rhythm of my hum - he knew there was no threat to Gina now. There were a million things I could have said to her just then, but instead I gave her a half-smile and turned around toward the restaurant, locking my arm in Julius's. Everything that needed to be said was said by Gina, and pointing out her faults at this point would have been redundant.

As we walked across the parking lot, Gina shouted in our direction. I wasn't sure what she said, but I knew that no matter what her words were they could no longer hurt me. I had Julius, and a group of friends who were waiting inside for us.

Chapter 9❖

The others had already put their drink orders in by the time Julius and I made it into the restaurant, and before we even sat down they were questioning why it took us so long. I decided that I had seen and heard enough from Gina for one night, and not wanting her to be the topic of our dinner conversation I opted not to tell them what had happened.

Instead of answering their questions, I shrugged while looking over the menu, leaving them to speculate for themselves.

Julius shot me a grin which I returned, causing the others to deduce that our tardiness had to do with nothing more than being wrapped up in one another, and neither of us corrected them.

Even though the seafood restaurant we were eating at was considered one of the best in town, I still wasn't crazy about the menu selections. To be honest, my taste for seafood wasn't exactly refined. I would have been happy with fish sticks and tarter sauce, but since that was only offered with the kids' menu I decided on the shrimp linguine. Julius ordered the grilled tilapia, which I tasted. It was actually very good, although I still preferred the pasta.

After we were finished with our entrees, Kaitlyn and Grady ordered desserts, and while they were eating, the rest of us talked about how our parents' acted before we left for dinner.

To no one's surprise April's mother bawled, devastated yet delighted that her baby was growing up so fast.

Alexis's parents actually decorated their gazebo and instructed her and Troy how to pose while they took pictures of the two of them with professional cameras. (Her parents were photographers who owned their own studio and did all of the senior pictures for our class.)

My parents suddenly seemed very normal in comparison to everyone else's, and for that I was grateful.

By the time everyone had finished eating, it was going on nine, and that was when the dance was scheduled to start. Taking into account the twenty-five or so minutes it took to
drive back to Kentland, we were only going to be about ten minutes late, and none of us minded much.

Julius paid for our dinner when the bill came, which made me feel a little weird. I knew he couldn't have a whole lot of money, considering he was a mechanic who had to find a new garage to work in every couple of years. It couldn't be easy to support yourself for eternity - eventually job opportunities had to become scarce.

I decided then that the next day I would look for a part time job. Maybe April could help me get on at Murphy's.

Julius held his hand out for me then, which caused me to lose my train of thought. I took it with a smile, and let him lead me out the door and into the Challenger.

I figured the ride back would be filled with conversation about Gina, but evidently Julius had taken my shrug at the restaurant very seriously, and he didn't mention her once, which

I was glad for. I knew he wanted this night to be perfect for me, as much as I wanted it to be for him. Staring at him, I wondered if he had ever been to a dance before.

I must have been staring at him longer and much more intently than I noticed, because suddenly he chuckled and said, "What?"

"Hmm?"

"You've been staring at me for close to ten minutes now. Do I have something on my face?" His smile never wavered when he talked, even through the motions of wiping his face.

"No. I was just wondering if you'd ever been to a dance before."

Julius laughed. "I've done a lot of things in my seventy-eight years, but this is my very first homecoming dance."

I couldn't help but feel Julius was exercising some form of semantics with his answer, and before I could stop myself I said, "But - ?"

Julius sighed. "But yes, I have been to other functions in my life that could easily have been classified as a dance."

I felt bad for having dragged it out of him when he so clearly didn't want to tell me in the first place, and since I could tell that it made him uncomfortable, I attempted to make him feel better. "Julius, I didn't mean - I mean I wouldn't have expected you to not have - I mean, forget I asked, okay?"

Julius sighed and pulled the car over. He put it in park and let it idle, thinking to himself for a moment before speaking. "The moment I saw you, Gabby, I was instantly attracted to you." He halted, stroking the outline of his mouth with his thumb and forefinger before continuing. "I've been attracted to a lot of women in my lifetime, but the older I became, the more I struggled with the attractions. You see, I don't know if I'm forever twenty, or if I'm seventy-eight and going."

I interrupted him then. "You can't seriously think there's something wrong with us being in a relationship can you? I mean, I'm frozen in time now too, aren't I? Even if I weren't,

I'm eighteen anyway-"

"What does that have to do with anything? If I looked as old as I really am, you wouldn't be attracted to me at all."

There was nothing I could say to that.

"But you're right, Gabby. The two of us are one in the same now. Neither of us will ever get any older." He stared out the window momentarily, thinking to himself before going on. "The moment I touched your hand that first day I met you, I knew how I felt about you, but at the same time I was questioning whether or not it was *right* to feel that way about you. I figured that if I was lucky enough for you to feel the same way about me, I would have to let you make the first move." He chuckled to himself before adding, "I quickly decided that a smile from you was all the move I needed to justify my feelings for you. I don't worry about us at all, Gabby. I don't think our relationship is wrong in any way, but I do feel a little guilty."

I turned to look at him, my face twisted in confusion. "What? Why?"

"Because I've lived. I've been alive for a long time. For most of my life, I lived as virtuously as possible, but after a while, things started to get a little boring, and so I did the only thing I could think of - I searched for companionship." He paused before adding, almost apologetically, "And I've had a few companions."

"Oh," I said. Suddenly I felt very childish in comparison to Julius, although I knew I had no reason to. And I knew Julius had no reason to feel guilty. "Julius, I don't expect you to have been a saint, and I really don't need an explanation of your past. It isn't as if I expected you to be psychic and know that some day you would meet me." I stroked his cheek with the back of my hand. "You have nothing to feel guilty about."

"Sometimes you amaze me, Gabby."

"Why?" I asked.

Julius shrugged. "You're just different is all."

"Different from...?"

"From most people." He leaned in and kissed me softly, as if he thought I might break if he put too much pressure into it.

I opened my eyes slowly, as if they were connected to my heart and I was attempting to acclimate its rhythm to beat in time to Julius's. His eyes were on mine in a way they had never been before, whispering to me with words that had never been penned by poets or spoken between two lovers. It was in that moment that he told me he loved me - not with his voice, but through his soul, and I did my very best to mimic his gaze, conveying I felt the same way about him.

Julius bent down to kiss me once more, but this time he hesitated, pulling back before he even reached my face. He turned away from me, his face flushed, and sat back in his seat before buckling his seatbelt again.

"Did I do something to upset you?" I asked, hurt and confused.

He put the Challenger in drive and before pulling onto the highway he shook his head and laughed.

I was devastated. "What?" I demanded.

"Are you actually going to make me say it?"

"Say what?" I was angry now. Julius was making fun of me, and the embarrassment I felt in that moment surpassed any I had ever felt throughout the course of my lifetime. Obviously that thrilling moment we shared only seconds ago meant a lot less than I assumed. I could feel my face heating up and the beads of sweat threatening the back of my neck.

Julius exhaled deeply. "Gabby, I -" I watched his face contort into an expression of humiliation, and suddenly felt sorry for having been angry with him. "I couldn't kiss you again because -" he paused, searching for the right words. "I was afraid things could have gone too far."

This time I laughed.

"What?"

"That frightened you?"

"Well…yes."

"Why?"

"Because I love you, Gabby, and considering our recent conversation I really don't want you to think badly of me."

I chuckled again, but this time it was out of nervousness. I wanted to console him, but I wasn't sure I had the proficiency needed in order to make it sound sincere. I decided to say what was on my mind anyway, whether he could take it seriously or not. "I couldn't think badly of you Julius Carter. I may not have any experience, but that doesn't mean the thought never crosses my mind. Anyway, what would be so horrible about going too far?"

Julius's eyes widened significantly at my words. "You can't be serious?"

"Of course I'm serious." I was trying to sound nonchalant, but at the same time I couldn't look him in the eyes.

"Don't you pay any attention to those public service programs?"

"I honestly don't watch television all that often."

Julius rolled his eyes, exasperated. "Well besides that, there really isn't any reason why we shouldn't take it slow. We have eternity remember."

I smiled. "I wasn't suggesting it - I just wanted to know what would be so bad about it is all."

Julius shook his head as he pressed his foot hard on the accelerator, undoubtedly trying to get to the dance as quickly as possible in order to put an end to the conversation.

When we pulled up to the school, the music coming from the gym was loud enough that I could feel it pounding in my chest.

Julius was out of the car in a matter of seconds, opening my door for me. I was a little embarrassed whenever he did that, but I never let him suspect it. I knew it made him feel as if he were following the rules of opposite sex-relations, so I refrained from telling him it was unnecessary.

What I never did mind, however, was when he extended his hand and took mine by the fingers to help me out of the car before linking arms with me. For some reason, whenever he escorted me in that way, the world seemed to only consist of the two of us.

Although Dad had given me money earlier that day to pay for my own ticket, (even though I knew he only did it as a test to see just how chivalrous Julius really was) Julius still insisted on paying my way in. I would have argued with him a little further, but I really wanted him to pass Dad's test. He would have anyway, but with a little more persuasion I knew I could've gotten Julius to at least consider letting me pay my own way in.

I realized when we walked into the gym that my mother would probably have passed out with delight at the sight of the decorations. They were so traditionally typical. Blue and silver streamers were dangling from the ceiling, and clusters of balloons were placed on every table. In the left far corner, people were lining up to stand under an arch of balloons to have their pictures taken.

Julius led me to a table close to the open dance floor near an enormous speaker. *I really must have made him nervous,* I thought, which made me laugh to myself.

Not long after we sat down, the rest of our group found us and dragged us off to their table. Julius looked relieved at the sight of them; evidently he wasn't comfortable being alone with me for the time being.

April grabbed me by the arm before I even had a chance to sit down, and pulled me out onto the dance floor. Usually I didn't mind dancing, but to be honest, I was really out of touch with the newer music the D.J. was playing. I also felt a little awkward dancing in heels and my knee-length dress. I was glad when the song ended and I could sit back down.

Thankfully, April felt the same way I did about dancing in uncomfortable shoes, and she didn't protest when I suggested sitting the next one out.

When we made it back to the table, I noticed that Julius was laughing. Being with his friends must have calmed him down and helped him forget how nervous I made him on the ride here. He grabbed me by the waist when I approached him, an instinctual action that he was unaware of. He was too absorbed in the conversation he was having with Evan and the others to notice his own motions.

I took a seat beside him and turned to talk to April. She was talking to Travis, though, and I didn't want to interrupt them. Kaitlyn and Alexis were still on the dance floor, and Ashley was hanging onto Evan's every word, so I decided to get Julius and I some punch rather than sit and stare at everyone. If Julius thought I looked bored he would probably stop talking to the guys, and I didn't want to ruin his fun.

Thankfully, someone put some thought into the floor plan, because I didn't have to make my way through the dance crowd to find the punch table.

A few people were hanging around the table; freshmen who were nervous to be at their first dance, and upperclassmen who came by themselves. The older ones without dates always stayed close to the freshmen - they felt more sophisticated and less down on themselves when there were people to look up to them. I couldn't blame them for that. If I had the guts to come to a dance without a date, I would be right where they were.

I said hi to a few people as I poured Julius and I some punch, and found myself stuck in a conversation with a boy named Conway that was in my sculpting class. He was telling me how he was on the dance committee for the student council, and that the punch was his mother's recipe. The conversation went on this way for several minutes, but I couldn't make myself interrupt him. I could tell he hadn't talked to anyone all night, and as bored as I was listening to him, I couldn't be rude.

Finally his eyes started scanning the crowd, and I knew he was running out of things to say. But before I could take this opportunity to return to my table he spoke up once more. "Man! I wonder what kid *that* chaperone's related to!"

I followed his gaze until my eyes finally fell on the person he was referring to.

I gasped, dropping one of the cups on the floor and splattering most of its contents on Conway's leather shoes. "I'm sorry!" I said, distracted by what I had done.

By the time I looked back into the crowd again, the mystery chaperone was gone. Maybe I only imagined it, but I was sure that the old woman who I'd seen only a second ago was the remorseful one who accosted me at *The Pizza Shoppe*.

My blood was running through my veins like ice water and my knees were starting to shake.

"My dad's gonna freak! He told me not to get anything on his shoes." Conway was standing in his socks now, shoes in hand. His words brought me from my thoughts, and although I knew I should've helped him clean them, or at least offered up another apology, I still couldn't completely shake the image of the remorseful one from my mind.

I told myself I had only imagined her. The chaperone had resembled her, that was all. I breathed slowly through my nose, willing my body to stop shaking.

Julius came up behind me then, placing his warm hand on the small of my back. For a moment I expected him to give me the hum, but when he didn't, I realized he had no idea how uneasy I was.

"I thought maybe you'd like to dance with me," he said with a sweet smile that instantaneously washed away all of my anxieties. It was hard to remember my uneasiness when Julius spoke to me that way.

I was suddenly aware of the music as Julius led me across the gymnasium to the dance floor. The song had a familiar melody, but I was too interested in him to pay it much attention. His hands were resting comfortably on my waist, and his eyes were boring deeply into mine. I smiled at him sweetly before resting my head on his chest. It felt good when he slid his right hand up my back, holding me to him. The moment was perfect, and like any other girl in the same situation, I didn't want it to end.

The music stopped much too soon, and I sighed as we were on our way back to our seats, Julius practically having to drag me from the dance floor.

I was sulking playfully and Julius was consoling me when the most peculiar feeling came over me. I stopped dead in my tracks, listening to the pulsating hum that was streaming throughout my body, leaving me feeling as if I were a beacon. I looked over at Julius quizzically, and noticed that his face no longer held an expression of happiness. Now he looked worried, and I knew that he was feeling it too.

"We have to go," he said sternly, as if I weren't compliant.

I nodded and the two of us headed for the door with unnatural litheness, my heart hammering in my chest.

Evan and Ashley stopped us on our way out, and I hoped that Julius could think of something before I had to. My lies always seemed to snowball past the point of no return, and I had the feeling that Evan and Ashley weren't as easily fooled as my parents.

"Where's the fire?" Evan asked jokingly.

Julius gave him a look of steep seriousness.

Evan looked shocked - frightened even, but he seemed to understand, which mystified me. He grabbed Ashley by the arm, her expression pure bewilderment, and walked her toward the table before Julius and I left the gym.

As we walked through the doors, we were stopped by Mr. Wilcoxen. "Where are the two of you going?"

Without missing a beat, Julius said, "Cordele needs me."

He and I continued to walk, albeit a lot less hastily.

"Is everything alright?" Mr. Wilcoxen looked worried now.

"I'm not sure just yet. He didn't sound good; it was really hard to understand what he was saying." Julius pulled the keys from his pocket and unlocked the car with his keychain before we even reached it.

Just as we were climbing into the car, Julius's cell phone

rang. Mr. Wilcoxen was standing just outside of the car, listening intently.

"I'm on my way, Nayana," he said. "Has he told you what's wrong?" He paused, listening to what she was saying. "Okay, I'll be right there." He closed his phone and threw it on the dashboard.

To our principal, the conversation sounded like Cordele was having some type of health problem, and he was genuinely concerned. "Do you know what's wrong?" He asked.

"Nayana is only six. I couldn't get it out of her." He pulled his door shut and buckled his seatbelt. Rolling down his window he added, "I'm going to take Gabby home on my way there."

We started to pull out of the parking lot when I heard the sound of the fire alarms going off inside the school. Julius acted as if he'd never heard them, and headed down the road.

"Why did the alarms go off?" I asked frantically.

"Evan did it," Julius answered stoically.

"Does he know what's going on?" I was stunned.

"I recruited him for you."

"You aren't seriously dropping me off at home are you?" I'd had enough surprise answers for one night, so instead of insisting on hearing the whole story about Evan, I asked a question that I could get a simple yes or no answer from.

"Only half of you," he answered impassively.

Fear was swelling within me, but I didn't tell Julius. Instead, I tried to focus on figuring out the events that could have unfolded during the past few hours that led to what was now some type of serious chaos.

"Julius!" I practically screamed it.

"What is it?" he asked, shaken by my sudden outburst.

"The old hag - the remorseful one - from *The Pizza Shoppe*. She was at the dance! Conway pointed her out to me, but then I spilled punch, and by the time I looked up again, she was gone."

Julius's emotions were coming back to him now. He looked confused when he asked, "Did she see you?"

"I'm not sure, I think so. I mean, she disappeared a second after I spotted her."

I watched as Julius furrowed his brow, thinking. He was so deep in thought that I wondered how he managed to follow the road so perfectly. Finally, he spoke.

"I don't think she was there to fight you. If she wanted to, she would have attacked you without caring who was there to see it."

"Then what was she doing there?"

"I think she may have been trying to warn you," Julius said, his tone hinting at surprise.

"This is the same woman who said 'everyone must be prepared for the upheaval she will place upon us.' Do you really think someone who is so sure I'm going to do all that is trying to warn me?"

Julius sighed. "Cordele and Nayana have been building an army, Gabby. The first place to start, no matter what side you're on, is with the remorseful ones. Cordele probably found her and explained it to her in a way that made her reconsider where she stood."

I was thinking about that when I felt the car slow dramatically. I clutched my seat instinctively, and at once my eyes refocused on my surroundings. My adrenaline pumping once more, I noticed something in the road. It was a row of people, and Julius finally got the car stopped inches from them.

"Stay here, they're obviously remorseful ones, but I need to be sure what side they're on before they see you." He got out of the car hesitantly, not wanting to leave me vulnerable.

Out of the crowd of what had to be no less than a dozen people, walked a dark skinned man in a flannel jacket. He seemed to be the elected spokesperson for the group, and I cracked the window to hear what he was saying.

His voice was deep, yet soft, as if he was trying to hide the amount of fear he felt. "They say his power surpasses that of any other before him, is that true?" The man tried to hide it, but I could still hear the quiver in his voice as he spoke.

"We think so. Things are very different this time," Julius answered tranquilly.

A low mumble came from the crowd, and the man quieted them.

He raised his finger slowly, until it was pointing straight at me.

I gulped from the fright it caused, and I noticed Julius slowly making his way in front of the man to block me from his sight.

"And what about her? Does her power compare to his?"

I felt my heart in my throat. What could Julius possibly say to that? What would they say to him if he didn't tell them what they wanted to hear? What would they do to him?

"It has to doesn't it? The real question is whether or not his army is stronger than ours. Can we count on you?"

This time the mumble from the crowd continued for nearly a minute with no interruptions. Finally, the man turned around to face Julius again. "We will fight alongside of you, but we will not go to the forefront as has happened in the past. If we fight, she fights." He nodded toward the car.

I don't know what was going through my mind, but I stepped out of the car. Julius was by my side in an instant, his arm locked tight around the back of my waist. Trying to sound confident, I said, "I will fight."

Someone in the crowd stirred, making their way to the front. I recognized the twisted frame of the old hag at once, and I stiffened at the sight of her. Timidly, she approached me. "An apology," was all she said, and I nodded in response. At once she retreated back into the crowd, but my posture never relaxed.

"We will come when it is time," the spokesman said.

With that, the crowd dispersed, twelve people walking off in different directions into the night.

Julius opened my door for me, and I climbed in. I didn't realize until that moment that I was shaking. I was having trouble buckling my seatbelt, which Julius noticed immediately.

Placing his hand on mine, he filled me with the hum, a soothing sensation running throughout my body. He didn't let go until he heard the click of my seatbelt.

"They will convince others," he said, stomping on the accelerator once more.

"You said a few minutes ago that the remorseful ones will fight for either side. Why would they fight for Hell if they didn't want to stay there in the first place?"

"Well first of all, many of them retreat. They know what Hell is like, and therefore don't want to be a part of fighting against it. They find it hard to believe that it can't win, and they are frightened about what could happen to them if they side with Heaven, and Heaven loses. A lot of them know that if they fight on Hell's side, they still have a chance of coming back if they lose. Then there are the kind that we just ran onto. They are the ones who really want to prevent Hell from prevailing. According to them, they know how Hell is too, and they don't want anything more to do with it. They care if Hell wins, because they know they will be stuck in it for all of eternity, with no chance of escape. They don't want to take that chance."

We rounded the corner to my street, and at once I panicked. "What do I tell my parents? It's only ten-thirty."

"I'll go in with you, and we'll tell them the dance was cancelled because the fire alarms went off." He paused before adding, "The dance was cancelled, Gabby. There really was a fire. Don't ask me how I know, because I can't tell you. I know how you are and if I let you in on it and your parents ask…"

I sighed. "I know, don't tell me. I don't think I want to know anyway." I started to get out of the car, and then stopped. "Wait, was anyone hurt?"

"Of course not. It was just a little fire. It was controlled by professionals, I swear."

I gave him a look of disbelief.

He smiled and through his hands in the air. "I *swear*," he insisted.

My parents were very surprised to see us when we walked in the house, and even more surprised with the news of the fire, which Julius had to tell them about. He was right, if I had to tell them, it would have probably ended up with all of us piling into the Buick to make sure the entire school didn't burn down. All of my lies ended with me taking a trip in a car.

Julius and I bi-located to Cordele's the moment my parents walked into the kitchen.

Nayana was waiting for us, wringing her hands anxiously. "What took you so long? I was just about to come to you!"

"You aren't with Cordele?" Julius asked, the intonation in his voice filled with disbelief.

Nayana shook her head. "Daniel's with him. They went to Dublin and told me to bring you two as soon as you showed up. Cordele says someone needs to stay here, and I figured the two of you would be stuck with Gabby's parents."

"Do you know what's going on yet?" I asked with trepidation.

"Only that it has something to do with Devon and his army. I think they've been attacking." She paused before adding, "I think it's a gimmick, Gabby. I think he's getting impatient; trying to do whatever he can to get you to come to him."

"But she's not ready! It's only been a few weeks since she's known. We haven't even come up with a proper plan yet!"

Nayana rolled her eyes. "Well it isn't as if he's going to fight fair, Julius. He obviously thinks she's getting close to a solution, or he wouldn't be so impatient." She stood between the two of us and grabbed our hands. "Let's go, they're waiting on us."

My mind was so clouded with images of Devon's attacks that I had a hard time concentrating on Dublin. We had to try three times before we made it there successfully.

When I opened my eyes, I couldn't fathom the destruction that had befallen this place. Through the dense fog that enveloped the area, I could make out what looked to be marble statues and slabs, broken and scattered across a green and brown lawn.

I looked, but couldn't see any people, and my heart started to race. I hoped that there weren't any casualties, that the stillness in the night had nothing to do with death.

I wrapped my arms around myself, rubbing the upper part of my arms in order to warm me up. I thought at first that the chill that had come over me was due to the anxiety I was feeling, but I quickly realized that the temperature here in Ireland couldn't have been any higher than forty-five. Julius draped me in his suit jacket when he noticed me shivering. Nayana, at least, had taken into account the difference in temperatures, and had dressed appropriately before coming.

"What is this place?" I asked, watching my breath float out in front of me with every word I spoke.

"Glasnevin Cemetery," Nayana answered. There was a sadness in her voice that tore through my chest when she said those words.

I'd heard of Glasnevin Cemetery before. It was the largest cemetery in all of Ireland, and was the final resting place of many who had helped shape its country's history. It was founded in the early 1830's, and I could understand Nayana's disappointment over the destruction of such an old and influential landmark.

From somewhere amidst the opaque fog, a familiar voice called to the three of us. It was Cordele, but we didn't dare move for fear of losing him in the density of the atmosphere. Instead, Nayana called back to him, and I wondered why neither of them had thought to use the hum - it was our natural GPS locater after all.

"Ah, there you are," he said, and at once his silhouette came into view. Following behind him was Daniel, a red-haired, blue-eyed man who looked to be in his late thirties. He wasn't very tall - in fact, he was very average in frame and build. He could easily have faded into a crowd.

Perhaps noticing my stare, as it was extremely obvious, he

extended his hand. "Daniel O'Rourke," he said with a heavy Irish accent.

"Gabby Spencer." I shook his hand, pleased to have finally met him, and a little embarrassed about my ogling.

"Daniel and I have been busy repairing the damage, but I don't know if we can finish it before people start showing up. It's only five-thirty in the morning, but you never can tell about people. I detest doing memory modifications."

I felt out of place amongst the four of them. The most I'd done in terms of being a sentinel was flatten Julius during our rustic strength training course and nearly killing him with my hum while we were making out. Fixing priceless marble headstones and modifying memories was completely out of my jurisdiction as far as I was concerned.

"Has anyone been hurt?" Julius asked.

"No. It seems to have been deserted."

"Then what was the reason for them to attack?"

"Perhaps they're getting restless. Maybe they've given up on Gabby finding the gate for them, and decided to search for it themselves." Looking around he added, "A cemetery seems a likely spot for such a ghastly thing, doesn't it?" He shrugged his shoulders after one last look around and continued. "Julius, Nayana, and Daniel - the three of you should spread out and do as much as you can. Remember - don't use the hum unless it's an emergency - we don't know who could be lurking about."

The three of them nodded their heads in agreement before marching off in different directions, leaving me alone with Cordele.

"Why can't you use the hum?" I asked unrelentingly.

"You remember I called it electromagnetic remedial waves?" He started walking, and I followed after him.

"Yes."

"Well, there are certain atmospheric conditions that interfere with electromagnetism." He chuckled to himself before adding, "The reception is a little off here."

"So it doesn't work very well here?"

"Actually, it works a little too well. If I were to give you the hum right now, you would be able to see it. And if we used it to call one another, the five of us would start flashing like lighthouses."

I considered that. "That's exactly how it felt when you - or Nayana - called me. I felt like I was a beacon."

"Indeed we are when we need to assemble."

We walked in silence for a long time after that. I wasn't sure where we were going, or even if I was supposed to be following him, but Cordele hadn't objected, so I continued alongside him, remaining quiet.

"Gabby, have you ever heard of Glasnevin Cemetery before tonight?" He eventually asked.

"Yes. In junior high I had to do a social studies report on any country I liked, and I picked Ireland. I wrote a sentence or two about Glasnevin in it."

"Is that the only time you've ever heard of it?"

I thought for a second. "No," I finally said. "I've also heard about it somewhere else. *Ulysses*, I think. Episode 6, Hades, from *the Odyssey*."

"Do you know *Ulysses* well?"

"No," I answered truthfully. "My Grandma Fran has this hat - she said it always made her think of Episode 6 - you know - the guy with the MacIntosh. Anyway, I had no idea what she was talking about, so she made me read it. Not the whole book, just Episode 6."

Cordele raised an eyebrow. "You don't find that significant in any way?"

My intelligence took a beating while I spoke to Cordele. He wasn't boastful or condescending in any way, but I couldn't help but feel inferior next to him in the intellect department. I couldn't figure out what he was asking me. "What, the Episode itself, or the fact that I'd heard about it before?"

"The fact that the only part of *Ulysses* that you read was

titled *Hades,* and now here you are, in Glasnevin, where *Hades* was set, trying to undo what Hell has unleashed on it."

"Are you suggesting that I was meant to have read that?"

"Possibly. Actually, I was asking your opinion on the matter, as opposed to suggesting it. Do you think it's possible?"

"I suppose so. I guess I could take it as some type of affirmation that I am what I'm supposed to be."

Cordele smiled. "I think that maybe you're right. There are too many coincidences in life to shrug off."

We walked in silence once more as I reflected on this revelation that Cordele instilled in me. I was starting to question my part in the universe, and why I was such an oddity among the rarest set of humans that I had ever known to exist. That thought branched off into another one entirely, and I decided to ask his opinion on the matter.

"Cordele, do you think we're human?" I asked morosely.

He smiled, as if he had been patiently waiting for me to ask this very question. "I think we just might be," he answered, with a jovial inflection to his tone. "You know," he continued, "there are black bears and brown bears, Kodiaks and Grizzlies - they're all bears. I believe we're human, perhaps we belong in a separate phylum, but human on some level."

Finally, after what seemed to be hours, we stopped. The spot in which we were standing seemed no more different from the rest of the cemetery. We had traversed over many headstones without stopping to fix them, and I wondered what was so special about the one Cordele was leaning over now. We had passed mausoleums and ornate Celtic crosses, tall marble monuments, and countless other markers, but the one he stopped at was nothing more than a simple stone slab that was settled into the turf. The corners of it were grown over with grass, and the only thing written on it was 'O'Reilly'. There was a single, hairline crack down the center of it, which was hard to notice even under the beam of light from Cordele's flashlight.

"Do you see the damage?" he asked me, without looking up

from the stone.

"Yes."

"Place your hands on it," he instructed.

I did what I was told, but I was doubtful anything would come of it.

"Would you be surprised if that crack disappeared just by laying your hands on it?"

I wanted to roll my eyes - obviously I would be surprised. "Yes, I would."

"Why?" he asked me patiently.

"Because I don't feel anything." I thought that was all I was going to say, but before I could stop myself, I blurted, "And because I'm no good at this. I'm not like the rest of you. I'm the outsider in a group of outsiders. The rest of you can do great things, and you do them effortlessly, without being taught." I felt tears prickling my eyes, which only made me angry. "I barely made it here tonight. It took me three tries to bi-locate."

"But you did it," Cordele said softly.

I huffed through the tears that I so longed would go away. "Yeah, well, it is the easiest thing for us to do isn't it? How am I supposed to eliminate Devon by bi-locating? At best I could avoid him for eternity." At once it hit me, and the tears stopped. I was awestruck, enlightened. "I could, couldn't I?" With my hands still on the stone, I looked up to see Cordele's face. His expression was radiant. "That's what he's scared of, isn't it? He's attacking because he knows that I could spend eternity hiding from him, and Hell would never break free!"

"Lift your hands, Gabby."

The minute crack was gone, and a glossy shine covered the stone now.

"It's a very austere stone - not elaborate or complex - but there were fresh flowers on it. Someone comes here to visit, and that tiny little crack that wasn't so easy to spot would have upset them. How easy it was to fix; how happy the visitors would be if they'd known you fixed it. The task may be simple, Gabby, but the reward is great."

I was stunned. That was it. All I had to do was avoid him forever. Could it really be that simple?

"I think that we had it wrong, Gabby. Initially I thought that Devon had evolved, but now, I think it is you who have done the advancing. Without that instinct to find and eliminate him, you have put an end to another malefactor ever being created again, and if he doesn't conquer you, Hell will have to stay put."

I exhaled, noticing the reality of his words. "But he will continue to attack, and maybe it didn't happen tonight, but sometime innocent lives will be lost. If I don't eliminate him, who's to say he won't create a Hell of his own?"

Cordele looked off into the distance. "Maybe, maybe not. Remember the coincidences, Gabby. This evolution thing can't be for nothing."

"Then this evolution thing is what we need to build on, right?"

He smiled again.

Chapter 10 ❖

It was almost daylight before we finished repairing the cemetery. It was 120 acres of total destruction, which seemed impossible at first, but once I realized that all I had to do was touch whatever Devon's army had destroyed to fix it, the task went rather quickly. Nayana was the quickest of all, and it was so cute to watch her skip around, touching everything. She probably could have fixed the entire cemetery herself.

Back in Kentland, it was one-thirty and I was asleep. Julius was sleeping on the floor beside my bed; he snuck in after my parents went to bed so we could go back to his apartment in Cleveland without waking him up.

As soon as we made it back to Cleveland, I told him everything Cordele and I had discussed. He agreed with Cordele that it was an evolvement on my part, but also agreed with me that Devon would create as much chaos as possible until I finally eliminated him.

Julius was much less happy about this new evolvement theory than I would have imagined. He worried that Devon would use it to his advantage. "If you haven't felt the instinct to eliminate him yet, who says you ever will? Devon could know this. If he really thinks you didn't wake up with the instinct, he's going to keep attacking until you finally come out of the woodwork. Then…" He couldn't say the words.

"I don't think he knows about the instinct thing yet. I still think he's trying to get me to unlock the gates. I think that's why they attacked last night. If he could get me to unlock the gates, he wouldn't have to worry about fighting me."

"You could be right," Julius said, although I could tell he wasn't completely convinced.

I changed the subject quickly, not wanting to think about eliminating Devon. "So tell me about how you managed to recruit Evan. Oh, and I want to know everything about this professional fire bug you were talking about last night."

Julius laughed. "Those are both fairly long stories, but I'll tell you anyway," he said, pulling me close to him on the couch. "First of all, Evan and I took a little trip the other day."

"What day?" I interrupted.

"The day I asked you to get some pizza, and you said you needed to spend time with your parents. Last Tuesday or Wednesday."

"Where did you go?"

"Well," he said with a smirk, "Evan was talking about Curtis, and how he hoped he was alright. He was really worried they would lose the game since Curtis was laid up and couldn't play. He could tell I really didn't care one way or the other, and he asked me why I had a problem with him. I told him, thinking that if he didn't believe me, I could just modify his memory. He acted like he really wanted to believe me, but didn't know if he could; I guess it really does sound far-fetched if you haven't been in the middle of it for almost eighty years. Anyway, I decided that if I took him to see Curtis, maybe he would be completely convinced, sooo..."

"The two of you went to see Curtis?"

Julius nodded with a smile. "I didn't even have to say anything. Curtis was convinced that Evan was a part of your army as soon as he saw the two of us together. He was pleading with Evan not to finish him off, and spilled his guts about Devon. He's terrified that Devon's going to kill him." He turned to look at me then, knowing that I would have been upset over that. "I promised him we wouldn't let that happen. I didn't want to; after what he tried to do to you I couldn't care less what Devon did to him, but I knew you'd want me to offer."

"Thank you," I said sincerely.

"You're welcome."

After a long pause, I urged him to continue. "I wasn't sure Evan was completely convinced, even after everything Curtis had said, so I gave him the hum. That really freaked him out, but he believed me, and so I called Cordele and Nayana. They came straightaway and initiated him."

"Initiated him?" That was new to me.

"Sure. You see, everything that's supposed to happen, does - for the most part anyway. Evan was supposed to be a part of your army. His powers are there, but until he acknowledges them, he can't use them."

"Sort of like how we can only use our physical strength for defense?"

"Exactly, except Evan could never use his at all if he didn't know about them. It's a kind of safety net. We all have free will, so even though Evan was committed to being a part of your army before he was even born, he could have changed his mind, and until he acknowledged that he *was* a part of your army, his powers were moot."

"But you just said that you were the one who told him about this; that you were prepared to modify his memory if he didn't believe you." I was starting to find this a little hard to follow.

"Yes, but the fact that I asked him was a part of *my* free will, and I exercised it. Evan had every opportunity to say he didn't want any part of it. That was *his* free will when he accepted it."

I acted like I understood, even though I wasn't sure I did. It really wasn't important, I guessed, as long as Evan was on our side. "Okay - the initiation."

"Well, all he had to do was say he wanted to be a part of your army, and his powers kicked in." Julius chuckled to himself. "Of course, Nayana likes to make a big ceremony out of these types of things, so we all gave him a shot of the hum at once as he bent down on one knee like he was being knighted or something. I didn't tell him it was unnecessary though, so don't say anything."

I couldn't help but laugh.

I did get to thinking about what Julius had said about how Evan's powers kicked in just because he said he wanted to be a part of our army. "What if he lied?"

"What, you don't trust Evan?"

"I trust *him*, what I meant was, what would happen if someone did lie? What if they didn't want to be a part of our army at all and said they did?"

"I don't know. That's never happened before. Anyway, it wouldn't matter, because as long as they tell us they want to be a part of our army, they can't use their powers against us."

"How do you know?"

"Because we're the ones who allow them to come to fruition. It's a sort of sacred contract we have between ourselves and the powers we invoke."

I was starting to get a headache from trying to understand and keep track of everything he was telling me, so I decided to give up on learning the ins and outs of the business. Instead, I changed the subject again. "You still haven't told me about the fire."

"Evan started the fire," he said simply, as if that was all I needed to know.

"How? Why? How do you know?"

Julius sighed. "You are relentless Gabby." He stretched his head back to where it rested on the top cushion of the couch. "It was our plan. I told him if there was ever a problem at the school, the first thing to do would be to evacuate the building. He suggested pulling the fire alarm, but I knew the farthest we would get with that would be lining up outside. I suggested an actual fire. I told him to light it in the bathroom, inside one of those metal trashcans. Once everyone saw the smoke, they would run, and then he had to put it out."

I shook my head angrily at him.

"What? It was a good plan!"

"You two were lucky no one got hurt! You swore to me it was a professional who started that fire!"

"First of all, no one *could* have gotten hurt because Evan has super strength now, remember? He could have saved *everyone* if it got out of hand. Second of all, I think the whole super-human power thing *does* qualify Evan as a professional."

I couldn't believe what I was hearing, but I didn't want to argue with him about it.
"Could you at least come up with a better plan for future instances?" I asked politely.

Julius sighed. "If it makes you feel better, I'll discuss it with Evan tomorrow." He stood up. "In the meantime, I'm hungry. Let's eat something."

He walked over to his refrigerator and opened the door. He shifted a few things back and forth before pulling out a plastic container filled with spaghetti. He dumped the cold gelatinous mass into a pot; it kept the shape of its container before he added a little more spaghetti sauce and stirred it with a wooden spoon.

I loved the way Julius cooked. He didn't chop fresh herbs and vegetables or add things to the mixture that most normal people would never have in their cupboards or refrigerators. He made everything simple. His spaghetti consisted of ground hamburger, sauce from a jar, and noodles. The only way it could be done any easier would be to buy it frozen.

We ate in silence, and for a while I assumed it was because he was angry with me for being upset about the irresponsible fire incident. After we finished eating, however, and I started doing the dishes, he walked up behind me and wrapped his arms around my waist, resting his chin on my shoulder. He didn't say anything, but I could tell something was on his mind. He seemed sad, and I turned from my task and faced him.

"What is it?" I was almost whispering.

He studied my face for a moment, as if he was trying to guess what my reaction would be before he said what was on his mind. His expression was serious, his eyes squinted. "I think that maybe you should stay here… permanently."

I was shocked, mostly by the severity with which he suggested it rather than with the suggestion itself. His somber approach frightened me, and I gulped. "Why?"

Julius sighed. "Gabby, I know you're aware of the severity of your situation, so I know you'll understand it if I say I think it's time we stopped waiting for something to happen. There are still things you need to learn, tactics that should be implemented. I think that maybe we should prepare for the worst." His eyes fell when he said it, as if it caused him immense pain to admit his fear.

I hated to see Julius like this, and as much as what he said scared me, the more pressing issue to me was putting his mind at ease. If that meant I had to act as if nothing about Devon scared me, then so be it.

Trying to act as casual as possible, I cleared my throat. "If you think that's best, I'll stay." I cupped his face in my hands and stared into his olive eyes, willing him to feel my words as I said them. "Anything it takes. I won't let Devon win."

Our eyes locked. For a few seconds, he was trying to figure out if I really believed what I was saying. I'm not sure what his conclusion was, but he wrapped his arms around my middle then and kissed me intensely. It was a wonderful kiss, sending currents of pleasure surging through my bloodstream, but remembering our little discussion we had on our way to the dance, I turned to finish the dishes as soon as it was over.

"So how is this going to work?" I asked, trying to get my mind off of the feeling that was left over from the kiss.

"Well, obviously you will have to be separated from yourself until it's over. I have everything here that you need, except for your clothes… and you can have the bed."

I wasn't really worried about sleeping arrangements.

"If you are at school and work most of the time, then why will I have to be in both places at once all the time? Why don't I just come here whenever you have some free time?"

Julius's face turned blank. He was searching his mind for a way to respond to that, and I could tell by his expression that he didn't want to disclose the actual reasoning behind that particular idea. When he couldn't think of anything to say, he changed the subject altogether. "There are a lot of things to work on. As soon as Cordele and Daniel have finished up their research and I know they've had some sleep, I'll call them. I want to try connecting our hums."

My eyes widened with a sudden pang of fright. Remembering what had happened to Julius the night our hums momentarily connected sent cold chills throughout my system. "Do you really think that's such a good idea? What if something goes wrong?"

Julius took me by the hands, calming me with the half smile that always seemed to divert my attention from the panic that intermittently plagued me. "There will be five of us, Gabby. Just remember that we were created to save the world. I highly doubt that you'll be able to single-handedly destroy all of us with your hum."

Not only did his words serve to relinquish my doubts, they made me feel foolish for ever having thought there was a possibility that I could harm the others. My face turned red, and I turned to rinse the dishes.

That evening, true to his word, Julius summoned the others. I'd given up on the fear of hurting them, only to have it replaced by an anxious feeling of inadequacy. What if it didn't work at all? What if it never actually happened between me and Julius? I was worried that maybe we had both been feeling our own hums and somehow mistook the feeling for a connection that never actually happened. Julius was very reassuring, promising that I had, indeed, linked our hums.

Cordele, Nayana, and Daniel were awestruck with the news, and very eager to see a demonstration, which did nothing to soothe my agitated nerves.

My first attempt was on Julius, of course. He reminded me that the only thing I needed to do was transfer my hum to him, and nothing else. He stood in the large, open space of his apartment, and I closed my eyes. Reaching out to him, I willed the current of my hum to flow from my extended fingertips. A burst of euphoria erupted throughout me the moment I made the connection to Julius, the power of it threatening to take on a life of its own. As before, I wanted it to stay. Breaking the connection wasn't an option. While in this state, I became the very essence of happiness - love in its concentrated form, and it became harder and harder to discern my real self from this new being I was creating.

This time, it was Julius who ended it. Breathless and perspiring, he fell to his knees. The others rushed to his side, worried. The entire episode was surreal to the rest of them; never had they witnessed something so strange.

Julius waved them away, insisting he wasn't in any pain. "It takes a couple of minutes to become acclimated to reality. The peace is...unfathomable while we're connected." Getting to his feet he tried to explain. "It's almost like there are an infinite amount of ways to feel it, and I'm getting millions all at once...it is so far past indescribable..."

A hush settled while Cordele, Nayana, and Daniel attempted to decipher his words, fascinated by the wonderment of his expression.

Finally, Cordele cleared his throat. "Forgive me, Julius, but have you considered the possibility that this…connection…could serve as more of a distraction to us rather than a weapon against our enemy?"

The rest of us turned to look at Julius, trying to gauge his reaction to Cordele's question. Certainly, it was an equitable concern.

"Perhaps it could be - if it had the same effect on them as it does on us. But I don't think it can. Peace, love, goodness - these things are pleasant for us, but not for them. These are the things they loathe - the reason they are our adversaries. No - I'm sure that the incapacitation will be far worse on them than on us. I'm certain of it."

I was staggered by the fervidness in his tone as he spoke, and surprised by the seriousness in his expression as he defended his idea. It wasn't maddening, as we all expected it to be; not a certifiable obsession. It was certainty, and we all accepted it.

"Of course. Forgive me, Julius, you know how skeptic I can be at times." Cordele's apology extended to his eyes, his sincerity apparent.

"Do you think this can only be done by Gabby, or is it possible for the rest of us to do it?" Daniel asked.

"I'm not sure," Julius answered, rubbing his chin. "I assumed Gabby was the control, but now that you mention it, I guess it's possible that the rest of us just never knew it could be done. It was only by accident that we discovered it at all."

"Really? How?" Daniel asked, his voice blazing with interest.

My face reddened. Of course Daniel didn't know that Julius and I were in a relationship, I'd only met him last night. And now that the thought occurred to me, I wasn't sure if Cordele and Nayana knew about it either. It was true we were both dressed in formal attire the night before; after having went to the dance together, but that didn't necessarily mean anything by relationship standards. Also, we were all so preoccupied by what had happened in the cemetery that the others probably didn't even notice how we were dressed.

I held my breath, waiting for Julius's explanation. Would he tell them that we were lip-locked while I discovered my hum? Or would he spare me the embarrassment?

"Well," he began, looking at me from the corner of his eyes. "She needed instructions...she didn't wake up with the same type of knowledge that the rest of us did, and I let her practice on me."

"Oh," Daniel said, but I could tell by his expression that he interpreted something more from Julius's timbre.

"Anyway," Nayana interjected, "I agree with Julius. This new...weapon...could be revolutionary, and I think we should all have a practice round with Gabby before attempting to make a group effort of it. We should at least have an idea of how it feels before we take a chance on strengthening it."

Cordele agreed. "If two hums can do that to Julius, it has to be extremely powerful, and we can't be sure that a larger number of people could equalize it."

Satisfied with Cordele's statement, Nayana jumped up eagerly and made her way to the center of the open space. Her long curls bounced against her back as she trembled with anticipation. "I don't have to do anything?" She asked Julius, her chocolate colored eyes sparkling with enthusiasm.

"Just make sure you're emitting your hum."

I gave her a moment to prepare, and she nodded at me when she was ready. I grabbed her hand carefully, worried that her small size required a touch of delicacy. The connection was made instantaneously, but unlike with Julius, the intensity began subtly, gradually increasing until it reached the point that I had to let go. I felt that if I held on for a fraction of a second longer, we would have been locked much in the same way a person would have been pulled into an electrical charge.

Nayana stood still, a reverent expression adhered to her face.

"I always thought the hum was the most pleasant thing I had ever experienced - until now. This…connection…is more. It's a…thing. A…creation."

Julius held a colossal smile. "Didn't I tell you?"

Cordele and Daniel traded looks of confused awe. It was clear they were much more curious now that Nayana concurred with Julius.

"It was different with her," I told Julius. "More…subtle I think, at least in the beginning. The end was much more intense. I got the feeling that if I didn't release her when I did, we may have…conjoined."

The others stared at me in disbelief. What did this mean? Could the connection turn against us after all? Was it possible that Nayana, being so much smaller than Julius and I, was just too fragile to handle it?

Cordele broke the silence. "I guess I will be the next volunteer." He took Nayana's place, and although I was sure he had to have some, affixed a no-expectations look upon his face and calmly waited until I was ready. This time, the connection started out extremely intense, as it did with Julius, then calmed, making the release as easy as the initial touch was. After it was over, Cordele stepped back. "Phenomenal," he said with a smile.

Daniel's experience was very similar, except when the intensity of the connection started to ebb, and I was about to release him, it skyrocketed again, and like Julius, he was the one to break it.

It was odd how everyone had a different experience with it. We discussed the perplexity of this, and it was Cordele who pointed out that no matter who felt what, I was the only one who never felt it my own way. "It stands to reason, then, that you must be the control."

I pointed out that the only way to be sure of that would be to experience the connection in a combined effort, and Cordele seemed pleased with the idea.

We all prepared ourselves before collecting in the center of the open space. The other four held hands as they performed their hums communally. They offered that nothing extraordinary was happening as they did this, proving that it was, indeed, an evolved strength on my part. Slowly I closed in on the circle, simultaneously grabbing Julius and Daniel's hands, becoming a live wire.

The result was nothing less than unparalleled. Every individual's experience was surging throughout me, hissing and crackling with the severity of an electrical storm. Every cell within me danced and collided until they were thrust forward into the center of our circle, mingling with the cells of the others. My entire anatomy was intermittently pulsating with energy, an electrical surge that started in my abdomen and spread south until it reached my toes, then north until it reached my scalp. My heart was racing, and I suddenly turned my attention to the center of our circle to discover the greatest anomaly of all.

There, floating amongst the volts of electricity that were flowing freely from the five of us, was the sphere of my dreams, that perfect orb that dominated my nights only a few weeks earlier. I knew now why I couldn't touch it in my dream; if I were to let go of anyone's hand, the connection would be lost, and the orb would disappear. Collectively we were one entity, and it was this one being that had the power to defeat Devon. With this realization, I broke the connection, satisfied that I had all the answers I needed.

The others slumped to their knees, breathless and exhausted.

Between gasps, Daniel managed to ask the one question they all needed an answer to. "What - was - that - thing?"

"It was…us," I said, the astonishment of my own words sending goose bumps across my chilled skin. "I used to dream of it." My voice was barely above a whisper as I attempted an explanation.

"That thing we created is what you told us about the first night we met you?" Cordele asked, a look of shock covering his face.

I nodded.

"Well, Gabby, excuse me for saying so, but you might have given us a better description. When you said you dreamed of a beautiful orb I pictured something that resembled a crystal ball."

I had no retort. Cordele was right. But it was one of those things you had to see to fully understand. It was impossible to describe, because there were no words in any written language that could have given it an ounce of the justice it deserved.

Later that night, after everyone had gone to their homes and the sun had descended in the sky, when we all were left to our own thoughts and surmises - when we were bedded down and our reflections of the day drifted us into sleep, the five of us dreamed of the hum.

Chapter 11 ❖

The next few months came and went with the swiftness of a howling winter wind.

My days at the apartment were exhaustive, as I spent nearly every waking moment honing my skills as a sentinel. Cordele, Nayana and Daniel spent hours coaching me while Julius was working, and stayed well into the nights after he returned. I was happy to have their assistance, but I couldn't help but think they spent so much time there in order to keep Julius and me at arms length. I wasn't sure if it was because they didn't approve of our relationship, or thought that we could get too preoccupied in each other to remember the objective. Whatever the reason, it could be a tad agitating at times. If it weren't for the fact that the other half of me was living a normal teenage life back in Kentland, I'm sure I would have gone mad. The cabin fever alone would have been enough to earn me a bed at an asylum.

Back in Kentland, the winter had thawed, but the spring rain had settled in, much more persistent than any other year. It was the beginning of May, and I was hoping that the next sunny day would occur when I had a day off from Murphy's. I liked working, especially since April and I always shared the same shift, but I was craving some alone time with Julius, and I spent my spare time daydreaming of walks in the park with him.

There hadn't been another attack since the one back in September, but I seemed to be the only one of us who was baffled by the lack of activity. Cordele was determined that Devon hadn't initiated the attack; that he had probably been furious with his army for being so restless and therefore threatened them if they ever let it happen again.

Julius, however, wasn't as convinced, although he tried his best to conceal his apprehension from me.

One Thursday evening, after we were through practicing defensive training, (I finally managed to plow Daniel into the floor - his stealth was extremely mastered) Cordele and Nayana announced that they would be vacationing in Florida. They too had grown tired of the cold precipitation of the north, and were too impatient to wait on the sun.

Daniel was glad to have some time off, too; he announced that he missed his home near the River Liffey, and intended to catch up on his fishing. He and Cordele had spent enough time doing research in Egypt, he mused, and made no effort to find a nice way to say he was exhausted.

The three of them left at dusk, leaving Julius and I alone together for the first time in months. The silence they left was deafening, and I was suddenly aware of how used I had gotten to being around them. Suddenly, the part of me that had been so eager to be alone with Julius was now nervous. I'd forgotten how to act like a girlfriend, and I blushed when he patted the empty space on the couch next to him, beckoning me to sit.

He threw his arm around my shoulder the moment I sat, and gently pulled my head against his chest. Instantly my anxiety trickled away, and I was left with relieved happiness. I exhaled, ridding myself of the stale air that had accumulated in my lungs after having held my breath in worried anticipation.

"Can you believe everyone's gone?" He asked with a smile that extended to his ears.

"It's hard to believe," I answered, stifling laughter. I wrapped my free arm around his stomach and closed my eyes. "How long do you think we have?" I asked lazily.

"A week at least," he promised. "Usually when they go to Florida they end up staying longer than they intended. Nayana loves the theme parks, and Cordele hates to let her down. And Daniel's been getting cranky lately - he's used to being by himself most of the time; I think he needs some time alone. We won't be seeing him again until Cordele calls for him." He chuckled.

I yawned. "Sorry, I know it's not that late, but between the all-night practice sessions, school, work and homework, I can barely keep my eyes open. If I could get some sleep in Kentland, I'd probably be alright."

"Just think," Julius said thoughtfully, "A couple more weeks, and we'll graduate."

I heaved a sigh of relief. "I can't wait."

"Cordele, Nayana and Daniel will be there. Cordele's always been telling me to finish school - I bet he'll be glad."

I jerked up then. "What?" My face was full of surprise. "You never finished school?"

He shook his head. "It wasn't such a big deal to finish school in the 1940's. There were a lot of us Carter's, remember, and the sooner we were able to fend for ourselves, the better off our parents were. I got a job in a grocery store a few days after I turned sixteen. I'd had a lot of odd jobs before that - but this one offered full time hours, so I quit school in order to earn a living."

"Wow. That seems so unreal," I mused.

"Yeah, I suppose it does."

I thought for awhile, trying to imagine Julius in one of those striped hats, bagging groceries for elderly people. I could actually see it, and I was surprised at how attracted I was to him even in my daydream. "Did you enjoy it?"

"It wasn't so bad," he replied with a shrug. "I didn't make a lot of money, but it was better than delivering papers."

"How much did you make?" I was curious. Inflation fascinated me.

"Forty cents an hour."

"Wow. Doesn't that surprise you?" I asked.

"I suppose it would if I hadn't lived through it, but I did, so..."

I rested my head against his chest again, thinking. It was odd, really, that two people could spend so much time together, yet barely even know one another. I wondered if that was normal. Surely it would take much longer getting to know Julius than it would most guys. He'd lived long enough that I could find out something new about him everyday.

Sometime while I was thinking, I fell asleep. It'd been a long time since my dreams were more than just flashes of undecipherable blurs. Usually they seemed like someone had pushed a fast-forward button in my mind, and the pictures reeled by so quickly that I couldn't make out what they were. This time though, my dream was extremely vivid.

I was walking alone on a cobblestone lane, the moon bright and larger than I had ever noticed it to be. Everything around me was still, and the more conscious I became of the eerie silence the slower I walked, until finally, I stopped, frozen with fear. I felt as if I was in an abyss of solitude, and the dread that encompassed me was unbearable. I yelled out, calling for someone, anyone, to rescue me from this abysmal absence of everything that I was lost in. No sooner had I called out than something came to me, beautiful and loving - a perfect sphere that shined like the moon and glittered like the sun on the ripples of a river. It was the orb, but this time, I couldn't feel it inside of my chest, filling me with the hum. I was stunned that its beauty wasn't radiating throughout me, hurt that its energy wasn't pulsating my every nerve with its absolute peace. It lowered itself to my eye level, and at once my head was careening back and forth, the orb forcing its way in. I was laughing, knowing that it was giving me some of itself, and thinking that it was such a ridiculously easy exchange. I had to laugh, because the complexity to which one would have thought it needed to manage such a task was hilarious in comparison to the effortlessness in which it actually took. When it was finished infiltrating my head, I giggled once more, and the orb trailed off into the distance, leaving me giddy and satisfied.

"Gabby!" Julius was shaking me awake feverishly, and the moment our eyes locked I jumped in fright, briefly unable to distinguish between the graphic mental images that had dominated my sleep, and the reality I had woken up to. I squinted my eyes, trying to focus him in, and reached out to test his tangibility.

"Gabby?" His voice held a hint of panic, whether I was frightening him or he was afraid for me I couldn't tell. His voice finally found its way through my muddled brain, and slowly I acclimated to my surroundings.

"Julius?"

"Are you alright?" I could sense the trepidation in his voice, and I wished I hadn't upset him.

"Yeah, I'm fine." My frame was trembling, although I couldn't come up with a rational explanation as to why.

"You had a nightmare." I was sitting upright on his bed, and he was on his knees next to me, his arms wrapped around my shoulders, coddling my head against his bare chest.

"No," I said, pulling away from him. "It was something different."

"What do you mean?" His hands were on my forearms now, his voice soothing, as if he were talking to a child.

"It was a dream, but…" I was searching for a way to explain it correctly, and in a way that described how it felt. "It was so real."

"Do you want to tell me about it?" He climbed under the blanket with me, and gently urged my head against the pillow. Never in the eight months that I had been staying here had we ever lie next to one another. He always insisted I take the bed, and whenever I refused, he didn't sleep well. Tonight he must have carried me to it after I fell asleep against him on the couch.

"I was alone. I was walking along a stone pathway, and I was scared, because I knew I was the only thing that existed. I started calling for help, and the orb came. It transferred…bits of itself…into my brain. It was infusing me with secrets or knowledge or something." It seemed so ridiculous after I said it that I wished I would've kept it to myself.

"I kept trying to wake you up, but it was like you were…stuck. You were screaming at first, and then you started this spine-chilling laugh." I felt him shudder as he recalled my maniacal façade. "What was so funny?"

I was glad it was dark, so he couldn't see the embarrassment creep across my face as I remembered the image of my head rocking back and forth in my dream. "I don't know," I lied.

"Well, it doesn't matter. It was just a dream, and it's over now." He was stroking my cheek tenderly, indulging me, attempting to swathe me in serenity. His touch, though very soothing against my skin, did little to calm my nerves however. In fact, my heart was racing riotously in reaction to his affection.

I stopped his hand mid-stroke, and entwined our fingers. I strained to see his face in the dark, finally focusing in on his silhouette, the contour of his features illuminated by the subtle glow of the moonlight. I turned onto my side to face him. "Have you been here all night?" I asked it timidly, hoping I wouldn't scare him away.

"No," he kissed the back of my hand before curling it up to his chest. "I was sleeping on the couch before you woke me up." I could feel his breath in my face as he inched closer to me. "But I like this far too much to go back - unless you would rather I leave you." He pressed his lips against mine delicately, as if I were as fragile as porcelain, and then released them slowly, leaving my heart to pound violently beneath my chest.

"I don't want you to go anywhere," I managed, my breath betraying me.

I pulled him closer to, kissing him vehemently. I let my fingertips trail down his back, expecting him to tell me to stop, thrilled when he didn't. The fervor within me escalated as I kissed him, until finally, with the stealth of a panther, he was over top of me, pinning me down delicately.

My chest was heaving as I panted, something I was unable to disguise. I tried to slow my breath, but my body insisted on being a renegade. I was sure Julius was ashamed of me, chagrined by my obvious lack of self control. But when I looked up into his face, expecting to see his reprimanding glare, I saw something entirely different. His expression was soft, silently posing a question, and expecting an honest answer.

Finally my breath slowed as I understood what it was he was asking me, and immediately I knew the answer. I placed my hand around the back of his neck and pulled him close to me, letting him know that, yes, I was sure.

The smell of coffee and burnt toast brought me out of a deep sleep, and I fought for the episodes of lucidity that intermittently broke through my dreams. Julius's voice finally conquered my exhaustion, my eyes fluttering open involuntarily the moment it hit my ears.

"Gabby, the coffee's ready. Sorry about the toast, I forgot to turn the setting down after I made those frozen waffles yesterday."

The sight of him in nothing but his boxers brought back the thrilling memories of the night before, and I couldn't contain the smile that threatened to take my face hostage. I dressed hastily, my inhibitions seizing me in the daylight hours. I grabbed my coffee and toast, and in a pathetic attempt to prevent my eyes from dancing all over Julius, I rushed to the couch to distract myself with my breakfast.

Julius sat down beside me, and from the corner of my eye I caught a flicker of a smile on his face. "How are you this morning?"

It was impossible to contain my smile any longer. "Better than I've ever been on any other morning of my life." I blushed.

"Me too." The left corner of his mouth raised in a half-smile before he took a sip of his coffee.

The hairs on the back of my neck stood at attention to his ridiculously simple yet enticing expression. I was surprised though, and verbalized my thought before I had a chance to stop myself. "Really?"

"Yes," he answered. Then, with one eyebrow cocked, he asked, "Why wouldn't you think so?"

I hesitated, not wanting to upset him or ruin the moment. But I had already opened my big mouth, and there was no way he would let it go with a shrug. "I just meant, I know this isn't exactly new to you and -"

Julius cut me off. "Gabby, there was a big difference between last night and the... other times. For one thing, I love you." He lifted my chin with his finger until we were at eye level. "And for another, this time I wasn't searching for anything." My favorite smile returned, and I watched his eyes look past me as he recalled the details of the previous night. "And also, the fact that we're both sentinels made it extremely...different."

"Are you saying that what we had last night is something normal humans don't?"

"Yes. Although I would say that the way you put it is a huge understatement." He put a big emphasis on the word 'huge'.

My eyes widened. "Really?"

He nodded.

"What was different?"

His face reddened. "Well, it's a little embarrassing to say."

I rolled my eyes. He was such a guy. "Just tell me, please."

He shifted his eyes to his feet, too embarrassed to look at me directly. I watched his face cringe before he said, "It was...miraculous...like...ugh, this is so embarrassing." He looked up at me with pleading eyes, begging me to let him stop talking.

"Julius, it's me you're talking to. It isn't as if I'm going to grab a bullhorn and tell everyone what you said." I rolled my eyes.

He sighed, and then let the words gush from his mouth quickly. "I guess it was like you were a lock and I was a key, and we opened up some hidden door that we'd been looking for all of our lives." He didn't meet my eyes, too sour with me for urging his words out of him.

"That's exactly what it felt like," I agreed.

His eyes were accusing, bitter as he whipped his head up to meet my gaze. "Then why didn't *you* say so? Why did *I* have to say it?"

"Because I'm a girl. If I had said it, it wouldn't have meant a whole lot. Girls are supposed to just naturally feel that way. I would never have known if it was just my hormones talking, or if it was something more."

"Still," he grumbled.

"I'm sorry," I offered sincerely.

He smiled back at me. "I guess I can let it slide."

I knew I was treading on thin ice with him, but something Julius said earlier was nagging at me, and while I had him smiling, I figured it was the best time to ask. "What did you mean when you said this time you weren't searching for something?"

He shrugged. "Just what I told you a few months ago - that I was searching for companionship." He sipped on his coffee then, and I knew he was uncomfortable talking about this with me. I let it go, thinking that if I had been him, I probably wouldn't want to talk about it either.

I finished my toast in silence, hoping that if I stayed quiet

Julius would forgive me for prying. As I made my way over to the coffee pot to refill our mugs, however, he surprised me by breaking the silence.

"I was angry," he said, as if he was offering a confession to some horrible crime.

"I'm sorry, Julius, I shouldn't have asked -," I started, only to be interrupted by him.

"No, that's not what I meant." He slumped back into the couch, and I could tell he was struggling with his thoughts. I brought his coffee to him and took a seat on the couch, patiently waiting for him to explain.

Finally, he sat up and sighed. "When I was searching. I did it because I was angry. I was angry with God."

"Why?" My voice was more consoling than I meant for it to be. I had planned on trying to sound nonchalant.

Julius turned to me with sadness in his eyes. "My family and I were Lutheran. I was baptized as a baby and went to church faithfully. I followed all the rules, knew every hymn by heart, and studied the Bible loyally. The day I woke up and realized what Suzanne and I were, I was so thankful that I hadn't let God down before that - I was so glad that I had been a good person." The volume of his voice dropped significantly before he continued. "And when the instinct to eliminate her took over all of my senses, even though the remorse I felt over having my sister killed was agonizing, I thanked Him for choosing me as his servant - for giving me the opportunity to oblige Him."

"But the years passed, and the pain didn't go away, and I didn't age. New obstacles cluttered my life. I couldn't stay in one place for more than a few years. Keeping a job was extremely difficult. I could never make any real friends - Cordele and Nayana are great, I've always liked them, loved them even, but I resented the fact that they were my only options. I could no longer be a part of my family's life." He looked up at me, his eyes hesitant. "I couldn't get married and have my own family."

"Eventually, I started questioning Him. What was the

purpose of my existence? Had I not served Him well? Did I not deserve to be rewarded in some way? The Bible taught me that good people were rewarded with an eternal life in Heaven, but I had been damned to an eternal life on Earth. I had to watch as friends I had as a child passed away, and their children grew older than me."

"I felt used and forgotten. The pity I felt for myself slowly turned to anger, and I decided to rebel. I went against all of my teachings. I didn't kill or steal or break the law. I wasn't trying to hurt God; I just decided that I was going to give myself the things normal men had. I was going to make myself as happy as other men 'my age' seemed to be. I started hanging out with a couple of guys I worked with, taking their lead. I smoked, drank, gambled, swore, lied, manipulated people, ignored everyone else's feelings but my own…gave in to the sins of the flesh. After a while, though, I realized these things weren't making me happy at all. Instead, they were making me feel horrible about myself."

"I visited Cordele and told him the things I had done and the reasons I had for doing them. He told me that he had similar feelings for a time before Nayana was created, but when he philosophized her creation, he came up with a conclusion that erased all of his resentment."

"He said that maybe we weren't living in vain at all, but living long enough to help the others that would come after our times. He thought that maybe we *weren't* going to live forever, but perhaps just long enough to find a solution to keep Hell from ever breaking free at all. Maybe if we could eradicate every possibility of them ever winning, we could earn our place in Heaven. I thought about what he said, and decided it sounded like a plausible idea."

"Since then, I've been trying to help him discover a possibility. That's why he spends so much time doing research. He's hoping he'll find something that gives him an idea as to how we're to go about doing it."

"Of course, I was still a little bitter. We didn't seem to be getting anywhere, and the research was exhausting." He lowered his eyes. "Please don't take what I'm about to say the wrong way, but when we felt you coming, I was happy. I know it's a horrible thing to have to deal with what you're dealing with, and so it's selfish of me to feel that way, but with you came excitement. Cordele could tell I was growing tired of the research, so he suggested that perhaps I should approach you without any help from the rest of them. You were different than we were, and he was afraid of what might happen to you if we weren't careful. I was glad to do it, to finally feel like I had a purpose."

"It was easier enrolling in school than it was to find a job. I modified the principal's memory, making him think I was a new student, and that I was in every class you were in. The guidance counselor handed me my schedule after a few minutes, and I was off to Government. The classroom was empty when I got there, as I hoped it would be, and I closed my eyes and called to you."

"I never bargained for what happened when I saw you. I am a man, a human on some level, so I had been attracted to women before, but you were different. The attraction I felt for you was like a magnetic field, making it impossible for me to stray from you for too long." He raised his head, smiling until it reached his eyes. "Not once since the day I saw you have I felt resentment about what I am. All of the anger I felt before is gone, even the faint traces of bitterness. When I met you, I apologized to God for being angry with Him, and thanked Him for creating me. If I weren't a sentinel, I'd be a seventy-eight year old man who could never have a chance with you."

I was speechless. What could I have said to that? I crawled into his lap and wrapped my hand around his neck, stroking his face with my free one. "Thank you for telling me that. All of it." I kissed his mouth softly, and then held his face in my hands. "Just in case I haven't made myself clear, I love you, Julius Carter."

The corner of his mouth lifted into a smile and he let out an impish groan. "You have no idea what it does to me when you say my entire name like that." His eyes drifted to the bed suggestively.

I cocked my eyebrows in response, and at once I was out of his lap and in his arms as he carried me to the bed.

Chapter 12 ❖

It was difficult to stay awake during Economics. Mr. Enoch's voice was a dreary monotone that seemed to merge with the bleak rain that pelted against the window of his classroom.

I tried to keep myself occupied by counting the number of times he crossed his arms in comparison to how many times he tapped the blackboard with his chalk. It kept my eyes on him, making it seem as if I was interested in what he was lecturing about. I was just about to make another tally mark in my notebook - another point for arm crossing - when the bell finally rang.

Mr. Enoch stopped us before we made it to the door. "Don't forget, your year end reports on elasticity in economics are due in one week. Make it good, people; this report could be the deciding factor between graduation and summer school."

Julius caught up with me in the hallway and threw his arm around my shoulder. "What was the final tally?" He loved the fact that I could always find a way to amuse myself.

"Fifteen blackboard taps and twenty-seven arm crosses. He's slacking. Yesterday he crossed his arms twenty-three times and tapped the blackboard nineteen times."

Julius laughed. "How is it that you only have a C average in probability and statistics? I bet if you showed your 'Mr. Enoch scorecard' to Mr. Howell, he'd probably give you extra credit."

A gave him a grin. "I like the way you think, Julius Car-"

He cut me off by placing a finger over my mouth. "You are wearing me out Gabrielle Spencer."

My smile widened under his electric touch. "Is that really possible?" I managed to mumble.

We started walking again. "Not really, but it's hard to stay focused here when so much is going on back in Cleveland."

I sighed playfully. "Yeah, I know."

We slipped into Chemistry II just before the bell rang, sheathed in reprimanding glares from Mrs. Barnes. She must have been in a good mood, though, because she refrained from making embarrassing remarks at our expense.

I quickly took my seat beside April, doing my best to concentrate on what Mrs. Barnes was teaching. I didn't want to give her any ammunition, certain she would be searching for something to use against me in her never ending quest to annihilate my self confidence.

Creative Writing went well; Mrs. Jameson complimented my mock college admittance form essay in front of the entire class. It was a lot less embarrassing than I thought it would be - she didn't make a big fuss.

When the lunch bell rang, Julius caught up with Evan, racing the other students to the cafeteria to be first in line. Earlier in the school year I reached the conclusion that when it came to the male species, everything took a backseat to their hunger.

By the time I reached the lunch room, Julius was already at our table, an extra tray of food beside him for me. He and Evan were already deep in conversation.

Julius assured me that he and Evan had come up with a new evacuation plan, although he wouldn't tell me what it was, which made me think it probably wasn't any better than the first one. He did promise me, however, that if their plan ever did need to be implemented, it would not be done in haste. They ruined the homecoming dance for everyone by evacuating the school when it was completely unnecessary, and they promised there would be no more false alarms.

I was glad when April finally made it to the table, relieved to have someone to talk to. "I'll be so glad when exams are over," she said, opening her Chemistry book before shoving a spoonful of mashed potatoes in her mouth. After swallowing she added, "I'm not worried about any of them but Chemistry."

"Why would you be worried about Chemistry? You've had an A average in that class all year," I reminded her.

She looked at me and rolled her eyes. "You know Mrs. Barnes. She'll probably make the entire exam about the last chapter of the book, which we haven't even covered."

I sighed. April was probably right. I hadn't been worried about exams until now. Mr. Enoch only wanted a report, which wouldn't be difficult at all, and Sculpture and Creative Writing weren't going to be hard, but Chemistry, English, and Probability and Statistics were going to be rough.

"If my A average gets screwed up over her exam I'll be furious," April said, shaking her head at the thought. "Can you imagine? My entire high school career I'm on the honor roll, and then two weeks before I graduate I get a B…or worse." Her eyes widened with fear at this sudden, albeit unlikely probability.

I rolled my eyes at her. "April, that isn't going to happen, besides, you know the book front to back already. Even if she did test us on what we haven't covered yet you'd still ace it."

She finally released the breath she'd been holding, and a smile appeared on her face in place of the anxious expression that had kidnapped it moments earlier. "You're right." She closed her book and shoved it aside. "There's no way I'm going to fail it." She added that last part to herself, more as an affirmation than a statement of fact. "Do you want to do something after work tonight? Catch a movie or something?"

April was definitely feeling better.

"Yeah, that would be fun," I said. "What's playing? Is there anything funny?"

"I don't know. I'm completely out of touch. Between work and studying, it's like I've been hibernating." April was practically squealing with delight at the promise of taking a break from the tedious routine she'd inadvertently developed.

"Well, we get off at nine, and something's bound to be playing at nine-thirty. We'll just pick the first one we can get into."

Travis overheard us making plans, and turned his attention away from Evan and Julius. "Are you seriously going to the movies tonight?" He asked April, surprised.

"Yeah. We don't even know what's playing, but we're going to go straight after work." April could barely contain her excitement, and she talked in a rapid whisper, as if she was leading some type of secret resistance against all things work related.

"Is it going to be just the two of you, or a group thing?" Travis asked. He was trying to sound nonchalant, but I could tell he was a little hurt. He and April hadn't spent much time together during the last month, and he hoped to be invited.

Before April could intervene, I jumped in. "Why don't we all go? We'll boycott studying for one night. It will be an ode to rash decisions and irresponsibility."

April laughed. "Just as soon as we're finished with work." She was pointing out the flaw in my statement.

A huge smile enveloped my face. "Well, April, it *will* be rash and irresponsible just as soon as we call off."

Everyone at our table was listening now.

"Are you serious?" April's eyes were wide with disbelief.

"Why not?" I challenged.

April was struggling with the concept. "But, won't it be obvious if we both call off at the same time?"

For what seemed like the hundredth time today, I rolled my eyes. "Come on April, you deserve this. What's the worst that could happen?"

"We could get fired!"

I laughed. "Yeah, right. You've worked there for two years without ever having missed a day. I've worked there for eight months and never missed a day. We aren't going to get fired. Besides, there are plenty of people to cover for us." Then, just because I knew how sympathetic April could be I pointed out, "People who could really use the hours."

My guilt trip seemed to work a little. April stared at me through winced eyes. "I don't know."

Travis groaned. "Come on April, it'll be fun. And tomorrow's Saturday so you can pull a double shift if you feel too guilty."

She smiled, giving into Travis's suave persuasion. "Okay, I'm in."

The table erupted in cheers just before the bell rang.

I came up with a plan while I was waiting for the end of the day bell to ring. I was going to go into the manager's office at Murphy's after school on the pretense of calling off, and if I could get her alone, I was going to modify our manager, Janette's, memory. I was going to make her think that she had given us a day off with pay.

When I discussed it with Julius, he suggested I skip the part about still getting paid, but agreed that it would be good practice for me.

My hands were sweating when I pulled into the parking lot, making the steering wheel slippery and hard to grip. I wiped my palms against my jeans before getting out, and took a deep breath before walking into the store.

Janette was behind the desk in her office, talking on the

phone. She was winding her shoulder length gray hair around a pencil as she talked, so I knew it wasn't a personal call - she was bored.

I tapped on the door so she would notice me, and she smiled and waved me in. "Okay, I'll take care of that," she was saying, while making hand gestures toward the phone that suggested the person on the other end wouldn't quit talking. "Okay, I'll let you know next Friday. Mmm-hmm." I always liked the way she ended a call. She never said 'Bye' but she never just hung up without letting someone know she was going to.

"Hey, Janette, I just wanted you to know I won't be able to work tonight," I blurted out before she had a chance to ask what I was doing there.

She raised an eyebrow. "Why not?"

Beads of sweat started to form on my brow. I was nervous about performing the memory modification, and I had just realized that I hadn't really come up with a plan on how to go about doing it.

"Well?" She asked impatiently.

I stepped closer to her, and my eyes went straight to her name tag. "Let me fix that for you." I reached forward, acting as if I were about to adjust it, but instead, I laid my hands on her shoulders. "You gave April and I the day off, because we've been working so hard," I said, my voice quivering slightly. I was just about to release her when another idea entered my head. "And you said that you were going to give April the employee of the month award."

I felt extremely stupid, especially since I felt nothing significant as I performed the modification. I expected to feel something similar to the hum, and I when I didn't, I was sure I'd done it wrong.

But Janette's expression quickly turned from confusion to understanding. "Oh, that's right. That reminds me, I'm gonna need a picture of her. Do you think she'll mind giving me one? I'd take a Polaroid, but I'm fresh out of film."

I exhaled. "No, she won't mind." I started to walk out of the office. "Oh, and you know April, she'll probably call to remind you she won't be coming in."

"That's why she's the employee of the month," Janette said, shaking her finger in the air. "You girls go do something fun tonight, okay?"

"Will do," I said, smiling with giddy relief at having done the modification correctly. I was still a little stunned that nothing out of the ordinary happened while I was doing it, but happy all the same.

My adrenaline was still pumping when I pulled in my driveway. I tried to calm myself down by breathing through my nose, hoping it would work well enough that my excitement wouldn't alarm my parents.

They seemed to notice every subtle detail about me now, especially my mother, who joined a support group for missing children. The group urged its members not to neglect their other children. There were two reasons behind this logic: the first one was to make sure the other children recognized they were just as important as the missing child, and the second one was that by focusing on the other children, the parents are thankful for what they still have, as opposed to distraught over what they lost.

I wasn't sure I agreed with the logic at first; I felt as if the group was using me as a tool rather than seeing me as a victim of his disappearance also, but as time went on, I could definitely see a change in my mother, and I was glad she had me to help her get through it. I couldn't imagine what it would have been like for her had Devon been her only child. (Although if that were the case he wouldn't have disappeared.)

When I thought of my mother's progress, I was frightened about her future. What would happen to her if I didn't succeed in eliminating Devon? What if something happened to me? Of course, if I didn't eliminate him, I knew what would happen to the entire world, so it seemed ridiculous to worry about my mother in that aspect, but how would she handle it if something were to happen to me before the process was complete?

I shook the thought from my head. I mustn't think like that.

I took one more deep breath to clear my head before stepping out of the car and into the house.

A pleasant botanical scent greeted me when I walked through the doorway, and I didn't have to look long before I found the source. Flowers covered the kitchen table and counter tops, and every inch of furniture in the living room.

"Mom?" I tossed my backpack onto the floor as I shut the door behind me and called to her. "What are all these flowers doing here?"

I heard something hit the bottom of the kitchen sink, and the water turn on. I walked into the kitchen and found my mother at the sink, filling up a vase.

"Hey, Gabs. Remember how I told you about the woman in my support group, Crystal, who was getting married?" She never looked up from the vase as she lifted it from the sink and carried it over to the table.

"Yeah."

"Well, I told her if there was anything she needed help with to call me. It turns out that her uncle owns a flower shop in Watseka, and the lady that was working for him quit yesterday afternoon, so Crystal called me in tears this morning to ask if I could help with the flowers. I agreed of course, and she and I drove over there. Greg - that's her uncle - was leery about me helping at first, but once he saw the arrangement I made...he offered me a job!" She couldn't keep the excitement from her expression any longer. She smiled with her teeth as her grin took on a life of its own.

"That's great Mom!" I flung my arms around her in a hug, genuinely pleased for her. "When do you start?"

I couldn't get over the intensity of her smile as I released her.

"Well, the wedding's tomorrow, and I insisted that what I'm doing now is strictly on a volunteer basis. I offered my help, and getting paid for it just seems wrong, so I guess I'm not officially employed until Monday." She nodded when she said Monday, putting a business-like emphasis on the word.

"Wow, Mom, I can't believe it. Have you told Dad yet?"

I knew he would be just as ecstatic. Seeing Mom happy sent him on an expedited track to utopia.

"No, I want to surprise him. I'd like to get this all done before he comes home. It's getting warmer in here and I don't want the flowers to wilt. We'll have to take them back to the flower shop as soon as he gets here."

I looked around once more at the staggering amount of flowers that covered the kitchen and living room. "Mom, there is no way all of these flowers are going to fit in the Buick."

"We'll have to make two trips," she shrugged.

"Probably more like four." I looked around once more, trying to imagine the number of flowers that could actually fit in the car. "If you took my car, too, it might only take a couple of trips."

"I thought you had to work."

I shrugged. "Janette gave April and I the day off. April's going to be employee of the month, but she doesn't know it yet." Somehow, although I thought it would, it didn't feel like a lie.

"Good for her. Do you have any plans now that you've got the night off?" She was gracefully placing a white rose in the center of a bouquet.

"Yeah. A few of us are going to see a movie in Watseka, but I can have Julius pick me up so you can take my car."

"He hasn't been here for a few days, has he?" She continued to focus on the flowers while she talked, which seemed eerie to me on some level.

"Well, I've been working and doing homework. He doesn't want to come over so late."

Actually, if he and I hadn't been spending so much time together in Cleveland, I probably would have skipped a few study sessions just to see him.

"Hmm," she responded. The intonation in her voice was bordering on snide, which surprised me.

"What?" My eyebrows were cocked, my defenses drawn.

"What does Julius do in the evenings? Does he work at all?"

"Mother!" I snapped.

"I just meant that he has that nice car and all of this free time on his hands. I'm just a little curious." She continued her duties nonchalantly as she talked.

"He repairs cars at his uncle's house. He's very good at it, and he earns a decent amount of money." My arms were crossed and my tone was harsh.

Mom finally looked up from her flowers. Her expression was serious. "Graduation is in a couple of weeks, Gabrielle. You haven't applied to college. Do you and Julius have any plans…together? Perhaps something you haven't told us about?"

A few seconds passed before the initial confusion wore off and the true meaning behind my mother's inquisition registered. My eyes widened. "What? You think we're secretly engaged or something?"

"Are you?"

I honestly couldn't believe what my mother was asking. My jaw dropped, leaving my mouth hanging open for a split second before I could answer her. "Mom! I'm only eighteen!"

Mom looked at me with squinted, accusing eyes. "I didn't ask how old you are Gabby."

I couldn't remember the last time I had been angry with my mom. It seemed like years had passed since she and I had been in an argument, and I couldn't remember how to deal with it.

I glared at her, challenging her facial expression. "No. Julius and I have never discussed anything of the sort."

Her eyes relaxed, but her stance didn't. I could tell there was more on her mind, but she was afraid she had already crossed the line.

"What now?" As soon as the words were out of my mouth, I wished I could've taken them back. It suddenly dawned on me what was nagging at her, and I had given her an open invitation to lay it on the table.

"You two have been together for awhile now. I want to know how serious your relationship has gotten." Her tone was softer, less accusing now, and she looked me in the eyes. Somehow, this made me feel better. Had she looked away from me, I would have felt shameful.

I inhaled and sighed through my nose, relaxing my shoulders. "Serious."

For a moment she stood completely still. She didn't breathe or even blink, and I knew she was struggling with herself to find the perfect way to handle this. Finally, she swallowed. "I know I don't need to tell you how important it is to protect yourself; you're a smart girl and I don't think you've been irresponsible. But I think I should make you an appointment with my doctor, just as an added precaution."

I nodded.

She was about to say more, but just then Dad walked in, putting an abrupt end to our unfinished conversation.

"Nina, what is all this?" He called to my mother.

She looked at me and put her palm to my cheek, signaling that she loved me, and that she wasn't disappointed in me.

I smiled back at her and ran upstairs to my room to call Julius and ask him to pick me up.

I was quiet for most of the ride to Watseka, which Julius finally called me on. I wasn't going to tell him about the conversation I'd had with my mom, but he eventually dragged it out of me. He was genuinely concerned, and I couldn't allow him to think my detachment had anything to do with him.

He shook his head when I told him. "I am so sorry Gabby."

I was shocked at his apology - it wasn't what I expected to hear from him.

"Sorry for what?" I asked sharply.

"For not thinking this through clearly enough. For letting my hormones get in the way of rationality. For my part in making your mother suspicious of you. For -"

I cut him off. "Enough!" The harshness in my tone surprised both of us, but I continued anyway. "There is nothing to be sorry about. We both have hormones, remember? And *most* teenagers have suspicious parents, or at least they should. The only parents that aren't are the ones who don't care. I'm actually kind of grateful on some level. And anyway, my parents were our age once too, and I'm sure they weren't perfect." I continued to stare out the window at the trees flashing by. I couldn't look at Julius, I was much too embarrassed.

He didn't say anything else for the remaining five minutes it took us to get to the movie theatre. I wasn't sure if he was upset with me for the way I yelled at him, or if he was still thinking about what my mother had said.

Kaitlyn and Grady were already there, the early birds that they were. Julius immediately started up a conversation with Grady, and I was sure he was only doing it so he wouldn't have to talk to me. I sighed, suddenly very sorry about the way I talked to Julius.

"So what do you think we should see?" Kaitlyn was just as enthusiastic about our outing now as she had been at lunch. "There's that one about the girl who helps her family immigrate, it looks pretty good."

"It sounds like something Mr. Enoch would show in class. I'd rather not see anything that could be considered educational."

My uncaring demeanor had just killed Kaitlyn's buzz.

"Oh. Okay, whatever then." She turned toward Grady.

Immediately the pang of guilt began. "Ugh, Kaitlyn, I'm sorry. I've just got something on my mind right now. I shouldn't have snapped at you like that."

She cocked one eyebrow at me in concern. "Is everything okay?"

"Yeah. It's just that my mom's upset with me about not applying for college yet." It was half the truth anyway. I didn't want to go into detail about my personal business.

She rolled her eyes. "Why do parents get so mad about that? I told mine I was going to the community college and they exploded. It's like they don't even think it's a real school or something."

"I think mine would be pretty proud of me right now if I told them that's where I was going." I scanned the parking lot as I talked, hoping to see April. I really did like Kaitlyn, but I enjoyed her company more when I wasn't so upset.

"I wish the rest of them would hurry up," she said, catching me watching the parking lot. "They have the best popcorn here; I can't wait to get some."

Finally I spotted April's silver car glide into an empty parking space, and I sighed with relief. If anyone could cut the tension between Julius and I - or at least make me forget about it - it was her.

She bounded toward me in a way which told me she was dying to tell me something.

"Can you believe Janette gave us the day off? I didn't even have to make something up! We lucked out!"

I noticed Julius look in our direction when April said that, and I could have sworn I saw a smile on his face. I forgot to tell him about how well the memory modification went.

"I know - it's weird isn't it?"

Travis finally caught up to us. "Can you believe it? The girl finally tries to be a rebel and somehow she gets off the hook." He kissed April on the cheek then and put his arm around her shoulders.

Troy, Alexis, Evan and Ashley pulled up just then, and we all discussed what movie to see. In the end, Kaitlyn won, and after stocking up on popcorn and drinks, we made our way into the theatre.

Julius grabbed my hand as we settled into our seats. Leaning into my ear he whispered, "It seems as if everything went well at Murphy's."

I nodded. "It was easier than I thought. I just lied and she believed it."

Julius smiled. "I told you it was simple."

He squeezed my hand tighter as the previews started, and in that instant, every ounce of friction between us melted away.

The next couple of weeks flew by. I passed every exam, even getting a B in Chemistry. I honestly don't know how I did it; I had to guess on at least twenty-five percent of the questions. Probability and Statistics was the other one I was worried about, but I managed a B on that one too.

Julius told Mr. Howell about the little game I played in Economics, and after he was convinced I passed Mr. Enoch's class with an A average, Mr. Howell actually did give me extra credit. Even so it was still embarrassing.

The night before graduation I couldn't sleep. It didn't have to do with excitement or even worry; I just couldn't stop thinking about Devon. I kept asking myself what would be going on right now if he were here. What would we be talking about? What college would he be planning on attending in the fall? What scholarships would he have gotten?

Mr. Wilcoxen stopped me in the hall a week before graduation to say that the student council wanted to mention him at the ceremony. They wanted to honor him in some way, and he asked if I would be okay with it. I told him I didn't mind, but asked if he would please let me discuss it with my parents first. I didn't want them to be ambushed.

It was a difficult conversation to have.

I mentioned it at dinner, of course, and at once an ominous silence fell. My mom's eyes filled with tears and my dad let his salad sit in his mouth for an entire minute before he realized it was still in there and finally swallowed.

"I think that would be nice," Mom finally choked out.

Dad grunted a nod.

The three of us sat in silence for the next fifteen minutes, pretending to eat until I finally offered to clear the table and do the dishes.

My mother wasn't as distraught over the conversation as I imagined she'd be, unless she was just hiding it well.

Dad was the one who really surprised me. He spent four days working overtime at the paper, then coming home and going straight to bed. He didn't speak to me or my mother at all, and I never saw him eat anything. I was so relieved when he finally started to join the real world again.

I finally fell asleep sometime after two in the morning, and after having my dreams perforated with images of Devon, I didn't wake up until eleven.

My eyes were heavy and swollen from lack of sleep, and by two in the afternoon I fell asleep on the couch while I watched reality show reruns.

Dad woke me up at four-thirty, for which I was immensely grateful. Graduation was at six, and I hadn't done anything to get ready.

April called me at five, right after I was done blow drying my hair, to go over her valedictorian speech and ask me for pointers. I laughed and told her the stress must be messing with the chemicals in her brain. The valedictorian shouldn't have to ask the average student for advice on speech-writing.

She pointed out the A I received in creative writing, but I told her that was just a technicality. It was her speech, and I happened to think it was brilliant.

Somehow I managed to put on my makeup, curl my hair and get dressed all by five-thirty, which was when we were supposed to leave.

We were a couple of miles down the road when we had to turn back; Mom forgot the camera.

By the time we arrived at the school, most of the students were already seated on the chairs in the football field. I was glad the rainy weather had finally started to break, otherwise we would have been cramped in the gym, and getting to my seat would have meant traversing an obstacle course.

Julius was already seated, and I called to him with my hum to let him know I finally made it. He turned around from his place in the first row and waved at me, a monumental smile on his face.

Just as the ceremony was about to start, I felt Cordele, Nayana, and Daniel's hum, and turned to look for them in the stands. They were easy to spot - Nayana's long dark curls were bouncing around as she waved excitedly in my direction. I waved back before turning around to listen to the Superintendent's opening speech.

His words were dull, of course, and no matter how strict I was with myself, I was unable to focus on them.

Instead, I looked to the seat next me, empty and forlorn. It was Devon's seat, and I couldn't help but picture him there to my left, wondering if he would look any different than he did the last time I saw him alive. Tears threatened my eyelashes, and in that moment I realized that among all the mixed emotions I was feeling - anger, sadness, desperation, guilt - the most prominent was love.

I snapped my head back toward the boring man in the grey suit and closed my eyes, trying to persuade my unkempt emotions back into the hollow place inside of me - the place that Devon created.

April was on stage now, shaking the Superintendent's hand and taking her rightful place in front of the microphone. It was a relief to see her up there, and although I hoped she would be able to hold my attention, I knew she wouldn't. I'd heard her speech just a little over an hour ago, so I knew my mind would wander.

I was still arguing with myself about how to stay focused on April's words by the time her speech was over, which was a huge surprise to me. I stood and clapped for her with the rest of the student body, feeling a little guilty about not actually hearing anything she said.

I finally lost the battle between reality and fantasy. I never heard another word until Devon was mentioned.

It was nothing more than a simple statement. Someone's voice boomed into the microphone, Devon's name echoing across the silent field. The ominous tone asked that we remember him, and to keep in mind that there was a strong possibility that he was still out there. "*Missing*," the solemn voice stressed, "But not forgotten."

Tears trickled down my face as I looked into the empty chair to the left of me, knowing he could never have this moment back, but desperately wishing he could.

I wanted to look out into the stands and find my parents, to see their faces at this moment. I wanted to console them, but I knew there was no use. The three of us had our own separate ways of dealing with this.

I wondered momentarily about their inner turmoil. Had they stopped hoping yet? Had they given up on hope altogether and started wishing instead? Did they still scan the faces of every teenage boy that they came across? Did they still pray? If they did, what did they say? Did they beg for his return? His safety? His happiness? What were they feeling right now?

I was yanked from my thoughts by the girl to the right of me. She nudged me and pointed to the stage.

I looked up just as Mr. Wilcoxen was leaning into the microphone. "Julius Eugene Carter," his voice boomed.

When his diploma was handed to him, Julius shook the principal's hand with his usual style of easygoing sophistication, but no matter how hard he tried, he couldn't suppress the smile that came to his face. This was his proudest moment, an achievement that was well deserved, and his grin refused to deny him this moment of accomplishment.

The crowd was told at the beginning of the ceremony to hold their applause until the end, but they refused to obey such a ridiculous instruction. No one would let their child walk off the stage without a standing ovation, and Julius's family was no different.

Nayana's supportive yells could be heard over Daniel's

whistles and Cordele's booming claps, and my parents weren't afraid to add their encouragement either. I clapped and yelled right along with them, as did the rest of Julius's friends; although Evan's bass tone drowned me out.

My knees started shaking when it was time for my row to stand and make our way to the stage, and I suddenly felt very warm under my crimson cap and gown.

When Mr. Wilcoxen called my name, I couldn't hear the applause for the ringing in my ears. My feeble smile and timid handshake as I accepted my diploma were all products of my nerves, and although I wanted to make it off the stage quickly, in case I would faint, my legs felt as if they'd suddenly become fifty pounds heavier.

I held on to the railing as I made my way down the steps on the other side of the stage, willing a breeze to hit my face and bring me out of this embarrassing episode.

Somehow I made it back to my seat without collapsing, and I found myself praying to God to give me the strength to get through the last ten minutes of the ceremony.

My body eventually calmed down, my breathing becoming steady once more, but my legs were still a little shaky.

Finally, the last name was called and when we were all seated as one again, the principal spoke his congratulations, giving us the cue to toss our hats.

And just like that, it was the end of Kentland High.

Chapter 13 ❖

The day after graduation was the official end to Cordele and Nayana's vacation. They were back at Julius's apartment by seven that morning, although Daniel refused to be there until eight. He wasn't quite ready to hang up his fishing rod.

By the time he arrived, Julius and I had already filled the others in on my latest accomplishment - memory modification. There weren't many details to it, but somehow we found a way to discuss it for nearly an hour.

I thought that the two weeks Daniel spent relaxing would have eased his grouchiness, so I was surprised when he showed up looking weary and irritated. His brow was furrowed the entire time he was there, and he snapped at everyone.

Whether it had to do with Daniel's attitude or everyone's lack of energy from being back in a normal routine I wasn't sure, but our day together ended by three in the afternoon.

Julius and I were eating hamburgers for dinner late that

evening when I brought the subject of Daniel up. "Don't you think there's something strange about the way he's acting? It's almost as if he's gone from cranky to…paranoid."

"I noticed that too. He hasn't been himself for the last month or so." He paused to take another bite. "I think Cordele is going to talk to him. I know he's noticed the change in Daniel, and I can't think of any other reason why he would let us off the hook so early."

I rolled my eyes. "Is there really any point to going over the same exact things day in and day out? I mean other than the fact that I know how to do memory modification now, what else is there to improve?"

Julius raised an eyebrow. "I know. At first I thought they were just coming over every day as a ruse to keep an eye on the two of us, but now…" He trailed off in thought.

"It seemed so obvious at first," I said. "Especially since Cordele made it clear that he thought my situation was a catch twenty-two. He was adamant that I would never have to eliminate Devon at all, and then the very next day he insisted on these defensive strength training sessions that last for *hours*."

Julius put his hamburger down and curled into his *The Thinker* position I admired so much. He tapped his chin a few times before squinting his eyes. "Maybe we were wrong. Maybe this doesn't have anything to do with us at all." His eyes looked upward into mine. "Did Daniel overhear the conversation between you and Cordele that night?"

"No, I don't think so. He was off repairing the cemetery."

"Hmm. Did he say anything about Daniel to you at all?"

"Nothing. He just asked me more or less if I believed in signs from God. We thought that maybe the fact that I'd heard references to Glasnevin Cemetery before were 'signposts' telling me I was on the right track. That was before he told me that he thought I wouldn't have to eliminate Devon after all." I took another bite of my hamburger, chewing it slowly as I tried to make sense of Julius's thought process.

"I'm not sure how, but I think all of this ties in together somehow, and I think the fact that Cordele's words and actions are a complete contradiction to one another are proof. He knows you and I are smart enough to figure out that he's not calling these meetings together everyday for your benefit. I could teach you everything you need to know without any help from the rest of them. I think he was *hoping* we would think he was here to keep a close eye on us."

I met Julius's eyes. "Why?"

"So we wouldn't figure out the real reason he really wanted us all here together."

"Which would be?"

"Daniel." He stood and started pacing. "Think about it. Daniel lives in Dublin, which is where the attack was, right? And he mentioned that he didn't think you would have to fight Devon, but Glasnevin Cemetery was where you were supposed to be." His eyes widened then, filled with the coldest fear I had ever noticed from him. "Gabby, Devon's army wasn't restless; they were following a direct order - looking for Daniel. He thinks Daniel's the easiest target of the five of us. I think they're trying to pick us off one by one until you finally come to him."

His words seemed to bore through my heart, ripping and tearing at every hope I'd ever clung to. The reality of my situation suddenly crashed down on me with the force of a wrecking ball, but for all of my wild internal emotions, my exterior was calm with shock.

"Cordele knows. That's why he insists on having us in one spot as much as possible. He's trying to keep Daniel safe. I bet Daniel has no idea that's what Cordele's doing."

Finally, I found my voice, and a tiny shred of hope to hang onto. "But what about their vacation? If Cordele really thought Daniel was in trouble he wouldn't have left for two weeks."

Julius shook his head at me. "Daniel needed some alone time. He needed to recuperate from all of the meetings. He's a loner and it was making him cranky. I'll bet anything in the world that Cordele and Nayana never went to Florida. They were in Dublin the entire time, standing guard over Daniel without him ever knowing it."

I slumped back into the couch, devastated by these new revelations. Julius was making perfect sense, and with every new disclosure came another bout of internal torture.

"Come on, we have to go." He grabbed his tee-shirt and pulled it on in a hurry, then grabbed a jacket for me.

"Where are we going?" I asked frantically as I pulled on the jacket.

"To Daniel's. I bet Cordele's there right now."

"But it must me two or three in the morning there. What could he possibly be doing?"

"That's what we're about to find out."

He grabbed my hand as we closed our eyes and thought of Daniel.

We were there in an instant, ending up at his bedside.

Julius was right, Cordele was right beside Daniel's bed, sitting in an old wooden rocker. He smiled when he saw us, as if our arrival was expected.

"You know," he started, "love can do funny things. If the two of you weren't so interested in each other, I wouldn't have gotten away with this for more than a week." He laughed at himself before putting a finger to his lips to signal for quiet, and then turned his attention back to Daniel.

We watched closely as a small smile appeared on his face as he was sleeping. Slowly it grew wider, until even the wrinkles around his eyes were grinning. Then, with shocking abruptness, it was replaced with an agonizing grimace. Whimpers escaped him, quiet and forlorn, as if he were in pain, then rising in volume and texture until they became screams of horror.

I wanted to wake him, but the moment Cordele saw my face he held up his hand, cautioning me against it.

His torturous cries soon faded back into the small whimpers once again, and slowly the smile returned, as if someone had pushed a rewind button on his face.

I assumed at that point that he would return to his normal state of sleep, the peaceful one he had been in just seconds before we arrived, but I was mistaken. Instead, I watched in horror as his head rocked back and forth on his pillow, and listened to the maniacal laughter that was coming from his throat.

I buried my head in Julius's chest to quiet the gasp that threatened to escape me. I knew what he was dreaming, and I was appalled by the experience.

What could this mean? Up until this point, I thought the dream I'd had was nothing more than that - a dream. But now that Daniel was having it as well, I was positive that it was more like an out-of-body experience than anything else.

"He'll be waking up any minute now," Cordele whispered. "Let's meet back at your place, shall we?"

Julius bombarded Cordele the moment we arrived back in Cleveland. "You should have told us about this!"

"Daniel hasn't even told *me* about it yet. I didn't think it was appropriate to discuss his personal matter with the entire group when he hasn't come to terms with it himself. He'll talk when he's ready."

Julius laughed sarcastically. "Sure, let's do the *appropriate* thing. He's only being hunted by the Devil's army. Let's not try and get to the bottom of this thing and perhaps save the man's life because it wouldn't be *mannerly*!"

"Julius! How dare you speak to me as if I know nothing! As if I'm naïve enough to assume grace over humanity! If he hasn't shared it with the rest of us it means he hasn't figured it out yet, and if the rest of us were to try to help him with it, it might only make him more confused!"

Julius wasn't about to back down. "If you had mentioned it earlier you may have gained insight. The exact same thing happened to Gabby the night you left for your *vacation*."

Cordele's eyes grew wide with shock, and for the first time

since I met him he was speechless.

"I'll go," I offered, breaking the silence. "He won't like it - knowing that we know - but the sooner we find out what it means, the better."

I had just closed my eyes when Cordele startled me. "Gabby, wait!"

"Cordele, we need to know-"

"That's not why I'm stopping you. I just don't think it's a good idea for you to go alone. It could be a trap, something to lure you to Daniel. If they know the two of you are alone…"

I sighed. "Okay then. The two of you can come, but you'll stay outside, keeping watch."

"Good enough," Julius said.

This time, when I bi-located, I purposely positioned myself in front of Daniel's front door. I didn't want to scare him by leaning over his bedside while he was sleeping, and I didn't want to feel like an intruder.

I knocked on the heavy oak door forcefully. I wanted to make sure he heard me in his sleep. It took a couple of times, but he eventually made it to the door, shocked to see me.

"Gabby, is everything alright?" His red hair was tousled, his eyes puffy and aching to close. He waved me in and shut the door behind him.

"Actually, Daniel, I came to tell you something important. Can we sit down?"

He rubbed his face vigorously in irritation. "Can't this wait until morning?"

"No, I'm afraid it can't. We have to talk about this while your dream is still fresh in your mind." I sat down on his couch and removed my jacket to let him know I had no intentions of leaving just yet.

"My dream?" He looked confused. He couldn't understand why his dream had anything to do with me.

"Yes," I answered. "You know, the one about the orb finding you while you're the only person in the world? The one where you're walking all alone down a cobblestone path at night."

His jaw dropped and he stared at me with a mixture of anger and disbelief. "How do you know about that?"

"Actually, we all know." My face reddened. "We were worried about you."

His face gnarled in anger as he was about to protest, but before he could interject I continued quickly. "I had the same dream. It was two weeks ago, the night of our last meeting before Cordele and Nayana left."

With this, his livid expression softened, as I hoped it would. He slumped into the worn-out easy chair opposite me, and sighed. He ran his fingers through the tangled mass of hair on his scalp and asked, with a hint of desperation, "Do you have any idea what it's about?"

I shook my head. "No. That's why I wanted to talk to you. I thought that maybe you and I could figure it out together. Two heads are better than one, or so they say."

He tilted his head back to let it rest on the back of the chair. "I've been having this dream since they came to Glasnevin. It's turned my nights into pure torture. I'm scared to sleep, and the only time I do is when I can't force myself to stay awake any longer. It's like I'm being haunted or something."

"Does it feel like a dream to you? Because when I had it, it felt more like an out-of-body experience. It was almost as if it was dreaming of me instead, and I was yanked from my body to be there for it in person." It felt just as ridiculous when I talked about it as it did when it was no more than a thought.

He sat up in alarm, as if he'd just had an epiphany. "That's exactly what it feels like!" He laughed from exhaustion. "I just wish I knew what it was taking from me. That's the scary part. It's like I'm being operated on against my will, and my head rolls around insanely, then I start laughing for some reason. It's like I think the whole process is so simple that it's ridiculously funny."

Now I was confused. "Did you say it *took* something from

you?"

"Yeah. Isn't that what it did to you?" He looked worried.

"I got the impression that it was *giving* me something," I said, surprised at this knew revelation.

"Really? Isn't it odd how two people can have the same experience and both see it from a totally different perspective?"

Is that what it was? Just a different perspective? I wasn't sure I believed that.

I stood to leave.

"Where are you going? I thought we were going to try to figure this thing out." Daniel was on his feet, hurt that I wasn't going to discuss this anymore tonight.

"We *will* figure it out. But to be honest, I kind of want to try something first."

"What?

"Well, the night I had the dream, I told Julius about it immediately, and I haven't had it since. I'm wondering if now that you've admitted it to me, you'll keep having them."

"Do you really think that's possible?" His face was disbelieving.

I shrugged. "I don't know. I was watching something on television once where these people kept having reoccurring dreams. This psychiatrist told them that sometimes when people acknowledge these dreams, they go away."

"I'm not sure I buy it, but I'll let you know," Daniel said with a hint of sarcasm.

"I'll see you tomorrow, Daniel. First thing in the morning - Cleveland time."

When I made it back to Cleveland, I called Julius with my hum, letting him know I was no longer at Daniel's. I didn't want to explain to him why I was walking out his front door when I could just bi-locate from his living room.

"Well? What did he say?" Julius asked as soon as he and Cordele appeared.

"He was obviously upset when I told him why I was there,

but he was relieved when he found out he wasn't the only one who had the dream."

"That's it?" He was disappointed.

"There's more. He said in his dream the orb was *taking* something from him. In my dream, it felt like it was *giving* me something. He thought it was no big deal - that we were both just seeing it from a different perspective - but I can't help but think there's something more to it than that."

Cordele looked worried. "I would imagine so," he said gravely.

"Now what?" Julius asked.

"I told him I would talk to him in the morning. I want to know if he's still having the dream or not. I haven't had it since that first night, when I told you about it, and I thought maybe now that he's got it off his chest, it will go away."

Cordele sighed. "I'm not sure it's that easy, Gabby, but it's worth a try. He isn't doing well at the moment, and the first thing we've got to do is make him feel better."

I shrugged. "That's what I thought."

He smiled. "Well, I'll leave the two of you alone. I think I'll catch up on some sleep, so don't look for me to be here in the morning. However, I will want to know how things go with Daniel."

"Of course," I said.

He was gone before my gaze reached Julius's.

"So you didn't tell him they were after him?"

"No, I couldn't bring myself to do it just then. He is such a mess, Julius. I've never seen anyone so...desperate in my life."

"I figured he would be. But if you and Cordele won't tell him I guess I'll have to. The man needs to know."

I nodded in agreement.

The next morning, just after dawn, I was frantically shaken awake by Julius.

"Gabby, come on, get up. Daniel just called me." His voice was panic stricken, and I knew what he was thinking.

Immediately I threw the covers off and began to dress.

"What could he want?" I asked absentmindedly. I knew Julius thought Devon's army was after him. Just then I felt Daniel call me, too. I pulled my jeans on as fast as I could, and didn't even bother to change out of the tee-shirt I wore to bed. "He just called me, too. What is going on?"

"I don't know, but Daniel rarely ever uses his hum. Something has to be up. Let's go."

Daniel was calmly sitting at his kitchen table when we showed up, sipping a cup of tea. "Would you like a cup?" he offered, lifting his toward us.

Ignoring his question completely, Julius said, "What did you call us for?" He was clearly astonished that we hadn't found Daniel half-dead.

"I have a few things to ask," Daniel said casually between sips.

"What things?" Julius's expression was still one of shock, but he was definitely making an effort to remove the panic from his voice.

"Well first of all," he started, turning to face me, "You were half right about acknowledging my dream."

"How so?"

"I did have the dream again after you left, but this time, it was just that - a dream. I didn't feel like I was physically there this time." He took another sip of his tea. "It's a lot less intense that way, let me tell you."

"So you actually slept, then?" I was relieved that he seemed to be feeling better.

"Better than I have in eight and a half months."

"But you're still having it in some form."

"Exactly - this is what I wanted to talk to the two of you about." He turned toward Julius. "That night she had the dream, did she act it out?"

Julius nodded. "It was unnerving, strange."

Daniel turned back to me. "But since that night you haven't

even had it in its simpler form?"

I racked my brain. I always did have a hard time remembering what my dreams were about, unless they were extremely vivid or completely absurd. "The last dream I can remember was about Devon, the night before graduation. Before that, the dream about the orb is the only one I can remember. I can't be positive that I didn't, though; I have a tough time remembering what I dream of."

He turned his attention back to Julius. "And she hasn't acted out that way since?"

Julius shook his head.

Daniel shrugged. "Well, I still don't understand what it means, or why it's so persistent. It's almost as if it's showing me something important, something I need to know and I'm just not getting it. If I could just figure out what it's telling me, I think I would stop having the dream altogether."

I suddenly remembered something. "Hey, Julius. Remember how I told you that it felt like the orb was infusing me with knowledge?"

"Yeah, you did say that."

"Well maybe that's why I haven't had it again. Maybe I already figured out what it meant." I turned to Daniel. "You said it felt like it was taking something from you. Do you have any idea what that something was?"

"It felt like it was taking my *mind*, Gabby. Like it was performing brain surgery on me or something." He sighed in frustration.

"Well, what's in your mind?"

"How the hell should I know? I've got a lot of things in my mind. Do you have any idea how old I am? Think of all the research I've done with Cordele during my ridiculously long life span. My head probably has more useless facts stored in it than a hundred set of encyclopedias." He shoved his cup of tea away from him, aggravated that we didn't seem to be getting anywhere.

Julius agreed. "He's right, Gabby, it could take an eternity to figure that one out."

We sat quietly for a couple of minutes, each deep in our own thoughts, until Daniel broke the silence.

"Well, I guess that's it. I'm never gonna figure it out. You two go on home. There's nothing else you can do, I'll just have to sift through my thoughts and hope I get lucky."

I stood to leave, but Julius tensed. I knew he was going to stick around to tell Daniel the worst part of our revelation, and it made me nervous. I could have stayed, but I thought Daniel might be more comfortable hearing it without me around, so I gave Julius an encouraging look and a short wave, signaling my departure before leaving.

I put on a pot of coffee and took a shower while I waited for Julius to return.

The warm water pelting against my skin was refreshing, but it did little to soothe my nerves.

It seemed that for every mistake Devon made, a loophole popped up and erased it. Every piece of good news was infected with a hidden clause, written in fine print and bound by a universal contract.

I was certain that the dream Daniel kept having was the key to his survival, and I desperately wished he could figure it out before Devon's army closed in on him.

By the time I was finished with my shower, Julius still hadn't returned, so I decided to kill some time by doing my makeup and fixing my hair.

It seemed to take forever to blow dry my hair now that it was so long, but I didn't mind today. I was trying to keep myself occupied as long as it took for Julius to get back.

By noon I had done everything humanly possible that I could do to myself, and since there was no sign of Julius I decided to tidy up the apartment.

We were both pretty organized, tidy people, so general cleaning didn't take up more than twenty minutes of my time. I decided that I would have to clean the most unobvious places if I really wanted the day to pass quickly, so I started with the refrigerator. I took everything off the shelves and scrubbed it down with soapy water, then dried it with hand towels and put everything back neatly. After I was finished with that, I started on the stove. I removed all the knobs and scrubbed them first, then I washed the range, and thankfully, by the time I was scrubbing down the inside (which didn't even need it), Julius appeared.

"You know, it's a little scary when I come home and find my girlfriend with her head in the oven. I hope you're not doing that because of something I said." He had a smile on his face - the crooked one that sent goose bumps up my spine.

"Ha, ha," I said, crawling out of the oven. "How did it go?"

"Way better than I expected, even for Daniel. It seems the promise of being hunted by a large group of wild entities with supernatural powers really makes a three-hundred year old man feel like he's got a purpose in life."

"You mean he's excited about it?" I couldn't believe what I was hearing.

"Thrilled is more like it. We spent two hours talking battle tactics."

I rolled my eyes. "Men."

"Well, at least he's got a plan. I wouldn't call it the best one, but it's certainly good." He grabbed a mug and filled it with the rest of the coffee. After taking a drink he licked his lips and said, "I'll still never get why this hasn't caught on in Daniel's neck of the woods."

"What do you mean by his plan is good but not the best?"

"Well, the best plan would be for him to stay here or with Cordele. The whole reason he's being targeted is because he's alone. But he adamantly refuses to leave his home, so even though he does have a really good plan, the fact that he's being stubborn makes it a little less effective."

I blew a few stray hairs out of my eyes and took off the

yellow rubber gloves I'd been wearing to clean the stove. "Well, at least now he'll probably be in a better mood. It's funny what things will do that to a man."

Julius grabbed me by the waist and pulled me close to him. "Is it?" He gently pulled my face close to his. "You don't find the things that entice a man to be utterly predictable?" He was running his fingers through the waves in my hair, offering an example.

My heart was pounding underneath my chest as I assessed his suggestive smile. "Apparently not," I managed, finally remembering how to breathe. "I didn't even consider a reaction from you. Evidently I'm more naïve than I thought."

"You know, people who are naïve are easily surprised, and in some situations, surprises can be a lot of fun." His chin was millimeters from my cheek as he whispered in my ear, the promise of his touch and his warm breath a fiery mixture which concocted a desirous reaction within me.

I wrapped my arms around his neck. "And what situation would that be?"

I was off the floor and in his arms in less than a second. His lips against mine were a welcome relief, and I reacted to them in the same way someone would react to water after being stranded in the desert. His kiss was thirst quenching, and I couldn't get enough.

He hoisted me onto the bed, never breaking our kiss, and there we stayed until the moon was high in the night sky.

I woke up twice before midnight, the blankets twisted around me so fiercely I could no longer toss and turn. I fought hard to remember the images that had filled my mind as I slept, but the best I could come up with were fleeting scenes of color that disappeared from my memory as fast as I recognized them.

I told myself that whatever I was dreaming, it couldn't have been the same one Daniel and I had. The colors were much too bright and vibrant to have hosted a night time setting.

As I rolled over onto my stomach for the second time, trying to force myself back to sleep, a sudden realization hit me from out of nowhere. I rolled over onto my back quickly, throwing the blankets aside.

I jumped out of bed and dressed swiftly, trying to do it quietly so as not to wake Julius, then bi-located to Daniel's house.

This time, I made sure I was in his living room rather than outside his door. I was sure he had the house surrounded in case of a surprise attack, and I didn't want to startle anyone.

"Daniel?" I called out in the darkened living room. "It's me, Gabby. I think I just figured something out."

I heard him mumble sleepily from his bedroom, and waited patiently for him to get dressed and meet me.

"I was sleeping pretty good," he grumbled as he made his way into the living room, irritated that I woke him.

"Sorry, but I think we need to talk."

He plopped down in the easy chair, fighting against sleep to hear what I had to say. "What is it?" He asked through a yawn.

"Our dream. You said it was taking something from you, but I thought it was giving something to me."

He growled. "You woke me up to tell me that for the umpteenth time?"

"What I mean is, what if we weren't seeing it from two different perspectives at all? What if it was taking something from you and giving it to me?"

He was quiet for a few seconds as he contemplated this new possibility. "Like what? What would I need to give you?"

"I don't know for sure, but I got to thinking about something. Cordele, Nayana and Julius all told me about themselves, and I don't know anything about you, really. Maybe something about your case will help me find a way to eliminate Devon."

He huffed in disbelief. "Gabby, everything I did to eliminate my sister is very similar to the way Cordele, Nayana, and Julius eliminated their malefactors. I don't think there's anything I could tell you that would do you any good."

"It wouldn't hurt to try." I waited for him to say something, but when he didn't, I changed the subject. "Were you having the dream again?"

He nodded in response. "At least it isn't like it was. I swear it was killing me before."

Another few minutes passed in silence, and finally, Daniel sighed. He reached for something on the end table beside his chair. It was a picture in a silver, oval frame, and he looked at it fondly before handing it to me.

"My wife, Loraine," he said sadly. "Denise took her out first. She knew that no matter what she did to get me to fight, it wouldn't work if Loraine didn't want me to."

He tilted his head back and smiled as he reminisced about his wife. "Loraine always got her way with me, even in that prudish era when sensibility and proper etiquette clashed. Back then it was a man's world, and wives were supposed to be eager to please. But Loraine was different. She did what *she* thought was best, but always with elegance and grace. She wasn't forceful or overbearing, she was kind. And anything done with kindness was right in my book."

I handed the picture back to him. "She was very lovely."

"Aye," he agreed as he let his gaze linger on her image a little longer.

"Anyway," he said, placing his most prized possession back on the end table with great care. "I was thirty-one when I woke up. My Malefactor lived more than a hundred miles from where I was, and I thought I had enough time to come up with something sensible before she came looking for me. See, usually they wait for you to come to them, but Denise was always impatient, so I knew she didn't have it in her to wait. It was hard to fight the urges to find her, but I couldn't leave Loraine alone long enough to do it. We'd just lost our daughter, Margaret, to tuberculosis. She was only five, and Loraine and I were devastated. She was our only child." Tears were welling in his eyes, and he looked away from me.

"So I fought the urges, and waited. Eventually she did come, but it was Loraine who greeted her at the door. She saw the hostility in Denise's eyes and immediately knew there was something wrong. I think that maybe, somehow, she knew exactly what was going on, because the moment she saw the hatred that flooded my sister's eyes she tried to close the door on her and screamed for me to run." He had to take a minute to regain his composure. The memories of that day were hideous to him; a vault of disparaging emotions that he'd spent most of his life trying to hide from himself.

"My malefactor knew Loraine was the only thing standing in the way of our fight, and she killed her with one swing of her arm. I screamed out to my wife as I saw her lying there in the foyer near the bottom of the stairs, her head cocked at an unnatural angle. And then I heard Denise laughing. I wanted nothing more than to kill her myself; to wrap my fingers around her skinny little neck and slowly squeeze the life from her with my bare hands, but my body wouldn't allow it. I fought against my internal makeup as a sentinel, willing the goodness out of me so I could kill the monster that stole Loraine's life. I finally made it two feet from her when I realized what would happen to the world if I let her kill me, which she could have done in my moment of selfish fury, and I bi-located just as she tore at my flesh. One of her minions had made his way behind me just as I disappeared, and the disgusting thing was so eager to please, selfishly attempting to obtain glory. He jabbed at me with a pitchfork, hoping to kill me so that he would be praised by Denise, but it was too late. I had already vanished, and the pitchfork landed in Denise's gut." Daniel's eyes were no more than dark slits, squinted with wrath as he recalled those past events. His voice became a low growl as he spoke between clenched teeth.

"The half of me that saw my malefactor's demise was cradling Loraine's head, and the other half was with Cordele and

Nayana. If I had called to them earlier, the three of us could have prevented Loraine's death, but the part of me that's human seemed to take over. My emotions stood in the way of logic, and for that, I will never forgive myself."

I tried to swallow back the lump that had formed in my throat, but the harder I tried to force it away, the faster the tears threatened to spill from my eyes. I didn't know what to say to him, so I stayed silent.

"It wasn't until after she was buried that it dawned on me that I could possibly have saved Loraine. She was destroyed by a malefactor, so it stood to reason that being a sentinel, I could have fixed her. That was the hardest part to come to terms with. Every decision I made that day failed her."

"What good was I as a sentinel? Why was I chosen? I live with these questions everyday. What is my *true* purpose? There has to be a reason why someone as dimwitted as I am had to go through the things I did, and I ask God everyday to show me the answer."

Suddenly his demeanor changed. He was trying to collect his emotions and put them away as they were before I showed up. "I know they're after me, and I think that maybe this is the answer I was looking for. I think that maybe I'm being given a second chance to do it right and do it well, but if it's not to be…"

"Daniel! Don't say that!" It was hard to keep the tears from my voice at this point, but I did the best I could. I didn't want Daniel to be upset with me, but at the same time I wanted to shout at him for even considering anything less than a good outcome.

"I've already told Cordele. If something should happen to me, I don't want anyone to try and fix it. For one thing, I wouldn't be any use to anyone after that - after knowing for sure I could have saved her, and for another thing…" He looked up at me, his eyes intense. "I miss them. I want to see my wife and child again someday, and while I'll fight to the death to protect the four of you and everyone on the planet, I don't want the opportunity to be reunited with my family taken away."

I turned away from him so he couldn't see the shock on my face. Did he really expect us to just stand by and do nothing? Did he know how selfish a request he was making?

When I didn't say anything he said almost sharply, "Gabby?"

I sighed. "It's not going to make a difference, because everything's going to go smoothly. But if it makes you feel better – I understand what you need, and I won't interfere."

He looked out over the river and nodded. "Thank you."

Chapter 14❖

Julius was angry with me when he found out I'd left in the middle of the night to go to Daniel's.

"I can't believe you did that after the precautions we took the last time!"

"Julius, I would have wakened you if I really thought I was in danger. You said Daniel had a plan, so I assumed he would have his house surrounded with people he recruited." I kept my arms crossed against my chest defiantly.

"That's not the point. If Devon found out you were there alone with him, he could've sped up the process."

I hadn't thought about that at all. Thinking of how I could have expedited what we thought was an inevitable attack on Daniel made me sick to my stomach. "I'm sorry, I wasn't thinking."

He sighed. "You know I can't stay mad at you."

Having him mad at me wasn't what stung. The fact that I had

disappointed him was what hurt.

"So, do you think anything he told you is going to help?" He was trying hard to keep the exasperation from his tone, and I was grateful for that.

"I don't know." I dropped my arms in defeat. "I keep thinking about the way he eliminated his malefactor, and even though he thinks it was nothing more than lucky timing, I can't help but think it happened the way it did for a reason."

Julius nodded in agreement. "Well, there's one way of finding out if your theory holds water."

I looked at him in surprise. "How?"

"You need to talk to Daniel again. Find out if he had the dream again. If he didn't, then you could be right, and the key to eliminating Devon could be in whatever Daniel said."

"He kept stressing how *human* he felt when Denise came to find him. I think that whatever he did right had something to do with that."

I didn't talk to Daniel again for a couple of days. I wanted him to get as much sleep as he could, giving him what I thought was ample time to have the dream again.

On Thursday, I called to him around noon. It would be close to evening in Dublin, and I didn't want to interfere with his daytime tasks or his sleeping at night. Also, I promised Julius that I would stay out of Dublin unless the five of us were together.

Daniel looked much better than he had a few days prior. His color was good, and the bags under his eyes weren't nearly as heavy. His attitude was much better now; a few nights of catching up on his sleep did wonders to terminate the cranky episodes he'd been having. The best improvement was the presence of a smile on his freckled face. I wasn't sure if I'd ever seen a legitimate grin from him in all the time I'd known him.

"Not one single dream," he said, before I had a chance to ask.

Relief flooded throughout my system at his words.

"So maybe you were right, Gabby," Julius said with a hint of triumph in his voice. "Maybe there is something in what Daniel told you that will help."

"I hope so," I said. Then, with a sudden pang of ineptitude, I dropped my head. "But it won't make a difference until I figure it out. I haven't come close to finding a way to decipher a hidden meaning from any of it."

Daniel's optimism was not to be defeated. "You will, Gabby, I know it. You've already come this far." His expression turned soft, consoling as he grabbed my hand. "If you hadn't talked to me about this, hadn't told me your theories, I'm certain that the experience I was having would have tortured the life out of me, and I mean that literally."

I still wasn't convinced, but I smiled anyway. Daniel was feeling too good for me to crush his newfound exhilaration.

"We should let Cordele and Nayana know about this," Julius interrupted, sensing my trepidation and wanting to change the subject before Daniel caught on. "Maybe they can add some insight."

Cordele and Nayana arrived a few seconds later, pleased when they heard the latest developments.

"Ooh, Gabby, how ridiculously clever of you," Nayana said, her eyes wide with surprise. Then, throwing Cordele a smug look, she added, "So there is something to be learned from new-age theories and daytime television."

Cordele's face reddened. "I haven't got the slightest grudge against new-age theories," Cordele said confidently. "However I am very surprised that the public has found a place for them in television programs. What show was it that gave you the idea that acknowledging a dream could be beneficial Gabby?"

I shrugged. "I don't remember to be honest. It was one of the talk-shows though, and they change topics daily."

Cordele felt better about himself when I told him that. He figured it wouldn't do them any good to start flipping through the channels, being on the lookout for some stray bit of useful information.

"What do you think, Cordele?" Julius asked. "You know Daniel's story, is there anything in there that we've overlooked?"

"Have you considered the human characteristics that dominated…?"

Daniel, Julius and I were nodding before he even finished his sentence.

"What about the similarities between the two of you? Have you considered those?"

To be honest, I had tried to consider them, but I hadn't come up with anything I thought to be similar between the two of us.

"I'm not sure we have a lot in common," Daniel said, echoing my thoughts.

Cordele looked shocked. "What about the love factor?"

Our faces twisted into confusion in unison.

"Love factor?" Julius was just as astonished as Daniel and I.

Nayana sighed with impatience. "Yes. Daniel and Loraine were hopelessly in love, just as you and Gabby are. Perhaps that's what invoked the feelings of humanity. Maybe the dreams are cautionary. Maybe the orb is afraid that Gabby's love for you could jeopardize Devon's elimination."

The rest of us looked at her in astonishment.

"What? It's something to consider isn't it?" The innocence in her eyes was hard to look away from.

"Maybe it's the other way around," Daniel said, enlightenment in his eyes. "Maybe *Julius's* love for Gabby is what is getting in the way." He turned his gaze to Julius. "You *are* very protective of her. Maybe she isn't able to reach her full potential because she's worried about upsetting you. She knows if she gets hurt, you'll be devastated."

I didn't like being talked about like I wasn't even in the room, and what Nayana and Daniel were saying worried me. I was afraid Julius was going to take their advice too far, and suggest we stop seeing one another. I held my breath as I waited for Julius to speak up.

"Gabby isn't like the rest of us, remember? There are so many differences that make it necessary to be…cautious."

Cordele nodded. "It would be unwise for us to assume she's perfectly capable of relying on her own instincts." Then, for added emphasis he said, "Let's not forget that it was Julius who insisted on being cautious with you, Daniel. The moment he realized you were Devon's target, he demanded that you be informed. He knew you would take the appropriate action to keep yourself safe."

I sighed with relief at Cordele's words, but just as I thought I was in the clear, he began again.

"However, I do believe that Nayana and Daniel have a point…Devon is sure to use your relationship to his advantage." His eyes filled with anxiety as he talked.

I swallowed. It wasn't difficult to read between those lines. It was very possible that Devon would try to get rid of Julius if he found out about our relationship. Targeting Daniel was proof that he was trying to lull me out of hiding, and the sooner he realized that I was in love with Julius, the sooner he would move on to him.

Silence filled the apartment now as the significance of Cordele's words sunk in.

Quietly, Julius finally spoke up. "What should we do?"

Cordele sighed, knowing the pain he was about to inflict with his next words. "I think Gabby needs to find a new place to stay." He winced as he predicted the outcome of his next suggestion. "The best place for her, in my opinion, is with Daniel."

"No!" The two of them objected in unison.

Cordele raised a hand, signaling quiet. "Let me explain, please."

"There's no need for explanations, we all know what you're thinking," Daniel growled through clenched teeth. "I've already been targeted, and you think that if Gabby is found with me, it will throw the scent off the rest of you. What good will that do if

Gabby is killed in the process? Devon will have already won!"

Calmly, Cordele said, "Daniel, I hope you never decide to take up profession as a psychic hotline operator."

Nayana laughed at Cordele's joke, but the rest of us weren't quick enough to find the humor in it.

Cordele cleared his throat, signaling Nayana to stop giggling. "I have faith in you, Daniel. I know how strong you are, and your battle tactics are superb. I have no doubt that you will win the battle, but we all know that the battle is inevitable. There will be casualties. What better way to prevent them than a surprise? When you defeat them, they will not stop, they will only move on. And they will be sure to bring even more recruits with them. If they find Gabby with you, which is sure to astonish them, they'll be too afraid to retreat, because they'll think that the minute they go, Gabby will flee. They will stay and fight to the death - their death - rather than take a chance on losing her. They will have no time to gather reinforcements, no time to waste on tending to their wounds. Their casualties will be great, their army significantly smaller. And there will be no harm to Gabby, because unless the malefactor defeats her himself, Hell can not win. I'm sure Devon has already told them that Gabby is off limits. Why delay the inevitable? So many lives can be spared this way."

The rest of us were silent as we pondered his side of the argument. I looked at Julius's face as he thought. I could tell Cordele had convinced him that it would work, but he was agonizing over the thought of putting me in the middle of it.

Finally, Daniel nodded in agreement. "Okay, but I have a stipulation."

Smiling in such a way as to make Daniel feel at ease, Cordele asked, "And what would your stipulation be?"

"Everything we've got. Not just the ones *I've* recruited, but everyone. If this is going to work, we'll need to inflict enough horror on them to never try it again. They'll never believe I brought the entire army to protect me. They'll be convinced that the one's they're fighting are only a fraction of what we've got. They'll be much too scared to attempt another battle."

Cordele nodded, his smile widening with pride for Daniel. "A very good plan, Daniel, very good indeed."

Daniel tried to be a good host to me, but he just wasn't used to having a visitor in his home. I felt like an intruder, knowing that solitude was his sanctuary, so I tried to avoid him as much as I possibly could. It wasn't as hard to be invisible as I thought it would be; I missed seeing Julius everyday, and spent most of my waking hours in silent reflection of him, my sadness increasing until I finally reached a stage of constant melancholy.

I had only been there a week when Daniel decided to chastise me for my despondent demeanor. "Give it another week, Gabby," he insisted. "It'll be okay to visit then. Maybe we can start our meetings again, that would probably confuse them the most. I bet that's the reason they haven't attacked again; they might think we were planning an attack on them for all the times we congregated."

I sighed in an attempt to exhale the overwhelming sadness. "I think Cordele wants this over with as soon as possible. He's right, there's no reason to prolong the inevitable. The sooner we get it over with, the better."

"Aye. But in the meantime, could you perk up a little bit? Depression is catching, you know."

I gave him a weak smile. "I'll do my best."

That night, I woke up to a surprise. I'd been sleeping in the one spare bedroom which was right next to Daniel's room, so when I was shaken awake, I assumed it was him, warning me of an attack. I bolted upright immediately, the terrorizing thought sobering. Strong hands clamped tightly around my mouth, and the only thing that kept me from using my defenses was the soft tone whispering in my ear.

"Julius!" I said in a stage whisper as soon as he released his hands.

"Shh! Daniel will be furious if he knows I'm here. I'm

putting the entire plan at risk, sneaking in. If anyone finds out, all of our efforts will have been in vain."

I nodded, trying to sift through my own selfish feelings to unearth the truth that was hidden in his words.

"Anyone could be watching, it's very possible that they could have infiltrated, watching your and Daniel's every actions."

I had to stifle a laugh then, thinking of an old spy movie I'd seen when I was younger. Julius sounded so serious that it was funny to me.

"You think this is funny?"

His harsh whisper in the dark sent a wave of silent giggles through my system. After a few minutes, when I finally felt like I had my laughter under control, I said, "I don't know why I'm laughing. I think I'm just so happy to see you that I could find something wonderful in whatever you said to me."

He scooted me over and crawled in bed next to me, laying his head next to mine on the pillow. "Well, I *was* overdoing it a bit. I hoped you wouldn't question me, but I guess a sudden downward spiral in your intellect was too much to ask for. I swear you can see through anyone."

"A virtue," I said jokingly.

"A gift."

"I miss you."

"I miss you too."

"Do you think it will be over soon?"

"Hopefully."

"Will it ever be over for good? Even if I do eliminate Devon, another malefactor will take his place, won't it?" I yawned. I thought that having Julius next to me would keep me wide awake, but it had the opposite effect. It felt so right, so natural to have his arms wrapped around me that his presence was slowly putting me to sleep.

"Unless we find a way to keep the gates from ever opening at all, there will always be sentinels and malefactors." His tone was solemn, and before I drifted off to sleep once again, I wished I hadn't brought it up - I'd been sad enough for the both of us lately.

Julius was gone in the morning, which didn't surprise me in the least. What was surprising was the fact that I was relieved by his absence. I was glad that he hadn't fallen asleep next to me and forgotten to leave. It would have frightened me to know that his love for me could muddle his judgment.

I wasn't ready to leave the bed just yet though. I rolled over, pressing my face into the pillow where his head had rested, trying to inhale his scent. Finally, I gave into reason and got out of bed. The longer I lie there, the longer the day would go, and I hated the thought of an extension of time.

I did feel much better this morning. Seeing Julius the night before left me glowing.

Daniel noticed my better mood at once, happy with himself for giving me a pep talk that seemed to be working. "You know," he said in his deep Irish accent, "I thought at first that you might be a thorn in my side. I hated the thought of having to entertain someone, but I don't think you're too much different than I am in that respect. You don't mind being alone when you have to, do you?"

I didn't look up at him while I buttered my toast. "I was kind of getting used to being invisible, right before Julius showed up. My family kind of retreated inside themselves when Devon went missing."

He nodded. "Aye. I remember the feeling."

You're still living in the feeling, I thought to myself, and I wondered why he never took to Cordele the way Nayana and Julius had. Was it guilt? Did he feel as if he didn't deserve to have any type of companion at all because he wasn't able to save his wife?

Daniel interrupted my thoughts. "The river's going to be great for fishing today. You're welcome to come along if you like."

I contemplated his invitation for a moment before accepting. I'd only been fishing once before, and I liked it well enough if I remembered right. Also, I figured that if Devon's army were hiding out in watch, it wouldn't hurt to let them see us together. "Sure," I said, and I couldn't help but wonder if Daniel was thinking the same way I was.

The river was beautiful, but the fog was thick and chilly. I didn't mind baiting my own hook, but my fingers were shaking from the unexpected cold, so Daniel volunteered to do it for me rather than watch me struggle. He didn't act as if he minded, but I hoped I wouldn't get it snagged too soon, I didn't want to have to interrupt him while he was in the middle of his peaceful excursion.

As it turned out, I caught a fairly large fish after having my line in the water for only five minutes. Daniel helped me reel it in, and the excitement on his face was well worth the trip. I tossed the fish, a bass, back into the river easily, then settled back into the small motor boat and baited my hook myself.

"Loraine liked the river," Daniel said after a few minutes of silence. "We brought Margaret here when we had her with us. Every Sunday after church she packed a basket of food for us and we'd lay a quilt under an old tree. We'd eat our lunch and Margaret would throw bits of food out for the ducks. Those were the happiest times of my life, and I think of them every time I come here."

I waited for him to say something more, but when he didn't, I spoke up. "I'm not looking forward to it. The four of you - your stories - are gut-wrenching. It doesn't seem fair, to save the world only to live forever with the horrible memories of what you left behind. I think about my parents all the time. How long will it be before they start to notice that I don't age? They've already lost a son, what will happen to them when they have to lose me too? I can't imagine the devastation they'll go through. It's my biggest fear." I laughed at the irony of the situation. "I have the potential to save the world, but I'll kill my parents' spirits in the process."

"Aye. It can make you bitter if you let it. When you read the newspaper and you hear about a man who burned his family alive, or a mother who threw her newborn in the trash, or a young man on trial for beating his own brother to death, it makes you angry. You read these stories and think, 'I saved these people - these wretched, evil people,' and you wonder why you were ever created in the first place. Why is it so important to save these people?

"But then you remember the people you know, the people you love, you imagine the smile on the face of a child, and the laughter of an elderly couple as they reminisce about the old days, and you know why you were created. All the doubt is erased in those moments."

I smiled. "I'll always remember this day. I don't know that I've ever seen a more beautiful place than this."

"I've been around for three hundred and sixty years, Gabby, and I've never found a more beautiful spot. Of course, I'm a little biased. The River Liffey and I share a history."

That night, I fell asleep not bitter about missing Julius, but happy that by being here I was keeping him safe.

I was shaken awake once again before dawn, and my memories of Julius's visit the night before put a smile on my face. But the more lucid I became, the more I was aware of the urgency that was forcing me to open my eyes.

"Gabby, get up! It's time!" Daniel was still attempting to shake me even as I was rising.

"What do I do?" I asked, the fright in my voice apparent as I jumped from the bed.

"I've already called the others; they'll be here as soon as they can get everyone gathered up. Stay in this room until they get here."

Our words were coming in rapid stage whispers, the conversation filled with panicked inflections.

"What? The remorseful ones and the other recruits aren't

here yet?" How were they going to get here in time?

"Everyone's here in Ireland, it's just a matter of convincing them that what we've planned is for the best."

I understood immediately. The others were only willing to fight if they knew they weren't being used. I promised I would fight in the frontlines, and they weren't happy with the change of plans. They didn't trust us now.

"I have to go with you," I said, not taking into consideration any other alternatives.

"No! We have to stick with the plan!"

"If I don't go, the others won't fight. Besides, I have immunity. No one's going to hurt me. And anyway, I thought part of the plan was for them to see me here."

"They already have! Why do you think they're here? Besides, anything could happen, Gabby!" Daniel wasn't trying to keep his voice down any longer. "Just because they aren't supposed to hurt you doesn't mean there can't be an accident! Stay put!"

My heart was racing as he left the room, and I shuddered as I heard the front door slam behind him ominously.

I pulled my jeans on hastily, and pulled the stretched-out hair bind from my pocket, tying my hair up in a thick knot on the back of my head. I pulled my tennis shoes on quickly, tying the laces in double knots for good measure.

I ran to the front door, peeking out the window at the horrifying scene. Daniel was doing a good job with one of Devon's recruits, kicking him under the chin repeatedly until the man's body fell limp on the dew covered grass.

Daniel's recruits seemed to have Devon's outnumbered, and even though it took everything I had not to open that door, I promised myself I would only deviate from the original plan if things started to go downhill.

My fingernails dug into my palms as I balled my hands into fists, the anxiety that flooded through me my dominant emotion.

Daniel took a kick to the face, and then retaliated with five or six punches to the gut. Another one found him as the first one fell, but this one didn't even attempt an infliction before Daniel's closed fist came down hard on the top of his head, leaving the enemy cold and stunned on top of the first and second one.

Please come, please come, I thought to myself as Julius, Cordele and Nayana entered my thoughts.

I bit my fist as I chanced a glance outside and saw Daniel fall to his knees when someone from Devon's army kicked him hard in the stomach. Just as I reached for the knob, he composed himself long enough to punch the guy in the nose with extreme force, knocking him out cold.

Some of Daniel's recruits were down, showing no signs of getting up again. I tried to count, but with the bodies of so many of Devon's army lying around as well, it was hard to tell who was who. *A dozen of our guys' maybe?* I couldn't tell for sure.

At some point, I became aware of a dull rumbling, slow and quiet at first but gaining momentum. It was a familiar feeling, and when I felt the house shaking I was finally able to place the memory. The last time I experienced this, I had been in Kentland with Julius. It was an earthquake.

Instinctively, I fell to my knees and crawled under the coffee table, seeking shelter from the inevitable shrapnel that the house was sure to become. As the house shook, however, I became aware that it wasn't coming down around me, and the rumbling, while still in existence, had dispersed.

I made my way out from under my inept shelter and looked out the window again, discovering that what I thought had been an earthquake was actually the reinforcements the others had persuaded to come.

I sighed with relief as I realized the numbers. I knew this couldn't be all of them, that there were some who refused to come, but the amount that did was staggering. Thousands of remorseful ones were fighting on our behalf, mingled with a couple of faces I recognized.

I gasped as I noticed Evan and Travis. I knew Evan was a

recruit, but it still surprised me to see him in the middle of battle. Travis's appearance nearly threw my body into shock, though. Did April know about this? She would be inconsolable if something were to happen to him.

I scanned the crowd for Julius, my body shaking when I wasn't able to find him, but my anxiety eased a bit when I saw Nayana, small and beautiful, fighting with more expertise than a full grown man who'd been professionally trained in martial arts.

The sound was deafening. Screams of agony pierced the night sky, leaving goose bumps on my skin and knots in my stomach.

I wondered momentarily about the citizens of Dublin. How was this going on without their knowledge? I would have to ask the others when this was all over.

I wanted so badly for this to be finished, for my friends to defeat our enemies, and I suddenly became aware of the tears that were streaming down my face as I looked out at the people risking their lives to save the planet from the most horrible state it could ever come to be in.

I could think of nothing worse than what was happening right at this moment, and I cringed when I realized that if I couldn't eliminate Devon, the world would be so much worse than the scene that was playing out in Daniel's small section of the earth right now.

Finally, I screamed with relief as I saw Julius lift two men at once and slam them into the ground, their bodies sinking into the soft soil. My heart leapt at the sight of him, and I wanted nothing more than to run to him now.

My moment of relief was only temporary. The moment he injured the two men, three more took their place. I watched in agonizing disbelief as they ambushed Julius from behind, knocking him out and dragging his wilted body beyond my vision.

I screamed in horror, slumping over against the door as the pain in my chest suggested my heart was being shredded into a million tiny pieces.

My hand was on the doorknob now, ready to tear the door from its hinges and sprint to Julius's side, offering my defenses.

There was no need, however. Just as I was about to betray the promise I'd made to the others, Devon's army retreated, carrying their wounded away with them, leaving their dead behind.

Impulsively, I scanned the faces of our army as I made my way through the crowd, looking for Julius and the others.

Travis grabbed my arm mid-stride, as I made my way through the cool mist of the early morning, my feet flying upward from the momentum of my run. I was on the ground, unhurt, and too worried to mention it anyway. "Where's Julius?" My face was twisted with fear, and the grievous look on Travis's face caused my heart rate to increase.

"Gabby, maybe you should come with me," he said consolingly.

"NO!" I screamed, a hundred heads turning in my direction. "I want to see him now!"

"At the end of the right field," he said, dropping his head.

The insinuation in Travis's words left my body numb, my eyes stinging from the tears that threatened to spill down my cheeks. *Not Julius, please not Julius!* The rhythm of my feet pounded out every syllable as I ran with a swiftness that was powered by concentrated adrenaline.

The sun was rising, peeking through the trees at the edge of the field, blinding me intermittently as I leaped over wounded bodies in pursuit of the one hope I held on to.

I tripped over someone as I ran, a sickening moan escaping the portly man as the toe of my left foot jabbed him in the ribs. Hastily I touched him, willing him to heal, but not sticking around to see if it worked. I felt sorry for him, but I had to find Julius before my mind would allow me to do anything else.

Finally, I found the edge of the field, and the scene that I witnessed made my stomach lurch. I fell to my knees slowly, the bile in my throat flowing from me involuntarily.

There, on the edge of the field, silhouetted against the early morning sun, was a body, limp and lifeless, and hovering over it were three people - my people.

A sharp ringing sounded through my ears as my head began to spin, and my body became heavy. The last thought that ran through my mind before the darkness overcame me was, *not my Julius*.

Chapter 15❖

"Gabby, can you hear me?"

The warm hands that cradled my face were unwelcome. I preferred the dark abyss of nothingness to the sharp pain of this horrific reality. "*Julius, Julius,*" I groaned, the pain in my chest growing unbearable with every syllable of his name.

"That's right, it's Julius. Can you open your eyes for me?"

How cruel this world could be. How selfish this person was, to ask for my lucidity by offering painful lies and distressing trickery. I would never open my eyes; never accept the reality that Julius was gone.

"Please, Gabby. If you don't let me know you're okay, we're going to have to use the hum on you, and given the current situation, it's going to put a huge strain on us."

I'd heard this voice before, knew it from somewhere. It sounded familiar, but the cracks and moroseness in it were all wrong. Suddenly, realization set in, and I allowed my eyes to flutter open.

Even through the bruises and the blood that was dried to his forehead, even through the darkness that was in his eyes now and the tightness in his jaw, I saw him, beautiful and alive. My Julius. They saved him, brought him back to me, to us, and the cry that escaped my throat now was one of happiness.

I touched his face, testing reality, and he winced from the pain. I was confused. If they fixed him, why were his wounds still there? How was it that his face was gnarled into an expression of hurt?

I sat up slowly, not wanting to faint again, and looked in his eyes.

He was using our unspoken language to answer my questions, telling me through his mournful expression of the grave news. He couldn't hold my gaze for long. Tears were welling in his eyes and he looked away.

I understood immediately. It wasn't Julius's body that had been lying in the field, it was Daniel's.

Guilt washed through me with the potency akin to being punched in the gut by a full grown man. I should have helped him before the others came. I shouldn't have let him convince me to stay in the house. I shouldn't have ignored him while I was staying in his home. I should have thanked him for letting me stay with him.

Tears spilled down my cheeks, dangling from my chin until they fell with little splashes against my chest. I remembered the words he spoke to me the night I asked him to tell me about his story, and a new emotion ripped through me, harsh and unbelievably poignant.

He didn't want to be fixed.

"Stupid old man," Julius sputtered angrily, seeming to read my mind. "This is what we're here for, to save lives, and he wouldn't even let us do that for him."

I grabbed Julius's hand. "He missed Loraine so much. He felt so guilty for not saving her. He didn't want to have to go on for the rest of eternity knowing for sure that it could have been done." I remembered the way I felt a few short minutes ago when I thought Julius had died. "He was right, if we had saved him, he wouldn't have been a sentinel any longer - the pain of knowing would have prevented him from being able to function that way."

Julius nodded. "I know. When I saw you lying here in the field, I thought you'd joined the fight. I thought you were…" He trailed off, unwilling to say the words out loud. "I've never felt so useless, so helpless in all my life."

I wrapped my arms around his neck, and rested my head on his shoulder. "I thought it was you in the field. I saw those three men knock you out and drag you away, and when I ran into Travis, the way he was talking to me…"

Julius rubbed the back of my arm. "Shh. We're both okay. Let's focus on Daniel now. That's the only thing we can do."

We stood at the same time, using one another for support, and then slowly trudged through the field to meet Cordele and Nayana.

Nayana threw herself into my legs and wrapped herself around them the moment she saw me. She was sobbing quietly, her small frame shaking against me. I picked her up, consoling her the way a child should be, letting her bury her face in my hair as she cried. Never had she seemed so helpless and childlike. Her pain sent tears cascading down my face, wishing there was something I could do to alleviate her grief.

Cordele's red rimmed eyes never swayed from Daniel's body, and I knew he was torturing himself over his decision to follow through with Daniel's wishes. How could he not feel guilty about that? It was one of the most powerful human emotions, and we were all feeling it right now.

He swallowed back tears unsuccessfully, the majority of them landing with little pats against his stiff, beige overcoat. "I don't know where his wife and child were buried," he managed to choke out, "but he loved his home, the nature that surrounded it, especially the River Liffey. We'll find a spot for him somewhere out here." He inhaled deeply, his chin quivering as he tried to take a cleansing breath. "Let's carry him to the back of the house for now. I don't like the thought of him out in the open like this."

Carrying Daniel's dead body back to the house filled the four of us with the deepest sense of sorrow we'd ever known. For me, not even Devon's initial disappearance or being informed of his death and eternal life in Hell inflicted heartache such as this. This was one of our own, the loss of one of the scarcest, rarest creatures on Earth, an unexpected and tragic deficit to our kind.

We cleared the workbench in his shed and placed him on top of it, which gave us all an eerie feeling. He fit it perfectly, and the four of us hovering over top of him made me think of an autopsy. I grimaced at the thought, goose bumps trailing down my spine as the gruesome image entered my mind before I could stop it.

Cordele cleared his throat. "I think somewhere near the bank of the river would be nice. Maybe a spot close to where he kept his boat."

Cordele's bereft tone was too much for Nayana. She buried her face in Julius's stomach and wept into his shirt, allowing him to wrap one of his arms around her torso and cradle her head with the other. "Shh," he whispered, fighting back his own grievous sobs.

The scene before me was brutal; a mass of sadness so deep in nature that it almost became a tangible object, a repugnant entity whose sole purpose was to invoke lamentation and mourning. It was as if we had inadvertently created the opposite of our orb, and the thought sickened me.

I wiped the newest of my tears away from my face and released a quivering sigh. "When?" I asked, without looking up.

"As soon as possible. We don't have much more time to waste. Devon's army retreated only because they reached their objective. It won't be long until they're under new orders." Cordele's expression was hard, an anomaly on his normally kind face.

At these words, Nayana spun to face him, her eyes fierce. "Why wait? Let's go after *them*; they would never expect it. Besides, we shouldn't be allowing those monsters time to celebrate."

Julius shook his head. "We were too unprepared this time. We took our army for granted and got here too late. Let's not allow our emotions to get in the way of logic. We need better tactics."

"I agree. And this time, no one can convince me not to fight. It's my fault most of our recruits didn't show up. I should have kept my word to them." I dropped my head in shame.

"That fault doesn't belong to you, Gabby, and this is no time to be placing blame." Cordele looked back down at Daniel's body. "We'll leave him here while we dig the grave. He preferred solitude; I don't want to begrudge him that now."

I led the way to the spot where Daniel kept his boat. Cordele hadn't been fishing with him in quite some time and couldn't remember the way.

It was Julius who suggested a spot on the hill east to the river. Flooding wasn't uncommon, and we all cringed when he brought this up.

It was a beautiful plot; the view of the river was breathtaking.

When we were agreed that this was the place for Daniel's interment, we each started digging with the shovels we brought along from the shed.

The task took longer than we intended; each of us knowing that the faster it was done, the sooner we would never see Daniel again. On one hand, it was a labor of love, the final act of kindness for a dear friend, but from the other perspective, we shouldn't *have* to be doing this, and that thought created fury within the four of us.

We all sat around the grave when it was finished, the noon sun warm on our faces, the dried sweat, blood, and tears sticking to us uncomfortably. No one said anything for a long time. Everyone was wishing for more time, wishing for the preservation of our stability. But we couldn't put it off forever, so with a nod from Cordele an hour after we finished our unpleasant job, we trekked down the hill and across the field until we reached the shed.

I tried not to look at him when we stepped into the cool shade of the shed. I tried to separate myself from this moment, to consider this a task and nothing more. The emotions that would flood through me, through all of us, when the time came to put him to rest in the makeshift grave would come all too soon, and I tried to preserve what little calmness I had left until it was no longer containable.

Tenderly we lifted Daniel's body from his temporary resting spot on the workbench. The strength that was usually reserved for moments of defense applied to this moment, perhaps because by burying one of our own, we were defending his honor.

The hike back was long, but not as tedious as I expected, and by the time we reached Daniel's final resting spot, none of us had even broken a sweat.

Gently, we released him into the cool, damp hole in the ground, the weightiness of his body causing the soil to cradle his frame, as if the earth were hugging him in welcome.

At last I allowed myself to look at Daniel's face, and the serenity that seemed to be there was undeniable. It was almost as if his final expression was one of gratitude, a silent thank-you to the four of us for complying with his final wishes, and in that moment, the guilt I had felt earlier was washed from my system. That we had done the right thing by allowing him to perish was unquestionable now. Somewhere in the universe he was reuniting with his wife and child, and he was happy.

The dam I had built to keep my emotions away broke then, a torrential flood of suffering filling every crevice of my system. I did not feel sorrow for my friend, but my own selfish grief at knowing I would never see his face on this plane of existence, never hear his rich accent, and never get to spend another quiet morning on the river with him again.

Nayana's soft sobs pierced the quiet reflection we had all had delved into, giving our bereavement a voice. No longer could we hide our woeful tears from one another. Together we wept, a unit of grief. The loss of our friend was great, and each tear that fell from our cheeks and was absorbed by the soil that had become host to the body of our comrade was like a talisman, offering love to the one who had fallen.

"I think it's time to say a few words," Cordele managed to choke out between dispersed breaths.

Nayana, Julius and I turned our attention to him, wiping away our tears to make way for the new ones which were sure to come with his words.

"Daniel was much more than just a good man. He was a treasured friend, an exceptional asset, and a loyal comrade in arms. His devotion to our cause was second only to the memory of his family, love being his highest and most admiring quality. It is love which is at the core of life itself - that which created not only us, as sentinels, but every being and creature known to mankind and beyond - the fundamental justification of our very existence. Daniel hosted love with a greatness not to be outdone by any, and equaled by few.

"His death is not his loss, but ours, for I am certain that God has a place for him - a place where love is not an emotion, but a state of being, and in that great state, there is no sorrow, no guilt, no grief, no pain that can penetrate the walls of his deserved sanctuary. There is only happiness for him now.

"Good-bye, our dear friend, we will keep you in our hearts forever, and always remember what you taught us - love is the key." He stifled a sob as he tossed a handful of dirt into the hole.

We each took a moment after that to say our own words before throwing our own handful of soil in the grave.

"I will always remember your bravery. You will forever be a legend to me," Julius said quietly.

"I love the way you were always in your truest form, never afraid to be who you were. It was an admirable quality that I will always remember you for." Tears streaked down Nayana's cheeks as she tossed in her bit of earth.

I sighed when I closed in on the grave once more. What could I say that hadn't already been said? "Thank you for telling me about yourself. And thank you for the fishing trip. You helped me see things from a different perspective - gave me a reason to hope for the best, even when it seems there isn't any room for it." I tossed my handful of dirt and backed away quickly, joining the others in an embrace before we finished the burial.

The next few days were the hardest. Cordele and Nayana stayed with Julius and me at the apartment in Cleveland. Not knowing when or where the next attack would be left us at a disadvantage, and we figured there was a better chance of survival if we all stuck together.

The atmosphere that surrounded us there was always quiet, each of us in our own separate mode of mourning. Even though we were cramped for space, it was as if none of us noticed each other's existence.

In the few instances in which we did become aware of one another, it was always easy to tell when someone was thinking of Daniel. A quivering chin, a thoughtful smile, or a morose sigh were always telltale signs.

A week after Daniel's death, however, Cordele woke us all up at seven in the morning, offering coffee to Julius and I, and orange juice to Nayana. It was a huge surprise to see him in such an eager spirit. He took Daniels death...not harder, but...differently than the rest of us.

"Enough of this useless moping. Daniel would be offended by it. We need to find out what Devon's army is up to," he said, making it sound more like an order than a suggestion.

"How are we supposed to do that? They're scattered all over the place, and the only thing they care about is Devon. Pulling them out of the woodwork is pretty impossible." Julius was groggy, talking through a yawn.

Cordele scrunched his face. "Nothing is impossible, Julius, we just need bait, something that will draw his army to us."

I sat up from the couch which Nayana and I had been sharing. "What he wants more than anything is me."

"Naturally. But that isn't going to help us this time. It's been a week and you haven't opened the gates. This time, they won't stop at just one of us; they'll want to eliminate everyone *but* you. If getting rid of us one at a time isn't working for him, he's sure to assume that getting us all out of the way at once will."

I froze at Cordele's words. This was a situation which I had never envisioned. But as soon as he mentioned it, I recognized just how possible it was.

I started thinking about all the things Devon would do to try to lure me to him, putting myself in his place.

He would start with the others, and when that didn't work, he would do the same to April and my parents. I suddenly realized that this was no longer just *our* fight; everyone I loved was at risk. The severity of the situation hit me with tremendous force right then, and the necessity of quick action was duly noted.

Suddenly, the pieces began to fall into place.

The reason why Daniel was really targeted.

The reason for the attack at Glesnevin Cemetery.

The meaning of the dream.

Why human emotions were so important.

All of it was starting to make sense to me, the cloud of confusion drifting away as desperation for an answer fueled my brain in every possible direction, searching for a solution.

I jumped from the couch, adrenaline pumping through my veins. "They don't know where the gates are, right?"

Cordele, Nayana and Julius all looked at me in confusion.

"No," Cordele answered, his eyebrow raised.

"And we don't either, right?"

"That's true." His voice raised in pitch, wondering what idea I had possibly come up with.

"Then we need to let them know we have no idea where it is. That will give us more time. Devon has to know I can't possibly find it on my own. He'll leave the rest of you alone once he realizes I need your help to find it."

Cordele's face fell, his hope that I had come up with something we could use lost.

"Gabby, the gates are irrelevant. You know that. Looking for them won't make any difference. Even if we did find them, there would be no way we could open them. Like you said, they would win by default." Julius slumped back into the bed.

"I don't want to find them; I don't even want to look for them. I'm just trying to buy us a little more time until I can figure out a way to destroy the key."

Chapter 16❖

My heart was pounding so hard I could feel my pulse in my neck.

Cordele's eyes were wide with awe; the meaning of my words seeping into his mind quickly. "Of course," he managed in a reverent whisper. "Destroying the key. How could that never have occurred to me?"

"I only mentioned the key to you once, and we ended up getting side-tracked, remember?"

Cordele began ruffling his thin hair as he paced the floor. "Is it really that effortless though? Destroying the key would definitely prevent the gates from ever opening again, but surely it can't be that simple."

Julius interrupted. "Cordele's right. It can't be that easy. Devon would never have given you that key if all you had to do was destroy it. There has to be more to it than that."

I shook my head. "You're wrong, in a sense. Devon didn't

give me that key - Daniel did."

Cordele stopped walking abruptly. "What?"

"He found it while he was researching. He tried to destroy it, knowing that by doing so, the gates would never open again, but he could never find out how to do it; it's made up of some kind of metal I've never even seen.

"The underworld knew he had it, but there was nothing they could do until Devon woke up. That's why he went straight to Hell instead of trying to kill me immediately. They needed to use *him* as bait. The key doesn't just *unlock* the gates, it *locks* them too. They want the key destroyed as badly as we do, but they want to make sure the gates are open first. If someone actually did unlock the gates for them, the first thing the underworld would do would be to destroy the key so they could never be imprisoned again."

Julius's mouth was hanging open, and he was struggling to make his body catch up with his mind and ask the question that was nagging at him. "What makes you...How did you...?"

"How did I figure it out?"

He nodded.

"Well, a few different ways. I was thinking about how Cordele said, 'love is the key,' which somehow triggered the thought of the key, I guess. And then there's the dream."

"You figured it out?" Nayana's eyes were bright with wonder; she loved hearing about the metaphysical aspects of life.

I nodded. "Remember the orb we made?" I continued without waiting for an answer. "Well I don't know why it hasn't occurred to me before now - maybe because I was frightened of it in the dream - but somehow it dawned on me that even in the dream it was *us*. I was dreaming that the orb was giving me something- secrets and knowledge, but Daniel dreamed that it was taking something from his mind. I realized that this was it - I was dreaming of him, and he was dreaming of me - he was passing the secret on to me."

"That's why Daniel was targeted. They knew he had the key,

and they wanted it back. They knew he hadn't found a way to destroy it, because Devon became a malefactor, and they were hoping he hadn't mentioned the key to the rest of us at all. If they killed him before he got a chance to tell anyone, it would give them enough time to find it before we ever even knew about it."

When I looked over at Cordele, his face was long, his eyebrows low on his forehead. "Why didn't he tell anyone? If he'd said something…"

My heart dropped as I caught on to his train of thought. If the four of them had worked together on it to find a solution before things got out of hand, Daniel would still be alive.

I bent down to him and squeezed his hand. "You know how Daniel felt about the way his malefactor was eliminated. He thought he won by a technicality, that he hadn't actually accomplished what he was created for. He wanted a second chance to make it right. He needed to try to do it himself. And when he couldn't figure it out, he was too ashamed to tell the rest of you, so he gave it to me, hoping I would mention it and we could all figure it out together with no one ever knowing he'd had it in his possession once."

"But you did mention it," Julius said, still not convinced.

"Yes, the very day you told me I was a sentinel, but Daniel wasn't there. And when it was never mentioned to *him*, he probably assumed that I hadn't found it yet."

Cordele exhaled a deep, sad sigh that signaled the acceptance of a difficult truth. "But why the attack on Glasnevin?"

"I think maybe his family is buried there. He had to have spent a lot of time there for Devon's army to assume that's where they might find him. Maybe they thought he hid the key there?"

Cordele nodded. "He already had a few of the headstones fixed by the time I arrived. When I offered to help him in that same area he shooed me away. I thought he was just being stubborn."

Nayana smiled. "He *was* stubborn."

The corner of Cordele's mouth turned upward slowly. "Yes - yes he was."

Julius interjected then. "Wait - won't they know you have the key when we let them know we're looking for the gates? Once they do, they aren't going to give us time - they're going to try to kill us."

"They're going to try to kill us anyway, Julius. They know I spent at least the last week of Daniel's life with him, and they didn't find the key. I'd bet my life that they think I have it anyway. But if we tell them we're looking for the gates, they might think I'm going to open them, so they'll leave us alone."

"I agree with Julius, Gabby," Nayana said. "They aren't going to believe you're planning to open the gates. They might even assume it would be best to kill you. I'm not sure they're aware of what would happen if they did. It's possible they could theorize another malefactor would be created. It would be a win-win situation for them."

It was Cordele's turn to talk now. "I don't believe they killed Daniel in hopes that the secret of the key would die with him. They had to assume that as long as he knew of its existence, the rest of us did too. I think they killed him as a warning to the rest of us. If we flaunt the key in their faces, they'll come after us harder than they did before."

I sighed in frustration. "So it's inevitable that there will be another attack, they have free reign to kill us all, and there's nothing we can do about it?"

"Not exactly nothing," Julius said. "We could always go back to our old tactics - using them against each other."

"How so?" Cordele was interested.

"What if we found a way for them to hand Devon over?"

"Is that even possible?" I asked. "I thought you said once he was in there, he couldn't come back out."

Cordele's face lightened once again. "He's a human soul - he can come and go as he pleases."

"But you said souls were unstable without a body. And how could I go about eliminating a soul?"

Julius shrugged. "It would have to find a body."

A smile etched its way onto Cordele's face, and I hoped he wasn't thinking what I thought he was.

"Please don't tell me we're going to go grave robbing."

It was odd, being back at Daniel's house. We were all talking at once, which is what gave it an eerie feeling; Daniel's house was never this loud.

"When do you think they'll be here?" I asked. Waiting was the worst part.

"Curtis said he couldn't promise us anything - he's not sure they trust him anymore." Julius was the one who came up with this idea.

Curtis curled up in the fetal position the moment he saw him, screaming that he hadn't been at the battle; hadn't been the one to kill our friend.

"But they didn't kill him - that's something, right?" Nayana always had a way of making the obvious seem funny somehow.

"We still can't be sure they won't," Cordele said with a smile.

Just then we heard something outside, and Cordele got up to look out the window. "They're here," he said.

"How many of them?" Julius asked, blocking me from view. He wasn't sure if they were convinced of what would happen if they killed me, and he wanted to keep me safe until he was certain they understood.

"Five. That's one more than us, and Curtis is with them."

My blood ran cold as the three of them stepped out of the house, leaving me inside. There were only five of them, not enough to cause any real damage, but it still made me uneasy to know how close we were to the enemy.

"This better be good," I heard a high-pitched, female voice say.

"That depends on what your definition of good is," Nayana retorted. I could hear the anger in her voice, and I hoped she could keep it under control.

"Good would be your youngest sentinel incinerated in our father's prison."

I could almost hear the blood in Julius's veins go from a calm simmer to a rapid boil. "That will *never* happen. Not only because we won't allow it, but because your malefactor has made it impossible." His voice was full of anger, but I had to admit, not killing her on the spot proved his self control.

"We aren't as convinced about that as you seem to be."

"But convinced enough to come here tonight." I rolled my eyes at Nayana's obvious haughtiness.

Why didn't the two of them just shut up and let Cordele talk? He was so much nicer than that.

It dawned on me then that that was *why* he'd kept silent. These sorts of people didn't respond to kindness. They would have considered his soft approach as a weakness and milked it for all it was worth.

The woman made a sound similar to a snarl.

"The only way you could possibly benefit from the death of our sentinel would be for her malefactor to do it himself. If our sentinel is killed by someone other than her own malefactor, that will put an end to the entire cycle. We win, you lose. Hell is kept under lock and key for all eternity and there's nothing you can do about it, except maybe spend that infinite span of time being tortured by your...*father* for being the ones to ruin a great opportunity for him." Julius's tone was thick with smugness.

A faint gasp escaped the female, which she quickly tried to recover from. "I don't believe you. A malefactor has never died by the hands of their own sentinel, and yet, they still continue to be born. Besides, why would you care? If it's true your world would be better off if we killed her, then why would you try to convince us to spare her? The fact that you are desperate enough to negotiate with us makes me suspicious. There is obviously an ulterior motive."

"Our world is always better with someone like her in it. We happen to love her enough to selfishly want her to live. It doesn't surprise me that you wouldn't understand love, but I'm sure selfishness is a term you can understand?" Cordele was trying to his best to sound sinister, but he wasn't doing a great job of it. I could only assume that the reason he'd interjected when he did was so Julius didn't have to say the word *love* when he spoke of me. It would have been too obvious and ended up as a weapon in their hands.

"And just so you know, if we could figure out a way to kill our malefactors without any help, they wouldn't ever be *born* again. The reason they continue being created is because we can't find a way to do it ourselves. Aren't you aware of the opposite factor?" I could almost feel the glare in Nayana's eyes as she spoke.

The evil woman tapped her toes against the wooden porch, contemplating what she had just been told. After a few seconds, she spoke up. "What do you think, Blondie?"

She was speaking to Curtis, and my posture stiffened. If she didn't trust him, it wouldn't matter what he said - any response from him could turn fatal.

"If they're right and we kill the youngest one, we'll never be able to prove ourselves. If we pull Devon out, there *is* a chance he'll defeat her; we'll be seen as heroes. If we pull him out and she defeats him, another malefactor *will* be created. I don't think we should take the chance of killing her." Curtis's voice was barely above a whisper, and I hoped the woman was too self absorbed to hear the fear in it.

Another moment of toe-tapping went by.

"What about the rest of you? Do you agree with Blondie here?"

Everyone was mumbling at once. I couldn't tell what they were saying, but evidently they all agreed with Curtis, because I heard an irritated sigh escape the woman's throat.

"Fine," the woman said tartly. "We will bring Devon to you. Blondie will let you know when."

I heard her heals against the porch as she turned to leave.

"And a body - preferably fresh. Devon can't fight without one," Julius reminded her.

"But don't kill anyone! There are plenty of morgues!" I had to laugh at Cordele for that one.

They didn't come back in the house until they were sure Devon's mutinous minions were gone.

"It sounded like it went well. Do you think they'll actually follow through with it?" My fingers were curled around my mouth as I gushed my words out in one breath.

Julius shrugged. "I can't see how they won't, they're too afraid of what would happen if they killed you. Plus they're extremely self-centered. Every single one of them would do anything to get noticed by that wretched beast they call their father. It's unbelievably disgusting."

"I think Julius is right, but let's not get ahead of ourselves. Devon was made for trickery; it's possible he could find a way to turn this around." Even as he said the words, Cordele didn't believe them. He was confident they would bring Devon to us.

"Even if they don't bring him out, we still bought a little bit of time," Nayana said reassuringly.

"All we have to do now is figure out how to destroy the key," I said sarcastically. If Daniel hadn't found out how it was done, I didn't see how we were going to be able to do it.

"Preferably before you eliminate Devon," Cordele added. "Another malefactor could still be created in the meantime, and we want to prevent that if at all possible."

I turned my head away from him before he could see the doubt on my face.

"Gabby, I think it's time you brought us the key," Julius said.

"You're right, Gabby, it's made from something I don't

recognize at all."

We were back at Julius's apartment, and Cordele was holding the key up to the light, turning it over and over, giving it a thorough examination.

"Daniel would have tried to destroy it in every normal way first. I wish we knew the other ideas he came up with that didn't work, though. It would save us a lot of time if we didn't have to go through the same things he did." Julius was looking over Cordele's shoulder, trying to get a look at the key himself.

"Yes, well, assuming he tried bashing it with hammers and roasting it with propane torches, we'll have to think of something less obvious," Cordele said before handing the key over to Julius with a defeated shrug.

"Heat obviously wouldn't do the trick," Nayana offered. "It is the key to Hell. Maybe we should try ice?"

"How would freezing it help? It would still be whole, wouldn't it?" Julius said with disbelief.

"Maybe it would help. Maybe the jewels on there would crack or something. If we got those off, the key wouldn't be in its entirety anymore. I wonder if that counts." I was trying to make Nayana feel better with my suggestion.

"I don't think it necessarily has to be in its entire form. As long as it still unlocks the gates it will be in working order, but that's just my opinion. But perhaps it wouldn't hurt to try it Nayana's way." Cordele said.

Julius headed to the freezer with the key, and then stopped. "Should we just...stick it in there? Or should we try freezing it in ice?"

"Fill up a cup with water and put the key in it before you stick it in the freezer. It would probably be more effective," Nayana said, although I could tell from her tone that even she was doubtful.

We thawed it out the next morning, giving it enough time to freeze solid. I have to admit I was a little hopeful. We were all anxious to see what happened, but as the ice slowly melted, we were filled with disappointment. Nothing about the key had changed.

"What should we try next?" Julius asked when it was obvious the ice didn't work.

"There has to be a way of melting it," I said. "How else would it have been made?"

"I have a feeling that nothing short of the temperature from the surface of the sun could melt this key," Cordele said.

"We could try flattening it on a train track," Julius said. "I used to do it with pennies all the time."

This was definitely not your easy-to-mangle zinc and copper penny, but we all had hopes that the weight and force of the train could somehow render the key unusable. All it would take was a small dent and it wouldn't likely be able to fit in the hole.

We all agreed it was worth a shot, so the four of us bi-located back to Kentland when it was time for the train to come through.

Julius waited until he was sure the operator of the train couldn't see him before he raced to the track and placed the key on the rail.

My heart was pumping fast when he did this, fearful of what would happen to him if he wasn't quick enough. His stealth was phenomenal, though, and I was breathing again in a fraction of a second.

He hadn't even had time to turn back in our direction, though, when the wheel of one of the train cars ran over the key. We covered our ears when the ear-splitting screech sounded.

I'd never heard anything like it. My ears were in agony.

The train started to slow down, and before it could come to a complete stop, the noise had died down and Julius made a leap for the key, which was lying in the gravel now on the outer side of the track.

We were back in Cleveland seconds later.

"Okay, I'm just going to say it. That was the worst idea you've ever come up with."

Nayana was talking very loudly, her temporary deafness still fresh.

Julius rubbed his brow. "I deserved that. We almost lost the key under the train. I never thought about that."

"How does it look? Is there any damage?" Cordele's voice was hopeful.

Julius opened his palm and turned the key over repeatedly to inspect it.

"No. Not even a scratch." His voice was full of disappointment, and he dropped his head in exasperation.

"We'll just have to keep thinking. It might take awhile, but we're bound to come up with something," I said optimistically.

Over the next few days, we exhausted our minds of every idea we could come up with. Even though the train didn't work, we were desperate enough to try smashing it with a hammer. We knew it wouldn't work but we were out of ideas and refused to sit around doing nothing.

We stuck it in the broiler once, but that didn't work either, not that we were surprised. We didn't even check on it. Nayana just turned the oven off without even looking at it.

After a week of wasted efforts, we decided to stop spending our time trying things we knew wouldn't work and start thinking instead. We put the key out of sight in one of the light fixtures, forcing ourselves to come up with new ideas.

One evening, as we were eating pizza for dinner, Julius tossed his half-eaten slice back on his plate. Out of frustration he said, "Maybe one of us should swallow the damn key. Maybe our stomach acid would digest it."

He was being sarcastic, not meaning it at all, but his words caused a light to go on in my head. "Wait," I said, the idea I had starting to excite me, "It could work!"

Julius rolled his eyes at me. "No it couldn't, Gabby. I was just saying it to be stupid."

"I didn't mean swallowing it. I mean the four of us might be able to create something that *could* digest it!"

Nayana's eyes widened with this sudden epiphany. "The orb," she said reverently.

Cordele and Julius looked at one another as if trying to discern the other's thoughts on the subject.

"It's the best idea any of us has come up with. I think we should try it," Nayana said, her eyes alight with enthusiasm.

Julius pulled the key from the light fixture and set it on the coffee table. "How do we go about doing this? Should we put it on something a little higher up? The orb wasn't that low when we made it."

"Let's just put it on the empty floor in the open space first. If that doesn't work, we'll try it a different way," Nayana said, eager to get started.

"Do you think it will still be powerful enough?" Julius asked. "Do you think we'll still be able to do it?"

He was referring to the fact that Daniel would no longer be a part of the orb, and the four of us shared distressed glances.

What if it didn't work anymore?

"We'll find out soon enough," Cordele said, trying to sound cheerful. "What do you think, Gabby," he was asking as he carried the key to the open space, placing it in the middle of the floor, "you and Nayana across from one another? She's a bit small for such a direct shot from you."

Nayana shot him a glaring look that he refused to acknowledge.

Not wanting to hurt her feelings any further, I shrugged and said, "Whatever you think."

We all took a deep breath as we joined hands around the key, the apprehension we felt thick in the atmosphere.

I made eye contact with each of them, and one by one they nodded, signaling that they were ready.

I breathed through my nose and exhaled through my mouth before closing my eyes and invoking my hum.

Just as before, I was aware of everyone's unique currents running through my system in unison, a euphoric sensation that buzzed within me until my body was no longer able to contain it. The energy thrust itself forward then, and simultaneously merged with the energy of the others.

The hissing and crackling of electricity was like beautiful music, the most pleasant sound I had ever encountered, and it was this sound that made me open my eyes, eager to see the orb in all its magnificence.

I watched in awe as the tendrils of electricity danced all around us, the white-blue colors alive with energy, love in its purest form.

The feeling of happiness was so strong it was almost unbearable. I felt as if I didn't deserve this, that no one could deserve this incredible state of utopia.

An earsplitting crack erupted then, and I watched in awe as the orb imploded, becoming nothing more than a single strand of electricity that my eyes followed to the floor. In that same moment, the electricity was gone, the orb no longer existing, and with the gust of a gale force wind the key flew across the floor.

My heart sank when I heard a *plink* as it hit the baseboard of the wall. But a fraction of a second later, elation was coursing through me as I heard another plink.

The orb worked.

The key was now split into two separate parts, each one lying on opposite sides of the floor as if they were the polar ends of a magnet, forced apart by nature.

The four of us stood completely still, not breathing. We were trying to see both parts at once, trying to convince ourselves that this was really, truly, happening. We exchanged glances, asking each other if what we were seeing was an illusion or reality.

Finally, Cordele's expression changed from awe to relief, and he walked to the left side of the room and picked up half of the key.

I held my breath, waiting for the results of his examination. I was worried that it hadn't broken properly; that the ridges were still in place on the body of it, and the head of the key had been the part that detached. If that was the case, we would be back at square one, because it would still be able to unlock the gate.

"Oh, my," Cordele said, stunned.

My posture slumped in defeat. "It didn't work."

"Oh it worked. In fact, it did a much better job than I thought. Look." He held out his open palm, half of the key reflecting the light overhead.

Nayana, Julius and I all gasped at once when we saw it.

"But I distinctly heard two clatters," Nayana said.

Julius and I nodded in agreement.

"So did I, but I guess our ears deceived us," Cordele said, as he held out his half of the key, proving that it was broken into two sections.

Julius ran to over to the other half, still lying on the floor, and picked it up. "Same thing with this one," he said, smiling.

"Four parts," I whispered.

Julius grabbed my face and kissed me on the mouth. "I would have done that even if you weren't my girlfriend. You have to be one of the smartest people I've ever met in my life."

"I'll second that," Cordele said with a huge grin.

Chapter 17❖

I wiped the sweat from my forehead and tightened my ponytail. It was the end of July and Julius's apartment was sweltering, making this training session miserable.

"Let's all take a break," Nayana suggested. "You haven't eaten anything since breakfast Gabby, and all you had then was a piece of toast." Her voice was filled with worry, though she tried to hide it.

I knew what she was thinking, and I could feel Julius and Cordele's eyes on me as I slumped into the couch grumpily.

The others had never tired so easily, never broken a sweat this way. They were worried that something was wrong with me - with my internal makeup as a sentinel.

I heard them whispering about it at night after they thought I'd fallen asleep. They already had another plan in place - one I wasn't supposed to know about - to defeat Devon, just in case I wasn't able to do it.

They were worried this would happen. They thought I'd started to get cold feet, that my nerves were getting the best of me, and since I couldn't bring myself to tell them they were wrong, I pretended not to notice their concern.

"How about a baloney sandwich?" Julius offered.

My stomach turned at the thought of the wretched, pink, processed meat. "I hate baloney."

"You ate it yesterday," he said sourly.

"Because I didn't want to hurt your feelings. You already made it for me."

"Oh," he said. "Well, how about peanut butter and jelly?"

I rolled my eyes. "You don't have to make my lunch for me, Julius, I'm not a child." I made my way over to the refrigerator and pulled out the first thing I saw - a jar of olives. I didn't particularly want to eat them, but if they thought I grabbed them absentmindedly, their eyes would start darting back and forth again.

"Um, wouldn't you rather eat something with a little more...sustenance?" Nayana asked me timidly.

I struggled with the lid. "I'm really not all that hungry. Besides, all that sweating I did has me craving something salty." I finally won the battle with the jar, and I speared a few of the olives with a fork before shoving them into my mouth.

The room was quiet again as they gossiped silently with their eyes about my pitiful bout with the olive jar.

My neck started to heat up as my irritation rose.

"You know, Cordele, we really should go check on the house. Anything could have happened while we've been away," Nayana said, as if she were reading lines from a cue card.

"I don't think that's a bad idea," he agreed. Cordele wasn't much of an actor either. "See you in a bit."

I didn't even turn around to see if they were gone yet. I continued eating the olives, pretending as if I were really enjoying them.

"Gabby," Julius said, tugging lightly on the back of my tee-shirt, "I think we need to talk."

"About what, Julius?" I asked innocently. "About the fact that the three of you think I'm not strong enough? Or how about your theory that I have cold feet? There's always the topic of plan B - you know, the one where I sit on the sidelines while the three of you convince Curtis to kill Devon for me?"

"Gabby, I…"

I reeled around to face him. "You what, Julius? You didn't know I overheard you?" My innocent façade was gone, replaced with my actual state of irritation.

"No, that isn't what I was going to say," he said sternly. "I was going to say I don't know what has gotten into you."

I stiffened at his words, speechless.

After a few seconds, I pulled myself together. "I think I need some time alone, Julius."

He sighed morosely. "You think I don't know that? Don't you realize that I'd love to be able to give you that? But I can't, Gabby. We can't take the chance of leaving you all alone. Curtis and that woman could easily go back on their word, and what would happen if Devon's army came here and the rest of us weren't even given the chance to fight with you?"

For one brief moment, I wanted to point out that he thought I couldn't handle it on my own, but I immediately choked it back. All four of them were fighting when Daniel died, and I knew that Julius didn't mean that I couldn't handle myself. He meant he wouldn't be able to handle it if he wasn't there and something went wrong.

"I just need some time to think, Julius," I pleaded.

"I don't know how to say this without upsetting you, Gabby, so I'm just going to let it out the way I see it. You don't know what it's really like yet. I know right now you think you need to make a decision, but once you see him, you won't have a choice. It's your natural instinct, and it completely takes over. Thinking about it is irrelevant. It won't matter that you've spent every moment of your life contemplating what to do in that instant.

Everything in you will do what you're built for. Your mind will be screaming no, but your impulse will take over; you'll become a prisoner in your own body, and no amount of thinking will fix that." His hands were cupping my face now, consoling me as he admitted the disturbing facts he'd tried so hard to guard me from.

My eyes began to sting, and I hid my face in his chest so he wouldn't see my tears. "Will I?" I wished his words were true. I wished I would at least be able to blame my horrific urges on my body, to blame the wounds I would inflict on my brother on my instincts.

But I was different - they'd said it time and time again, and my biggest fear was that I would have nothing to rely on but my own logic. I was going to eliminate Devon - even had a plan on how to do it, thanks to Daniel - and what tortured me the most was the fact that even without the instincts I may be lacking, I was going to do it.

Could they have done it? If Cordele or Nayana or Julius didn't have the instincts it took to eliminate their malefactors, *would* they have done it?

What kind of person did it make me to know that I could? Even if I didn't come equipped with the same tools as the others did, I would still be able to eliminate my own brother, and that realization scared me more than anything else.

"I know you can do it, Gabs," Julius whispered in my ear, unaware that it was that exact fact that scared me the most.

I gulped back tears, not wanting him to get suspicious of my newest fear or the motivation behind it.

Instead, I pulled my head away from his chest and dried my eyes. "I love you, Julius."

"I love you too, Gabby," he said before kissing me. When he finally pulled away, he said, "I know you can't possibly be satisfied with olives. Let's go get something to eat."

That evening, Cordele and Nayana decided that there wasn't any real reason to stay with Julius and me any longer.

I felt bad about this, knowing that my behavior was at fault, and I tried to persuade them to stay.

"Really, Gabby, we can all be together in a matter of seconds if something should go wrong," Nayana insisted. Then with her face scrunched she added, "Besides, I detest sharing the couch with you - you kick me in your sleep."

"I'm sorry," I told her. "Why didn't you say something?"

She shrugged. "You would have insisted on sleeping on the floor. I would have felt guilty about that."

"We'll be back in the morning; we shouldn't slack off on the training," Cordele said.

I groaned quietly to myself as I watched them disappear.

I was quiet as I did the dishes, thinking about our friends from Kentland.

"What's on your mind?" Julius asked, wrapping his arms around my waist.

"Does April know? I've never mentioned it to her, just in case, but Travis…"

"Travis hasn't told her," he said. "He knows she'd want to join us, for you and him, and he would never be able to concentrate on the fight with her there. He would be too worried."

"Why didn't you tell me?" I asked, my eyebrows scrunched.

"I don't know. I guess I just think of you as too self sacrificing. If you knew everyone who was fighting for you, you'd try to talk them all out of it. Your army would dwindle down to the four of us."

"That's not true, I didn't try to talk the remorseful ones out of fighting," I reminded him.

"That's true, but they're different from friends. You don't know them."

"You're right," I said, appalled. "How awful!"

"It's okay, Gabby. If it were the other way around, they'd feel the same way about you," he said.

"Still…"

I let my mind wander again, back to my friends. "Julius, I

want you to tell me all the people you recruited that I know personally. Is it just Evan and Travis?"

Julius hesitated. "I'm not sure I should tell you."

"Why?" I demanded.

"Because I don't want you upset with me, that's why," he answered.

"I won't get upset with you." I bit my lip, wondering if I should tell him why I thought I needed to know. I figured it wouldn't hurt, so I said, "I could use the extra motivation."

Julius sighed. "If you really think it will help, I'll tell you. But not because I think it will do you any good during the fight; it won't make a difference then. If you think you need the motivation though, it might help now."

"Right. I know - the whole instinct thing. Go ahead," I said.

"Evan, Travis, Kaitlyn, Grady and Alexis."

I frowned.

"See, I knew you would be upset," he scolded when he noticed my expression.

"No I'm not. You just threw me off when you said Alexis. Why her and not Troy? Why not her *and* Troy?"

Julius laughed. "Troy didn't buy it. I had to modify his memory and make the others swear to never mention it in front of him."

"Really?" I had to laugh with him.

"Yeah. It really surprised me - Troy has a really creative mind. He comes up with the cleverest things. I figured he'd be the easiest to convince."

"I figured Travis would be the hardest," I said.

Julius laughed again. "Me too. He's so quiet most of the time; it's hard to read him. I think he was just humoring Evan and I at first, too nice to tell us he thought we were full of crap, but when Evan and I started fighting -"

I cut him off. "Wait - you and Evan were fighting?"

"Well, yeah. A demonstration. Travis said he'd never seen anything like it. And when Evan told him I was the one who beat up Curtis, he…shuddered. He stopped by Curtis's house the next day and told him he knew it was me that beat him up, and Curtis flipped out the same way he did with Evan."

"How did that boy ever find the guts to be in Devon's army?"

"He obviously didn't know what he was getting into," Julius said. "Otherwise I'm sure he would have stayed as far away from the dark side as possible."

Julius put the last of the dishes in the cupboard for me then, and we sat on the couch to rest.

"I hope they'll all be okay. I hope they're not like Curtis," I said, talking about my friends.

Julius sighed. "Curtis got into this for all the wrong reasons, Gabby. He was seeking glory and power, and the promise of those things got in the way of his judgment. Your friends aren't looking for those things. They couldn't be a part of your army if they were. They want to help protect you. They're doing it out of love, and that's the only motivation they need."

"I know. I just hope they know it's okay to back out if they need to. I love them for doing it, but I worry that someone will get hurt."

I rested my head on Julius's shoulder and closed my eyes.

"Tired?" he asked as he rubbed my arm with the tips of his fingers.

"Yeah," I sighed.

"Maybe you should see a doctor, Gabby. You're run down even by normal human standards."

My body stiffened. I remembered Julius telling me once that sentinels were naturally very healthy, and I hoped I still fell into that category.

"I'll be fine," I told him. "Once this is all over with Devon everything will get better."

"Maybe you're working too hard," he suggested. "There really isn't any need for you to keep the practices up. I know Cordele thinks it's for the best, but if you tell him you're confident enough-"

"No, Julius," I said quickly. "I need to do it everyday. I need to know that my abilities haven't changed."

"Why would they change?"

I shrugged. "I'm not like the rest of you."

"Just because your situation is different doesn't mean *you* are," he protested.

"But I am - you said so yourself many times. I can't rely on past situations to help me. I don't know what to expect. Anything could happen."

We were both quiet after that, and after a few minutes with my head on Julius's shoulder, the sound of his breathing lulled me to sleep.

When I woke up the next morning, the sunlight looked all wrong. The shadows were too small. I sat up and yawned, stretching my arms above my head, before throwing the covers aside and reluctantly climbing out of the bed.

Julius was just coming out of the bathroom as I was making my way over to the coffee pot. His expression was full of worry when he saw me.

"What?" I asked, looking myself over.

"It's noon," he said.

"You're kidding! How did I sleep this long?"

"Fourteen hours."

"What?" I was shocked. Had I ever slept that long?

"I told Cordele and Nayana to forget about training. You're obviously exhausted, Gabby."

I sighed, knowing this conversation would have to come sooner or later. I preferred later.

"Julius, I -"

"You don't have to say anything. I know what's wrong with you," he said.

"You do?" I didn't know what to say.

"Gabby, you've got to stop worrying. We all get a little down from time to time, but you're making yourself sick. You aren't eating right, and you're doing too much. I'm making you a big lunch, and you're going to eat everything, okay? I can't have you malnourished." The strain in his eyes told me that he was genuinely scared, and I couldn't stand it.

"Okay, you're right. No more worrying, I promise. When the day comes that I have to do what I have to do, then I'll worry, but not a moment sooner."

His face relaxed. "Thank you," he said, kissing me on the forehead.

True to his word, Julius made a very big lunch, and true to mine, I ate a lot.

Nothing really went together, but that's one reason I liked Julius's cooking. He didn't worry about making a meal that pleased the eye, he made what he liked. We had macaroni and cheese, salad, ham sandwiches, cottage cheese and applesauce.

I started to clear our dishes from the coffee table when we were done, but Julius stopped me.

"Not today," he said. "You relax." He took the dishes straight from my hands and over to the sink.

I hated having to watch him do something while I sat there like a lump. It made me feel lazy and useless, but I promised to take it easy today, so I picked up Julius's latest copy of *Motor Trend* and scanned through the pages, trying to keep myself occupied.

An article on the Dodge Challenger caught my eye, for no other reason than the fact that Julius owned one exactly like it. I was just getting to the part that compared the 1970 model to the newest 2009, when I was jolted by the sound of a plate hitting the empty basin of the sink that Julius was using to rinse the dishes in.

"Do you need some help?" I asked, returning to the article. I knew he would refuse.

"They've got him," he said in an eerie monotone.

"What?" I put the magazine back on the coffee table and turned to face Julius.

"Tonight. They're bringing him to Daniel's tonight. Curtis just told me." His tone was a mixture of fear and relief, torn between the apprehension of my coming fight and the liberation it would bring when it was all over.

My insides buckled with his words, the excessive emotions that flooded through me mixing with my big lunch, and I flew to the bathroom, hugging the toilet as I threw up.

Julius was behind me so quickly I thought that maybe he'd gotten there first, guessing the inevitable.

He held my hair for me, an act that both touched and embarrassed me at the same time. I knew I should have been thinking of more important things just then, the foremost being the issue that caused this onset of lurching, but all I could think in that moment was that the smell was so bad. I didn't want to make Julius sick, but he insisted on being there to watch my debut in *Lunch: Act I, Scene II.*

My head was pounding, the combination of stress and vomiting leaving me on the verge of a migraine.

I flushed the toilet before leaning against the vanity and closing my eyes, willing the room to stop spinning.

"Gabby?" Julius called quietly to me. I could sense the anguish in his voice, and it sliced through my heart like a knife.

"I'm fine, Julius, really. That was the worst of it, I promise. I got it all out of my system, and in a few minutes I'll be as good as new, you'll see." My voice was weak, which scared me. If I didn't get it together fast, Julius would leave me behind and proceed to plan B.

I took a deep breath, the bile that coated my throat stinging my esophagus with the intake of air.

With one hand on the sink and another on the wall, I pulled myself to a standing position and leaned over the sink, turning on the water. I cupped my hands under the tap, filling them with the lukewarm water, and then rinsed my mouth before grabbing my toothbrush for a more thorough cleansing.

I could feel Julius's eyes on me, questioning my health, both physical and mental, and I tried hard to make him feel at ease by remaining calm.

After splashing some water on my face, I took one more deep breath, composing myself. The fear that Julius was experiencing was the fuel I needed to make myself whole again, to collect the broken shards of myself and reconnect them. I used his feelings for me as medicine, a healing agent that put me on the fast track to recovery.

I exhaled slowly, ridding myself of the weak, fragile girl I was only moments ago, replacing her with a strong, healthy young woman.

I turned to look at Julius, and watched as his expression changed from frightened to relaxed.

"I'm good," I said seriously.

It was all the response he needed.

I knew that during the past few months, Julius, Cordele, Nayana, and Daniel had busied themselves gathering troops, but as I looked out at the crowd that had congregated at Daniel's place, I was immensely overwhelmed. The numbers were staggering.

There wasn't a patch of ground that wasn't covered within my range of vision, the once green scenery now hidden beneath shades of varying skin tones and hair colors. The mass of recruits expanded into the forest beyond the vast field and rolling hills, a flock of supporters so large in numbers that I wondered what part of the world's population could possibly be absent.

I was standing on Daniel's front porch, Julius by my side, his arm around my waist. It no longer mattered who in Devon's army found out about our relationship, about our feelings for one another. It would soon be over, and Julius was eager for them to know about it. He wanted to give them a reason to come after him, just in case things didn't go right. He wouldn't live in a world without me in it, and for that, my love for him expanded well beyond the depths of my soul.

"There are so many. Will it scare them off?" I whispered in his ear.

"No," he answered. "If anything they'll be too afraid to go back on their word."

I nodded in understanding.

"Where are our friends?" I asked. I really wanted to see them.

"Probably forcing themselves through the crowd to make their way up here," he said.

I smiled. Every word that came out of his mouth was spoken with tenderness, a soft vibration against my ear that sent chills cascading down my neck.

"How many will Devon bring?"

"I don't know. The rest of us never went through something like this. Our malefactors never had more than a dozen or so followers; they never had enough time to gather any more than that. We've never had so many either, though. A handful of remorseful ones and a couple of friends at the most."

"But the guy who stopped us in the street, the remorseful one on our side, he said they've always been the ones to be on the frontlines. What was he talking about?"

"Cordele and I sent them out to help us track down the strays - the ones that had left our malefactors armies before we had a chance to eliminate them. We didn't want to take the chance that they would recruit others. A few of the people in our armies didn't survive, and the remorseful ones have always remembered that. It wasn't that we didn't care; we didn't see them as expendable, we just couldn't physically kill anyone ourselves - there was no other way." He paused, looking out at the enormous crowd. "Devon will definitely be outnumbered. Your army will take him down easily."

Julius didn't know it yet, but there would be no reason for them to take Devon down. I had my own plan, one that I had kept a secret from the rest of them since the day we buried Daniel.

I knew it would work, but it had to be timed just right. If I was off by a second...

The crowd erupted with a roar, signaling Devon's arrival. Beside me, I could feel Julius tense, his arms around my waist getting tighter.

I thought that in this moment, the calmness that filled me would suddenly be replaced by anxiety and fear, but I was surprised when the only emotion that trickled through me was relief. It would soon be over.

As the crowd parted, letting Devon through, I released myself from Julius's hold. He was right - another surprise for me - my only impulse in that moment was to protect the world from my malefactor - I wanted to fight.

My lithe gait surprised me as I made my way through the throng of soldiers, my shoulders back and chin high. It was as if I were being pulled toward Devon by an invisible elastic cord that had just been stretched and released, tugging me toward him with a force I had almost no control over. My breathing became heavy as adrenaline coursed through my veins, a serum of animalism brought on by the promise of seeing my adversary.

Knowing that I couldn't allow myself to give into the insatiable appetite that was quickly engulfing me, I fought hard against my instincts, willing the human emotions that were the key to the survival of this world to come to the surface. I remembered Daniel, the strongest of us, the only one of us who was able to subdue the urges of the sentinel, and prayed for strength akin to his.

As the murky, green aura that surrounded Devon entered my vision, however, my eyes narrowed and the speed of my walk increased. I felt my nostrils flair of their own accord, my sense of smell heightening as the malefactor's scent assaulted the atmosphere.

From somewhere inside of my chest, emotion erupted. I thought of Julius, the love we shared and the future we would have together, my main motivation. I thought of Evan and

Travis, of Kaitlyn and Grady and Alexis, of what they were putting themselves through at this moment, and forced myself to think of the demise they could encounter. I thought of Cordele and Nayana - what would happen to them should I fail. It would just be the two of them if this didn't go right. Julius would see to that. I let all of these frightening images fill my mind, shoving every bit of optimism out. I needed the fear. The fear is what reminded me of the all the love I felt, and it was love that was going to win this fight.

Finally, the thought of my loved ones invoked the human emotion I knew I would need, although my reflexes hadn't entirely receded; my hands were still balled into clenched fists, and the little slits my eyes had become refused to change position.

I stopped walking then, knowing Devon would eventually appear in my range of vision. I wasn't sure if I would be able to stop myself when I saw him, and thought it best to prepare ahead of time. My sentinel instincts told me he was getting closer; the smell of his murky aura harsh and putrid, stinging my nose badly enough to make my eyes water. I stiffened my posture, the human side of me trying to take the sentinel side hostage.

As Devon came into view, my body jerked, the instinct that threatened to overwhelm me fighting against the rationality I was trying to impose upon it. I breathed deeply through my flared nostrils, a human habit of mine, and immediately regretted it. His smell momentarily overpowered me, and at once I went back into sentinel mode. A flash of dark hair and green eyes from the corner of my vision finally stopped me just before I was about to lunge; Julius was on my left, advancing toward Devon, and it was this visage that wrenched me from the depths of my weakness.

The body Devon was in was lean and tone, a male who looked to be in his early twenties, with sandy blonde hair. This was a body with the ability to kill, and my eyes betrayed me as the shock registered. I expected something more…dead looking.

The woman who had been the spokesperson at the meeting we'd had a few weeks ago was beside him, a satisfied grin on her face. It was the first time I'd actually seen her, and the moment our eyes connected I wanted to rip her short, red spikes from her scalp.

"Stole it from a hospital," she said, noticing my astonishment. "The guy went into cardiac arrest, and Devon slipped in just as his soul slipped out. The doctors resuscitated him rather quickly. Handsome, don't you think? And so young to have heart problems. But that's okay, who really needs a heart anyway?" She laughed then, her high pitched cackles causing fury to surge through my veins.

I balled my hands into fists, resisting my hostile urges.

Devon's - or rather the stolen body's - eyes widened at my lack of physical response. "It's true, then," he said, his surprise suddenly turning into sinister humor. "You don't have the instincts."

"I told you," the wretched woman mocked. "Any *normal* sentinel would have attempted to rip you to shreds by now."

"Enough, Stella," Devon growled at the woman, keeping his eyes on me. "Your annoying chatter is only wasting time." Then, with a laugh I knew was intended for me he said, "I bet you thought I was scared to come, afraid of what you might do to me, but I wasn't. I have longed for this day for almost two years. It's time for you to die."

His fist came at me with speed and agility, but I ducked just in time to hear it buzz past my ear, and I grasped him by the elbow with both of my hands and used my right leg to pull his feet out from under him, sending him crashing to the ground.

His free arm grabbed mine, flipping me over his body, but I landed on my feet in a crouched position before lunging at him with a high kick.

He caught my ankle before my kick landed against his chest, jabbing his foot into the back of my knee, and I knew the time had come to implement my plan as the pain from his infliction throbbed throughout my leg.

His kicks were strong, much more so than mine; lethal even. I blocked a few of them, testing the power behind them. Yes, they could kill me.

I fought back as best as I could, buying time.

I realized then that some of my army was fighting his, and I knew the time had come. I had to implement my plan soon, before anybody had a chance to intervene.

I kicked him in the chest one last time, knowing I couldn't stop his body's heart, but hoping for a minute shudder from him.

It worked.

In that moment, I put my plan into action. At once, I brought myself back from Kentland. I was whole, and it felt odd to be so. I had been separated for far too long, and I didn't have the time I needed to adjust to this feeling.

I didn't have time to brace myself for what was about to happen. Devon was quick, and I was glad; I didn't want the opportunity to change my mind.

Just then, another kick from Devon came across my face, and I could feel the bones in my neck crush, the most sickening feeling I'd ever felt in my entire life. My head felt so heavy; there was nothing to hold it up with. It landed against my shoulder before my knees buckled, and the last thing I heard before everything faded to black was Julius's heart wrenching bellows.

A victory cry erupted from Devon, deep and sinister; a baleful roar that reverberated across the span of recruits, stopping each and every one of them in their tracks.

I clamped my hand tightly around Julius's mouth from the spot behind him where I bi-located to. Before he had time to react to my touch, I whispered quickly, "It's me, don't move."

I knew that if I didn't time it just right, Julius would have gone after Devon, and he wouldn't have stopped until he earned the same fate half of me had.

I felt his warm tears trickle over the tops of my fingers as I relaxed my grip against his mouth, and I rested my head against his back to console him.

I had to blend in with the crowd, camouflage myself, and any sudden movements would alert them. They had to think I was gone, or there was no hope for the rest of my plan.

I'd known since the day we buried Daniel what I had to do.

I remembered clearly the way he talked of bi-locating at the last second, how his instinct refused to let him kill, and I wondered what would have happened to him if he hadn't gotten out of the way in time.

It occurred to me that half of him would have died, and half of him would have lived, and there was a good possibility that Cordele and Nayana could have fixed the half that was destroyed by his malefactor.

What would happen, I wondered, to a malefactor who actually *had* destroyed his sentinel?

I thought I knew the answer to that from Nayana's story. Her malefactor became a remorseful one when he accidentally killed their parents, and I was hoping Devon would come to the same fate.

Even if it didn't work out that way, he wouldn't live anyway. Our army was too large. He would be destroyed this evening one way or the other, and the world would be safe from him.

Finally I heard a thud and peeked over Julius shoulder.

A gasp escaped every recruit that was in seeing distance of Devon.

He had fallen to his knees, clutching my dead body, cradling it.

I was revolted by seeing my own body, head askew, limp and lifeless, and I had to look away.

"What are you doing you stupid, stupid creature?" Stella was screaming at him. "You've defeated her! Hell has been freed from the clutch of the righteous! Soon everything you see before you will be ours! You should be celebrating the coming of our father!"

A sound came from him, a soft whimper at first, gradually becoming louder and louder until he was wailing in agony.

"Get up! Get up!" Stella was yelling. "Release that vile sentinel!"

I heard a gasp from Julius and looked up. There, surrounding Stella, were our friends. I watched as Alexis grabbed her by the hair and slammed her into the ground.

Stella's eyes were alight with fire, angered at having been humiliated in what she thought was her time to shine. She lunged at Alexis, only to be brought down once again by Evan.

There were five of them and only one of her, so I knew that they were just playing cat and mouse.

Kaitlyn grabbed her hands and Travis grabbed her feet, carrying her writhing body into the crowd, which went wild for only a few moments.

I knew it wouldn't take them long to kill her.

Devon's cries were slowly dying down, now only soft sobs. I ached for him. He was my brother again, this soul who was crying over my body, crying with the remorse he felt for having killed me.

I wanted so badly to run to him, to tell him I was okay, but I knew I couldn't. His instincts as a malefactor would take control of him once again, and I couldn't take that chance.

I couldn't watch him wilt, but I knew when it happened; Julius pulled me around to face him, kissing me with vigorous lips, and then squeezed me against him so hard I thought I would burst.

He yelled for Cordele and Nayana with more excitement than I'd ever seen capable in a human being or a sentinel. He was dragging me by my arm into the clearing that was now host to two dead bodies. I clamped my eyes shut at the scene, my stomach rolling at the thought of what was lying there.

"Oh my," I heard Cordele say. "Oh my, oh my, oh my!" His excitement had reached an all time high, which made me glad he was a sentinel; a normal eighty year old man would probably have had a heart attack.

Nayana made a running leap in my direction, attaching herself to the front of me. She had no words of excitement, only tears of joy as she hid her face in my hair and wept. I squeezed her tightly; in this moment she was a child in need of reassurance, and I was glad to give it to her.

Julius came up beside the two of us then, wrapping his arms around us both. I could hear the relief in his tone when he whispered in my ear, "Did you have that planned this whole time?"

I nodded in response, too tired to go into detail.

Nayana climbed down then and ran to Cordele, whose arms were outstretched for her in anticipation of a hug.

The moment was nothing short of surreal, the emotions I was experiencing weaving in and out, a tapestry of inexplicable taste.

I had just lost Devon for good, and knowing now that I would never again have the chance to see him or hear his voice left a gaping wound in my heart.

The world was safe now, however, and the promise of never having to go through something this intense again was a relief. Getting on with my life was going to be tough, but at least now I stood a chance at living it with a hint of normalcy.

Then there was Julius - *my* Julius. With my head against his chest, I realized that I had reached the acme of what it was to be human. Love was much too simple a word to describe the feeling that flowed through me as his hands trailed up and down my back, reassuring himself that I truly existed.

Of course there was also the ever prevalent guilt, of which I harbored for more than one reason. Eliminating Devon was the foremost of these reasons. Even though I knew it had to be done, I wasn't quite sure if I could ever forgive myself for putting his soul through the pain that I did, although I did find consolation in knowing that I had given him a second chance. He wouldn't be in Hell, but have a human body and a new life as a remorseful one.

The other thing that made me feel guilty had to do with Julius. I had been keeping something from him for a few weeks now, and I was worried about how he would feel once he found out how long I'd been hiding it from him.

I shoved the thought from my mind. There would be plenty of time to explain - approximately nine months anyway.

Right now I wanted to be in this moment with him, celebrating the promise of a peaceful future.

I squeezed Julius tightly, smiling to myself as I reveled in his hum.

Epilogue ❖

It was hard to admit that my expectations for the future ended up to be laughable - which was by all means putting it lightly. In fact, if I were being honest I would have to say that 'laughable' was a colossal understatement. The truth was, except for the absence of fire and brimstone, my life *had* become Hell, despite my best efforts to prevent that.

The night that Devon was eliminated, Curtis admitted that he had been the one to kill him. His body was in the quarry, he told me, Devon having thought that the Kentland Crater would be the perfect place for his earthly life to end.

Curtis's face was pained as he disclosed the locality and details of Devon's death, which I couldn't bear listen to. It was obvious he had no idea what he was getting himself into when he agreed to be a part of Devon's army, and the reality of the situation didn't actually sink in until that September night almost two years ago when he killed Devon against his better judgment.

Logically I knew that the acceptable emotion for confronting the person who murdered my loved one would be hatred, contempt, and loathing, but none of those feelings stirred within me. Instead, I felt indifferent toward Curtis. He was nothing more than a pawn to Devon, and for some reason, I felt as if the actual act of killing him did not lay in the fault of Curtis for having done it, but in Devon for having insisted that it be done. Somehow I managed to feel sorry for Curtis, and it was the act of feeling sympathy for him that I struggled with. Surely I should not feel this way toward the person who killed my brother.

Curtis also admitted that it was desperation that led him to try to kill me with the earthquake. He figured that by killing Devon, he had set an irreversible plan into motion, and the only way he could prevent a war from happening would be to kill me. If there were no one for Devon to fight, it stood to reason that he could never prevail over the world. Oddly enough, I understood what he was saying, found nobility in his words somehow.

I had no intentions of looking for Devon's body myself, although I desperately wanted to find his remains; my parents would be devastated but at least they would know. Julius reminded me that geologists had been in and out of the crater for months, and that they would undoubtedly be the ones to find him.

He was right. Two weeks after I eliminated Devon, his remains were found in the quarry. My parents were inconsolable when the police contacted them with the news, and after the gut-wrenching funeral the police launched a full-scale investigation into my brother's death. My parents were looked at very closely, which was a horrible thing for them to have to go through, and eventually Julius and I performed memory modifications on the entire staff of the Kentland Police Department. We convinced them that my parents were not suspects in any way.

I told Julius about the baby the night I eliminated Devon. He was so shocked I had to perform the hum on him. When he finally came out of his shock-induced stupor, he smiled. He seemed genuinely pleased about the idea of being a father, but the anxiety about the prospect overwhelmed him.

We hadn't planned the baby, we weren't married, and neither of us had a college education. We had just buried Devon, so my parents were extremely fragile, and we both had apprehensions about telling them. I had already come to terms with being a teenage, unwed-mother, and now I had to watch Julius go through all the same emotions I had.

We decided it would be best to visit the doctor before we told anyone, and so I chose one from Lafayette. I couldn't have a doctor from Cleveland; my parents would need an explanation that I wouldn't be able to give them.

Dr. Kennon was a very nice man who treated Julius and I with respect, and he concluded that I was healthy and nearly three months along. The baby I was carrying, our child, was conceived sometime in May, before my mother put me on the pill. I told Dr. Kennon this, and he seemed surprised. After all, the doctor my mother sent me to gave me a pregnancy test before prescribing the birth control, and the results were negative at the time. Perhaps, he suggested, I conceived shortly after that particular day. Maybe I hadn't given the pills enough time to settle into my system, and there was always the possibility that my body had rejected them - they weren't one hundred percent effective. Of course there was also the possibility that I had been mistaken about my last menstrual cycle, so to get a better idea about just how far along I really was, Dr. Kennon decided to do a Doppler test to check for a fetal heartbeat.

The earliest a fetal heartbeat could be detected was about nine weeks, and by twelve weeks it should be strong and consistent, he told Julius and I, so the Doppler test should give us a better understanding about how far along I was into the pregnancy.

Finding the heartbeat wasn't hard, and Dr. Kennon guessed that I was somewhere around ten weeks along, but his face was scrunched as he tried to count the beats, and immediately I knew there was something wrong. Even to me, the quick fluttery sound seemed jumbled, and my body tensed at the odd rhythm.

Julius and I looked at each other with fright as Dr. Kennon announced the ominous word - twins.

My hope for the future was shattered. Could it possibly be true? Was this really happening? Surely it was just a fluke, nothing more than a heaping dose of my mother's genes.

No amount of optimism could break through the fear that had encompassed me at this point, though. Somehow I knew that there was no hope. Perhaps it was intuition, but I knew what I was carrying. In six months I would be giving birth to the next generation of sentinels and malefactors, and as soon as that realization set in, I passed out.

Made in the USA
Charleston, SC
09 April 2010